➤YOU'VE GOT M_[

The PERILS
of
PIGEON POST

WRITTEN BY
Blackegg

COVER ILLUSTRATION BY
Leila

INTERIOR ILLUSTRATIONS BY
Ninemoon

TRANSLATED BY
alexsh

Seven Seas Entertainment

You've Got Mail: The Perils of Pigeon Post - Fei Ge Jiao You Xu Jin Shen (Novel) Vol. 1

Published originally under the title of 《飛鴿交友須謹慎》
Author©黑蛋白 (Blackegg)
Illustrations granted under license granted by I Yao Co. Ltd.
Cover Illustrations by Leila
Interior illustrations by Ninemoon
English edition rights under license granted by 愛呦文創有限公司 (I Yao Co. Ltd.)
English edition copyright © 2024 Seven Seas Entertainment, Inc
Arranged through JS Agency Co., Ltd
All rights reserved

Seven Seas press and purchase enquiries can be sent
to Marketing Manager Lauren Hill at press@gomanga.com.
Information regarding the distribution and purchase of digital editions is available
from Digital Manager CK Russell at digital@gomanga.com.

Seven Seas and the Seven Seas logo are trademarks of
Seven Seas Entertainment. All rights reserved.

Follow Seven Seas Entertainment online at
sevenseasentertainment.com.

TRANSLATION: alexsh
ADAPTATION: Abigail Clark
COVER DESIGN: G. A. Slight
INTERIOR DESIGN & LAYOUT: Clay Gardner
COPY EDITOR: Vera Klimt
PROOFREADER: Imogen Vale, Nino Cipri
EDITOR: Hardleigh Hewmann
PREPRESS TECHNICIAN: Melanie Ujimori, Jules Valera
MANAGING EDITOR: Alyssa Scavetta
EDITOR-IN-CHIEF: Julie Davis
PUBLISHER: Lianne Sentar
VICE PRESIDENT: Adam Arnold
PRESIDENT: Jason DeAngelis

ISBN: 979-8-88843-975-3
Printed in Canada
First Printing: August 2024
10 9 8 7 6 5 4 3 2 1

YOU'VE GOT MAIL
The PERILS
of
PIGEN
POST

1

CONTENTS

"Wu Xingzi," he called out.

The name tasted rather sweet rolling across the tip of his tongue.

Inexplicably, this person now held a place in his heart—something he would have never imagined was possible.

WU XINGZI, an adviser to the magistrate of the remote Qingcheng County, had recently come to the conclusion that life was not worth living. Both of his parents were dead, and he didn't have a single property to his name. Not only was he attracted to other men, he was a virgin to boot, and his looks... well, they were rather forgettable. He felt like he might as well just die. With all of this weighing on him, Wu Xingzi decided to kill himself on his fortieth birthday.

Before committing suicide, he ventured out one last time to confess his long-time affection for the local fellow who sold tofu. While on this final errand, he discovered the existence of a secret association that matched male couples through messenger pigeon: the Peng Society for Gentlemen. After a few bouts of hesitation, he joined the ranks of these men becoming pen pals through the pigeon post, searching for his springtime lover.

Spring hadn't even sprung when he was faced with a field of blooming flowers, allowing him to finally experience the joy life had to offer. How could he bear to kill himself when there was such a blissful collection of cocks to explore?!

One day, he received an illustration that claimed to portray the prick of the Lanling Prince of the Peng Society. His heart aflutter, Wu Xingzi could no longer suppress his erotic desires—he had to get to know the owner of this magnificent meat! Before he knew it, he was entangled in a passionate tryst.

Wu Xingzi felt that meeting General Guan Shanjin for that brief dalliance was truly one of the luckiest things to happen to him. When he arrived home in complete satisfaction, he was surprised to see that not only had the general followed him home, but he also wanted to stay—despite the fact both of them had already gotten what they wanted. Instead, the other man continued to circle around him, refusing to leave him alone...

Thus, a philandering pengornis[1] met a timid little quail holed up in the bottom of a well. One man treated life like a game because he had never obtained his heart's true desire; the other was isolated, robbed of money and companionship. Two people who had never known romance were now stumbling toward a journey of love.

---

1   Pengornis houi is a large prehistoric bird that lived alongside dinosaurs in what is today northeast China. It is named for the Peng, a giant bird from Chinese mythology.

CHAPTER ONE

THE FIRST ENCOUNTER WITH THE PENGORNISSEUR

Dear Sir,
If I may be so bold, with just one glance at The Pengornisseur,
I was captivated by your looks and charm. I hope for us to forge
a friendship through the pigeon post; perhaps this may result in
a happy union.

SOMETHING ODD was going on with Adviser Wu Xingzi of the magistrate's office.

Every other day, he hired Old Liu's cart and headed to Goose City, which was half a day away. He didn't stay for long, always ready to head home again before Old Liu was even halfway done smoking his pipe.

At first, Old Liu didn't mind, since he earned more money when someone hired his cart. Winter was fast approaching, and it was never a bad thing to have more cash for the New Year. However, this had gone on for ten days, and Old Liu was growing concerned. He was worried that Wu Xingzi had fallen for some kind of scam.

After all, everyone in Qingcheng County knew Wu Xingzi. He lived alone and penniless and had been working as an adviser in the magistrate's office for the past twenty-odd years. He was about to turn forty, but he had no one to take care of him; there was no sign of any companion by his side.

The more Old Liu thought about it, the more likely it seemed that Wu Xingzi was being scammed out of his money. He doubted Wu Xingzi was seeing a lover every other day... How embarrassing would that be, if he couldn't last for more than a quarter of an hour every time?

In the beginning, Old Liu had only mentioned this issue to his wife in passing. Who would have guessed that within a couple of days, the matter would become known to half the county? Qingcheng County really was too small; its citizens had nothing better to do.

When Wu Xingzi came to look for Old Liu again today, he was pulled aside by Auntie Liu.

"Xingzi," she called out, her eyes reddening before she could continue.

Wu Xingzi became alarmed. "What's wrong, Auntie? Did someone upset you? Do you need me to write a citation for you?"

This was not the first time his neighbors had come crying to him for help. Having been working in the magistrate's office for more than half his life, Wu Xingzi could write citations in his sleep.

"Xingzi..." Auntie Liu wailed, tears beginning to flow.

Wu Xingzi raised both his hands in bewilderment and threw a pleading look at Old Liu, who was brushing his cow. Old Liu returned Wu Xingzi's gaze before turning to look at his wife. Shaking his head, he heaved a soft sigh.

This matter seemed quite serious. Wu Xingzi hurriedly recalled various incidents from the past few days.

The Wang family and the Shi family argued in the magistrate's office due to their children pledging themselves to each other in secret, but when they finally settled on the bride price and the dowry, both families cheerfully started discussing the wedding banquet.

A young child of the An family stole some persimmons off the tree that grew next to the Xu family's courtyard. When the An family discovered that the child had been shoved around by the Xu family, they brought the case to the magistrate's office. Wu Xingzi wrote a citation, but in the time it would take an incense stick to burn, the county magistrate had dealt with the matter. Both families amicably left to enjoy the persimmons together.

Sister Li and Old Wang had some minor land disputes. Widow Zhou and her eldest daughter-in-law had some disagreements. Li San owed the head of his clan three silver ingots and refused to pay it back, offering his life instead of coughing up the cash... Wu Xingzi wracked his brain, but he couldn't remember any incidents that involved the Liu family.

But Auntie Liu cried until her eyes were swollen and her shoulders trembled. Wu Xingzi tried to console her. "Don't cry, Auntie Liu. What can I do to help you?"

Old Liu could not watch this go on any longer. He coughed loudly. Only then did Auntie Liu force down her sobs, wiping her tears away as she stared at Wu Xingzi. Her profound gaze gave Wu Xingzi an ominous feeling.

"Xingzi," Auntie Liu called out. "Oh, Xingzi!"

"Yes, Auntie." *Please say something else!* Wu Xingzi had never had his name repeated so many times in his life.

"Xingzi... Tell me the truth, are you...interested in a girl?" Auntie Liu didn't want to scare Wu Xingzi, so she didn't ask directly if he had been swindled out of his money.

Wu Xingzi blinked helplessly. Sighing, he said, "Auntie, did...did you forget? I don't like girls."

Auntie Liu blinked back, stunned for a moment. However, she quickly started crying again. "Oh, poor Xingzi, did you get conned by a man, then?"

Even Old Liu had a sympathetic expression on his face as he shook his head, smoking his pipe off to the side.

Wu Xingzi's face flushed. "It's not that, Auntie. Why do you think I was cheated by a man?"

"What? *You* swindled a man instead? Xingzi! What have you become? I've told you before, you're no spring chicken. Whether it's a man or a woman, it's good to have someone by your side. But you... If you've started cheating people..."

What? You can't think of anything other than me cheating people or being cheated? Wu Xingzi thought. *How big a failure have I been these past thirty-odd years?*

"Auntie, you're overthinking things. I didn't cheat anyone, and nobody cheated me." Wu Xingzi rubbed his face helplessly. Hunching his shoulders, he looked around and lowered his voice. "Auntie, please don't tell anyone what I'm about to tell you."

Auntie Liu nodded vigorously, her eyes shining brightly as she clasped onto Wu Xingzi's hands. "Go ahead, go ahead. I won't tell a soul."

After some hesitation, Wu Xingzi continued, his voice quiet. "Auntie, I've made some pen pals through the pigeon post."

"Pen pals through the pigeon post?" Auntie Liu stared at Wu Xingzi, bewildered.

"Ah, yes." Wu Xingzi scratched at his cheek. He might as well spill everything. "Auntie, you know I'm turning forty soon. I have no prospects, no money, and I like men. It's really not easy for someone like me to find a life companion."

"That's true." Auntie Liu nodded.

Wu Xingzi's face paled, and he felt even more hopeless about his future. Silently, he picked up the pieces of his broken heart.

"So, through the pigeon post, I hoped I could find a partner..." His tone was light, almost as if he was talking about someone else.

"Yes, yes." Auntie Liu nodded again, then asked, "Is it safe to make friends through the pigeon post?"

This was something new to her, and it was hard for Auntie Liu to get her head around it. In Qingcheng County, pigeons were food. What poor and hungry person would have the energy to raise pigeons for carrying letters? *Pigeons are so delicious, fat, and tender...* Saliva pooled in Auntie Liu's mouth.

"Uh, it should be safe." Wu Xingzi said, his ears reddening faintly. "I've been visiting Goose City to collect mail from the pigeon post."

"Oh, so it's like that..." Auntie Liu muttered. "Xingzi, I don't know much about writing to pen pals, but it's somewhat worrying that you're not able to see the other person's face. You have to be careful. If you really want to look for a partner, I can ask around."

"No need to trouble yourself for me, Auntie." Wu Xingzi patted the back of Auntie Liu's hand to placate her. He looked up, seeing the sun rising high in the sky. It was too late for him to make his way to Goose City, and he looked a little lonely.

"Uncle Liu, I'll trouble you to drive me to Goose City tomorrow."

Old Liu said nothing, just puffed away at his pipe as he gave a small nod of his head.

Wu Xingzi decided to go to the magistrate's office to work after their conversation. Qingcheng County was small, and the living conditions were so harsh that even thieves avoided coming to the county. Other than the occasional squabble within families and between neighbors, there was really nothing much to handle at work, and Wu Xingzi was able to run off to Goose City every other day without the county magistrate showing any disapproval. He felt a little disappointed that he hadn't been able to go collect his mail today, though.

Having gotten all the information she wanted, Auntie Liu let Wu Xingzi go. She stuffed a basketful of steamed buns into his arms, then waved him off. Once she was certain that Wu Xingzi was far enough away, she picked up a basket of mountain vegetables and ran over to Zhang A-Niu next door for a chat.

It didn't take long for the gossip to spread. Within a few days, half of Qingcheng County knew about Wu Xingzi making friends through the pigeon post. (For some reason, it brought about a trend of raising pigeons for mail delivery, but that was another story.)

This matter, making pen pals through the pigeon post, started about a month ago.

In general, there was no issue with Wu Xingzi's appearance. His eyes flanked his nose, his eyebrows tilted down, and his nose was fleshy and slightly round. His short philtrum made his mouth and nose look a little too close together. His lips were plump and full, and according to the art of face-reading, this was a sign that he was prone to money troubles.

Although Wu Xingzi's face wasn't exactly handsome, he looked very approachable. It was because of this that he landed the job of adviser to the magistrate.

When Wu Xingzi was sixteen years old, his entire family perished, leaving him with nothing. His father was once a scholar who passed the country's imperial examinations, but his journey had stopped there. He didn't have the money to continue the examinations, and he wasn't talented enough to achieve higher honors. However, Father Wu was a practical person. He decided to open a private school in his hometown instead, managing to take care of his family with the income.

Since his youth, Wu Xingzi's talents had been average, and he neither stood out nor fell back. After passing the apprentice exams in his district, he amounted to nothing.

Every generation of the Wu family had only one son. After Wu Xingzi's grandparents passed away, there were only the three of them left. His mother's side of the family was small as well. They'd left Qingcheng County long ago, and no one knew where they'd moved. So when a tragic flood occurred, Wu Xingzi was left all alone at sixteen years old.

Since not many people in the county knew how to read or write, Wu Xingzi was considered a step above the rest. Thanks to his literacy, along with the magistrate's sympathy for him, he was hired as the magistrate's adviser. Although the salary was not high, it was enough for him to live on. Magistrates assigned to Qingcheng County tended to be free from corruption, and they usually could not bring advisers of their own. As such, Wu Xingzi's position was unshakeable, and he had maintained his job post for many years.

Wu Xingzi never found a problem with his way of living. However, as he slowly progressed from youth to middle age, his pockets and his house remained empty. One day, he suddenly felt that his life was too monotonous. He wondered if there was a point to living life so aimlessly. Once this thought surfaced, he could not shake it from his mind.

After staring blankly at his walls for hours on end, Wu Xingzi decided to commit suicide on the day he turned forty. With this decision made, he felt as free as a bird. After a satisfying meal and a good night's sleep, he started thinking about methods of suicide that would be the least bothersome to others.

As he was contemplating this, he suddenly thought of the young man who sold tofu jelly in the market. The fellow's appearance was very clean, just like the soybean curd he sold. Recalling the curve of his eyes, his white teeth as he smiled, and those pink, plump lips, Wu Xingzi felt his pants getting a little tight.

Since he was going to die anyway, he might as well do something daring!

Wu Xingzi grabbed his money pouch. First, he went to the jewelry store and bought a jade hairpin of relatively good quality. Then, he headed to the store that sold tofu jelly. By then, the sun was setting, and most of the stores in the market were closed. The tofu boy was bare-chested, wiping the day's sweat from his body. He smiled upon seeing Wu Xingzi, revealing his bright, white teeth.

"Xingzi-ge." The tofu boy called his name warmly.

"Ai." Wu Xingzi mopped at the sweat on his forehead. His mouth was so dry that his tongue stuck to the roof of his mouth. He snuck a glance at the lad's firm body, his form outlined by the rays of the setting sun.

The young man was about seventeen or eighteen years of age and tall, with long and slender limbs. With clothes on, he looked deceptively lean; bare chested, it was clear he was very muscular. He had perfectly defined abs, and there was a fine trail of hair on his belly that disappeared underneath his trousers.

Wu Xingzi gulped, his throat burning.

"Xingzi-ge, did you need me for something?" The lad casually tossed his shirt over his shoulder and walked over to Wu Xingzi.

"I-I... Y-you..." Wu Xingzi couldn't get the words out. He awkwardly clamped his legs shut and hunched over slightly, stealing a look at the boy's abs. They looked so defined! So strong, so robust... Wu Xingzi's hips trembled slightly.

This was not going well.

"Xingzi-ge?" The lad seemed a bit perplexed at Wu Xingzi's lack of response.

"Do... Do you like men?" Wu Xingzi blurted out, immediately feeling like running away.

The Great Xia Dynasty did not ban relations between men. There were some male couples that spent their lives together. However, the majority of people were heterosexual, and quite a few were still repelled by the idea of homosexuality.

Wu Xingzi could not believe he had just said what he did out loud.

The tofu boy was dumbfounded. Seeing that Wu Xingzi was about to turn and run, he reached out and grabbed him. "Xingzi-ge, don't panic. I...I also like men."

Hearing this, Wu Xingzi could not help but smile. He forgot about running, turning back with starry eyes. He opened his mouth to say something, but the young man interrupted him. "I already have a partner."

Looking at his shy yet blissful expression, Wu Xingzi's mind blanked. "Oh. In that case, um, congratulations..."

"Xingzi-ge..." The tofu boy could not bear to look at Wu Xingzi's despondent face, and he pulled him into the store. With a soft voice, he said, "Xingzi-ge, have you heard about the Peng Society for Gentlemen?"

"The Peng Society?" Wu Xingzi blinked, a look of confusion on his face.

"Yeah, the Peng Society for Gentlemen." The young man lowered his voice even further, whispering secretively. "The society has this book for men like us called *The Pengornisseur*. It lists pen pals you can exchange mail with through the pigeon post."

"Pen pals by pigeon post?" Wu Xingzi was still befuddled. He knew that pigeons were used to deliver mail; there were even a few pigeons kept at the magistrate's office. They were used for official communication between Qingcheng County and the state capital. Wu Xingzi also happened to be the one in charge of caring for these pigeons.

"That's right, using messenger pigeons to make friends." He explained the system to Wu Xingzi in detail.

The Peng Society for Gentlemen was a secret coalition of men interested in other men. Once you submitted your name, interests, a self-portrait, the preferred destination for your letters, and fifty coins, you would receive a copy of *The Pengornisseur*. The subscription was valid for one month. It listed men who were seeking life partners. Everyone was invited to write each other through the pigeon post. If things progressed well, they could choose to meet privately.

"That's how I met my man." The fellow's face was red, and his gleaming grin dazzled Wu Xingzi. Of course, he could have just been dazzled by the existence of *The Pengornisseur*. "Xingzi-ge, if you're interested, I can tell you more about it."

"More about it..." The jade hairpin he'd acquired earlier remained in Wu Xingzi's sleeve pocket, and he was still a little confused. "Let me think about it." He'd come here to confess to the young man, but now there were other things on his mind.

"Of course." The tofu boy gave him a comforting look. "Don't think about it too hard, Xingzi-ge. You'll meet him when the time is right."

Wu Xingzi nodded, his head in a daze. Waving goodbye, he headed back home in a stupor.

Wu Xingzi returned home with a lot on his mind. After dinner, he carefully placed the jade hairpin in a wooden box, locked it, and buried it under his bed. He then sat down and fell into a daze.

There was no doubt that he was interested. If the Peng Society for Gentlemen was real, it would be a true paradise for him. He would actually be able to make connections with other men who were looking for love.

Wu Xingzi had been lonely for many years, with not even a dog to keep him company. At the end of the workday, he would come home to long, arduous nights without a single soul for company.

Sighing, he bent over and retrieved a small pot from under his bed. Inside the container was his stash of ten taels of silver, the entirety of his life savings. He had never intended to touch the sum at all. He wanted to save up for a sturdy coffin made from a yellow-wood tree, or perhaps even elm—something to lie in comfortably while he rotted away.

Fifty coins... Wu Xingzi was extremely torn. That was the total sum of his expenditures for ten days! That money included his allowance to buy a bowl of tofu at the market every few days, where he could admire the charming smile of the fellow who sold it to him... It was unfortunate that he had already found someone before Wu Xingzi could even confess his feelings. Wu Xingzi's shoulders sagged as he shrank into himself, looking like a shriveled eggplant.

Time passed, and Wu Xingzi remained stuck in deliberation. By the time he made up his mind, five entire days had passed.

Well, he was planning to die at forty anyway, so what was the point of worrying about a few coins? If he spent the money, he might find someone willing to settle down with him. With the hope of spending their futures together, he would no longer long for death.

The more he thought about it, the more agreeable it seemed. Wu Xingzi gritted his teeth. After counting out fifty coins and placing them in his pouch, he ran off to the tofu boy for more details.

The lad was about to head home, having packed up and closed his shop for the day. He turned around and was surprised to see Wu Xingzi, red faced and panting hard from running.

"Xingzi-ge," the young man said.

"Would you please tell me more about...the Peng Society?" Wu Xingzi said in a low voice, eyes darting around nervously. His palms were sweaty. He was terrified of being discovered.

After a moment of astonishment, the lad smiled. "Sure. This really isn't a good place to talk about it, though. Xingzi-ge, why don't you come home with me?"

Follow the boy home? Wu Xingzi blushed red. This was not just a polite invitation from a friendly neighbor; this was a proposition from his crush!

"C-can I?" Wu Xingzi stuttered.

"I'm just worried my place isn't nice enough for you." The lad bashfully scratched the back of his head. Wu Xingzi was charmed by the sight and became lightheaded with joy, his heart fluttering.

"No, no, how could that be? You're much too polite," Wu Xingzi responded at once, happily following the tofu boy. Along the way, he even took the initiative to buy a jug of wine and two dishes for dinner, hoping to prolong their chat.

The young man's home was located in Jinghua Alley on the west side of the city, not far from the market. A row of houses dotted the street, half of them empty. As the sky darkened, the unlit houses looked somewhat unnerving.

"We're here, Xingzi-ge." The lad stopped outside a house with warm light glowing through the windows. "My man has a bit of a temper. Don't mind him, he just...gets jealous easily."

This sudden display of affection pulled Wu Xingzi's head out of the clouds.

"No, I'm the one imposing on the two of you." His expression dimmed. How could he forget that this young man was already taken?

"Don't say that." The lad patted him on the shoulder before turning to push the door open. "I'm back!" he called out. "I also brought Xingzi-ge with me."

"Xingzi-ge?" The voice that drifted out from inside the house was deep and sullen and did not say much else. With a few muffled steps, its owner walked to the door and glanced outward. "Adviser Wu?"

Wu Xingzi's jaw dropped. He knew this man! Wasn't this Constable Zhang? They'd been colleagues for twenty years and counting!

"You met each other through *The Pengornisseur*?" Wu Xingzi said. A match like this could be made through the pigeon post? Wu Xingzi's spirits lifted a little. There were more homosexuals around him than he realized!

"That's right," the tofu boy said. Smiling, the lad reached out and held Constable Zhang by the hand while motioning for Wu Xingzi to come inside. "Come in, Xingzi-ge. Make yourself at home."

Wu Xingzi nodded profusely and entered the house under the constable's somewhat embarrassed gaze.

Wu Xingzi took a seat at the table. There were already two entrées and a bowl of soup waiting. Smelling the aroma of the meat and vegetables, Wu Xingzi swallowed and hurriedly laid out the two dishes he had brought as well.

Perhaps uncovering a secret about one's coworker was too unpleasant a surprise. The mood remained rather awkward throughout the meal, all three keeping their heads down and eating frantically. Only after they had eaten their fill did the lad send Constable Zhang away to wash the dishes. Wu Xingzi heaved a breath of relief.

"This Peng Society is really impressive," Wu Xingzi said.

"It is. I'm sure you'll find a good man from *The Pengornisseur*." The lad nodded in encouragement. "Feel free to ask me anything you want to know."

Wu Xingzi gulped before asking the young man for further details about the Peng Society.

According to the tofu boy, divisions of the Peng Society for Gentlemen existed all over the country, and its subdivisions could be found in even the most remote corners of the borderlands. The closest branch to Qingcheng County was located in Goose City.

Of course, since it was a secret association, there were no prominent signboards declaring its location. The chapter in Goose City was concealed in the back of an antique store. The tofu boy gave Wu Xingzi precise instructions on how to find the store, what code words to say to the manager, and what he needed to bring with him. Once again, he reassured Wu Xingzi that *The Pengornisseur* was completely confidential and very rich in content.

He finished his explanation and patted the older man's shoulder. "Xingzi-ge, it's not easy for men like us to find someone to spend our lives with. Since it's something you've been thinking about, why don't you give it a shot? Life is short!"

"That's true, that's true," Wu Xingzi said with a nod. He noted everything down before departing the house, hope blooming in his heart.

The next day, Wu Xingzi woke up early and hired Old Liu's cart to reach Goose City.

Goose City was originally called Xuanyi Town. It used to be as poor as Qingcheng County, only its condition was even more grim. After all, Qingcheng County was still an entire county. Eventually, however, a goose farmer by the surname Huang became the richest person in the district by farming poultry. No one knew how he managed to grow such a successful business. With all that money, he rebuilt his hometown into a much more respectable place, transforming it into the most prosperous and lively city in the area.

As a result, people started calling the town Goose City instead of Xuanyi Town. In time, the original name was forgotten entirely.

This was not Wu Xingzi's first trip to Goose City. After all, Qingcheng County was small and poor; if one wished to stock up on goods and necessities for major festivals, one had no choice but to travel to Goose City to purchase them. Each time he was here, Wu Xingzi felt awkward. It seemed like people were staring at him, mocking him in silence for being a country bumpkin. Wu Xingzi couldn't help thinking it even though he knew he was being ridiculous.

Following the tofu boy's directions, he hastily made his way down the busiest street in town. Wu Xingzi had never set foot in this part of the city before. The beautiful stone-paved roads here felt comfortable under his feet, and the streets were lined with resplendent stores as far as his eyes could see. Intriguing, unfamiliar fragrances hung on the breeze. It was all so novel and remarkable that Wu Xingzi could barely move his feet.

Before long, he found the antique shop that acted as a front for the Peng Society for Gentlemen. The store was magnificent and huge, standing tall with elegant and ornate architecture.

After pacing in circles in front of the shop for some time, Wu Xingzi finally mustered his courage and went inside.

However, upon entering, he immediately regretted it.

He froze. All he saw around him were priceless items he didn't recognize. It terrified him to the point that he didn't dare move a muscle.

"Are you looking for anything in particular, sir?" The store attendant was very welcoming, as if he hadn't noticed that Wu Xingzi's clothes were old and fraying from being washed too many times.

Wu Xingzi choked a little before responding. He almost forgot the code words the tofu boy taught him. "I-I... Do you have a jade pagoda from the Han Dynasty?"

The attendant's eyes lit up, but he didn't tip his hand. He was still smiling warmly, his expression not revealing anything. "What kind of Han jade pagoda would you like, sir?"

"O-one that Dong Xian used to play with," Wu Xingzi replied.

"Oh, Dong Xian?" The attendant chuckled. "Sir, I'm afraid that I'm not too familiar with such an item. Would you like to come to the back and speak to our manager?"

"Of course." Wu Xingzi wiped the sweat off his brow.

Without any further small talk, the attendant led Wu Xingzi to the back of the shop.

As he was about to leave the front hall, a pleasant voice rang out. "Dong Xian?"

Wu Xingzi turned to see a man dressed entirely in black.

He was at least a head taller than everyone around him. His demeanor was as sharp and cold as ice, but he had a handsome face that dazzled with the splendor of springtime. His eyes held an amorous glimmer, as dreamy as blossoming flowers in the mist.

He stared directly into Wu Xingzi's furtive eyes.

Cheeks burning, Wu Xingzi hurriedly turned away, hiding from this face that made his pulse race. "How beautiful," he murmured under his breath. The attendant glanced at him, smiling cryptically.

After guiding Wu Xingzi to the garden at the back of the shop, the attendant respectfully asked him to wait in the pavilion. He served

Wu Xingzi a cup of fragrant tea along with some exquisite-looking snacks.

It took Wu Xingzi a moment before he cautiously lifted the cup to sip his tea. Then, he picked up a snack and began nibbling on it. It was sweet, but not cloyingly so, and the burst of fragrance in his mouth was almost floral. He had never tasted anything so delicious in his life.

The wait was quite long. Wu Xingzi drank two cups of tea and finished all the snacks before someone finally sat across from him.

"Enjoying yourself?" the newcomer asked with a smile. His voice was as beautiful as birdsong.

Wu Xingzi immediately tensed up, sitting ramrod straight in his stone seat. "Ah, yes. They're delicious."

The mysterious man burst into laughter, his beauty leaving Wu Xingzi breathless. He was totally entranced by the man's smile, completely unaware that he was turning as pink as a prawn.

"I'm Rancui," the beautiful man said, lifting his teacup for a sip. "And you are?"

"I-I..." Wu Xingzi's throat burned. Unable to speak, he coughed dryly instead.

Rancui chuckled and refilled Wu Xingzi's cup. "Please, soothe your throat. There's no need to rush."

"Thank you." Wu Xingzi picked up his cup and gulped the tea down. Only then did he feel a little better. Embarrassed, he bowed his head and thanked Rancui.

"So polite," Rancui said. He didn't seem to mind Wu Xingzi's awkwardness at all. "Did you come for the Peng Society?"

"Ah, yes," Wu Xingzi said. "I-I brought the money and a self-portrait. I know the rules!"

"Really?" Rancui said. "Since you've done your research, I'll get right to the point. *The Pengornisseur* is published on the tenth of every month, and each edition costs fifty coins. If you'd like to stop your subscription, you'll need to return all previous copies."

"I understand." Wu Xingzi bobbed his head eagerly, hurriedly removing his money pouch from his waist and placing it on the table. "There are fifty coins in here, Rancui-gongzi. Please take them."

Rancui picked up the pouch with a slender hand and opened it, looking inside. Breaking into a smile, he said, "Now that the payment is taken care of, please provide me with your name, hobbies, and self-portrait. Your copy of *The Pengornisseur* will be ready for collection on the tenth."

"Of course." Wu Xingzi quickly passed the drawing and information over to Rancui. It felt like a weight had finally been lifted from his chest; a true sense of relief washed over him.

"Wu-gongzi, right?" Rancui glanced at Wu Xingzi's name. "What a lovely name, Wu-gongzi. I'm sure you'll find a compatible partner in *The Pengornisseur*."

"Thank you for your kind words," Wu Xingzi said, with a foolish smile. For the first time in his life, he was looking forward to the future.

Next, Rancui explained the process of becoming pen pals through the pigeon post.

To protect the identity of the society's members, letters were sent to the local Peng Society branch. Members could use their own pigeons or the pigeons kept by the organization to deliver their letters.

"You will be charged a total of three coins for the first five letters. After that, every letter will cost one coin each," Rancui said.

Wu Xingzi noted everything down with great diligence. He would definitely have to make use of the special rates!

Although there was a fee to use the society's pigeons, the birds were fast and highly reliable; society members typically received their letters within a span of two days. Using the society's pigeons prevented members from being tracked down, protecting their privacy.

"You know, anything can happen in this world. Who hasn't flirted around?" Rancui chuckled, raising a hand to cover his mouth.

Wu Xingzi nodded in agreement, making up his mind to spend some of his money to use the Peng Society's pigeons. He didn't love the extra charge, but it was better to be safe than sorry. If his identity were revealed, he would be in real trouble.

Having explained all the rules in detail, Rancui went on to share the stories of some happy couples who had met through the society. Finally, he bade farewell to a deliriously happy Wu Xingzi.

Knowing he would receive his copy of *The Pengornisseur* on the tenth of the month, Wu Xingzi beamed all the way home, his smile blossoming like a spring flower.

The tenth arrived very quickly. Wu Xingzi woke before the sun was even up. He tidied up his house, polishing his furniture until it shone. He then hurried to a nearby mountain waterfall and washed himself clean. Once he was done, he hired Old Liu's cart to head to Goose City, brimming with joy.

Wu Xingzi fidgeted for the entire journey, countless butterflies fluttering in his stomach. It wasn't until the third glance Old Liu shot him that he realized he'd been humming.

Wu Xingzi didn't know many songs. He only knew the story-telling tunes his father had taught him when he was still alive. For some unknown reason, he was humming the melody from *The Injustice to Dou'e*.[2]

2 　竇娥冤, *a Yuan dynasty opera about the unjust execution of a young woman and the unnatural phenomena that follow until her spirit is vindicated.*

Blushing, Wu Xingzi rubbed the back of his neck and tried to play it cool. He attempted to focus on the familiar scenery around him, but his heart had already flown ahead to the antique shop in Goose City.

This was probably the most arduous, yet pleasant trip Wu Xingzi had ever endured. Upon reaching the city gate, he hastily leapt off the cart. "Uncle Liu, is there anything you wish to buy in Goose City?"

Biting at his pipe, Old Liu placidly watched the restless Wu Xingzi. "No, not really. If you need more time, I'll just wait for you."

"I'm just picking up something. I'll be back soon." Wu Xingzi gave a few firm nods of his head before running off.

Before Old Liu finished smoking his pipe, Wu Xingzi returned, carrying a moderately sized parcel.

"Uncle Liu, please try this."

Wu Xingzi climbed into the cart and pulled out a little bag with four exquisite-looking pastries inside. Old Liu's face looked slightly surprised as he studied Wu Xingzi's bright black eyes and flushed cheeks.

"I'll have some." Although he had no idea where he'd gotten these snacks, Old Liu knew Wu Xingzi wasn't a troublemaker, so he took a piece.

Wu Xingzi carefully placed the package he was carrying on his knee. He stroked it quite a few times, as though he was smoothing out invisible creases; happiness was very evident on his face. It looked as if he could float up into the sky in delight.

When they arrived back at Qingcheng County, Wu Xingzi handed all the pastries to Old Liu. He also arranged for another trip to Goose City for the next day, before leaving with the parcel in his arms.

Old Liu smoked his pipe, watching the usually quiet and restrained Wu Xingzi walk away. He didn't say anything to him, despite how strangely he felt the younger man was acting today.

Back home, Wu Xingzi prepared a basin of water to wipe his body clean. He then washed his hands twice, drying them with a clean cloth. Only after making sure his hands were completely dry did he carefully open the package.

Inside the parcel was a book.

It wasn't too thick, numbering about a hundred pages. The cover of the book was simple and elegant, with the words "The Pengornisseur" written on it in lively, graceful penmanship. The words were well-proportioned and beautiful, their strokes striking; the characters were austere, yet also held a pleasant and casual feeling. Wu Xingzi glided a trembling finger along the words a few times. The paper was high quality, too. Wu Xingzi couldn't identify what type it was, but it felt soft, like cotton.

Wu Xingzi took a deep breath, about to open the book, when he suddenly remembered something. He pulled his hand back and ran over to the door to make sure that it was securely locked, then to the windows to ensure they were shut. Only then did he pat his chest in relief and return to the table, finally opening *The Pengornisseur*.

So this is paradise! Fifteen minutes later, that was the only thought in Wu Xingzi's head. He was giddy with joy, smiling like a drunkard.

There was a total of one hundred and twenty pages in *The Pengornisseur*. Besides the first and last two pages, the rest each had a portrait of a man and his information.

Some descriptions spared no detail, covering their likes and dislikes, the way they dressed, and even their family background. Others only mentioned their names and interests.

Wu Xingzi found his own portrait on page ninety-six.

It was not the drawing he had originally submitted. Instead, it seemed that Rancui had found a professional artist to redraw his portrait. It looked so vivid, so real, it was as if he could walk out from the page. Sheepish yet pleased, he stroked the drawing over and over again. *I don't look that bad,* Wu Xingzi thought. He might really be able to find a man to spend his life with.

He had already forgotten about his plan to commit suicide on his fortieth birthday.

The other illustrations also looked professionally drawn. The Peng Society was very meticulous when it came to their work. It seemed they sincerely wanted their members to find life partners.

After quickly scanning through, Wu Xingzi went back to the front, carefully studying each page.

It wasn't until the sky turned dark and he could no longer see anything that Wu Xingzi put *The Pengornisseur* down. Lighting a lamp, he rubbed at his growling stomach. He quickly cooked a bowl of noodles, adding an egg and two fistfuls of vegetables into the pot. He slurped everything up, filling his belly, before promptly returning to *The Pengornisseur*.

By the time Wu Xingzi had picked out five people, wracked his brains over five whole letters, dried the ink, and rolled the letters up, he was so tired he could barely keep his eyes open. However, lying on his bed, his delight was so overwhelming it kept him awake. Finally, when the crowing of a rooster sounded in the distance, he fell asleep.

The next day, when Old Liu saw how energetic Wu Xingzi looked despite his swollen and bloodshot eyes, he only gave a gentle raise of his brow. Silently, he stuffed two buns and an egg into Wu Xingzi's hands, hoping he could have a good meal along the way.

Once they reached Goose City, Old Liu waited under the shade of the trees outside the gates. Wu Xingzi thanked him before running off into the city.

He took a little longer than he did yesterday. By the time he hurried back with a bag in his hand, the sun had shifted from its earlier position.

"Sorry to keep you waiting, Uncle Liu." Wu Xingzi's eyes were shining, completely different from his usual calm and dreary self. He presented two large meat buns and a bamboo container of cool water to Old Liu. "Please, take these. The buns are delicious."

Old Liu kept feeling that something was amiss, but he didn't say anything. Accepting the buns and water, he thanked Wu Xingzi, and they headed back to Qingcheng County.

On the way back, Wu Xingzi started humming again. He recalled the salesman's instructions when sending the letters. "Sir, replies usually take about three days. However, since letters are delivered so early in the day here, you should be able to receive replies within two days. Please remember to come collect them."

Wu Xingzi had nodded vigorously. "Of course."

He did not pull his eyes away until the pigeons carrying his letters had disappeared from sight.

He had it all planned out. Although there were many men in *The Pengornisseur* who held his interest, he knew his age and lack of assets put him at a disadvantage. As an adviser his salary was only enough to cover his daily necessities, so he had to be careful with the amount he spent on the letters.

These five men were carefully selected. They were close to him in age, the youngest being around thirty-four. All of them were scholars, and two of them had even passed entry-level imperial examinations. They didn't live too far away from him, either, seeing as the receiving point for their letters was in Fragrance City, only a day's travel from Goose City.

All five of them were the only living members of their family, with neither parents nor siblings. They seemed honest and upright, and one of them was even rather handsome. Wu Xingzi privately hoped that he would make friends with the good-looking one.

During the two-day wait, Wu Xingzi was euphoric. He felt as if he were floating on clouds. He smiled more frequently, growing more personable. On the afternoon of the second day, Constable Zhang brought him a bowl of mutton soup with tofu and patted him on the shoulder encouragingly. Overwhelmed by his kindness, Wu Xingzi thought the soup tasted even better than usual.

However, he had yet to realize why Constable Zhang was making a special effort to encourage him. Was it not just a simple issue of making pen pals through the pigeon post?

When Wu Xingzi finally received the replies, he gleefully returned home, locking all his windows and doors.

He opened all five letters, laying each of them flat... And he was stunned at their contents, unable to believe his eyes. His smile remained frozen on his face, which made him look somewhat frightening. Rubbing his eyes, he inhaled deeply, then rolled up each letter with trembling hands and placed them neatly on the table. He went to the kitchen to prepare a bowl of noodles, quickly eating before returning to the table and spreading the letters out flat again.

As the drawings in the letters were revealed, Wu Xingzi's eyes widened more and more, almost falling out of their sockets.

He took a deep breath. His vision dimmed, and he felt like he was going to faint. However, his hands still held those letters flat against the table.

What is going on here? he thought. In front of him were...were... *Are these not five drawings of male anatomy?!*

Wu Xingzi was about to go crazy. He tried to recall what he had written in the letters: "Dear Sir, if I may be so bold, with just one glance at *The Pengornisseur*, I was captivated by your looks and charm. I hope for us to forge a friendship through the pigeon post; perhaps this may result in a happy union."

He felt that his words had been too direct, feeling rather embarrassed when posting the letters. However, he was worried that if he did not express enough sincerity, the other man might think he just wanted to be friends. If that happened, it would have been a huge waste of his money.

Could it be that he had been *too* direct?

Wu Xingzi gripped the five letters, his body shaking so much that his teeth clacked together. It took a long time before he recovered from the shock. Releasing the sheets of paper, he went back into the kitchen to prepare another big bowl of noodles, slurping it all down before returning to the letters. His stomach was so full that it hurt, but he managed to regain some of his usual calm.

Now, he was finally able to carefully consider the cocks before him.

He had to admit, the technique used to draw them was...striking. The illustrations were so realistic that he could almost feel them exuding heat.

Wu Xingzi was a little suspicious. There was no way the Peng Society's artist had redrawn these as well, right? If it were true, those fifty coins were truly well spent.

It was said that there were as many different faces as there were people in the world, and everyone had their own preference. However, Wu Xingzi had never imagined that was also the case for cocks.

The first phallus was neat and clean, the foreskin retreating to show a rounded head. The slit was pink and tender, as if it had never been used before. It looked like the owner rarely masturbated. Wu Xingzi also belonged to this category of cocks, but his own wasn't as big.

The second one was a lot thicker and sturdier, its veins evident through the skin. It looked somewhat threatening, with a huge head, tapering slightly toward the root. It wasn't as long as the first one, and its slit gaped slightly. Darting his eyes across the drawing a couple of times, Wu Xingzi unconsciously gulped.

The third penis belonged to the good-looking gentleman. It was a little smaller, not as thick and long as the previous two. However, it was very aesthetically pleasing, just like a beautiful jade carving. From the root to the tip, and even the slit, it looked exquisite, glowing with an inner warmth. It was a flawless phallus. Wu Xingzi marveled over the way the artist had managed to imbue the illustration with the texture of jade. It was so realistic that he wanted to reach out and touch it.

The fourth was a little different. The foreskin was longer, covering the tip of the penis, and the slit peeked out from within. It was rather thick and long, but not as frightful as the second one. The hair at the root was lush; the artist had deliberately drawn each distinct strand. It looked wild and untamed. If one were to press it against a certain tender part of the body, it was bound to feel ticklish.

Wu Xingzi squirmed in his seat.

The final phallus was an eye-opener for Wu Xingzi. The drawings were all on sheets of the same size, but this one barely fit within the page. The cock was so colossal it looked as if it might burst from the page. The balls looked weighty and full, and the head was about the size of an egg, round and sturdy. The shaft was not straight; it curved slightly upward.

Wu Xingzi breathed heavily. Flustered, he put the drawings down. He vigorously rubbed his hands together, as though flames were licking at his palms. He could not fathom why he'd received such explicit replies through the pigeon post. Were such erotic letters to be expected? Wu Xingzi's body felt hot. He glanced down at his crotch.

Uhh...uhh... He definitely wouldn't be able to draw his own prick in response! For Wu Xingzi, a man who'd lived in a remote village his entire life, the outside world was truly staggering.

Despite being overwhelmed, Wu Xingzi felt a yearning rising within him and a fire blazing in his belly. He stared at the five letters, his throat bobbing as he swallowed.

Wu Xingzi was starting to tent his trousers. Fretfully, he twice walked from one end of his house to the other. The flames did not recede, only burning even more fiercely.

Pushing the windows open, he looked outside. The sky was already dark. No one would drop by his place, right?

With that thought, Wu Xingzi sucked in a deep breath. Once again, he made sure that his door and windows were securely locked before bringing the five phalluses and a candle back to his bedroom. Shucking off his trousers, he climbed into bed.

Wu Xingzi was about to turn forty and he had barely masturbated his whole life. This was the first time he had felt so eager...

Tonight, Wu Xingzi finally tasted a pleasure he had never experienced before.

Wu Xingzi slept better than he had in ages.

Ever since the tragic flood, he had not slept well. However, waking up that morning, he felt refreshed and invigorated. All the gloom was expelled from him, and his body felt bright and nimble.

There was still time after breakfast before he had to report to work. He studied those five drawings he had repeatedly looked at the night before. As he did so, something emerged in his mind.

Does this mean I have to send a drawing of my cock, too? He didn't think he could go through with it. Exhaling, he stacked the five drawings neatly together and carefully placed them in an empty rattan box. He even added a scent pouch to repel insects.

He picked up *The Pengornisseur* and came to a decision.

Last night's enlightening experience had brought Wu Xingzi to an epiphany: his life had been too mundane. Now that he knew there were so many fascinating things out there in the world, not trying any of them out would be such a waste.

There were over a hundred men listed in *The Pengornisseur*. Although not everyone was outstanding, they were all proper and respectable individuals. At first, Wu Xingzi's goal had been to find a life partner or a friend to talk with, so he had carefully made his selections with this in mind.

But...what if everyone was accustomed to sending drawings like these? Even if he was unable to become pen pals with the jewelry store manager on page seventeen, it would not stop him from admiring his...pengornis.

After all, desire for food and sex was just part of human nature.

Wu Xingzi might have been introverted and insecure, but that didn't mean he wasn't interested in sleeping around. The more "birds," the merrier!

Wu Xingzi made up his mind to send a letter to everyone in *The Pengornisseur*, not realizing that he was completely deviating from his original plan. A hundred-odd drawings of phalluses would last him for years! If he had to actually interact with a bunch of men face-to-face, there was no way he could do it. But checking out these cocks in the privacy of his own home? Very exciting indeed.

A few days ago, he'd agonized over spending fifty coins. That was not the case today. Wu Xingzi took the half hour he had before work and wrote ten letters in one go. Thankfully, he had bought a brush, ink, and paper the day he went to pick up *The Pengornisseur*, so he had plenty of supplies to use with reckless abandon.

Wu Xingzi had never once splashed out on anything nice, even buying the cheapest possible New Year's supplies. But now, money was no object as Wu Xingzi dove headfirst into the unexplored world of the pigeon post. From that day on, Wu Xingzi hitched a ride on Old Liu's cart every other day, sending letters and collecting replies. He never spent a second coin on the same person.

After half a month, he'd collected about fifty drawings. Storing them neatly in the rattan case, he flipped through them every night before bed, selecting two or three for that night's enjoyment.

However, Wu Xingzi had never expected that his little form of entertainment would attract the suspicions of Auntie Liu. Having wasted a day waiting for Old Liu's cart, Wu Xingzi finally left the Lius' place, full of regrets.

Without new cocks to admire, how was he supposed to weather the long nights ahead?

Sluggishly, he went to the magistrate's office to settle some paperwork. Soon, the sun set in the sky. Just as he started to head home, Constable Zhang stopped by.

"Adviser Wu," Constable Zhang said.

"Evening, Constable Zhang." Wu Xingzi gave a feeble smile.

Constable Zhang frowned as he looked at him. "Would you like to come over for dinner tonight?" Constable Zhang's expression was tender and sympathetic. However, Wu Xingzi didn't notice at first, still upset that he hadn't collected his letters that day.

"Uhh..." Wu Xingzi blinked. He was delighted, but shyness soon overtook him. "I'd only be intruding."

He was not exactly friendly with Constable Zhang. Despite being colleagues for twenty years, they had barely exchanged more than a few dozen words about anything not work-related. Besides, Zhang knew about Wu Xingzi's previous crush on the tofu seller. He had completely dispelled any notion of becoming close with the constable.

"It's okay," Constable Zhang said. "There's not a big difference between two people having dinner and three. Besides, Ansheng is worried about you." Ansheng was the name of the tofu boy, something Wu Xingzi had discovered the day he learned about the Peng Society.

Constable Zhang looked so calm and even-tempered that Wu Xingzi couldn't refuse him. The two men left the magistrate's office together, heading to the market.

Arriving at the tofu stall, they found Ansheng wiping the tables. The sight of his bare chest, with the rays of the setting sun casting a glow over his sweaty torso, was spectacular. Wu Xingzi rubbed his eyes, quickly turning away to avoid arousing any suspicion. Still, he couldn't help but sneak a peek.

Constable Zhang didn't seem to mind. He went up and hugged Ansheng's waist, kissing him on the forehead. Witnessing such a warm and charming scene, Wu Xingzi felt a pang of envy.

"Xingzi-ge." Ansheng quickly noticed Wu Xingzi was there, blushing as he firmly pushed Constable Zhang away. "How have you been?"

"Very well, thank you." Wu Xingzi bobbed his head. Thinking of the fifty phallus drawings in his house, the smile on his face turned brighter.

"Auntie Liu says you've been going to Goose City a lot." Ansheng winked at him with a cheeky smile.

Wu Xingzi flushed, rubbing the back of his neck. He admitted to it with an embarrassed nod.

"Adviser Wu is having dinner with us tonight. Is there anything you'd like to eat?" Constable Zhang took over the cleaning for Ansheng, scrubbing at the chairs.

"That's great! Xingzi-ge, what sounds good? Fu-ge is a great cook, he can make any dish," Ansheng said. The pleased look on his face made Wu Xingzi even more jealous.

Seeing Ansheng and the constable together made Wu Xingzi feel a little discomfited. When he first joined the Peng Society, his objective was to find a life partner, yet now he only cared about dicks. He didn't pay attention to the people he was sending his letters to ever since he decided to start judging their cocks instead. To him, those hundred-odd men in *The Pengornisseur* were now just variously shaped pengornises. There was no emotion or affection to be had, but he did gain quite a bit of physical satisfaction from it.

"Xingzi-ge?" Ansheng called out to Wu Xingzi in concern, noticing that he was in some sort of daze.

"Hmm? Oh, it's fine. I eat everything. I'm not picky." Wu Xingzi came back to his senses, his response a little awkward.

Ansheng and Constable Zhang exchanged a look. They seemed worried, but neither said anything. They warmly welcomed Wu Xingzi to their home.

Constable Zhang was quite the chef. His simple stir-fried mountain vegetables, fried long beans, and pickled vegetables with meat could hold their own against the food served at restaurants in Goose City. Wu Xingzi's meals usually consisted of a bowl of noodles, buns, or pancakes with eggs. He didn't spend too much effort on food, seeing as he only cooked for himself.

After dinner, just like last time, Constable Zhang went to wash the dishes while Ansheng pulled Wu Xingzi away for a chat.

"Xingzi-ge, have you met someone you like?" Ansheng asked the question after some deliberation.

"Huh?" Wu Xingzi blinked. He was drinking the wine he'd brought along, and his train of thought had strayed. Reflexively, he nodded.

"Really?!" Ansheng sighed in relief, his eyes shining. "What kind of person is he?"

"Umm..." Wu Xingzi was unable to answer. The truth was...he didn't like a *person*, but a person's *penis*.

"Hmm?" Anticipation was written all over Ansheng's face. Wu Xingzi blushed. He felt he had to try to come up with an answer no matter what.

"He's a very...powerful and magnificent man." Flashing across Wu Xingzi's mind was that thick and weighty phallus he'd seen the first time, the one that nearly filled up the entire page. By now, he had already collected fifty drawings, but none could compare to that particular prick.

He thought of it fondly: the thickness and the length, the slightly curved shape, that full and round tip; the slit was almost shy, and the balls were heavy and full. Each time he held that drawing, it felt like it was burning in his hand.

"Is he someone like Fu-ge?" Ansheng asked, clearly curious. He was familiar with *The Pengornisseur*, so he knew it was rare for a tall, muscular man like Constable Zhang to appear within its pages.

Wu Xingzi's brain almost imploded at Ansheng's words. He could not help but attach the image of that phallus to Constable Zhang. A thick and weighty object like that... It suited him. Quietly, Wu Xingzi savored the image in his mind, nodding his head firmly.

"So Xingzi-ge also likes tall and muscular men," Ansheng said, a little surprised. He wasn't very close to Wu Xingzi, but he still had a good understanding of the older man. This man in front of him was warm, gentle, and somewhat shy. He always seemed nervous when he saw those tall, strong constables at the magistrate's office, quietly distancing himself from them. Ansheng always thought that Wu Xingzi would prefer a gentle, mild sort of man.

"Ummm... I quite...quite like them..." Wu Xingzi shifted about uneasily. The drawings he favored all belonged to the thick and strong category. He was burning to know what it would be like to touch the real thing. Would it be just how he imagined it, heavy and scorching in his palm?

"That's great, Xingzi-ge." Ansheng sincerely expressed his congratulations.

Wu Xingzi felt a stab of guilt. "It's nothing, really," he said. When he thought about it, everyone on *The Pengornisseur* was looking to make friends. The fact that he only cared about collecting the drawings seemed rather reprehensible.

Believing that they'd gotten a good answer, Ansheng and Constable Zhang's worries were put to rest. When they finished the wine, Wu Xingzi said his farewells and made his way home.

Upon reaching home, Wu Xingzi locked all his doors and windows. He took out that special rattan case and spread the fifty drawings across his table, comparing them one by one alongside their owners' portraits in *The Pengornisseur*.

He had not paid much attention to most of the men's faces. Some of them were from places quite a distance away, and it would take four or five days for the pigeons to return with responses.

His favorite pengornis picture belonged to a private tutor. From his portrait, he looked fair and refined, his face exuding a sense of righteousness. His shoulders were a little narrow; Wu Xingzi estimated that the width of the man's shoulders was similar to his own. He was slim and tall, if a little bony.

This private tutor was also a scholar, and he was close to forty. He liked reading, the art of tea, and drinking with his old friends every few days. He did not plan on going after any more scholastic honors, only wanting to stay in his hometown and be a good teacher, peacefully spending the rest of his life there.

For some reason, an image of his own father popped up in Wu Xingzi's mind. At this image, he firmly closed *The Pengornisseur*. Staring at the picture of the pengornis, he giggled.

Life was truly too fragile. He thought about how his parents had been swallowed up by the swelling river in the blink of an eye, their bodies never found to this day. He was about to turn forty. Even if he looked for someone just past the age of thirty to spend his life with, there was no guarantee that one day he wouldn't wake up alone.

But these pengornis pictures were different. Even if he were to perish tomorrow, these drawings would join him in that yellowwood coffin, accompanying him to the afterlife.

With these thoughts, Wu Xingzi cheered up again. He pushed the memory of the affectionate behavior between Ansheng and Constable Zhang down into a deep corner of his mind, rolling a large boulder on top to trap it there.

Remembering he would again be able to collect new drawings from Goose City tomorrow, Wu Xingzi was in a state of bliss.

He picked up the drawing he liked the best, peeled off his pants, and climbed onto his bed. He wrapped his hand around his cock and started stroking.

The moment the salesman from the Peng Society saw Wu Xingzi, he welcomed him with a smile. "Wu-gongzi, you're here!"

"Ah, yes, yes." Wu Xingzi smiled bashfully. Nervously wringing his hands, he followed the salesman's familiar steps to the parlor at the back of the shop.

"Please, Wu-gongzi, take a seat. I'll go get your letters." The salesman collected the letters that Wu Xingzi wanted to send and left him with tea and snacks.

Wu Xingzi sat on the chair, his feet tapping continuously on the ground. He lifted the teacup a few times but didn't even bring it to his lips before he put it back down again. With the butterflies fluttering in his stomach, he couldn't stop staring at the closed door.

There were quite a number of such parlors at the back of this shop that were used as waiting rooms. Although they weren't very spacious, they weren't cramped either. They were perfectly comfortable to wait in for about a quarter to half an hour, especially with drinks and snacks provided.

Although he had been here a few times already to collect his replies, Wu Xingzi still wasn't used to being in such fancy surroundings as the Peng Society. He was filled with anticipation for the letters, but he felt uneasy about having someone basically running errands for him.

After a quarter of an hour that felt more like an eternity, the door finally opened. Wu Xingzi nearly leapt up from his seat, barely managing to hold himself back.

"Wu-gongzi, you have a few more letters today. Some even from Bastion City!" The salesman gestured at the letters before gathering them up and passing them to Wu Xingzi.

Bastion City? Wu Xingzi was a little taken aback before he remembered that he did send three letters to the Peng Society in Bastion City about seven or eight days ago. Bastion City was Great Xia's southernmost city, and its most prosperous. It was probably the furthest place possible from Goose City. An indescribable hopefulness welled up within him.

Wu Xingzi thanked the salesman for the letters before passing him a few coins. Just like last time, he packed up the leftover snacks and left feeling satisfied.

Wu Xingzi had never met any other members of the Peng Society, likely because very few of them came as early as he did. He'd learned from his casual chats with the salesman that most members only dropped by in the afternoon. Therefore, when he heard the door of the parlor beside him open at the same moment he was leaving, Wu Xingzi started. He shrank back and contemplated retreating into the room. However, the salesman stood directly behind him. He was stuck, one foot beyond the threshold and one foot still inside, completely frozen.

"Wu-gongzi?" The salesman was quick on his feet, managing to avoid colliding with Wu Xingzi.

"Umm..." Wu Xingzi felt so awkward. He wanted nothing more than to dig a hole and bury himself in it. Flustered, he didn't know what to do next.

The customer from the parlor next door casually stopped, and upon seeing Wu Xingzi's pale, sweaty face, he asked, "What's wrong?"

Wu Xingzi shivered as he heard that voice, his ears instantly reddening.

Never before had he heard such a pleasant voice. It sounded like jade pieces striking together. It was melodious and flowing like a clear spring, yet warm and gentle like a lover's whisper. Even though it was just a simple question, it dug its hooks straight into Wu Xingzi's heart.

Wu Xingzi dared not look toward the owner of that voice. He covered his ears in abashment, his head hanging so low his chin dug into his chest. From the corner of his eye, he caught a glimpse of a black robe embroidered with dark, elegant patterns.

"It's fine, it's fine. Please go ahead." With some effort, Wu Xingzi gestured at the other man to walk ahead of him, but his body was so stiff he ended up twisting his arm. A loud creak was heard. It was truly impossible for Wu Xingzi to reach higher levels of embarrassment today.

The man did not respond, and the black robe soon disappeared from Wu Xingzi's sight.

The salesman waited until the other man was some distance away before cautiously calling out to Wu Xingzi. "Wu-gongzi, are you all right? Should we call a physician here to take a look at you?"

"No need. I'm fine..." Wu Xingzi no longer cared about his humiliation. He hurriedly waved the salesman off. Clutching at his package of letters, he stiffly headed out of the shop, nearly tripping over the threshold in the process.

He couldn't fathom why he was reacting this way. There were over a hundred members of the Peng Society, and twenty or thirty of them listed Goose City as their location. Meeting a member really shouldn't be a big deal; there was truly no need to feel flustered. Furthermore, if they ran into each other and each man found the other satisfactory, they might even have a chance to start a relationship.

Wu Xingzi couldn't make himself take that step.

He felt ashamed for no reason at all. By being so shy, he might lose his chance to collect more phallus illustrations. Especially a person like him, who was old and far from handsome...

He could still console himself that his features were nothing out of the ordinary. However, that man he saw just now... His voice was music to the ears, and his looks were definitely above average. With the existence of such a man in *The Pengornisseur*, what business did Wu Xingzi have appearing within the same pages?

Clinging to his letters, Wu Xingzi fled the Peng Society. He did not notice the pair of eyes closely following him. They stared in his direction, even as the crowd swallowed him up. It was a long time before those mysterious eyes shifted away.

CHAPTER TWO

THE LANLING PRINCE OF PENGORNISES

Wu Xingzi didn't know what was wrong with him. It was just a drawing of a cock... No, no, no, he immediately refuted himself. This wasn't an ordinary penis picture, this was the Lanling Prince of pengornises![3] He was now a city conquered by the Prince of Lanling, utterly defeated and thoroughly vanquished, yet completely willing to be destroyed. He was bewitched by its devastating beauty.

JUST LIKE USUAL, after passing Old Liu a meat bun and some cool water, Wu Xingzi sat on the swaying cart and chewed on his own bun. For once, his attention was not on his food. Instead, it was occupied by that melodious voice. A faint, silly grin appeared on his face.

Old Liu glanced at him but didn't say anything, just kept moving the cart along.

They returned to Qingcheng County earlier than usual. Since the letters had to travel a little further this time, Wu Xingzi made arrangements with Old Liu to head to Goose City three days from now. He then headed to the magistrate's office to deal with his work.

---

3   This is a reference to Gao Xiaoguan, a general of the Northern Qi dynasty who was also known as the Prince of Lanling. He was purportedly so beautiful that he wore a fearsome mask into battle to conceal his face.

It wasn't until the sun had nearly set completely that Wu Xingzi hurried home from the magistrate's office.

He quickly prepared a bowl of noodles and ate it. Then he fetched some water and took a bath. The weather had started to turn colder, but he was too lazy to heat up the water. He ended up so chilled that his teeth chattered; it took him a long time huddling under a blanket to finally warm up.

Once he felt warm enough, he excitedly opened the letters he'd received today. As expected, they were all drawings of cocks. There were eight in total.

Five of them were average looking. After a quick glance, Wu Xingzi put them down. Having studied quite a few penis pictures, Wu Xingzi did not spend much time appraising the less impressive ones. The artist's skill was as exemplary as usual; even though they looked plain, they were still decent, and they could be put to use on ordinary days. However, Wu Xingzi's mood was rather feverish tonight, and he needed a very provocative pengornis to soothe himself.

The next three drawings were truly eye-catching. Each one hailed from Bastion City, and after the artist's retouching, they were all awe-inspiringly noble and handsome. *Especially that one...* Wu Xingzi gulped down excess saliva, his eyes fixed on the phallus that left him breathless. To even blink would be a waste.

At first glance, Wu Xingzi noticed that this prick was definitely comparable to the one that currently held the number-one spot in his heart. All its characteristics were beautiful; whether it was the length, the thickness, the heft, or the curvature, Wu Xingzi could not pull his eyes away. His throat felt so dry, it was as if a fire had blazed through it.

After studying the drawing carefully again, Wu Xingzi was deeply shaken. It was then that he noticed this sheet of paper was nearly an inch longer than the rest of the letters. Despite the extra space, this phallus filled up most of the paper, almost exploding out from it. Although it was just a drawing, it looked almost as big as a child's arm. Wu Xingzi blushed deeply.

Not only did it look weighty, but Wu Xingzi could also practically feel its heat emanating from the paper. The bulbous head was the size of a chicken's egg, adorned with a slightly gaping slit; it was practically begging him to suck on it. A throbbing vein ran along the thick shaft, and two full, round balls hung at the bottom. It was as savage and alluring as could be. It was perfect—neither too big nor too small. It was full of masculine vigor, yet it did not feel boorish; the curve looked as though it could hook him in the heart. It carried itself with the elegance of a scholar and the might of a warrior.

Wu Xingzi looked at the drawing in his hand, then at his pants. His cock was so swollen it hurt. It drooled heavily from the tip, forming a large wet patch on his trousers. He hadn't even touched himself. Just looking at this drawing and imagining the phallus's weight, heat, and scent was nearly enough to make him orgasm.

He finally understood what people meant when they said something was indescribable. The prick he was looking at now was exactly that.

Wu Xingzi didn't know what to do. He only knew that he had been completely captured by the cock in the drawing.

No matter how much time he spent gazing at it, it wasn't enough. He had long forgotten about the other two drawings from today's mail, and the fifty drawings in his rattan case completely lost their allure. Wu Xingzi grabbed his teapot and poured the tea directly into his mouth, finishing half the pot in one gulp. His dry, burning throat finally felt soothed.

His eyes stayed fixed on the drawing as he drank his tea, greedily ogling every inch. Those plump, round balls... Wu Xingzi pursed his lips and sucked in air. His tongue rolled around, as though he was actually sucking that bulging sack into his mouth.

Next was the thick shaft with its pulsing vein... Wu Xingzi opened his mouth slightly, his bright red tongue curling up, licking his lips. But just pretending wasn't enough; he felt an emptiness in his heart and a tingling in his throat. How he wished he could pull that phallus off the paper and put it into his mouth. He longed to lick and suck at it, to taste the fluid dripping from the tip.

It was like he was a man possessed.

Wu Xingzi panted heavily. He curled up on his bed, pumping his cock vigorously, and bit down on his blanket, sucking and licking at it.

It was the first time he had ever felt like this. Having appraised over fifty cocks, he had never before lost his composure so severely. He had other favorites and wanted to know their tastes as well, but that was only in his head. Looking at those drawings while rubbing himself off, then having a good sleep afterward was enough for him.

Wu Xingzi had never had a partner before. He was a complete virgin from head to toe. He'd learned about cocksucking from the erotic drawings that Manager Rancui had given him some time ago.

"Ahhh!" His hips quivered and his pale, slender thighs jerked on the bed. Almost winded, his body was weak after his orgasm, and his hand was full of white, sticky fluid.

His mind only cleared once he caught his breath. He stared vacantly at the blanket, at the imprints his teeth had left, then raised his hand to look at the cooling semen on it. His entire body was out of strength, but deep within him was a relentlessly squirming restlessness.

He didn't know what had brought on this behavior. After all, it was only a drawing... *No,* Wu Xingzi immediately refuted himself. This was not some ordinary pengornis picture, this was the Pan An of all pengornis pictures![4]

Or perhaps this was the Lanling Prince of all pengornises. Exceedingly beautiful, yet within its elegant exterior lay a hidden strength that was powerful enough to topple cities. Wu Xingzi was now one of those destroyed cities. He was willingly defeated by its intoxicating charm.

Wu Xingzi rested on his bed for a while before he finally regained some energy. He carefully placed the drawing by his bedside then stood up and washed the sticky fluid off himself. He changed his clothes and made sure his hands were clean before carefully picking up the drawing again, unwilling to let it go.

Only when the moon was high in the night sky and the stars were distant did Wu Xingzi reluctantly place the drawing in his rattan case and go to sleep.

Wu Xingzi was not sure if he slept well that night. In his dreams, at first, the owner of that voice appeared. As he hadn't seen his face, just his robe, the man in his dream was blurry, but he had a vague impression that the man was very handsome, so much so that he was unable to find the words to describe it. The man was somewhat aloof. When Wu Xingzi asked for his name, the man ignored him. He took a seat some distance away from Wu Xingzi, looking just like a painting as he drank his tea.

Somehow, though, the next moment, the man leaned forward, laughing quietly into his ear. The laugh left Wu Xingzi feeling weak, his entire body turning red as a beet. Then, the man removed his

---

4   Pan An is a common name for the Western Jin dynasty poet Pan Yue, who was known for being particularly good looking.

black robe, exposing his fearsome phallus, and it just happened to be the one Wu Xingzi had become so enraptured with.

Wu Xingzi's eyes widened, and his brain went blank.

"Do you want to touch it?" the man asked with a smile. Wu Xingzi nodded eagerly, his legs collapsing under him. He kneeled between the man's thighs and reached out with a trembling hand to touch that mysterious member.

It was hot—so hot that his palm tingled.

Wu Xingzi carefully dragged his hand from the root to the tip, letting that hefty weight slide across his palm, while his other hand lightly caressed the man's swelling balls.

The man's breathing became slightly strained. At the sound of his groaning, Wu Xingzi hardened in his pants, the sweat on his forehead rolling down his face. His abdomen tingled, and he wished someone could soothe the restlessness inside.

"Lick it," the man directed gently, and Wu Xingzi willingly obeyed. He opened his mouth, feeling eager yet also shy. He drew closer to the hot, swollen head, about to swallow it in...

And woke up with a violent start, choking.

Still only half awake, he felt trapped in the surroundings of the dream. He sat there in a daze with his mouth open, sucking in air. His breath came out in a hiss.

It took him a while to recover his senses. His body was bright red, and he felt almost powerless.

Did I really just have a wet dream? Forget about that, exactly how much do I want to suck that cock?! He harshly pinched his cheeks, only letting go after leaving bruises.

His trousers were once again stained with semen. Wu Xingzi climbed out from his bed in shame and frustration. Once he'd changed his pants, he realized that it was already dawn. He secretively carried his clothes to the riverside and washed them clean before running home to dry them out in the sun.

Oh, Wu Xingzi, he reproached himself silently. *Forget about the fact that you've achieved nothing in your life, and forget about your hobby of collecting dick pictures. Why would you fall in love at first sight with a cock?!*

But still, he tried to justify it to himself. That was no ordinary cock, after all! *Think about it! If Lord Longyang stood in front of you today, would you not fall in love with him immediately?*[5]

This might be difficult. Wu Xingzi slapped himself hard, but he still couldn't rid himself of that lingering dream. He had to admit defeat.

This was the first time Wu Xingzi decided to spend a second coin on the same man.

The question was, should he draw his own cock in response? Or should he act in a civilized manner and write a sentimental letter offering to be friends? Wu Xingzi struggled with this dilemma for three days.

On the third day, which was also the day he had arranged with Old Liu to go to Goose City, Wi Xingzi woke up early, finally making his decision.

He inhaled a few sharp breaths, prepared his writing materials, pulled his trousers off, and stroked himself until he got hard— it wasn't difficult to do. All he had to do was think of that Lanling Prince of pengornises and he'd get so hard he leaked. He used slow brushstrokes to paint his own dick on the paper, making sure to include every detail, then folded it up after it dried.

Bastion City was far away, located along the country's border. It neighbored Nanman and stationed nearly twenty thousand soldiers.

---

5   Lord Longyang was the Warring States era lover of an unnamed king of Wei.

The commanding general of the city, who was heir to the protector general, had achieved great feats in war. In just five years, he'd pushed the Nanman army back and forced their king to pay tribute to the capital. Nanman dared not test the border again.

Because of the massacres that had taken place during the war, just hearing the general's name would make children cry at night. It was said that he looked like a vile and sinister demon. He protected the southern border as if there was an iron wall around it.

Wu Xingzi had heard of him, but he had never paid much attention. After all, Qingcheng County was a tiny place in the middle of nowhere, and they rarely received news or messages. This notorious general of the Southern Garrison would never in his life have any business in a place like Qingcheng County.

However, Wu Xingzi was still very grateful for him. It was only thanks to the military presence in Bastion City that he had been able to gaze on such a perfect pengornis.

He had been waiting four days for a reply now. In that time, he'd barely had any appetite for food or drink; he only counted the days in anticipation. Knowing that he still had to endure three more days of waiting, he was rather irritable. He'd even lost a fair bit of weight.

Compared to how enjoyable his life had been only a few days ago, Wu Xingzi now felt his days were incredibly monotonous. In fact, the time spent waiting was possibly more arduous than his life before joining the Peng Society had been.

It was said that when one became accustomed to luxury, it was hard to return to a frugal life. How could one go back to simple vegetarian fare after growing used to hearty meat dishes? Wu Xingzi gazed at that drawing from Bastion City every day, often comforting himself with his hand. He dreamt of that phallus along with the mystery man in black. Although he knew that cock could not possibly belong to that man, he couldn't control his imagination. He ended up washing his trousers every morning after he woke.

Would his own cock be enough to pique the other person's interest? Wu Xingzi was pessimistic, especially when his was so... lackluster. It was plain, just like his face.

By the sixth day, Wu Xingzi was drifting about like a ghost, staring at people vacantly. Constable Zhang was concerned and asked after him many times. Rumors spread within Qingcheng County that Adviser Wu had lost his money and his heart through the pigeon post.

"Where'd you hear that?" Ansheng asked. He finally had some free time at work and overheard his customers gossiping. They vividly described how Adviser Wu was deceived by a sham of a man and had his heart broken and that this man swindled him out of every penny he owned. They insisted that making pen pals through the pigeon post was risky.

The customers' expressions became even more excited at Ansheng's question. "Ah, we heard it from Auntie Liu! You know her, right?"

"Auntie Liu? The wife of the guy who drives the cart?" Ansheng wiped his hands clean and sat at their table, full of curiosity. "What did Auntie Liu say?"

"It's about Adviser Wu! He kept going to Goose City. We heard that he was obsessed with making pen pals through that pigeon post. Tsk-tsk, why do they have to be so secretive with each other? You don't even know the exact background of the other person. Adviser Wu is rather daring." The first customer was so excited that spit went flying as he spoke, his eyes bright. He sounded sorrowful but his face was full of interest.

"Yes, exactly! This pigeon post pen pal thing is so bizarre. How can you believe what's written on those letters if you've never seen the other person's face? Adviser Wu is about to turn forty. I'm afraid he started this because he's been so lonely! To seek a solution this haphazardly... Now look at how he's suffered! He even lost his stash of cash!" The second customer patted his chest. It seemed he was compelled to spill all the gossip.

"Adviser Wu told all this to Auntie Liu?" Ansheng suppressed the urge to roll his eyes. Maintaining a look of interest on his face, he let the two customers continue speaking.

"Adviser Wu would never be so direct. However, the past few days, he hasn't hired the cart to go to Goose City. What other reason can there be?" The first customer shook his head.

"Exactly!" the second customer agreed. "You don't know how often Adviser Wu used to visit Goose City. He would go every other day! If he hadn't been completely foolish, why else would he run to Goose City so often? Who knows what kind of sweet words Adviser Wu fell for? It made him lose all sense."

"Don't you agree with us, young man?" asked the first customer.

Both customers looked at Ansheng. He smiled and nodded. He was smart enough to not reveal anything, but secretly he was worried.

He wasn't concerned about someone deceiving Wu Xingzi. The Peng Society was very meticulous with their business, and not everyone made it into *The Pengornisseur*. No one knew how they received their information, but all criminals were refused at the door. This policy was corroborated by Constable Zhang, so Ansheng didn't doubt it.

However, he was worried that Wu Xingzi had liked someone and been rejected. This was common when making friends through the pigeon post. With how timid and cautious Wu Xingzi was, it was likely that he wouldn't try again if he was rejected too many times.

He wouldn't make any friends that way, and that was the entire purpose of the pigeon post.

Ansheng noticed there was still some time left before he had to close the store, but he couldn't wait any longer. As soon as the two customers finished eating, he quickly packed up the shop.

By the time he reached the magistrate's office, it was nearing three in the afternoon. The entrance to the office was quiet. Even the guards who were supposed to be stationed at the door were nowhere to be seen. Sparrows perched in a row on the roof and chirped away as a cool breeze set a sleepy mood.

Ansheng paused for a moment, then entered the office from a side door. He did not know where to look for Wu Xingzi. Although he was Constable Zhang's partner, this was the first time he had come to the magistrate's office.

"Is that Ansheng?" A gentle and slightly nasal voice was heard. It sounded very friendly.

"Xingzi-ge!" Ansheng hurried over, delighted.

"Are you here for Constable Zhang?" Wu Xingzi's complexion was pale, but he still had a genial smile on his face.

"No, I was looking for you." Ansheng bit his lip and hesitated before he spoke. "Xingzi-ge, do you…have time to talk?"

"I do have some time…" Wu Xingzi looked troubled but didn't send him away. "Come, let's talk in my office."

"Okay."

Wu Xingzi led Ansheng into his office, which was a little room by the side of the hall. Inside was a table and two chairs. Many bookshelves stood against the wall, all crammed full. Even the table was stacked with dossiers.

"Sorry about the mess." Wu Xingzi's ears reddened a little. "Take a seat. I'll go prepare some tea."

"Don't trouble yourself, Xingzi-ge. I'm just here to discuss a small matter. It won't take long." Ansheng motioned for Wu Xingzi to sit down before taking a seat himself.

Both of them looked at each other in silence. Ansheng carefully studied Wu Xingzi, while Wu Xingzi puzzled over the reason for Ansheng's visit.

Wu Xingzi was uneasy and could not stop fidgeting. Ansheng finally let out a deep breath and spoke up. "Xingzi-ge, tell me the truth. Have you gotten into any trouble?"

"Trouble?" Wu Xingzi was confused. He did have some trouble with his favorite phallus, but that was hardly something he could talk about out loud.

"Yes, trouble with the pigeon post..." Ansheng tried to be subtle with his question. He didn't believe the rumors being spread, but he could not ignore how haggard Wu Xingzi looked. It had only been a few days since they last saw each other, but Wu Xingzi had lost so much weight. His build had never been exactly sturdy, but now he looked as though he could be blown away by a stiff breeze.

Wu Xingzi could not control the blush on his face at Ansheng's words. He rubbed the back of his neck in embarrassment, unable to say a word. But Ansheng was in no hurry. He sat there quietly and waited.

After a while, Wu Xingzi finally replied. "No, I'm fine. It's just..." He really could not mention his infatuation with a penis. He was easily embarrassed and wanted to continue living with his dignity intact.

"It's just?" Ansheng prompted Wu Xingzi.

Wu Xingzi adjusted his position and gulped. "A few days ago, I was attracted to a p...a person. I sent him a letter and now I'm waiting for a reply. I've been thinking about it so much that I've lost my appetite. Sorry if I made you worry."

"How many days ago did you send the letter?" Ansheng was a little less worried after hearing Wu Xingzi's explanation.

"It's been six days. The other man lives in Bastion City, so the pigeon takes longer. I think I'll finally get the reply tomorrow." Once Wu Xingzi started talking, the conversation flowed easily. After all, he wasn't an ill-tempered man. He'd gotten to know Ansheng quite well by now, so he told him everything that he could.

"Oh, so it's like that." Ansheng nodded, completely putting aside his worries. He blamed it on Auntie Liu. With those ridiculous rumors she was spreading around, people would end up saying all kinds of things.

"Xingzi-ge, there's something that I have to tell you," Ansheng said.

"What is it?" Wu Xingzi's face was still slightly flushed, but he looked more at ease.

"It's about Auntie Liu... Be more careful. There are some things you shouldn't tell her."

"Auntie Liu?" Wu Xingzi blinked, then smiled gently. "I know she likes to gossip, but she doesn't have bad intentions. Rumors always blow over after a while. I don't mind."

Qingcheng County was small and impoverished. Life was difficult for its people, and chitchatting was the only form of entertainment available. Wu Xingzi was well aware that his matters were treated as gossip fodder. Since he didn't hear about it directly, he pretended not to know about it. Such was life!

Ansheng sighed. "You've got such a good attitude. No wonder Auntie Liu likes to gossip about you."

"It's nothing. No one means any harm." Wu Xingzi patted Ansheng's shoulder. "Thank you for worrying about me."

"Ah, that's just what I do." Ansheng considered for a moment, then added, "Xingzi-ge, everyone in Qingcheng County knows you're a good person. You shouldn't look down on yourself. *The Pengornisseur* is only a means of introducing yourself to people. Don't think too much about it."

"Yes, I know." Wu Xingzi felt warmed by the concern. Although he and Ansheng were not destined to be partners, they had become good friends, which was its own kind of destiny.

"Come over to my place tomorrow for dinner," Ansheng suggested.

"Sure," Wu Xingzi replied.

They continued chatting about various daily trifles and didn't say their farewells until the sun and the sky began to darken. Wu Xingzi took Ansheng along to look for Constable Zhang, and they both went home separately.

Wu Xingzi woke bright and early when dawn broke through the sky the next morning. He was full of vigor, completely different from his dispirited state the past few days. He didn't even have a wet dream during the night, probably due to his anticipation over the incoming reply.

He prepared his breakfast at home, but his heart was already in Goose City.

Before he left, he went back to his room and counted out fifty coins. He had originally only planned to subscribe to *The Pengornisseur* for a month, but he decided to continue his subscription. He was secretly committed to collecting those pengornis drawings. That way, even if he couldn't be friends with that Prince of Lanling, there would be others to console him.

Who could say—he might just meet a Han Zigao, a Wei Jie, or a Ji Kang.[6] The world contained an abundant assortment of cocks; even without his current favorite, there were many others to come.

Just like last time, Wu Xingzi arrived at the Peng Society in the morning. A salesman brought him to one of the parlors in the back. He was excited—when he'd been here seven days ago, he'd only sent that single letter. If he was being asked to wait, that definitely meant there was a reply! Could the owner of this fantastic phallus also be attracted to his own? Ah, how embarrassing!

Wu Xingzi waited in anticipation for the salesman to return. He waited for quite some time. His enthusiasm gradually dimmed, and a sense of unease welled up within him. Before, he'd been sitting up properly in his seat, eager to receive his reply. Now, he was anxious, and his posture shriveled.

Could it be that the man had not replied? Had the salesman made a mistake? Was he hiding from him? No, the salesmen of the Peng Society were all smart people. If they made a mistake, they would be able to come up with a good solution. *Even if they can't, there's still Manager Rancui, right?* Wu Xingzi thought. *Rancui puts everyone at ease!*

He sighed, deflated.

Should he just go? It was getting late; he shouldn't leave Old Liu waiting like this. He could just pass the salesman the fifty coins and leave. There were cocks everywhere, why focus only on a single bird?

Having made his decision, Wu Xingzi drank a final mouthful of tea and headed out of the parlor dejectedly. At the same time, he heard the door to the parlor next to him opening.

---

6   Three male historical figures who were noted for their good looks. Han Zigao was the lover of Emperor Wen of Chen, who doted on him excessively; Wei Jie was a beautiful youth who was said to have been stared at so much that he died of it; and Ji Kang was a scholar from the Three Kingdoms period, recorded as being exceptionally tall and handsome.

Reflexively, he lifted his head to take a look, only to be left in shock.

Stepping out of the room was a man dressed in black. The material of his robe was like flowing water, and Wu Xingzi immediately thought of the black robe he'd seen the last time he was here.

The man was extremely tall, his clothes billowing in the wind. His silky black hair was bundled up plainly with a jade hairpin. His skin was as pale as snow. Wearing his black robe, he had an otherworldly demeanor.

Having apparently noticed Wu Xingzi's attention, the man glanced at him. His face was perfect. His cold eyes glittered like black crystals. His gaze made Wu Xingzi tremble, his legs weakening under him.

Realizing that he had acted indecently, he quickly averted his eyes. As he was about to raise his hands in apology, the man spoke first.

"Are you Adviser Wu from Qingcheng County?"

It was definitely the same melodious voice he had heard that day. Icy and lingering.

"Yes, yes, that's me. I'm sorry I offended you." Wu Xingzi hurriedly cupped his hands in apology, bowing his head until it was almost buried in his chest. The fact that the man recognized him didn't make him suspicious in the least. After all, men who frequented this establishment were all members of the Peng Society, and they had all seen *The Pengornisseur*. Wu Xingzi's portrait appeared in it!

However, the man in front of him was not featured in the pages of *The Pengornisseur*. Wu Xingzi would have remembered a man like him, who looked like he had descended from the heavens.

"There's no offense." The man paused. "My name is Guan Shanjin."

"Guan-gongzi..." Wu Xingzi could not resist lifting his head to peek at him, only to end up nearly stumbling and falling backward—

the man who'd originally stood quite a distance from him was now silently standing at only an arm's length. An intoxicating scent wafted toward Wu Xingzi, and he was compelled to inhale it again and again, his mind floating away.

"Yes." Guan Shanjin seemed to be smiling. It was as if his voice had claws, capable of scratching a person's heart.

"You're...also a member of the Peng Society?" Wu Xingzi was unsure of what to do next. He felt ashamed of his ungainly appearance, but still could not resist leaning closer. *Ah, this noble man smells magnificent.*

"I am, but I'm also not." The corners of Guan Shanjin's lips curled up. Those lips were sumptuous, neither too big nor too small, and perfectly thick. Their color was a faint red, just like the petals of a flower.

How would it feel to nibble on them? Having never kissed anyone before, Wu Xingzi started daydreaming.

The feeling this man gave him was similar to the one his favorite phallus gave him—a deep impression from just one glance. Everything else faded away.

"Guan-gongzi, do you plan on appearing in *The Pengornisseur*?" Wu Xingzi asked with a smile.

"I've done it already." Guan Shanjin spoke these words carefully, but Wu Xingzi did not notice. He only felt regretful hearing this answer.

If this man already made friends through the pigeon post, but Wu Xingzi had not seen him in the current edition of *The Pengornisseur*, did that mean he had found his partner?

"Oh..." Wu Xingzi said. Since this man already had someone, Wu Xingzi could only sigh and sniff quietly at the man's scent. "Then you're here to return *The Pengornisseur*?"

"No." Guan Shanjin's eyes crinkled. His icy demeanor melted away in a flash, and he emanated seductive charm. "I'm here to collect a letter."

"A letter?" Wu Xingzi said.

"Yes." Guan Shanjin pulled out a letter from his robes and opened it in front of Wu Xingzi. "Yours."

On that sheet of paper was clearly the cock illustration that Wu Xingzi had personally drawn.

His eyes widened, his entire body trembling. He retreated on unsteady feet, only to have Guan Shanjin put his arm around his waist.

No, no, no, this is definitely a misunderstanding! Wu Xingzi tried to struggle, but Guan Shanjin was unexpectedly strong. He easily carried him into the parlor, kicking the door closed behind them and giving the shy man a gorgeous smile.

"Since we've already seen each other in such a manner," Guan Shangin said, "why don't we take the next step?"

Huh? Wu Xingzi's eyes widened even more. While he was dazzled by that dimpled smile, something within him screamed in alarm.

When a soft and warm breath brushed against his lips, Wu Xingzi forgot all about struggling.

Wu Xingzi was a complete and utter virgin. He had never even kissed his own hand, let alone another person. It made him faint and giddy, and within a few moments, he completely melted.

Guan Shanjin's kisses were forceful, pressing firmly against Wu Xingzi's lips. His breath was so hot that Wu Xingzi shivered underneath him, but his lips were very soft, tasting almost sweet.

I must be in paradise... Wu Xingzi panted, his breath filled with the intoxicating scent of Guan Shanjin. It was as if he was immersed in a garden of gardenias, orange blossoms, and white sandalwood.

Wu Xingzi's mouth was dry, but those soft lips on his felt a little wet. He vaguely registered that something supple had slid across his lips.

Unconsciously, he opened his mouth, and Guan Shanjin's tongue instantly swept its way inside. It slid past his teeth, stroking his gums, then tangled with his flustered tongue. As it caressed his sensitive spots, he couldn't help but moan.

Guan Shanjin responded with a low, lustful laugh.

Wu Xingzi tried to snap out of it, but he was too inexperienced— or perhaps Guan Shanjin's beauty was too seductive. This kiss was deep and long, and the agile tongue that licked at the roof of his mouth felt like it could reach the back of his throat. Wu Xingzi luxuriated in the sensations, yet he felt a little terrified. His body trembled incessantly. All strength left him, his body completely under Guan Shanjin's control.

Just as Wu Xingzi thought he would asphyxiate from kissing, Guan Shanjin finally pulled back slightly. Using his soft, wet lips, he nuzzled against Wu Xingzi's mouth, letting him catch his breath. Seeing Wu Xingzi's eyes reddening as if he might cry, Guan Shanjin seemed very satisfied. He lightly pressed against Wu Xingzi's swollen lips again.

"Give me your tongue," Guan Shanjin said. The low and soft command was both alluring and passionate. Wu Xingzi's thin body shivered, the fire in his belly burning.

"No," Wu Xingzi replied. He was becoming dizzy from kissing. As he caught his breath, he remembered that he was still in the parlor of the Peng Society. Yes, he was a virgin about to turn forty, and he was hardly very picky, but...well, this would be the first time he experienced such intimate contact with someone else. At the very least, shouldn't there be...a bed?

"Am I not good enough for you?" Guan Shanjin laughed, then took Wu Xingzi's earlobe into his mouth and sucked on it.

"Ahh!" Wu Xingzi shuddered and moaned. It was unbearable. His legs almost gave out under him. He had never imagined that his ear could be so sensitive.

Guan Shanjin was also surprised by this discovery. The face of this ordinary man in front of him was flushed pink: those eyes, the tip of his nose, and even his ears. He possessed an indescribable appeal. The charm could make a man's heart melt, but also tempt him to do unconscionable things. It would be even better if he could make Wu Xingzi break down and cry until he could no longer utter a sound.

"Give me your tongue," that lustful voice breathed hotly in his ear. Wu Xingzi's eyes were blurry, and his thin shoulders trembled. Finally, he slowly pushed his little pink tongue out from between his lips.

"Good boy," Guan Shanjin purred, praising him in satisfaction. He bit on that pink tongue, teasing it, and the tingling pain almost made Wu Xingzi lose his breath. He shut his eyes, afraid to look into Guan Shanjin's passionate gaze. Giving in, he stuck his tongue out further, until it was completely taken into Guan Shanjin's mouth.

Guan Shanjin played with Wu Xingzi's shy, pink tongue as if he was eating a juicy piece of fruit, making wet sucking sounds. It was too embarrassing. Wu Xingzi could neither open his eyes nor keep them closed. Even if he wanted to hide, there was nowhere to go. Feeling the arms around him tightening and the kiss deepening, he believed that Guan Shanjin wanted to swallow him whole.

There was no way out for him now.

There was a large, round table in the parlor with a vase displayed in the center. On the vase was a painting of a hundred children playing. Every child looked sweet and innocent, vivid and lifelike;

their little mouths laughed, cried, or fussed. One could almost hear the sounds they were making.

Wu Xingzi had never dared to come close to this table. He did not know if it was appropriate for the vase to be displayed here, but it was a high-quality item of great craftsmanship. If he accidentally broke it, he wouldn't even be able to afford a straw mat for his corpse.

Guan Shanjin clearly did not share his concerns. He kept on attacking Wu Xingzi's mouth, even as he carried the smaller man, who had completely lost his strength to walk. Reaching the table, he swept the vase to the ground. That crash startled Wu Xingzi, who started writhing in Guan Shanjin's grasp, but with his slender limbs, it was a fruitless fight. Guan Shanjin shoved him down on the table, rendering him immobile; the intense kiss made Wu Xingzi's mouth overflow with saliva.

When Wu Xingzi felt he had completely lost his senses, Guan Shanjin finally seemed somewhat satisfied, and pulled back from the kiss. Long, glistening threads of spit stretched between their lips. Guan Shanjin licked and swallowed them all, his red, petal-like lips curving into a smile.

"Did you like that?" Guan Shanjin asked.

All Wu Xingzi could see were those white teeth, crimson lips, and wicked tongue. He felt he was about to faint, and no matter how hard he tried, he could not stop hyperventilating. In a daze, he stared at Guan Shanjin, then nodded woodenly.

"You're so obedient." Guan Shanjin chuckled, looking as luminous as the stars in the sky.

Wu Xingzi was incoherent; all he could do was savor the beauty in front of him.

"Um..." Entranced, Wu Xingzi nodded his head and said, like a man possessed, "I can be even more obedient. Would you like that?"

Guan Shanjin was surprised to hear a reply like that from Wu Xingzi. His smile sharpened, and he cocked his eyebrow slightly. He reached out and slid his hand around Wu Xingzi's slender throat, his thumb stroking along the faintly throbbing vein in his neck. Feeling that ragged pulse under the skin, he laughed again.

"Yes, I would." His fingers glided down Wu Xingzi's throat and flicked apart the robe's lapels, exposing collar bones as sharp as knives and Wu Xingzi's gaunt, pale chest.

Wu Xingzi was so thin you could almost see his ribs. Lying on the table like this, they became even more prominent, covered only by a thin layer of muscle. His soft, flat stomach rose and fell with each breath. He wanted to curl up and hide, but Guan Shanjin moved first, forcing his muscular figure between Wu Xingzi's thighs. He placed his heated palm upon the pale belly beneath him and pressed down firmly.

"Oh..." Wu Xingzi moaned. It felt like his stomach was pushed against a burning piece of metal. His whole body was awash in a flush of red. He tried to clamp his thighs together, but just ended up tightening his legs around the other man's trim waist. His clothes fell wide open, and he sprawled naked upon the pile of fabric, his entire body on display.

Wu Xingzi swallowed his spit. Despite how shy he felt, he was overwhelmed with anticipation. The fire that started in his belly blazed throughout his body, and his cock was shamelessly hard. Shining, crystalline fluid beaded at the light pink head, and under Guan Shanjin's heated gaze, it only dripped faster.

"Do you know what I'm about to do?" Guan Shanjin's fingers were long and slim, but rough to the touch. Wu Xingzi's belly twitched as the other man caressed him, his entire abdomen aflame.

"I...have the general idea," Wu Xingzi replied, sheepish. He was a virgin, but he still understood what sex entailed. Even if he had never tasted pork, he knew what a pig looked like.

"You really know what I'm about to do?" Guan Shanjin gave a low chuckle, his fingers tapping Wu Xingzi's abdomen. His half-lidded eyes glowed with lust. "I'll be this deep inside of you." His fingers drew upward. "Here, here...and all the way to here."

Wu Xingzi could not control the widening of his eyes when he realized how deep Guan Shanjin meant.

"Th-that's impossible... You'll pierce right through me." Wu Xingzi licked his lips, his trembling voice threaded with anticipation.

"That's right. I *want* to pierce right through you. Do you like the sound of that, hmm?" The lilt in Guan Shanjin's voice snared him like a hook.

"No..." Wu Xingzi said. He opened his mouth fruitlessly, confusion in his eyes. Guan Shanjin was in no hurry. Leaning down, he kissed Wu Xingzi's blushing cheeks and sucked on his swollen lips. Wu Xingzi gasped for breath as Guan Shanjin's tongue lapped at his ear lobes.

Then, Guan Shanjin licked his nipples. "D-don't lick me there," Wu Xingzi stuttered. He shivered, pleading for mercy as his nipples were sucked.

The little nubs perked up after a few moments. They looked soft to touch at first but hardened and swelled under Guan Shanjin's tongue. Wu Xingzi's mind blanked out, lost in pleasure. His hips twitched along with the nipping and sucking against his body, an unspeakable ache inside of him. Viscous fluid leaked continuously from his cock, trailing down the shaft. It dripped down his perineum, trickling down onto his hole.

Wu Xingzi had never been teased like this before, and he was startled by how sensitive his body was. No matter where he was touched, he leaked copiously. No matter where he was licked, he felt pleasure. Why did he keep himself pure for so many years? Why did he become an adviser? What was the point? He should have just looked for a strong man right from the start and built a relationship with him. He would have been able to enjoy this dripping wet pleasure his entire life!

Just as Guan Shanjin was about to bring Wu Xingzi to climax, he drew his cruel and ardent tongue away. He tapped on Wu Xingzi's abdomen. "You haven't answered me yet. Do you want me to pierce through you?"

Wu Xingzi could feel Guan Shanjin's thick and heated flesh pressing against him. He swallowed, no longer having the strength to restrain himself.

"I-I'm looking forward to it," he said. He was desperate to look at Guan Shanjin's cock. Feeling the heat and the size, it vaguely reminded him of the drawing he received from Bastion City...

Wait, hold on... If Guan Shanjin had his reply, that meant that his favorite dick picture belonged to Guan Shanjin! This was a gift from heaven! That beloved cock unexpectedly belonged to this beautiful man... He deeply desired to see it. He wanted to lick it, to touch it, to feel its heft and heat; his mouth tingled with desire at these thoughts.

Noticing Wu Xingzi's sudden excitement, Guan Shanjin creased his brows. "What are you thinking about?"

Caught off guard, he blurted out: "I'm thinking about your cock!"

Both of them were speechless. Wu Xingzi was extremely embarrassed by his outspokenness. Guan Shanjin looked vacant for a moment before his expression subtly changed.

"Why not?" Unabashed, he removed his robes, kicked off his shoes, and took off his socks. A strong, muscular body was soon revealed in front of Wu Xingzi.

There was nothing he could say. Guan Shanjin was incredibly handsome. Under that smooth, pale skin was an undeniable strength. He was as beautiful and sharp as a sword, especially between his legs. His cock was so hard, it lifted and pressed against his abdomen. It was definitely the Prince of Lanling!

Wu Xingzi's lower body writhed helplessly. His thighs tightened harder around Guan Shanjin.

Guan Shanjin could no longer hold back. Tugging at Wu Xingzi's thin legs, he pulled them further around his waist. His thick, savage cock dragged against Wu Xingzi's soaked perineum trailing up past his round, tight balls until he reached his cock, two sizes smaller than his own, and thrust against it.

"S-slow down," Wu Xingzi pleaded. With Guan Shanjin's hot, hard cock rubbing against his, Wu Xingzi was about to lose himself in pleasure. His body twitched and his back arched up from the table, only to be pushed back down.

"You'll want me to speed up later." Guan Shanjin smirked, his slick palm caressing Wu Xingzi's dripping cock. "I didn't bring any lubrication. Bear with it for now. I'll take care of you."

"Huh?" Dazed, Wu Xingzi didn't understand what Guan Shanjin was implying. As the Lanling Prince ground against him, his belly began to convulse, and it looked like his climax was near.

But Guan Shanjin didn't care if Wu Xingzi had understood him. Spreading his slender legs apart, he slid his hand along the hidden cleft. It was already drenched with his fluids, and together with the wetness on Guan Shanjin's hand, it was very slippery. An angular finger rubbed along Wu Xingzi's entrance a few times. The shy, tight hole quickly relaxed, and with a little pressure, Guan Shanjin's finger was swallowed up.

Guan Shanjin's face was slightly shadowed, and his alluring eyes darkened. Without warning, he shoved his finger fully inside.

The tip of Guan Shanjin's finger immediately struck a spot within him. Wu Xingzi gave a short, sharp cry. He instinctively began to curl his body up, only to be stopped by a hand on his stomach.

"Don't touch me there," Wu Xingzi moaned. The pressure on that spot made his vision turn white, a shockwave traveling from his hips to his heart. He was not sure exactly what had happened; he only knew that he nearly sobbed from the pleasure.

He was still in a state of shock, but Guan Shanjin refused to notice. With an enchanting smile, his finger continued teasing that place within him. Wu Xingzi cried himself hoarse as his body twitched and shuddered, his cock spurting as he climaxed.

"You're so sensitive," Guan Shanjin said, looking at the mess on his own thigh. Swiping it up with his fingers, he pushed it all into Wu Xingzi's hole, making squelching sounds with the movement of his fingers.

"Don't... I-I can't take it any longer!" Wu Xingzi cried, his belly convulsing under Guan Shanjin's hand. His legs tightened around Guan Shanjin's waist, his toes curling up. He had clearly gone beyond the peak of pleasure. Other than heavy breathing, he didn't react.

Guan Shanjin simply pushed a second and third finger into that loosened hole, not giving Wu Xingzi a chance to get used to it. He continued playing with the sensitive spot inside, and Wu Xingzi could only go along with it, his eyes blurry with tears.

It was not long before Wu Xingzi came a second time. Shudders ran through his body, the muscles along his thighs trembling. Crying for mercy, he choked on his saliva. Guan Shanjin finally pulled his fingers out.

His once shy and tight hole was now flushed bright red and gaping. Dripping with juices, it convulsed helplessly.

Wiping the remaining residue on his painfully hard cock, Guan Shanjin smacked Wu Xingzi's ass lightly. "You'd better relax. I'm going inside."

He tapped the place on his abdomen that he had previously marked out and put Wu Xingzi's feeble hand on his belly. "Leave your hand here and wait for me to fuck you."

"Ungh," Wu Xingzi moaned.

Before Wu Xingzi could get any words out, Guan Shanjin grabbed one of Wu Xingzi's thighs. With another hand on his thick cock, he pressed the heated tip against the little hole that had yet to regain its usual tightness, and quickly pushed all the way inside.

"Ah!" Wu Xingzi gave a quivering shriek. It was so painful! The flush on his face faded, his lips whitening in pain. He groaned weakly, reaching out to push Guan Shanjin away. However, his hand was caught and placed back on his belly. Guan Shanjin's palm brushed the back of his hand and their fingers interlocked, rubbing gently.

"It hurts?" Guan Shanjin asked.

"It hurts..." Wu Xingzi didn't realize he was whimpering, as if seeking sympathy.

"Behave." Guan Shanjin's forehead was covered in a sheen of sweat, a look of patient concentration on his face. He leaned down to kiss Wu Xingzi's cheek and spoke gently in a low voice. "If you can't endure this now," he said, "what will we do later?"

Hearing that honeyed tone, Wu Xingzi's tense body relaxed, but he failed to register the danger in Guan Shanjin's words.

Wu Xingzi had yet to catch his breath. Guan Shanjin gripped his waist tightly, and with a hard thrust, he buried himself deep inside Wu Xingzi, hitting his sweet spot. Under this assault, Wu Xingzi could only sob and pant, lacking the strength to fight back.

"Don't cry." Guan Shanjin placated him. "It'll stop hurting soon." He stayed still. The tight channel was clamping down painfully around him, and he knew that if he forced himself in any further, there would be blood. He had no choice but to hold back.

Heavy, heated breaths burst out of Wu Xingzi's chest. Painful shivers ran through his body. It felt as though his hips had been dislocated, and he didn't have the energy to tighten himself on Guan Shanjin.

Even through the pain, Wu Xingzi did not feel an ounce of regret. Panting and moaning, he tried to relax his rigid body. The erotic drawings that he had seen in the past flashed through his head.

Perhaps his hidden desires were exposed in his letters, as the two books of erotic drawings Manager Rancui had given him were filled with real heavyweight phalluses. Seeing the way people lost themselves in extreme pleasure under those cocks, Wu Xingzi yearned deeply to be in their place.

The pain was inevitable. However, once he pushed past it, immense pleasure would come. One of Wu Xingzi's admittedly few merits was that he was good at waiting things out.

After they both paused for a moment, the pain lessened greatly. Guan Shanjin's breath on his chest stoked the fire inside him again. Wu Xingzi gave a hoarse cry.

Guan Shanjin raised his brow as he felt Wu Xingzi relax. He did not expect this timid, quail-like man's body to be so suitable for sexual pleasure. After all, the thickness and the length of Guan Shanjin's cock was astounding. Wu Xingzi was the only person who had not bled after being deflowered by it. He even ground down on him nicely.

Guan Shanjin's laugh was a little strained as he lightly smacked Wu Xingzi's soft buttocks. "Does it still hurt?"

Wu Xingzi jerked a little at being spanked, and his softened hole tightened up again. Without any prompting, it started clamping down on Guan Shanjin's cock. Both of them exhaled heavily at the same time.

"You..." Guan Shanjin's expression darkened. Grabbing hold of Wu Xingzi's waist, he started pounding into him without restraint.

The once tight channel was completely stretched open. Thoroughly defeated, it gave in completely to the engorged cock thrusting its way inside. Aching, tingling, overwhelmed by both pain and pleasure, Wu Xingzi cried out. He tried to push away the arm around his waist, only for his hand to be caught and pressed into his abdomen.

"You're not going to feel it for yourself?" Guan Shanjin said. The taste of the man below him was remarkable. He pulled out slightly, their combined juices dripping out. Wu Xingzi's hole had expanded to become a perfect sheath of pleasure. Gaping slightly, it looked pink and tender, and Guan Shanjin reached out to pinch it.

"Ah!" Wu Xingzi yelped. There was a burning pain, but that pain held a sensation that made him ache for more. He had long since lost himself to pleasure, shuddering and moaning rhythmically along with Guan Shanjin's rough thrusts.

Although Wu Xingzi was thin, he was very flexible. His ass was so pliant and supple that it made Guan Shanjin lose control. Wu Xingzi's timidness, his shame, and his obvious desire mingled with his mumbled objections, all spurred Guan Shanjin to action. He harshly thrust and slowly pulled out, thrills running through his body. Wu Xingzi's hole sucked him in easily, letting Guan Shanjin ruthlessly invade his body. When Guan Shanjin retreated, Wu Xingzi's body was reluctant; he tightened his hole and refused to let go of his cock, clinging onto it as long as he could.

"You dirty boy," Guan Shanjin growled, biting Wu Xingzi's earlobe and spreading his buttocks further apart.

"Ahh!" Wu Xingzi yelped. His slender legs kicked out and his toes curled. Sprawled across the table, tremors ran throughout his entire body.

"Have I pierced through you yet?" Guan Shanjin laughed.

His savage cock shoved into Wu Xingzi's shy hole all the way to the root, his heavy balls smacking against Wu Xingzi's trembling buttocks. With his palm pressed against his belly, Wu Xingzi could feel the bulging shape of Guan Shanjin's cock through the thin layer of skin and muscles. He really had pierced right through him.

Wu Xingzi stared at the ceiling with unfocused eyes. The depth of Guan Shanjin's cock inside him combined with the dull ache of its invasion was utterly overwhelming. His mouth was wide open, yet he couldn't make a single sound. Drool dribbled from the corner of his lips. Guan Shanjin leaned forward to teasingly lick at the trail before pressing their mouths together and kissing him so deeply that Wu Xingzi nearly fainted.

Guan Shanjin was in no hurry to pull out. Wu Xingzi's body was warm and lithe, his hole clenching around him. Just being inside him felt so incredible that Guan Shanjin's desire deepened and his eyes turned bloodshot. He was like a wild beast that had tasted blood.

"No, d-don't get harder," Wu Xingzi mumbled, his hand rubbing against his belly. The mind-blowing satisfaction of Guan Shanjin's cock growing thicker within him made him whimper. Wu Xingzi came again despite not having fully recovered from his last orgasm.

"You had this coming," Guan Shanjin snarled.

Next came a brutal pounding. Guan Shanjin hammered so hard that Wu Xingzi started sliding up the table. He cried for mercy, only to be impaled even more ruthlessly. Guan Shanjin did not employ any special technique, just brushed past the sensitive spot each time he entered and retreated. The combination of his brute force and his skilled seduction had Wu Xingzi thoroughly intoxicated.

There was no fixed rhythm to the drilling of his hips. Wu Xingzi never knew when Guan Shanjin would shove in hard, nor how deep he would go. Finally, Guan Shanjin went on a full assault, pushing himself inside as far as he could before pulling out. Wu Xingzi's little hole was fucked into submission; it could only obey Guan Shanjin's cock. His belly was on fire, and he could barely tell if he felt pleasure or pain.

Before long, Wu Xingzi started getting hard again. On the table, his blushing pink body convulsed, and his eyes rolled to the back of his head. Whining and gasping, his legs kicked out before he climaxed again.

This time, the fluid that came out was thin like water. If anything else was going to come out, it would probably just be piss.

Guan Shanjin clearly did not give a damn if he could endure it. With reddened eyes, he tightened his arms around Wu Xingzi's waist, impaling him as deep as possible. Each time he pulled out, juices from within Wu Xingzi's body spilled out, dripping down the cleft of his ass to pool below him. Wu Xingzi felt like he was getting fucked to death. He tried writhing away, but it only resulted in him being fucked harder.

When Guan Shanjin finally shoved in his cock fully to the root and came inside him, Wu Xingzi blacked out, his body twitching and trembling. The fluid that dribbled out from his soft cock was the consistency of water.

Guan Shanjin quickly pulled out. The erotic expression on his face had yet to fade away, but his previously warm eyes had already turned frosty.

Guan Shanjin's cum mingled with the juices from Wu Xingzi's red and swollen hole, slowly dripping out of him. Guan Shanjin stared at Wu Xingzi's gaping, pulsing hole, his expression indifferent.

He finally bent down to pick his clothes up from the floor, and casually tugged on a pair of pants and his inner robe. He covered Wu Xingzi up with his own outer robe, then headed to the door and pushed it open.

Two tall and muscular men were waiting outside the door. Their expressions were cold and stern, and they exuded a deadly aura. On seeing Guan Shanjin, they lowered their heads respectfully and greeted him. "General."

"Tell Rancui I need a room, and to prepare some hot water," Guan Shanjin instructed. "Tell the old man with the ox cart outside the city to go back."

"Yes, General." The man on the left cupped his hands in front of his chest and retreated.

"Any news from Bastion City?" Guan Shanjin said to the man on the right, without looking at him. His tall figure leaned languidly against the door.

"No, General," the man said. "There's no news."

Guan Shanjin sneered, his eyes half-lidded. Curling his red lips, he spoke. "That man is rather patient... All right then, let him be." Waving the man off, Guan Shanjin stepped back into the room and closed the door. The man outside continued to stand guard, his expression unchanged.

When Guan Shanjin returned to the table, Wu Xingzi was still lying limply across it. His face was so flushed it was giving off heat. The lower half of his body still shuddered slightly.

"Interesting..." Guan Shanjin pinched the fleshy tip of Wu Xingzi's nose. Bundling him up in his robe, he gathered the man into his arms, then pushed the door open and walked out. "Lead the way."

The employees of the Peng Society were well trained. Guan Shanjin had only just instructed them to prepare a room, and a salesman was already present to bring them there. The salesman didn't seem to notice the wreckage of the room, nor did he even glance at the man in Guan Shanjin's arms.

Soon, the sun set.

Wu Xingzi woke up in a daze. Covered by a soft blanket, he felt like he was sleeping on a cloud; he figured he must be dreaming. If not for the aroma of freshly cooked food and the gurgling of his stomach, he would have definitely shut his eyes and gone back to sleep.

When he moved, though, the pain made him hiss. He almost teared up. It felt as though his whole body had been shattered and reassembled. It was agonizing, especially around his hips and buttocks.

It was only then that he recalled what happened yesterday.

When the memories hit him, he turned red as a beet. He dragged the blanket over his mouth and stifled a giggle.

Although his body hurt, it also felt refreshed. Someone had clearly cleaned him up. He was sure that Guan Shanjin wasn't actually the one who'd done the washing—that young man seemed used to being served by others and wouldn't have the patience to bother with cleaning—but that didn't make Wu Xingzi any less delighted. He secretly hoped that Guan Shanjin was the one who had wiped his body with a towel from head to toe, including the shameful area between his legs.

He remembered how Guan Shanjin came inside of him at the end. Perhaps during the process of cleaning up, those slender, jade-like fingers had reached into his hole and slowly scooped out the cum from inside... Wu Xingzi shivered, his legs nearly turning to jelly from his own imagination.

He bowed his head to look at his belly, and his hand couldn't resist caressing it. He had never expected that a cock could reach so deeply inside him. That feeling of his belly distending under the assault of Guan Shanjin's member was burned in his memory. That sturdy cock bulging out under his palm, so hot and so hard through his skin, nearly made him lose his mind... Thinking about it now, it was so embarrassing!

He hugged the blanket and burbled out a laugh.

"What's making you so happy?" Guan Shanjin's tender, affectionate words were laced with frost, turning Wu Xingzi weak. He shivered as his body, which had just learned the pleasures of sex, unexpectedly and shamefully reacted to that voice.

"Y-you are," Wu Xingzi said. He was a very shy person; the feeling of having his secrets exposed left him too bashful to speak.

"Really?" Guan Shanjin's lilted voice was bewitching. With a red face, Wu Xingzi covered himself further with the blanket, only exposing his eyes. He peeked at Guan Shanjin, who sat at the table.

"What is it? You seem surprised that I'm here."

Wu Xingzi nodded automatically, then hurriedly shook his head and smiled. "No, no, I just didn't expect..."

Guan Shanjin raised his brow at this but didn't ask Wu Xingzi to elaborate. Instead, he casually called him over. "Come, you must be hungry," he said. "Have some porridge."

"Ah, yes, I'm coming," Wu Xingzi said, hastily moving to get off the bed—but he wasn't expecting his body to disobey his intentions. Staggering, he nearly fell face first into the ground. Guan Shanjin was swift enough to stop his fall, though, and he picked Wu Xingzi up and carried him to the table.

That was too embarrassing... Wu Xingzi struggled inwardly for a moment before carefully sitting down, leaving a seat between him and Guan Shanjin.

Guan Shanjin glanced at the space between the two of them but did not say anything. He placed a spoon in front of Wu Xingzi. "Come, this rice porridge was specially prepared. Fish bones were boiled for two hours to make this, so you ought to be able to eat it. For now, you'll want to abstain from food that's too oily."

"Thank you, thank you." Wu Xingzi cupped his hands in thanks toward Guan Shanjin, then picked up the spoon and scooped up some porridge. The rice grains had been cooked till they were soft and sticky; they glistened like snow. The porridge was a light gold color. With just a slight stir, the grains clung to the spoon, and a delicious aroma wafted from the bowl. It was the tastiest porridge Wu Xingzi had ever eaten.

Once he started eating, he didn't think about anything else. He was truly ravenous, and the porridge was delectable...and he had no idea what to chat about with Guan Shanjin.

There was no way he could say, "Guan-gongzi, your pengornis and my hole seem to have fallen in love at first fuck. Why don't we pair up and spend our lives together, fulfilling our dreams?" Guan Shanjin would flee in terror for sure.

Ah, this porridge is so tasty, let's just have another bowl. Wu Xingzi's thoughts strayed again, and he scooped himself another bowl of porridge, burying his head in it.

"So, you're the adviser of Qingcheng County?" Guan Shanjin said.

The sudden question nearly made Wu Xingzi choke on his mouthful of porridge. He hurriedly swallowed and wiped his mouth. "Ah, yes. I am the adviser of Qingcheng County."

"What sort of place is Qingcheng County?" Guan Shanjin asked. It seemed like he was in the mood for casual conversation. He picked some stir-fried bean sprouts and placed them in Wu Xingzi's bowl.

To eat or not to eat, Wu Xingzi thought. In a dilemma, Wu Xingzi looked at the bean sprouts in his bowl, then at Guan Shanjin. At the same time, he was agonizing over how to introduce Qingcheng County to the man in front of him. He was stumped, his mind reeling.

This...this wasn't what he expected!

Wu Xingzi had gone into this just wanting to be pigeon pen pals with Guan Shanjin's penis. His desire was sincere and single minded. But seeing how tender and caring Ansheng and Constable Zhang were with each other, how could he not have been envious of their romance?

He had already planned it all out. He was going to mail the drawing of his own cock to the other man, and if he liked it, he might send a normal response back. With months of exchanging letters back and forth, they would begin to get to know each other better. Later, they might consider meeting face to face; if they got along, they would settle down together.

However, Guan Shanjin's zeal had come as a surprise. As soon as they met, he brought him to paradise over and over, making his entire body ache. He had no idea what would happen next. All he wanted was to hurry home and look through *The Pengornisseur* to calm his nerves.

He couldn't deny that he had greatly enjoyed what happened. He really had experienced overwhelming pleasure. Wu Xingzi's belly started to tingle, and he touched it unthinkingly.

Wu Xingzi knew his role in life. He was boring and ugly. As a small village's adviser, his salary was only enough for him to survive in a simple little house. He was clearly unworthy of Guan Shanjin; he didn't dare try to get close to him.

To be able to ascend such a peak with Guan Shanjin, Wu Xingzi must have offered countless blessings to the gods in his previous life.

At last, when Wu Xingzi had somewhat calmed down, he lowered his head and ate his vegetables. After swallowing a mouthful of porridge to settle his nerves, he replied, "Qingcheng County is a small village. Ever since Great Xia was formed 214 years ago, we've ranked last in the state system. We're small, poor, and have a tiny population, but we're all very close with each other. No major incidents have occurred, and everything happens as it should."

"Oh?" Guan Shanjin gave a nod. "Have you ever thought of leaving?" He picked more vegetables and placed them in Wu Xingzi's bowl.

"Huh?" Wu Xingzi blinked and shook his head. "No, never. I want to live out my life in Qingcheng County." *I even have my gravesite prepared!*

"Why do you not want to leave?"

Wu Xingzi was a little overwhelmed by all these questions. He couldn't eat and answer at the same time. The porridge was so delicious; it would be a waste to eat it cold... With no other alternative, Wu Xingzi lifted the bowl and gulped down the porridge. His stomach and nose were full of the porridge's pleasant warmth and aroma. He almost ladled himself another bowl, but he managed to resist.

"Are you that hungry?" Guan Shanjin watched this bold manner of eating. His smile was like a spring breeze. Along with the misty, easygoing look in his curved eyes, it made Wu Xingzi blush at the sight of him.

"Yes, yes..." In a stupor, he nodded his head.

To have such beauty accompanying him during a meal spurred his appetite. He should grab the opportunity to eat a few more bowls of porridge.

"All these dishes were prepared for you. There's no need to be polite; please have more." Guan Shanjin ladled another bowl of porridge for him, then placed a little portion from every dish onto the plate in front of Wu Xingzi. "Eat some more," he urged. "We'll talk once you're full."

Wu Xingzi's eyes followed Guan Shanjin's hand that held the chopsticks, his heart completely flustered.

The hospitality of the Peng Society was reliable and meticulous. Perhaps it was due to Guan Shanjin's status, or perhaps they were like that with everyone. The utensils on the table were all high-quality dinnerware, complementing the food perfectly. The stir-fried bean sprouts were served on a white, flawless, jade-like plate.

As for Guan Shanjin's chopsticks, they looked like they were made of ivory. The handiwork was exquisite, but not gaudy. Held in Guan Shanjin's hands, which looked like they could have been carved from jade, they were truly a feast for the eyes.

However, Wu Xingzi's hands were not suited for this pair of chopsticks. He gave them a try, and it turned out that ivory chopsticks were really quite slippery.

Since Guan Shanjin didn't seem to mind, Wu Xingzi dived into the food and ate as much as he wanted. For now, he pushed everything else to the back of his head, planning to take his leave when he was full.

It was already very late in the day. Wu Xingzi wasn't worried that Old Liu would still be waiting for him outside the city gates. Unless prior arrangements had been made, he would head back by himself after a certain amount of time. However, this meant that Wu Xingzi would have to rely on his own two legs to make his way back to Qingcheng County. He didn't know if he had enough money to stay the night in Goose City, either. If he didn't, then he would have to hurry back through the night.

As though seeing his plans, Guan Shanjin spoke. "This room is yours tonight. You should sleep here and leave in the morning."

I'm saved! Wu Xingzi expressed his gratitude toward Guan Shanjin continuously. Even more joyful, he gobbled up the entire table of dishes until his stomach was bulging. He slumped in his chair, panting.

Guan Shanjin didn't eat much, only slowly sipping from his teacup. His elegant fingers, red lips, and bamboo-straight back painted a lovely picture. Wu Xingzi stared at him, still not sure why Guan Shanjin had stayed in this room with him for so long.

"Can we talk?" Guan Shanjin asked, putting down his teacup. His lips pursed slightly, and he looked at Wu Xingzi with a faint smile in his eyes.

"Yes, yes... What would you like to talk about, Guan-gongzi?" With a glance from those sensual eyes, Wu Xingzi was compelled to sit up straight.

"Have you ever wanted to leave Qingcheng County?"

"Um..." Wu Xingzi rubbed at his full stomach, pondering over it for a short moment before shaking his head. "I don't want to."

"You really don't want to?" Guan Shanjin clearly did not believe him.

This time, Wu Xingzi shook his head with determination. "I don't. Guan-gongzi, I've lived my entire life there. The furthest I've ever been is Goose City. Do you know the story of the frog in the well?"[7]

Guan Shanjin smiled. "I do."

Realizing that he had asked a stupid question, Wu Xingzi flushed with embarrassment. Timidly, he lowered his head. "O-of course you've heard of it."

"Don't worry about it. Please continue." Guan Shanjin caressed Wu Xingzi's earlobe, startling the middle-aged man so much so that he nearly fell out of his chair. Bewildered, Wu Xingzi covered his ear and shifted another seat away before he managed to catch his breath.

There seemed to be amusement in Guan Shanjin's eyes, but there was also a deep indifference that frightened him.

Wu Xingzi looked down. He no longer wanted to see Guan Shanjin's face. He skittishly continued, "I'm that frog stuck in the well, and I'll remain there for the rest of my life. I have everything I need. I'll just look up at the sky and let the days go by."

"Don't you want to explore the world outside?" Guan Shanjin asked.

"The world outside?" Wu Xingzi said, quickly lifting his head and glancing at him. He then looked down again and shook his head. "Guan-gongzi, I know there are many things going on in the world outside, but it's none of my business. After all, how long can a frog that has lived in a well its whole life survive the world outside? He's not familiar with anything or anyone around him. There's not even a place he can be buried."

---

7   A Chinese fable in which a frog that has spent its whole life in a well brags to a turtle about how wonderful the well is, only for the turtle to shock the frog into silence by telling it about the sea. "A frog at the bottom of the well" is used as an idiom to describe someone with a very limited worldview.

Guan Shanjin chuckled. "But this old frog still dared to mail a drawing of his cock to someone. You've clearly jumped out of the well."

Hearing that, Wu Xingzi's face reddened, and he was unable to say a word. This was much, much too embarrassing! He bowed his head and did not dare to respond, praying for a hole to appear and bury him alive. Why was he so mesmerized by Guan Shanjin's cock—so mesmerized that he lost himself? He would never be able to show his face to anyone else again!

"Hmm?" Guan Shanjin refused to drop the subject. His questioning tone brushed across Wu Xingzi's heart. He trembled, then stood up.

"Guan-gongzi... Guan-gongzi..." Stammering, Wu Xingzi cupped his hands in submission. "Yesterday is in the past. Let's just forget about this little incident!"

"What 'little incident'? Pulling me into bed, or mailing a picture of your penis to seduce me?" At some point, Guan Shanjin had pulled himself closer to Wu Xingzi. His low and syrupy voice, along with his warm breath, brushed past Wu Xingzi's ear. Wu Xingzi flailed backward violently, nearly tripping over a chair.

It went without saying that Guan Shanjin caught him, once again cradling Wu Xingzi in his arms.

CHAPTER THREE

Like a Spring Breeze, We'll Come and Go

*Guan Shanjin had the utmost confidence in his handsome looks
and prowess in the bedroom. No one had ever left him like this
after spending a night of passion together.*

*Who would have thought that Wu Xingzi, a timid old quail
of a man, actually dared to run away after sleeping with him?*

*"Damn you, Wu Xingzi!" Guan Shanjin gnashed his teeth.
With a pound of his fist, the table crumbled beneath him.*

THIS WAS DIFFERENT from their intimacy earlier in the
afternoon. Guan Shanjin's intoxicating scent had dissipated;
he must have taken a bath. A faint whiff of sandalwood was
left on him, as well as a vague smell of rust. It was sharp and savage,
yet still alluring.

Wu Xingzi covered his face in an attempt to hide, and Guan Shanjin
laughed at his antics. Wu Xingzi's ear pressed against Guan Shanjin's
torso. When Guan Shanjin's chest shook with laughter, the sensation
made Wu Xingzi's entire body melt, and though his body still ached
from their previous sexual escapade, it did not deter his little pengornis. After a nourishing meal, it had decided to perk up.

"You're hard?" Guan Shanjin chuckled, seeming a little surprised.
"How lewd, darling."

Without waiting for Wu Xingzi's protests, Guan Shanjin lifted the man up into his arms, returning to the bed in several long strides. In the blink of an eye, he stripped Wu Xingzi bare. Sprawled on top of the bright red bedding, his pale, naked body looked absolutely obscene.

"Wait, hold on..." Wu Xingzi tried to push himself up, but he found it was impossible. The bed was as soft as a cloud; each time he struggled to get up, the bed engulfed him again within moments.

"Don't worry, I won't be unreasonable." This time, Guan Shanjin did not remove his own clothes. He looked at Wu Xingzi with a mischievous glint in his eyes. "Your hole is still too swollen. I don't want to injure you. Let's just have a little fun."

What?! Wu Xingzi thought. *The word "fun" doesn't make me any less worried!*

Wu Xingzi's face reddened instantly. The luxurious silk bedding felt like flowing water against his skin, making it tingle so much that he started panting heavily.

"Wh-what sort of fun?" he asked. Though his mind was thrown off balance, his body throbbed with great anticipation. At this point, he could barely recognize himself as he lay trembling on the bed.

"Take a guess." Guan Shanjin's smile was like the sun emerging in spring. The amorous look in his eyes completely shattered Wu Xingzi's resistance, and his brain turned to mush.

It was hardly as if he had never experienced sexual pleasure at the hands of this man; there was no need to be so shy about it now.

With a blush, Wu Xingzi looked at Guan Shanjin expectantly. "I can't think of anything. You can..." *You can do as you please.*

His openness mingled with embarrassment sparked a reaction in Guan Shanjin. At first, he only wanted to tease this old fellow in front of him, but now he was aroused. However, since Guan Shanjin had been a bit too enthusiastic during their previous round of activities, Wu Xingzi would not be able to endure any direct fucking for a couple of days. He'd have to hold himself back for now.

Guan Shanjin clicked his tongue and pulled the blanket away from Wu Xingzi's waist, exposing his lower body and embarrassing him. The older man's pink cock was already hard, shyly pointing toward Guan Shanjin's gorgeous face, delicate yet bold.

"Don't..." Wu Xingzi's legs dangled in the air, and in that moment, he knew he looked salacious. He writhed his hips, wanting to hide, but Guan Shanjin held him down instead.

"No need to be shy, now. We've only just begun." Guan Shanjin gave him a radiant smile. The lilt in his voice made Wu Xingzi give up his struggle, his hips relaxing.

He gazed at the beauty on top of him. Finding the sight of his own little cock distracting, he didn't know exactly what he was waiting for.

"You'll have to pay attention next time so you can learn properly, all right?" Guan Shanjin leaned down to kiss Wu Xingzi's cheek. He then bit at his reddened earlobe, listening to his husky moans in smug satisfaction.

Wu Xingzi assumed Guan Shanjin would continue kissing down from his ear like before, but instead he lifted Wu Xingzi's hips and parted his petal-like lips. In a single breath, he swallowed the twitching pink cock into his mouth.

"Oh! No, no..." Wu Xingzi's cock had never been inside anything before, but now it was suddenly enveloped in a soft, warm chamber. He scrabbled at the bedding, his rebuke punctuated with passionate cries.

Glorious... This feels glorious...

Wu Xingzi's brain dissolved into a sea of white.

A nimble tongue traced the shaft from root to tip a few times; the sensation was exquisite. Guan Shanjin's smooth, hot mouth bobbed along with his tongue's licking and sucking. When Wu Xingzi's cock was swallowed all the way down, his sensitive tip was trapped somewhere that felt even tighter.

Wu Xingzi gave a short, sharp cry. His buttocks twisted on the bed, his pale thighs tensed, and his entire body began to sweat.

He didn't know why Guan Shanjin was willing to lick his cock, and he couldn't tell if his technique was any good, but Wu Xingzi was losing his mind in the throes of ecstasy. This pleasure was completely different from being pierced all the way through. The overpowering feeling of being swallowed down to his root was like a drug.

"No, this is dirty..." Wu Xingzi whimpered. He barely knew what he was moaning about. He was weaker than Guan Shanjin, and in his current position, there was no way he could resist.

The soft tongue continued downward to tease his wrinkled balls. Wu Xingzi may have come too many times earlier; his shy little balls were a bit shriveled. Guan Shanjin rolled them on his tongue before sucking on them harshly.

Wu Xingzi couldn't hold back his lewd moans, his quivering thighs rubbing against Guan Shanjin's shoulders.

Guan Shanjin's large hands kneaded Wu Xingzi's buttocks. He continued licking down to his perineum, making the middle-aged man beneath him so satisfied he kicked his legs wildly, screaming and crying, his cock dripping.

Having been tossed around in bed a few times, Wu Xingzi collapsed onto his back, breathless. Bite marks littered his spasming inner thighs, and his perineum was swollen from Guan Shanjin's sucking and biting.

At last Guan Shanjin seemed to have had enough fun. He ended his torment, coming back up to swallow the pink tip of Wu Xingzi's cock back into his mouth.

"No more... Have mercy!" Wu Xingzi burst into tears, hiccupping as he cried. He could no longer endure it. His cock was oversensitive, unwilling to withstand any more of Guan Shanjin's exquisite attack.

But Wu Xingzi discovered he was too naïve. Guan Shanjin's terrible, agile tongue was so aggressive and passionate that he couldn't help but be enthralled.

Since there was almost no semen left inside of him, the little slit at the tip of his cock could only throb sadly, fluttering nonstop. The tip of Guan Shanjin's tongue circled the head before digging into the slit. The overstimulation made Wu Xingzi's eyes roll to the back of his head as tremors ran across his body.

Guan Shanjin continued to dig his tongue into that place, as if trying to see how deep he could go. Wu Xingzi shouted and feverishly kicked out his legs, but Guan Shanjin trapped him on the bed, making him come with his tongue before releasing him.

Thin juices pooled on Wu Xingzi's belly. Then, he convulsed again, and fluid with a musky odor spurted out intermittently from his cock, flowing over his stomach. He made a mess of the bedding, but the odor dissipated quickly in the air.

Guan Shanjin chuckled. "You pissed yourself."

Wu Xingzi collapsed on the bed, trying to get his wits about him. Guan Shanjin was in no hurry, removing the stained bedclothes. After casually wiping Wu Xingzi's body with them, he tossed the sheets onto the ground.

The bedframe was cold, hard, and a little uncomfortable. Wu Xingzi quickly recovered from his lightheadedness, and he stared in confusion at the beautiful man in front of him, who still had an affectionate twinkle in his eyes.

"Are you awake?" Guan Shanjin asked, gently patting Wu Xingzi's cheeks. Seeing him shake his head with half-opened eyes, Guan Shanjin picked him up in his arms and casually tossed the blanket onto the bedframe.

"You, you..." Wu Xingzi stuttered. Breathing in Guan Shanjin's scent, Wu Xingzi's brain finally started working again. He was so ashamed that he didn't know what to do. He had seen drawings of people playing the flute, but he had never thought that the flute could be played so hard that a man could lose his soul.

"Hmm?" Guan Shanjin patted Wu Xingzi's back. It was so thin that the ridge of his spine could be seen. He traced his fingers along Wu Xingzi's backbone and rubbed his fleshy buttocks.

Wu Xingzi groaned, shutting his eyes and hiding his face in Guan Shanjin's arms. Although he was naked, Guan Shanjin was still immaculately dressed, and it was a warmth that he had rarely felt. Humans always needed the warmth of human touch.

Even though Guan Shanjin was merciless when they had sex, fucking him ruthlessly and leaving marks all over him, he was always very gentle and caring afterward. Guan Shanjin wrapped around him like a comforting spring breeze. Wu Xingzi reveled in this feeling.

Wu Xingzi was unable to resist Guan Shanjin's affections. He was a lonely person. He had experienced no tenderness from anyone since the age of ten. His parents had been as courteously aloof with each other as one would be toward guests. They even treated their own child with distant affection. At first, his mother had loved hugging and kissing him, but once he turned ten years old and started attending school, his father stopped his mother from being so affectionate toward him.

After studying and learning about shame, he came to understand the distinctions between men and women. It was inappropriate for males and females to come in bodily contact with each other. He could no longer be a child who willingly threw himself into the arms of his parents.

Soon after that, the flood had taken his parents away, and Wu Xingzi had been alone ever since. He was also not attracted to the opposite sex. When he saw a man's body, he would avoid it in self-consciousness, building a wall between himself and temptation.

Guan Shanjin's warm embrace was the first he had felt in thirty years.

The man's body temperature was high, but it was not unpleasant. It was warm, like the sun in winter. Wu Xingzi nuzzled into his firm shoulder, whimpering and nearly drifting off to sleep.

He couldn't sleep now. He had reached his pleasure, but Guan Shanjin was still as hard as a rock!

Registering that Wu Xingzi was about to fall asleep, Guan Shanjin shook him awake, not bothering to be polite. He kissed him on his blushing ear. "How ungrateful. Shouldn't you reciprocate?"

Reciprocate? Wu Xingzi shuddered, becoming alert in an instant. *Does he mean...*

Wu Xingzi felt his tongue and mouth itch slightly. He started to drool, and his favorite drawing came into his mind: that Lanling Prince of pricks which he had been yearning to lick and touch! This was a gift from heaven! He did not expect Guan Shanjin to effortlessly fulfill his fantasies like this.

Wu Xingzi was very eager, but he was afraid that he would scare Guan Shanjin, so he feigned reluctance. "Yes... I-if you don't mind my mediocre skills, I'll do it for you."

Guan Shanjin narrowed his eyes coldly for a moment, but he swiftly hid the sharpness in his gaze. "Adviser Wu, please."

Cupping his hands together, Wu Xingzi did not care that he was completely naked. His eyes were ravenous as they stared straight at Guan Shanjin's crotch... His trousers were tented, but his cock was still concealed. Was he supposed to take it out for him? How kind of him to let Wu Xingzi do this!

Wu Xingzi licked his lips. His exhausted body and his sex-drunk mind recovered in a flash. His once-weak legs were instantly full of vigor, and his mind felt clearer than ever. This was truly a rare opportunity. He would record every single moment of this in his head.

Looking at Wu Xingzi's anxious and impatient face, Guan Shanjin's lips curved slightly. "Go ahead and do whatever you want—just don't use your teeth," he said, his voice quiet and gentle.

"Of course, of course..." Wu Xingzi gulped. As he was about to reach and pull the prick out, he suddenly realized that his palms were sweaty. He hurriedly wiped them on the blanket underneath him before cautiously undoing Guan Shanjin's pants. Almost reverently, he pulled that enormous cock out with both his hands.

This pengornis was even hotter, weightier, and more delightful to touch than he had imagined it would be. Reluctant to pull his hands away, he slowly stroked up and down the shaft. He caressed it from the two heavy balls at the bottom all the way to the tip, savoring every inch. It felt silky and exquisite in his palms. The throbbing vein looked quite imposing, and it was satisfying to touch.

"You're not going to kiss it?" Guan Shanjin's voice was slightly strained. His hand on Wu Xingzi's shoulder shifted to the back of his head, pushing him down.

"Kiss it... Yes, of course..." Wu Xingzi leaned closer. The heat of Guan Shanjin's cock mingled with the smell of soap and entered his nose. Wu Xingzi panted uncontrollably, his entire body drowning in the scent and warmth. It was more glorious than he could have ever imagined.

Guan Shanjin's cock was startlingly large. The round and full head was slightly angular, the slit on top pulsing a little. A thirst developed in Wu Xingzi's heart; he was unable to resist it. He had already kissed this little slit countless times in his mind.

Wu Xingzi wasted no more time. He pursed his lips and leaned in, giving it a kiss. The head of Guan Shanjin's cock was already flowing with fluid, and the juices seeped into Wu Xingzi's mouth through the seam of his lips. It tasted a little musky; he couldn't help but stick his tongue out and lick at it.

The slick tip of Wu Xingzi's tongue swept across the head of Guan Shanjin's cock. His tongue was inexperienced and a little bashful, but it made Guan Shanjin's breathing speed up sharply.

"Keep going," he said. He pushed Wu Xingzi's head down again, driving his cock deeper into his warm, wet mouth.

"Mm..." This was the first time that Wu Xingzi had ever sucked a cock. His mouth tingled with hunger, and he trembled at the feeling of the firm head directly thrusting inside. Unable to hold his saliva back, he drooled over the shaft, soaking Guan Shanjin's skin.

"Open your mouth wider, and use your tongue." Guan Shanjin's low and gentle voice was laced with erotic huskiness, brushing across Wu Xingzi's heart like a feather. He was already infatuated with the enormous organ in his mouth, but now, he was beside himself with want as he obediently followed Guan Shanjin's guidance. He opened his mouth wider, and with some effort, he slid his tongue around the shaft.

"Good boy," Guan Shanjin said.

Wu Xingzi placed his hands around the thick root, slowly attempting to swallow the unwieldy member into his mouth. He could feel Guan Shanjin's excitement from his tensed thighs. Unfortunately, Guan Shanjin's dick was just too big. Wu Xingzi had only taken half of it into his mouth, and it had already reached his throat. If he continued, he would choke on it.

He was a little fearful; he did not dare to swallow it down further. Using his hand to fondle what didn't fit, he sucked at the rest with loud, wet sounds. Blissful intoxication bloomed across his face.

To Guan Shanjin, such simple maneuvering only made it more unbearable.

There was not enough space in Wu Xingzi's mouth. He worked at licking that throbbing vein and the slit at the tip. With his cheeks hollowed, he sucked with all his might, his hands playing with Guan Shanjin's balls.

"Adviser Wu," Guan Shanjin said, his voice strained with a grudging self-control. This was essentially torture for him. He looked at Wu Xingzi with half-lidded, lustful eyes. It made Wu Xingzi weak, and he tried even harder to bring him pleasure with his mouth.

"Take me in deeper," Guan Shanjin instructed.

Deeper?

"Relax your throat, and take me in..." Guan Shanjin coaxed him, stroking Wu Xingzi's cheeks. His slender, calloused fingers slid down from his face to his throat. He scraped there with his nail. "Swallow."

No one could resist such a beauty in the flesh. Wu Xingzi certainly was unable to hold out against such temptation—not to mention the allure of that tremendous cock. Wu Xingzi's senses were so full of the scent of cock that he barely knew who he was, drunk on the heft and heat of it.

He tried his best to relax his throat, swallowing the rest of the shaft inch by inch until his narrow throat bulged out with its shape. His face was stained with snot and tears, his nose buried in Guan Shanjin's bushy pubic hair.

Wu Xingzi gagged to the point where he was nearly about to vomit. His throat burned in pain, but it gave him a ravishing sort of satisfaction. His tongue was immobile, forced down by the thick shaft. Wu Xingzi reached up to timidly touch the skin of his own neck, and it felt as though he was touching a flame.

"Such a good boy," Guan Shanjin praised him. One hand was tangled in his long hair, and the other held his throat, rubbing heavily at where his cock was bulging out.

In no time, Wu Xingzi went into a stupor, allowing Guan Shanjin to grab his head and thrust himself inside. At first, his throat contracted and he gagged, but as he got used to it, his throat completely relaxed, letting the shaft pump in at will. He sucked on it gladly, the tip of his tongue dragging past the head, licking at it as if he was savoring a delicacy.

Eventually, Wu Xingzi's body started convulsing. About to asphyxiate, his throat contracted tightly, and his eyes rolled to the back of his head. Guan Shanjin was clearly about to reach his peak; he slammed even more savagely into Wu Xingzi's throat, almost shoving his balls into Wu Xingzi's mouth. Then he came, the strength of the spurting semen making Wu Xingzi struggle and choke. The older man was unable to free himself as the musky, thick fluid shot straight down into his belly.

Nothing could be heard in the room except for the lurid sounds of heavy pants and coughs.

Guan Shanjin could not stop himself from thrusting the head of his cock lightly into Wu Xingzi's mouth one last time before he pulled out, cleaning the last bit of cum there.

Wu Xingzi had fainted.

After a short rest, Guan Shanjin got up. He called for his subordinate, who was guarding the door, to summon the attendant from the Peng Society. He replaced the sheets on the bed with a new set of bedclothes, prepared a basin of hot water, and cleaned both of them up before heading to bed.

Wu Xingzi always rose very early. He was normally awake when the sky was just starting to brighten.

Even though he had been thoroughly ravaged the night before, the bed in the Peng Society was fabulously comfortable; he had slept better than usual. Other than his mouth being a little sore and his muscles slightly aching, he was full of energy.

He stretched and got out of the bed, his footsteps a little shaky. Looking around, he found that his clothes and belongings had been folded neatly and left on the shelf. He deftly dressed himself before turning back to look at the bed.

Guan Shanjin lay there, his gorgeous, silky black hair scattered across the red bedclothes. As for the owner of that black hair, he was undeniably, heart-stirringly beautiful, despite being as cold as frost.

After staring at him for some time, Wu Xingzi turned and left the room.

It was time for him to return to Qingcheng County. Even though there were normally no complicated cases that kept him on his toes, there was still a lot of paperwork for him to handle as an adviser. He could not make his salary without working!

Outside the doors stood two towering guards. Hearing the door open, they turned toward him, but neither one said a word.

Facing their stares, Wu Xingzi was at a loss for what to do next. He shrank backward reflexively, then cupped his hands at them with a servile smile before quietly closing the door.

Just as he was about to ask where the exit was, a figure dressed in jade green waved at him from nearby. Looking closer, Wu Xingzi realized it was Manager Rancui. He was neatly dressed, looking at him with a bright smile.

Although he felt a little uneasy, Wu Xingzi still walked forward. "Good morning, Manager."

"Good morning to you as well, Adviser Wu." Rancui affably hooked his hand around Wu Xingzi's arm. "Don't hurry off—I have something I would like to discuss with you. When we're done talking, I will arrange for someone to send you back."

It just so happened that Wu Xingzi also had something to discuss with Rancui. He still had to pay the next month's subscription fee for *The Pengornisseur*, so he let Rancui pull him away.

Guan Shanjin's subordinates watched the two men depart. They did not stop them and continued guarding the door.

Rancui brought Wu Xingzi around a few turns and past a few courtyards, finally arriving at that small pavilion where they had met for the first time. Breakfast sat already prepared on the stone table of the pavilion, with plates of stuffed buns, mantou, and a few other dishes. They looked exquisite; the sight alone could whet one's appetite.

Rancui beckoned Wu Xingzi to sit down first before he sat across from him. He picked up a pastry and bit into it, his eyes urging Wu Xingzi to join. Since his host had started eating, Wu Xingzi ate without any worries. The meal was very satisfying, and the portions were perfect.

When they finished their breakfast, the mist in the air had dissipated. With clear skies, the weather looked nice.

It was only now that Rancui started talking business. "Adviser Wu, as the manager of the Peng Society, I have always wished for all gentlemen to find their fated partners."

"Thank you, thank you..." Wu Xingzi scratched at his face awkwardly. He did not dare to confirm if he had met his fated partner, but he definitely did have a destiny with Guan Shanjin's pengornis.

"So, I have no choice but to ask. After spending yesterday with General Guan, do you plan on being life partners with him? Or is this just a tryst?" Rancui was direct with his question. He knew that beating around the bush would not work with Wu Xingzi, as Wu Xingzi would never be able to intuit his meaning.

With this question posed to him, Wu Xingzi replied without hesitation. "It should be a one-time thing."

"Oh?" Rancui's brow raised slightly. He had certainly never expected that Wu Xingzi would answer so quickly without needing to dwell on it. It didn't seem like he was playing coy, either. However, the satisfaction and bashfulness on his face was evident, and it made it hard for Rancui to figure out what was going on in his head.

"So, Guan-gongzi is a general? It's no wonder," Wu Xingzi said. He naturally did not notice Rancui's prying. Instead, he was pleased with his ability to accurately judge people. He had already noticed that Guan Shanjin's status was out of the ordinary, and now, it turned out that he was a general of Horse-Face City.

"You...don't plan on getting to know General Guan better?" Rancui stared at Wu Xingzi's face.

"No, no." Wu Xingzi waved his hands. He then took out fifty coins from his money pouch and pushed them at Rancui. "Here's next month's subscription fee for *The Pengornisseur*. Please take it."

"Oh..." Rancui did not press further and pushed the fifty coins aside. "Since that's the case, I'll get someone to send you back to Qingcheng County."

"It's too much trouble," Wu Xingzi said, wanting to refuse.

Rancui smiled at him as he tapped at his lips. "It's part of the Peng Society's services."

Giving him no chance to argue, Rancui summoned one of his staff. After giving him a few instructions, he smiled at Wu Xingzi. "Don't worry. Since you and the general are not meant to be, the Peng Society will be responsible for the rest of it. I'll let my staff drive you back in the carriage, and we'll welcome you back on the tenth of next month."

"Thank you, thank you. I'm sorry if I've caused you trouble." Wu Xingzi hurriedly cupped his hands at him in thanks, then got onto the carriage and soon returned to Qingcheng County.

Wu Xingzi had no idea that Guan Shanjin raged upon waking up after he left, that he destroyed half the room and punished his guards, and that Manager Rancui had to cut him down for his behavior...

Ah, the tenth of next month will be arriving soon. Wu Xingzi opened his rattan case and flipped through the drawings kept inside. He spent some time stroking the drawing of Guan Shanjin's cock in satisfaction, then changed his clothes and happily left for the magistrate's office.

Stationed in Horse-Face City were the fiercest troops in all of Great Xia. Their presence was so strong and overpowering that they seemed to rule the land on which they stood. Even if the other three military forces in the territory were to be combined into a single army, it would pose little threat to the camp in Horse-Face City.

If not for the fact that the protector general had come from a line of ministers, and that he was thick as thieves with the emperor, the emperor might have become worried...but he wouldn't have been able to do much about those worries.

Before General Guan Shanjin took up guard at the borders of Nanjiang, they would be pillaged by the Nanman king on a yearly basis. However, within the space of five short years, Nanman had been completely subdued, obediently slinking back to the demarcated limits of their territory, accepting their defeat and paying tribute. The emperor doubted his own head was as hard as that of the Nanman king.

Of course, there were people who hated Guan Shanjin and were jealous of him, but this was of no concern. He was always in Horse-Face City and never returned to the capital, and he had the most fearsome troops in the Great Xia Dynasty under his hand. Just mentioning his name was enough to dry little children's fearful tears. Even a drunkard wouldn't have the guts to openly speak ill of Guan Shanjin.

As for the ones seeking his favor? There were many.

At first, they started sending him beautiful women. Plump ones, thin ones, all lovely in their own ways. There were all kinds of beauties amongst them, like a hundred blossoming flowers; even the emperor's harem could not compare.

However, Guan Shanjin was not interested.

When Guan Shanjin first made a name for himself, he was only sixteen years old. By then, he had already achieved military merit for himself in the northwest region—the honor could have gone to the general of the Western Garrison, but the Guan family army was so renowned that the Western Garrison general didn't dare to spearhead the campaign.

The Western Garrison general used to be a commander under the protector general. Later, the protector general promoted him, handing him command of his own troops. It was only natural for him to be more lenient toward his previous young master, Guan Shanjin.

Once he came of age, Guan Shanjin was finally willing to return to the capital city, where he idled around for a couple of years. Publicly, it looked as though the emperor had taken pity on him for having spent so much of his young life on the battlefield, never being able to enjoy the company of his family. It was also to conveniently settle his marital matters, father an heir, and soothe the protector general's love for his child.

In private, it was a lot simpler. The emperor was afraid that this young man would become too difficult to control, but it was a waste to leave his sword unused. He planned to let him marry and start a family as quickly as possible—that way, he would have a few more chips in his hand.

No one was sure if Guan Shanjin had seen through the emperor's plan, but young General Guan was completely uninterested in the portraits of gorgeous women that appeared at his door daily. The scrolls of paintings piled up in stacks in his study, and if there was no space on the wall for them to be hung up, they would be sent to a corner of the house and left to collect dust. A clever steward came up with the idea of replacing the paintings on the wall daily, so as to give a face to the names of various aristocratic families.

Time passed, and half the beauties in the paintings had found their marriage matches already. Young General Guan still did not pay a moment of attention to those drawings, let alone select one of them.

Of course, this was not difficult to understand. After all, these women might have been beautiful, but none of them were as good looking as young General Guan himself. Next to him, how could the beauties compare? All eyes would be drawn to young General Guan instead.

The protector general had no idea how to deal with his son. Beat him? This son of his was ruthless. Regardless of whether the protector general was able to physically punish him in the first place, even if he did manage it, he himself could lose a pound of flesh in the process. Scold him? The protector general was boorish and could not compare to the quick wit of his son, who was well-versed in both literature and military affairs. With accomplishments to rival a scholar's, his son might not leave his father with any dignity.

It wasn't as if the relationship between father and son was strained. However, he had brought Guan Shanjin up to be a strong-minded person, even as a child. As long as one could convince him with logic, everything was copacetic; he would listen to advice if it didn't push his limits. However, if someone tried to get their own way with him, he could hold a grudge until the end of time.

Still, the protector general could not let the matter drag on like this. He could only suggest to his wife to discuss it with their son, and to inquire if he had any preferences. This way, they could at least have an idea of how to proceed!

After the talk, they finally learned what Guan Shanjin liked: men.

Although the Great Xia Dynasty was at the peak of its prosperity, and there were quite a few famous instances of men with male lovers, the aristocratic families still disapproved somewhat of homosexuality. If a man was attracted to other men, they would see each other in secret, and would not consider accepting a man as a legal spouse. However, young General Guan did not care, and he was candid about his lack of interest in women. If they wanted him to get married in this life, it would have to be to a man.

When the emperor heard of this, he was much less worried. In Great Xia, the protector general was one of the rare few who chose to spend the rest of his life with only one wife—he didn't even have a companion maid to serve him in bed. The protector general and his wife were very loving toward each other and had married when they were young, and the general's wife gave birth to their only son, Guan Shanjin.

If the sole son of the protector general only wanted men and not women, that meant the family would no longer have any descendants. The emperor was hugely relieved, immediately declaring Guan Shanjin general of the Southern Garrison and sending him to Nanjiang. *Ah, the poor family,* the emperor thought.

After the protector general saw his son off to Nanjiang, he returned to the ancestral hall and kneeled for one night. The next day, he started seeking a good man for his son.

After all, he was a rather open-minded man.

As for Guan Shanjin, once he left the capital, he never returned. However, such a tremendous distance could not deter a father's love and concern for his son.

One day a few months back, Guan Shanjin had received a book that consisted of over four hundred pages. The workmanship was exquisite, and the pages within the book were made of Bailu paper, an expensive paper that was usually only used within the palace. The cover was made of Jinsu paper, which was usually reserved for important scrolls. On it was inscribed "The Pengornisseur," and at the bottom was a label as tiny as an insect—"The Capital and Nanjiang Edition."

Accompanying the book was a letter from his family. Guan Shanjin didn't feel like reading it himself, and instead gestured for his vice general, Man Yue, to read it on his behalf.

Just as his name suggested, Man Yue was round and fat like a full moon.[8] His smooth skin, flushed with a slight pink tint, was fair and could never hold a tan. Other than those in the Guan family army and the current Nanjiang army who knew him, no one could have guessed that this plump dumpling was Guan Shanjin's most valiant general.

Reading the letter, Man Yue burst out laughing. "General Guan, it's a letter from your father."

Guan Shanjin shot him a cold look, warning him to cut out his usual nonsense.

"Don't give me that look! Your beguiling eyes could make someone fall for you, you know. I'm still young; I couldn't bear it if I fell in love," he teased, clearly not taking Guan Shanjin's warning to heart. The relationship Guan Shanjin had with Man Yue was different from his other friendships; Man Yue could afford to tease him.

"Shut up." Guan Shanjin reached his hand out to pinch harshly at Man Yue's cheek. "Tell me about the letter."

He didn't let Man Yue read the letter verbatim, because Guan Shanjin understood his father too well. He was an ill-mannered oaf of an old man, and his letters always dragged on about trivial matters, such as how the little yellow dog at the city gates had given birth to a litter of puppies. There was nothing Guan Shanjin could do about his father's disposition.

Although Man Yue was a very lively and boisterous person, he could handle Guan Shanjin's temper with surprising grace. He laughed. "It's nothing that interesting. General Guan, do you know about the Peng Society?"

"Yes." Of course he knew—ever since Guan Shanjin came out with the news that he preferred men, someone from the Peng

---

8 Man Yue (滿月) means "full moon."

Society had sought him out, saying they wanted the honor of being his matchmaker.

Guan Shanjin sneered. Even random passersby were concerned with his marriage prospects. He suspected the emperor had a hand in this. As for who exactly the boss behind the Peng Society was, before he left the capital he had delegated the investigation to a trusted subordinate. He soon knew everything about the man in charge of the society, so he set it aside and no longer bothered with it.

Who would have thought that after so many years, the Peng Society would again appear in front of him—via his father, no less? They really did have a death wish.

"The Peng Society specializes in matchmaking men through this *Pengornisseur* book." Man Yue flipped through *The Pengornisseur* and clicked his tongue continuously in amazement. "Who do you think started the Peng Society? They really know their stuff."

"Dong Shucheng founded it," Guan Shanjin said, pursing his lips derisively. "If you're interested, you can take it. My old man just wants to marry me off."

"Dong Shucheng?" Man Yue asked, joyfully accepting the book. When he flipped through a few pages, he came across all sorts of outstanding men from proper family backgrounds. Having kept himself chaste for so many years, it seemed now might be the time for him to look for someone himself.

"The owner of Azure Pavilion," Guan Shanjin said, providing a little more information.

"Really?! The owner of Azure Pavilion?" Man Yue gasped in admiration. Almost everyone in the Great Xia Dynasty knew about the Azure Pavilion. It was a gentlemen's entertainment venue that reigned supreme across the land, and only the most distinguished elites were allowed to enter its premises. Even a person like Man Yue, who preferred men, was a little interested in checking it out. One could only imagine how impressive it was. This pavilion owner's influence was far-reaching. If he could even earn money off such intimate matters between men, he truly had sharp business acumen!

Man Yue owed the protector general a favor for inadvertently giving him a copy of *The Pengornisseur*, so he took a moment to speak on the man's behalf. "Let's get back on topic, General—you can't remain a bachelor for life."

"I won't." With a shadow of a smile on his face, Guan Shanjin looked at his deputy from the corner of his eye. "You know there's a man who has my heart."

"I do, but so what? He's in *your* heart, but you're not in *his*." If any other man had said this, he would be chopped into pieces and fed to the wolves, but Man Yue had the confidence to say such things. Still, he was unnerved by the murderous, cold glare that Guan Shanjin shot him. After a couple of jeering laughs, Man Yue grabbed *The Pengornisseur* and ran away with it.

Over the next few months, regardless of the weather, *The Pengornisseur* was delivered. Man Yue would receive it, then joyfully make friends through the pigeon post.

As time passed, Guan Shanjin finally understood the impressiveness of this *Pengornisseur* book. One day, he could not resist his curiosity any longer, asking Man Yue to lend him the latest edition.

"You're finally thinking of indulging in pleasures of the flesh?" Man Yue looked at Guan Shanjin with exaggerated astonishment, offering the book to him with both hands.

"Pah," Guan Shanjin spat. But if a person was beautiful, even such vulgar grunts were music to the ears. He reclined on the daybed next to the window, feeling somewhat lazy. After morning training, he had returned to his room for a bath. Without even tying up his hair, he dressed in a thin inner robe and lazed on the daybed, idly flipping through *The Pengornisseur*.

"How is it?" Man Yue asked as he sat nearby, itching to know the answer.

Guan Shanjin didn't reply, looking through the book page by page. He had always been well read and had a sharp memory; with one glance, he could read ten lines. Without much effort, he read through more than half of the book. There were only a few pages left.

Man Yue felt a pain in his heart. The men listed within *The Pengonisseur* were all good people. The ones he had contacted over the past few months were the cream of the crop. Among them, there were gentle and elegant ones, strong and heroic ones, and even ministers and other powerful men.

However, looking at how Guan Shanjin flipped through the pages, even a genuine pearl could be discarded as a fake.

Suddenly, Guan Shanjin straightened and stood up from the daybed. The apathetic expression on his face was gone, his alluring eyes gleaming.

Man Yue's heart thumped, realizing that something might have gone wrong. Of course, this was only in his imagination. He leapt up, reaching out to snatch *The Pengornisseur*... But his hand had only just made the slightest movement when a sharp, black sword was immediately at his throat. *Damn, will he ever stop taking his sword out when he gets upset?!*

Man Yue hurriedly took a couple of steps back before he dared to grumble a retort. "Put your sword away! No matter what, I'm still your vice general!"

"So?" Guan Shanjin shot him a look, but with a flex of his arm, he sheathed his sword.

"You..." Man Yue sighed. "Will you at least let me know who caught your eye?"

Although he wanted to lean closer, after evaluating the darkness in Guan Shanjin's eyes, Man Yue decided to not risk his neck.

Guan Shanjin did not reply to Man Yue's question, instead asking another question in response. "Tell me, what exactly does it mean to make friends through the pigeon post?"

"Hmm... Essentially, it's just writing a letter to the person you're interested in and mailing it to a collection point. Someone will take it from there." Man Yue had no choice but to answer obediently. He had to calm this man down to prevent a tragedy from happening.

"A collection point?" Guan Shanjin asked.

"Yes, isn't it all written in there? Goose City, Fragrance City, Horse-Face City, the capital, and so on. They're all Peng Society collection points." Man Yue could see that Guan Shanjin's mood had improved, so he took a few steps closer. "Why? Are you really going to indulge in worldly desires?"

Guan Shanjin still did not reply to his questions and only curled his lip. "Prepare the horses and find four men to accompany me. I want to go to Goose City."

"You want to go to Goose City?" Man Yue jumped, his soft flesh trembling. "If you really are interested in someone, you just need to send a letter! There's no need to travel so far!"

"Hmm?" Guan Shanjin's tone was gentle, and even Man Yue blushed upon hearing it. His heart raced and his mouth opened, but no words came out.

After all, Guan Shanjin was the general, so there was nothing Man Yue could do about this. Could he get someone to tie the general up and prevent him from leaving? The general's Chenyuan Sword would definitely have a good meal to slice through if he tried.

Although lives might not be taken, there was still a high possibility of him being bedbound for at least a couple of months afterward.

"General, aren't you afraid that Mr. Lu will be displeased once he hears about this?" Man Yue had no choice but to take one last stand. He was extremely unwilling to mention Mr. Lu in front of the general, as this man was the underlying cause to all this trouble! However, Man Yue could now only try to fix this problem in the worst way possible, like drinking poison to quench his thirst.

"Isn't this what you want?" Guan Shanjin scoffed and slammed *The Pengornisseur* closed. "When I'm gone, send someone to tell Mr. Lu where I'm going and what I plan to do. If any news comes, inform me through the mail."

"I don't know what you're planning to do." Man Yue was visibly upset, his usually cherubic and smiling face gloomy.

"I'm only going to pick up some male civilians." Guan Shanjin pinched Man Yue's cheek. "Ask someone to ready everything, quickly; when I'm done packing, I'll leave."

With Guan Shanjin being so urgent, Man Yue could only obey his orders.

With a swift horse, it would take about fifteen days to travel from Horse-Face City to Goose City, but Guan Shanjin made it in nine.

Travel-worn, his party reached Goose City and asked for three luxury rooms in the city's biggest inn. After washing off the dust of the journey and eating a meal, Guan Shanjin wanted to directly look for the Peng Society, but was persuaded not to do so by the subordinates who accompanied him. They said that those were the instructions of Vice General Man Yue, who didn't want Guan Shanjin to look for trouble at the Peng Society until he'd had a good rest and refreshed his mind.

Knowing that Man Yue and his subordinates were only thinking of his well-being, Guan Shanjin didn't trouble them and returned to his room to sleep.

He had no idea that his four subordinates couldn't sleep the entire night due to their anxiety, worried that he would sneak out in the middle of the night to make a fuss. The next morning, all four of them had bags under their eyes.

Goose City was a bustling place, and unlike Horse-Face City, it had not gone through the chaos of the war that took place five years ago. Although Horse-Face City had been recovering during the last five years, progress was slow since the damage was so severe. It was far behind Goose City in terms of peace and prosperity. The citizens, too, were different from those of Horse-Face City, who had a slightly cruel air to them. The citizens of Goose City were like quails: gentle, soft, and silly.

Having stayed by the border for so long, Guan Shanjin took a while to acclimate to this before strolling around the city streets.

When he finally reached Goose City's most prosperous street, he led his subordinates straight to the antique shop that was used as a cover for the Peng Society.

This place made him think of the capital.

The furnishings and atmosphere were sumptuous but not ostentatious, extremely delicate yet vibrant. Although the store was a front for a different business, there were many quite valuable items available. There were clusters of customers around the place, and from their clothes and temperaments, they were clearly from some of the most wealthy and influential families of Goose City.

"Hello, may I ask if you're looking for anything?" an attendant said, welcoming them in. He was pleasant-looking, his smile a little uncouth yet not dislikable.

This Dong Shucheng was really good at training his people.

"I just want to take a look. Don't stand there and be an eyesore." Guan Shanjin waved him off. Although he did secretly want to enter the Peng Society's parlor, he suddenly remembered that Man Yue had not told him the catchphrase to gain entry. Man Yue had gotten quite gutsy lately. But the information was not left out on purpose—it seemed he'd been in such a hurry that he'd forgotten about it.

Thinking Guan Shanjin was really a customer here to look at the antiques, the attendant apologized and retreated.

Just as he was trying to decide how to get the secret phrase from Man Yue, he heard a clear and gentle voice behind him, soft as a spring breeze in March.

"... Do you have a jade pagoda from the Han Dynasty?"

"What type of Han jade pagoda would you like, sir?" the attendant asked.

The unknown man said, "O-one that Dong Xian used to play with." His soft voice was laced with a little uneasiness.

"Oh? Dong Xian?" The attendant chuckled. "Sir, I'm afraid that I'm not too familiar with such an item. Would you like to come to the back and speak to our manager?"

"Of course." The man gave a huge sigh of relief. In a rare moment of curiosity, Guan Shanjin glanced in his direction.

He only saw the back of a man dressed in a somewhat old, dark green robe. His long hair was held in a neat bun by a simple bamboo hairpin. The back of his neck was so fair that Guan Shanjin could make out the greenish-blue veins under the skin.

The neck was very slender, looking as though it would break immediately if struck, and the man was very thin, making the robe gathered around his waist seem voluminous. He looked tempting.

"Dong Xian?" Guan Shanjin repeated quietly, but the man who was about to step into the back seemed to have heard him. His ears tinted red and he sneaked a peek at him.

That face left Guan Shanjin stunned. Even as the thin figure vanished behind the door, he was still in a daze.

He really looks very similar... Although his nose was a little fleshier and droopier, his lips thicker and his philtrum shorter, with dewy eyes like a startled deer, he really did look very similar to Mr. Lu.

"Is that...Mr. Lu?" A subordinate was unable to keep the surprise from his lowered voice, and that finally pulled Guan Shanjin out of his trance.

"No," he snorted coldly. At first glance, he did look like Mr. Lu, but after some contemplation, it was clear that these two people were as different as night and day. Ignoring the low-class, ordinary facial features, it was the man's innate shyness and timidity that stood in stark contrast to Mr. Lu's elegant demeanor.

"The general is right." The subordinates would certainly not refute what Guan Shanjin had said. They were simply surprised that there could be someone who looked so similar to Mr. Lu at first glance.

Guan Shanjin waved an attendant over and asked with a smile, "I'm looking for a jade pagoda from the Han Dynasty."

"What type of Han jade pagoda would you like, sir?" The attendant's eyes flashed, but it was not concealed from Guan Shanjin.

"One that Dong Xian used to play with," he replied.

Hearing that answer, this attendant did not respond the same way as the other one, leading him to the back. Instead, he observed Guan Shanjin and the four armed guards towering behind him. He only replied after a moment of pondering. "Sir, our little shop does not have a treasure like this. Why don't you take a look—"

"The Peng Society." Guan Shanjin bluntly cut off the salesman. Although the stranger's demeanor was very different from Mr. Lu's, ever since he laid eyes on the man, Guan Shanjin decided he must enter the Peng Society—even if he had to tear this shop apart.

The attendant immediately stopped and seemed unsure what to do. He cupped his hands toward Guan Shanjin. "Sir, I have to inform the manager first. Please wait a moment." He hurried away and did not dare to look back.

The attendants of the Peng Society were all very clever. Naturally, this attendant could see the murderous gleam in the eyes of this awe-inspiring, imposing beauty of a man. This went beyond what the average wealthy family could produce. It was so sharp it was almost tangible, and it made the fine hairs on his neck shiver.

Guan Shanjin waited leisurely, picking up some of the valuable objects in the shop and fiddling with them, before the attendant returned, panting with exertion.

"Sir, the manager would like to invite you for a chat. Please follow me." His somewhat fawning expression made a few customers standing by the side express curiosity, privately measuring up Guan Shanjin with their eyes.

"Lead the way." Guan Shanjin smirked. He was starting to become interested in this manager. From the way this attendant acted, it was likely that he knew Guan Shanjin's identity. He had only spent a short period of time in the back room, but he seemed to have gotten information on him already.

The back patio of the shop was a lot more spacious than Guan Shanjin had estimated. It was lush with greenery, with flowers blooming everywhere. Courtyards stretched in front of him. Ordinary people could easily lose their sense of direction entering this place.

Finally, they arrived at an ornamental lake. In the middle of that small and exquisite lake was a pavilion made of white jade. A green bamboo bridge connected it to the shore, its emerald-green reflection picturesque as it glimmered on the water beneath.

The attendant led the group of them to the pavilion before cupping his hands at them. "Please wait a moment, General Guan. The manager is still attending to a guest. He will join you shortly. Please enjoy the tea and snacks."

As expected, the Peng Society knew of his background. Guan Shanjin smiled. Naturally, he would not make trouble for the salesman; he simply waved him off.

The furniture of the pavilion was made of black bamboo, and the cool and smooth material gleamed in the light. On the bamboo table sat two steaming cups of tea. The pastries were exquisite looking, so intricate that one could hardly bear to eat them.

Guan Shanjin did not have a sweet tooth. He smiled at one of his guards. "I recall that you like sweet things, Hei-er. Take them."

"Thank you, General." Hei-er did not stand on ceremony, picking up the snacks and scarfing them down.

In no time at all, there was not a single crumb left. Hei-er licked his fingers, clearly wanting more. Guan Shanjin scolded him with a laugh, then shooed away his four guards. Everyone knew what was going to happen next, but Guan Shanjin did not wish to talk about such matters in front of his subordinates.

He didn't have to wait long. A slim and delicate figure drew closer from afar, crossing the bamboo bridge and stepping into the pavilion. The man greeted the imposing Guan Shanjin. "I, the ordinary civilian Rancui, greet the great Southern Garrison general."

"Manager Rancui," Guan Shanjin said, cupping his hands at him.

"I'm sorry to have let you wait so long, General. Please forgive me." Rancui gave a beguiling smile. Both his voice and manner of dress were somewhat androgynous. With bewitching eyes, he looked like a seasoned courtesan.

"You are too polite, Manager. Take a seat; let's talk." Guan Shanjin gestured for Rancui to sit down. Although Rancui was very handsome, he was unable to stir even a little bit of Guan Shanjin's heart. His attraction dampened further because his identity had been exposed. The general's eyes shot daggers at Rancui.

"Thank you, General." Rancui elegantly took his seat and picked up a teacup, holding it in front of his lips. "May I ask, because you went out of your way to come here—is there someone you're interested in?"

Guan Shanjin snorted lightly. "You're rather astute."

"I'm only vetting you for the safety of the members of the Peng Society. I had no choice but to pry into your identity." He covered his mouth as he smiled, his alluring eyes curving slightly. His figure was lithe, while his words were soft but forceful.

Guan Shanjin couldn't be bothered to spend any more time on this subject and gave him a cold glance. "I want to know who that man just now was," he asked directly.

"The man just now?" Rancui blinked, responding after some consideration. "Oh, so the great General Guan is interested in men like Old Master Bao? You really can't judge a man by his appearance."

"Old Master Bao?" Guan Shanjin frowned. Although he didn't know the name of the ordinary-looking man who shared a slight resemblance to Mr. Lu, he was sure that he could not be addressed as an old master. Going by his appearance, he was a village schoolteacher at most.

"Are you not attracted to him? Don't be shy, General. Although Old Master Bao is of a certain age, he has maintained his body very well. He also has multiple properties under his name. He's honest and devoted. If he hadn't become a widower, he would never have sought the Peng Society." It was as though Rancui had not noticed Guan Shanjin's darkening expression, continuing to introduce the man with a smile. "As for your preferences, the Peng Society never judges."

"I guess I can only thank you for that." Guan Shanjin smiled without humor, pulling out his Chenyuan Sword and pointing it at Rancui's neck. "I can't be bothered to spend any more time talking nonsense with you. Treasure your life, Manager. You should take note of the current situation."

The straightforward threat clearly stunned Rancui. His eyes froze in horror, only shifting to the side slowly after taking a few breaths. He smiled. "Calm down, General. I've simply misunderstood you. Just tell me what you want to know—there's no need for knives or spears here."

"This is the Chenyuan Sword. It's neither a knife nor a spear, so you needn't worry." Guan Shanjin's lips curved up as well, his tone consoling. He sounded as if he was flirting. However, that glinting sword tip never strayed from its position.

Rancui's hands, hidden in his sleeves, slowly tightened into fists. He knew he could no longer dodge the issue. This man in front of him was the famed demon of Great Xia. He could kill him in a blink of an eye, faster than anyone could protect him.

Rancui had no other choice. He gave a stiff smile. "Could it be that the general is asking about Qingcheng County's adviser, Adviser Wu Xingzi?"

"Adviser Wu..." Guan Shanjin chuckled softly.

Guan Shanjin had learned Adviser Wu's name and personal details but did not act immediately on the information. His original purpose in coming here was not for the adviser of Qingcheng County, but for a different person in *The Pengornisseur*.

There was another refined and gentle-looking man of nearly forty years; he had a quiet elegance and scholarly manner about him. He was an accountant in Sushui Village near Goose City, and his boss owned the biggest restaurant in the village. Other than two younger siblings who were already married, there was no one else in his family. His face was slightly longer, and he had a somewhat off-putting feel to him, with eyes that were somewhat dim and uneven. His facial features were rather lacking, but if one looked long enough, he did bear a resemblance to Mr. Lu. This was what surprised Guan Shanjin and had him insisting on traveling to Goose City despite Man Yue's objections.

He never expected to meet someone even more similar here.

He tapped his finger on Adviser Wu's portrait. It was obvious that the adviser was not good at drawing—his image was only about sixty percent similar to his actual appearance, and the spirit of the drawing was even worse. He looked lifeless, with soulless eyes, a bulbous nose, and a broad mouth. Adviser Wu seemed extremely dislikable.

Fortunately, to prevent the members' poor drawing skills from affecting their possible marriages, the Peng Society employed an expert painter to redo the drawing before it was published. Once that was done, Adviser Wu's portrait would become even more similar in appearance to Mr. Lu.

Guan Shanjin felt satisfied. He decided that before next month's copy of *The Pengornisseur* was published, he would first make friends and have some fun with the accountant in Sushui Village.

The great General Guan, who had lived by the borders, discovered that city folk really knew how to play. Making friends through the pigeon post was not just a simple exchange of mail—the first reply was often a drawing of a phallus. Despite being very experienced and having no lack of bedwarmers, this was truly an eye-opening experience for General Guan.

He even confirmed it with Man Yue. No one knew when the tradition started or from whom it originated, but dick pictures had become the standard form of greeting. Thinking of Man Yue drawing his own phallus and mailing it to several men made Guan Shanjin laugh aloud. However, his mood soon changed.

Naturally, he sent people to investigate Adviser Wu. Qingcheng County was a small place, and it was laughably easy to collect information there. He dug up Adviser Wu's background and everything else about him, and so of course he knew that this middle-aged man was an incredibly shy person. A man like him, with such a simple scholarly character, would get quite the shock if he were to receive such a drawing.

Needless to say, Guan Shanjin was not worried about shocking Wu Xingzi, but he was concerned about the older man following this trend. Guan Shanjin would not tolerate other people looking at the private parts of his chosen plaything.

They hadn't so much as officially met yet, but Guan Shanjin would make sure no one else could touch even a hair on his head.

The extremely cocky General Guan immediately sought out Manager Rancui, and they came to an agreement: whenever Adviser Wu mailed out a drawing of his own phallus, there was no need to forward it. Instead, it would be delivered straight to Guan Shanjin's hand. As for whether Manager Rancui agreed to it willingly or not, that was of no concern to Guan Shanjin. After all, he wasn't the one making the suggestion—his Chenyuan Sword was.

Guan Shanjin remained in Goose City for a while and had an affair with the accountant from Sushui Village, but grew tired of him in less than a month. After all, an imitation could never be as appealing as the genuine article.

This was also when he received the first letter Wu Xingzi mailed to him.

Wu Xingzi had never sent a second letter to the same person— out of tradition, or perhaps out of malice. This had become an interesting observation amongst the members of the Peng Society.

In reply to Wu Xingzi, Guan Shanjin mailed out a drawing of his cock for the first time. Then, Adviser Wu replied with an illustration of his own phallus. It was beyond Guan Shanjin's expectations, and he ate it up. Despite his annoyance that Wu Xingzi's expressions were not like that of Mr. Lu, he could not stop himself from hunting down the few traces that were similar.

After he spent a night of passion with Wu Xingzi, Guan Shanjin slept very deeply. Being stationed by the borders and having spent more than half his life on the battlefield, Guan Shanjin was not a man who could fall asleep easily. He was hypervigilant, and the smallest noise could alert him from his sleep. As such, when he woke up and discovered the bed empty and cool to the touch beside him, he was unprecedentedly horrified.

He didn't even bother to dress himself properly. He hastily pulled on his trousers and pushed the door open with his feet still bare. Glaring at his subordinates who stood guard outside, he questioned them harshly. "Where is he?!"

Shocked by his crazed appearance, the two guards looked at each other in dismay. They were stunned for a short moment, but then they saw he was about to draw his sword. "Manager Rancui invited Adviser Wu to have a chat," one guard hurriedly answered.

"Rancui?" Guan Shanjin was speechless. He slammed the door shut, quickly dressed, and haphazardly tied up his hair. The raging fire in his heart did not dwindle—it burned even brighter, like a snarling beast that wanted to burst out.

No one had ever left him like this after spending a night of passion together. Guan Shanjin had the utmost confidence in his handsome looks and prowess in the bedroom. There was no denying that he had always felt disdainful toward people who thought themselves better than him, but they all still ended up losing themselves in the pleasure he gave them.

There was nothing special about this Wu Xingzi. His timidly inexperienced yet enthusiastically wild behavior during their acts was completely different from the proper and upright way he held himself when he had his clothes on. Guan Shanjin knew too many people like this and had always felt fed up with them.

Who would have thought that Wu Xingzi, a timid old quail of a man, actually dared to run away after sleeping with him?

"Damn you, Wu Xingzi!" Guan Shanjin gnashed his teeth. With one pound of his fist, the table crumbled beneath him.

The display cabinet by the window wasn't safe from his swinging fists either, and together with the exquisite antiques, it all went crashing to the floor.

His subordinates outside listened to the cacophony of crashing furniture and trembled in their boots. Fifteen minutes later, Guan Shanjin finally opened the door and emerged from the room with bloodshot eyes. He glared at the Peng Society attendant who, after hearing the ruckus, quickly came over to investigate.

"Bring me to see Rancui," Guan Shanjin said, his voice as cold as ice.

"Uhh..." The attendant mopped at the cold sweat forming on his forehead, trying to avoid Guan Shanjin's sharp gaze.

"Is there a problem?" Guan Shanjin sneered, grabbing at the door panel with some force. Spiderweb cracks appeared through the panel, and in the next moment, it shattered.

The attendant quaked, staring stupefied at the wood chips on the ground and the wreckage in the room. His loud gasps sounded like bellows, and he looked like he was about to collapse onto the ground.

Naturally, the great General Guan would not let him escape. He strode forward, his clawed hand savagely gripping the salesman's throat. "If you faint," he said, his voice cold yet sickly sweet, "I'll break every single bone in your body one by one, starting with your fingers..." With his unoccupied hand, he reached out and stroked the attendant's little finger.

The attendant had experienced many an ordeal in his life, but right now he was panicked to the point of choking, nearly in tears. It was only by suppressing his fear as much as possible that he managed not to piss his pants. "R-r-right... P-p-please f-follow m-me..." The attendant was shivering so violently he could barely speak a word.

Guan Shanjin gave a faint smile and released the attendant's neck. "Lead the way."

Guan Shanjin's mood swung wildly from one extreme to the other, and the attendant had yet to get used to it. He was still shuddering as a smile appeared on Guan Shanjin's face. It was distorted and hideous.

Before he left, Guan Shanjin tossed some words indifferently toward his subordinates. "The two of you can go decide what self-imposed punishment you deserve," he said. The towering men stiffened up, but neither could find an excuse to get out of this. They both acknowledged him with murmured agreements.

Days had passed since Wu Xingzi's very first experience of sexual passion, and he still felt deeply satisfied. He slept better, no longer experiencing wet dreams.

With the temperature becoming cooler, it was time to start preparing for winter. Wu Xingzi went to the magistrate's office every day, dealing with case files and writing statements for his fellow villagers. After work, he went home and mended what needed to be fixed and strengthened what needed to be fortified. He nailed down his roof and repaired his windows. Although Qingcheng County was in Nanjiang, where it didn't snow in winter, the winds were still very cold and damp, and the bone-piercing chill could be unbearable.

On the publication day for the new edition of *The Pengornisseur*, though, he received a surprise.

He was on the way home, thinking about whether or not he should poach two eggs for that night's noodle soup. However, out of nowhere, he suddenly thought about the two hefty, round balls below a pengornis, and his pants tightened. He was nearly unable to walk and had no choice but to awkwardly bend over a little. He had to shrink into the corner of a wall for quite some time before he finally calmed down.

Who would be in the new edition of *The Pengornisseur*?

His already joyous heart became even more carefree. It was hard to believe that Wu Xingzi had once thought of dying by suicide at the age of forty.

Since the new issue of *The Pengornisseur* would be available, he planned to go to Goose City tomorrow. With this in mind, Wu Xingzi turned and walked toward Old Liu's place. He confirmed the departure time with Old Liu, and Auntie Liu shoved a bag of roasted chestnuts in his arms. He peeled the chestnuts and ate them as he walked home.

When Wu Xingzi arrived at his doorstep, only a sliver of red remained on the horizon. He was also down to his last chestnut, peeling it and stuffing it into his mouth. After tossing the chestnut shells where he stored his firewood, he opened his door.

"You're back?" a voice rang out.

"I'm back..." Wu Xingzi answered instinctively, then trembled at the realization that someone was there with him. As he stared with wide eyes into his simple little home, an indistinct silhouette stood inside.

Is that a person or a ghost?

He stood by the door in a trance. His hands and feet grew cold as he tried not to shiver. He rejoiced in the fact that there were still chestnuts in his mouth to muffle the noise if his teeth started chattering.

The person inside the house was considerate. After laughing lightly, he lit a candle, and the cramped room soon glowed with warm candlelight.

At the same time, an indescribably beautiful face was also illuminated.

"G-guan-gongzi! No, no, no, *General* Guan, General Guan..." Discovering that the mysterious silhouette was someone he knew, Wu Xingzi immediately sighed in relief and cupped his hands at him.

"Adviser Wu." Guan Shanjin remained seated, his expression imposing. His fingertips swept through the flame of the candle, and his fair skin instantly reddened. Wu Xingzi squinted his eyes from the imagined pain, but Guan Shanjin behaved as if he felt nothing.

"Adviser Wu," he said, "come in. Quickly, now. This is your home—why are you standing outside?"

He sounded very considerate, but something seemed amiss.

Wu Xingzi scratched his cheek and took two timid steps forward. He finally entered his home, but he did not know if he should close the door behind him. For some reason he felt apprehensive about turning and revealing his back to Guan Shanjin.

"Close the door, it's getting cold." Guan Shanjin glanced at him, his soft lips curved up in a faint smile. In the wavering candlelight, he looked eerily elegant.

"You're right, you're right." Wu Xingzi agreed. He reached behind him and spent quite some time fumbling for the door handle before finally managing to close the door.

"Have you eaten?" Guan Shanjin asked. He was very satisfied with Wu Xingzi's reaction to him, a bright delight shimmering in his forbidding eyes.

"Not really..." Wu Xingzi rubbed his belly and swallowed down what was left of the chestnuts in his mouth. He was still hungry. The chestnuts he'd just eaten weren't even enough to cushion his stomach, instead making him even hungrier.

"Has the general eaten yet?" he asked. After all, Guan Shanjin was technically his houseguest, so it was the polite thing to do.

"Not yet." Guan Shanjin smiled, brushing his fingertip through the flame again. "I wanted to wait for you to get home so we could dine together."

"Of course, of course. I'm just afraid you might not like the food." Although Wu Xingzi lived in poverty, he still had enough provisions in the house to be a good host. He could prepare some dumpling stew. "It might take some time before it's ready. If you're hungry now, General Guan, I can fry some vegetables first."

The leeks he had planted in the backyard were ready to be harvested. Now was the time of year when they were the most tender. He also happened to have those two eggs. A dish of scrambled eggs with leeks should be enough to satisfy Guan Shanjin's stomach.

Having made his decision, Wu Xingzi rolled up his sleeves. He wasn't as timid and shy as before—after all, the general's cock and his hole were already well acquainted, so there was nothing left to be awkward about. He went out to the backyard to cut the leeks.

Guan Shanjin did not stop him, staring at his silhouette as he bustled back and forth in the yard, his passionate eyes full of charm.

Soon, a plate of scrambled eggs with leeks arrived on the table. Wu Xingzi placed chopsticks on the table as well, saying, "Please eat, General Guan. I ate some chestnuts on my way back, so I'm not that hungry. The dumplings need some time to prepare. Don't go hungry in the meantime."

"Thanks." Guan Shanjin picked up his chopsticks, picking up some scrambled eggs and leeks. He put them into his mouth and chewed.

The freshly cut leeks were sweet and tender. They did not have the bitter taste of vegetables, and the heat of the fire used to cook the dish was perfect. The dish of crisp leeks together with the silky eggs, although not exactly a refined delicacy, was appetizing. After taking a bite, Guan Shanjin put his chopsticks down and stood up, walking to the entrance of the kitchen and staring at the man inside kneading dumpling dough.

The kitchen was tiny, filled to the brim with pots, bowls, ladles, and a stove. There was just enough space remaining for Wu Xingzi to squat down and start a fire.

Guan Shanjin had not seen Wu Xingzi in a while. He seemed to have gotten thinner, which made his mouth look wider. His pouty lips looked like they were smiling. Right now, he was kneading the dough with great effort, and the huge pot of water on the stove bubbled happily away. This seemed to leave Wu Xingzi a little flustered. He worked the dough more and rolled it into a plump ball, then started tearing off pieces and tossing them into the pot to cook.

It was clear that Wu Xingzi was an experienced cook. He quickly tossed the fat balls of dough into the pot, and within moments, they all bobbed up to the surface. He scooped them up, and next, all sorts of mountain vegetables and a small handful of minced bacon were thrown into the pot to braise. After everything had boiled, he returned the dough dumplings into the pot and simmered them for a while. Soon, the dish was ready.

Wu Xingzi turned his head and unexpectedly met Guan Shanjin's alluring eyes. "Uhh..." His body tilted, and the bowl in his hand looked like it was going to fall. But Guan Shanjin moved quickly. In the blink of an eye, he had one hand around Wu Xingzi and the other steadying the bowl, preventing a small catastrophe.

"Thank you." Wu Xingzi blushed lightly. Guan Shanjin's sweet scent wafted past his nose, his strong, warm body behind him. It was nearly impossible for him not to think about that night they'd shared!

"It's no bother," Guan Shanjin said, nudging the bowl back into Wu Xingzi's hand and pushing him out of the kitchen. He ladled a bowl of dumpling stew for himself, returning to his seat. "Let's eat."

The meal was quiet, but neither man was paying attention to the taste of their food.

CHAPTER FOUR

A BEAUTY'S FAVOR IS THE HARDEST TO ENJOY

Adviser Wu wearily made his way into his office. With a sigh, he fell into introspection. What had he done wrong?

The books always said that people in high positions would only ever have casual affairs with the common folk. He'd thought he'd really met a general who only wanted a fleeting dalliance. Who would have thought that once the tryst was over, Guan Shanjin would refuse to leave?

W HEN HIS STOMACH felt completely satisfied, Wu Xingzi tidied up the table and washed the dishes. He even prepared a new pot of tea before remembering that he should ask Guan Shanjin the reason for his visit.

"General Guan…"

"Call me Haiwang." Guan Shanjin sipped at his hot tea and cut him off composedly. "Your courtesy name?"

"Uhh… I don't have one. We're not so particular about it around here." Really, he should have been given a courtesy name when he started school, but for whatever reason, his father hadn't paid any attention to it and kept on calling him by his established name. Out in the village, people didn't care much about such matters—it was simply left unsettled.

"Hmm," Guan Shanjin hummed. He put his cup down after taking a sip of tea, seeming to be unsatisfied with the flavor. Looking at Wu Xingzi, he asked, "Why did you leave without saying anything?"

Leave without saying anything? Wu Xingzi looked back at him blankly, clearly not understanding the question. This made Guan Shanjin furrow his exquisite brows and tap his slender fingers heavily on the table. Each and every sound jarred Wu Xingzi's heart.

"You..." Wu Xingzi said.

Too impatient to let things drag on, Guan Shanjin went straight to the point. "Why did you leave before I woke up?"

"Uhh..." Wu Xingzi did not expect Guan Shanjin to ask this question. He awkwardly rubbed the back of his neck and apologized sincerely. "I was wrong. I should have waited and said goodbye to you when you woke up."

For some reason, at the time, Wu Xingzi had a feeling that if he didn't leave when he did that day, he might never get another chance to. Coincidentally, Rancui had also invited him for a chat, so he just accepted the invitation. When he thought about it, though, he could understand General Guan's anger. He had been too negligent. Spending a night like that together but leaving without a word—it was as if he had treated Guan Shanjin like a prostitute, and their time together as a frivolous fling.

"You never thought about staying by my side?" Guan Shanjin said out loud what Wu Xingzi had left unspoken. This old man really meant to sever all ties with him after they slept together! Flames of fury and embarrassment twined together, licking at Guan Shanjin's heart until it ached.

Guan Shanjin had been well-favored his entire life, the center of attention since his childhood. He was surrounded by people who clung to him, refusing to let go. Never had there been anyone who was so dismissive of him as this man—and he was the adviser of some small, poor village, no less! Not even Mr. Lu had behaved so indifferently toward him.

"No, no, definitely not!" Wu Xingzi took three steps back in panic, shaking his head as he spread his palms open. "I know that I'm not worthy of the great General Guan. I wouldn't dare to even dream of it."

Wu Xingzi was alarmed by Guan Shanjin. The general's cock was fantastic—whether it was in his mouth or screwing him senseless, it felt amazing. Any man could lose his self-control over it. However, Wu Xingzi had no illusions about his own status. Even if he liked the great General Guan Shanjin, he would never be worthy of him! A single night of passion had been enough for him to thank his ancestors for the blessing.

In case Guan Shanjin did not believe him, Wu Xingzi tried his best to repress his timid nature. He stared at those fierce yet alluring black eyes and spoke sincerely. "I know you are a noble and accomplished individual," he said. "General, please be assured that I've never thought of rising above my station."

Guan Shanjin was not assured at all. Wu Xingzi's thorough disavowal only embarrassed him further. He dearly wished to crush this reckless old man to death. Furious to see that Wu Xingzi planned to continue explaining, he cracked the table into two. "Shut up!"

Sucking in a deep lungful of air, Wu Xingzi watched as the solid wood table he had been using for twenty years lost half its surface under Guan Shanjin's hand.

Bang! The pieces fell to the ground, making Wu Xingzi tremble in shock.

U-u-uh... Wu Xingzi had no idea what to do. He did not know what part of his words had provoked the general like this—unless he thought that he had been too shameless about climbing into his bed. But Wu Xingzi could not be blamed for that! It was clearly the general who had pushed him down without a word that day. As a gentle and frail adviser, he was physically weak and utterly unable to withstand Guan Shanjin's might.

Maybe Wu Xingzi could still redeem himself. "G-great General, you..."

"I told you to shut up." Guan Shanjin's imposing aura loomed over him.

It was not reassuring at all. It made Wu Xingzi gasp for breath. His legs buckled beneath him, and he fell to the floor, timidly looking up at the beautifully threatening and demonic man above him.

"Take off your clothes," Guan Shanjin said. The four words sounded so smooth and pleasant that Wu Xingzi obeyed without thinking; it didn't even occur to him that there was anything wrong with the demand until he was already in his undergarments, faced with Guan Shanjin's satisfied smile. He froze in embarrassment, his exposed skin flushing a burning red.

Guan Shanjin was displeased. "Take them *all* off," he ordered, further emphasizing his command.

"Umm... Dare I ask the General what his intentions are?" *It can't be that he wants to do that again...* Wu Xingzi felt a great sense of shame that his mind came to that conclusion, but he couldn't deny that he was hopeful.

This great heap of fortune was absurd—surely his luck would run out soon, or he'd end up depleting the Wu family's store!

"You'll understand in a moment. Take your clothes off. *Now.*" Guan Shanjin remained regally seated in place. However, he now held a wooden box of about seven or eight inches in his hand, and the smile on his face was seductively charming. Just a glance at him had Wu Xingzi submitting completely, all doubts leaving him.

Adviser Wu stripped himself bare in short order, his pale skin glimmering under the dim candlelight. His waist was narrow and bony, but he didn't give off the impression of being sickly—rather, there was a delicateness and fragility about him that made Guan Shanjin eager to torment him.

In front of Guan Shanjin's smiling visage, Wu Xingzi's cock hardened, timidly raising its head. The pearly drops of fluid trickling down stood out prominently in the glow of the candlelight.

"Come here," Guan Shanjin said as he held his hand out to Wu Xingzi. Wu Xingzi felt light as a cloud as he drifted over to clasp that broad, flawless hand. His shoulders shrank as he touched the burning heat of Guan Shanjin's palm, but he still slowly drew in closer.

"Do you know what this is?"

Guan Shanjin pulled Wu Xingzi down to sit on his thigh and put his arm around him. He bit his sloping shoulder, admiring the feminine beauty of it, then opened the wooden box in his hand.

Wu Xingzi's eyes widened. "This is..." *What is this?*

He gazed in astonishment at the long, thick object within the wooden box. A cautious expression mingled with a trace of excitement gradually appeared on his face, his eyes glued to the item.

This had to be the "Mr. D" that Manager Rancui had once told him about! This was the first time he had seen it in person. Adviser Wu had to stop himself from reaching out to touch it. He licked his dry lips, showing no hint of the bashfulness that Guan Shanjin expected to see. Feeling inexplicably sullen, Guan Shanjin's smile turned a little savage.

"You seem rather interested in it."

"Yes, quite..." Wu Xingzi suddenly realized what he was saying, realizing that he had acted too audaciously. He hurriedly lowered his head. "N-no, not really..."

"This is Mr. D," Guan Shanjin said. He caught one of Adviser Wu's hands, spreading his palm open. He then took the object, which was made of some unknown material, out from the box and placed it in his hand. Laying his hand under Wu Xingzi's, Guan Shanjin curled his fingers over Mr. D.

"I-I've seen it in drawings before..." Drowning in the sensation coming from his palm, Wu Xingzi unknowingly exposed himself.

"Then you should know how to use it, yes?" The low, pleasant voice exhaled into his ear, the breathy sensation pleasurable yet intense. It was too much for Wu Xingzi, and he shuddered, his whole body tingling.

He cleared his throat, his voice hoarse. "I do..." he responded, sounding as though he was in a daze.

"Good." Guan Shanjin licked his blushing ear and spoke in a bewitching tone. "Show me."

"Yes..." Putting aside how Guan Shanjin's alluring voice overwhelmed him, Wu Xingzi was already very curious about Mr. D. He had already been considering whether or not to use some of his savings to purchase one to play with.

Wu Xingzi's breathing quickened as his ear was tongued at and sucked. His hand, holding onto Mr. D, shook so much that he could barely move.

Even though he was trembling, Guan Shanjin did not let him get away. His hand caressed the soft skin of Adviser Wu's slender waist as he opened the end segment of Mr. D. "You should quickly fill up Mr. D while the tea is still warm," he urged.

It was clear he meant that the object in his hand should be filled up with tea, but Wu Xingzi was struck by the memory of being filled with Guan Shanjin's cum just a few days ago, and the warm, bloated feeling that came with it. Lost in that recollection, his hand loosened its grip and his entire body almost melted. He snuggled into Guan Shanjin's heated embrace, intoxicated by his sandalwood scent.

Seeming amused by his behavior, Guan Shanjin chuckled softly. He grabbed Wu Xingzi's hands and placed them both around Mr. D. "Hold it tight, hmm?"

"Okay..." Wu Xingzi obediently tightened his hands around the toy.

"Good boy." Guan Shanjin kissed his forehead appreciatively and picked up the teapot. Placing the spout at the opening of Mr. D, he poured it full of the hot tea.

Brimming with liquid, the object grew warmer and swelled up to look just like a real penis. Its increasing weight nearly had it slipping out of Wu Xingzi's hand.

Subconsciously, Wu Xingzi's grip tightened, and the tea nearly spilled out. Guan Shanjin hurriedly closed the end section. The seal was perfect, and the tea didn't leak out at all.

"Go on, let me watch you use it." He lifted one of Wu Xingzi's legs onto the table. The table, having been split in half, was unsteady, and Adviser Wu's body swayed along with it. His buttocks were exposed, and Guan Shanjin could vaguely see his little hole winking slightly between them.

"Use it?" Wu Xingzi said. Despite feeling as though his brain had melted out of his ears, he still had some resistance left.

"You don't want to?" Guan Shanjin did not care about his hesitation. He took out a container of oil and rubbed some over Mr. D.

He then covered Wu Xingzi's fingers with the slippery substance as well. "Don't be afraid," he said. "We'll lubricate it this time. If you take it in slowly, it won't hurt."

After what he'd seen last time, he knew that Wu Xingzi was born to take cock. Adviser Wu hadn't been injured in the slightest by taking in his long, thick member; even without using oil, he imagined he would only feel pain for a moment. The only reason Guan Shanjin mentioned the lubricant was to embarrass him.

As expected, Adviser Wu shuddered. He breathed heavily, on the verge of tears. The oil on his hands mingled together with the oil on Mr. D, making it so slippery that he almost lost his grip. His body convulsed against Guan Shanjin's thigh.

"Stop dragging things out." He hastily grabbed Wu Xingzi's finger and shoved it into his hole.

Adviser Wu cried out hoarsely as his finger entered his hole. He had never touched himself there before. Once his finger went inside, his ass clamped down tightly. It felt soft and warm, and he shivered as he thrust his finger in deeper.

"Good boy," Guan Shanjin said, a smile tinging his voice. "Here, take Mr. D as well," he said, sucking on Wu Xingzi's ear. "Don't let that little hole go hungry."

With an exclamation, Wu Xingzi pressed the thick head of Mr. D against his cleft, but his arm wasn't long enough. In this position, half-sprawled in Guan Shanjin's arms with his buttocks raised high and his hand struggling to hold the slippery weight of Mr. D, he started cramping before he could even thrust the toy inside. Losing strength in his fingers, Adviser Wu dropped Mr. D on the floor.

"Ah..." Wu Xingzi was concerned that the toy had been damaged in the fall. However, Guan Shanjin caught the object and pushed it back into his hand. He gently held Mr. D along with Wu Xingzi, slowly feeding the egg-sized head into his hole.

"Ah!" Wu Xingzi let out a trembling moan as the thick, warm object impaled his body.

The toy wasn't as long as Guan Shanjin's cock, but the thickness was comparable. It might have even been a little thicker. It seemed ready to tear him apart, but his pliant, greedy hole gradually swallowed it in. Wu Xingzi could barely pull it back out. His hand slid off the end of Mr. D a few times before Guan Shanjin took over, moving Wu Xingzi's hands to his chest.

"Rub your nipples," he instructed. "You like that, don't you?"

"Yes..." Without any protest, Adviser Wu started rubbing his tender nipples.

Just a few days ago, his small, pink nipples had become swollen after Guan Shanjin played with them. Now Wu Xingzi stroked and caressed them with his own hands until he shivered, his chest tingling and his eyes cloudy. He couldn't stop.

Guan Shanjin's hand manipulated the toy inside him so deftly it was unbearable. Every time he thrust it in, it brushed past his sensitive spot straight into his core, grinding against it.

"Don't... I-it's too much..." Wu Xingzi moaned softly. He had no strength to struggle, no matter how he tried. He couldn't even close his legs. Guan Shanjin was much stronger and had complete mastery over Adviser Wu's body; he knew exactly which spots made him weak. Wu Xingzi's mind had melted completely. His senses registered nothing other than pleasure.

Guan Shanjin ignored his pleas for mercy and moved his hand faster and faster. Mr. D felt like a living thing, warm and weighty. The toy spread his tight hole open, then savagely pulled away, only to plunge back into his emptiness and impale itself deeply, making Wu Xingzi cry out.

The heat welling up in his body made him feel like he was burning to death.

"G-general Guan... General... I'm burning up!" When the toy thrust directly into his sensitive spot again, Wu Xingzi could only plead and cry. Thick white fluid spurted from his cock and landed on his belly, a few drops even reaching his face.

Completely spent, he lay feebly in Guan Shanjin's arms. The hand that had been playing with his nipples now sagged by his side, trembling too hard to grip anything. His hips twitched, his buttocks spasmed, and he clenched around Mr. D so tightly that it could barely be moved. Guan Shanjin decided to leave the toy inside him while his slender fingers moved to the front and started playing with Wu Xingzi's softened pink cock.

"This little prick of yours is quite interesting," Guan Shanjin said, placing a gentle kiss on Wu Xingzi's cheek. His kiss was soft as a lover's caress, but what he was doing with his hand made Adviser Wu whimper weakly.

Adviser Wu believed that this time, he was doomed. There was no escape. He opened his mouth, trying to speak to Guan Shanjin in his brief moments of lucidity, but Guan Shanjin had no plan to let him catch his breath. His fingers, warm yet torturous, seized his tender cock with substantial strength. He pinched at his slit, which had yet to recover from his recent orgasm. It was even more agonizing than a few days ago, when Guan Shanjin used his tongue there. His hard fingernail pressed forcefully into the tender tip, making Wu Xingzi let out a quavering shout.

Guan Shanjin lifted Wu Xingzi's chin in consolation, kissing him on the lips. "Here, look at this," he said.

"What is it?" Wu Xingzi's eyes were filled with tears, and he was almost unable to distinguish what was in front of him. With blurry vision, he managed to see that Guan Shanjin's fingers held a long, thin rod.

After blinking and looking at it again, Wu Xingzi finally saw that it was a rod made of jade, about three or four inches long, with one end curved into a hook. It was very thin, less than half an inch in diameter.

The jade was a pale green color, like a clear lake in spring. It looked so stunning in Guan Shanjin's hand that chills spread through Wu Xingzi at the sight.

He had a feeling that he had seen such an object before in certain erotic illustrations, but having endured Guan Shanjin's recent attentions, he could no longer recall what it was. He hunched his shoulders, subconsciously wanting to avoid it, but Guan Shanjin gripped his waist to keep him upright. He was held so tightly that marks were left on his skin.

"Do you know what this is for?" Guan Shanjin asked with a smile.

"Uhh..." With a dry mouth, Wu Xingzi swallowed. He had yet to fall from the peak of pleasure, and he blinked pitifully as he shook his head.

"This will be inserted into your urethra." Guan Shanjin tenderly caressed his hips and buttocks, dragging the jade rod along the pinched-red tip of his cock. "Relax, I've already slicked it up. I'll be gentle. Don't be scared, okay?"

"All right..." Wu Xingzi nodded obediently.

"Good boy." Guan Shanjin fondled Wu Xingzi's fatigued cock in satisfaction, his fingers pinching the tip to further expose the slit. Then he slid the jade rod into the tiny hole.

"Ohh!" Wu Xingzi's body convulsed, and Guan Shanjin held him more securely. The jade rod was cool and slippery to touch; although it didn't look thick, his urethra was tight around it. The tip of the rod scratched lightly past his tender insides, and the prickling sensation was as if he was being nibbled at by thousands of insects.

Wu Xingzi wailed out loud, his legs kicking out a couple of times before Guan Shanjin caught them. "Don't move," he ordered. "You don't want to start bleeding, do you?"

Bleeding?! Hearing that, Adviser Wu was scared to death. Even though it itched so much that he desperately wanted to scratch at it, he didn't dare make any more sudden movements. Gritting his teeth, he muffled his moans and experienced the incomparable tingling sensation of the jade rod lightly scraping the inside of his cock.

He felt like his body was about to melt. This was a completely different pleasure from getting fucked or having his cock sucked. It brought him to a high that left his mind blank.

"G-general Guan!"

"Haiwang," Guan Shanjin said, sucking on his earlobe.

"H-Haiwang..." Wu Xingzi shuddered. He could feel the jade rod reaching a spot that made his scalp prickle, but Guan Shanjin didn't stop, continuing to let it go deeper.

"Stop... Don't... It's too much..."

Adviser Wu reached out to push him away, but how could his strength compare to General Guan's? Instead, he accidentally bumped into the part of the jade rod that protruded from his cock. The part that was buried within his cock jolted, and the bone-jarring tingle of pleasure laced with pain made Wu Xingzi cry out, crazed.

"So eager," Guan Shanjin chuckled. He tugged the jade rod out a little, then pushed it back inside. After Guan Shanjin repeated this a few times, Wu Xingzi lay limp and lifeless, tears and drool staining his face. His mouth gaped open, but he was unable to make a sound, and the muscles of his inner thighs twitched violently. Finally, he let out a loud wail. "No more! I can't..."

"And why can't you?" Guan Shanjin said, pulling the jade rod out and back in again. This time, he pushed it in deeper than before, leaving only the curved hook outside.

Wu Xingzi's cock had been tormented so much that it turned a deep, dark red color. It stood half-erect and trembling.

Wu Xingzi did not know what he could do. He wanted to come. He wanted to piss. But he could do neither. The jade rod firmly obstructed his urges.

Guan Shanjin had teased his holes so thoroughly that they were unbearably swollen.

He convulsed a few times, but Mr. D and the jade rod had him trapped on the edge of orgasm, always one step away from bliss. He couldn't touch himself anywhere; a mere brush against his skin would cause him to spasm. Other than crying and pleading for the man behind him to show him mercy, there was nothing he could do.

Guan Shanjin simply kissed his eyelids and brows and consoled him superficially with honeyed words, making Wu Xingzi even more agitated.

"Please... Please, can I come?" Wu Xingzi's face was full of tears, completely terrified to be trapped at the edge of pleasure like this. He couldn't stop begging, to the point where he was no longer conscious of what he was saying.

"You don't like it?" Guan Shanjin held Wu Xingzi's half hard cock, twisting the jade rod inside it. He immediately heard a cry.

"Don't! Stop, don't..." The muscles of Wu Xingzi's inner thighs spasmed. He reached out to push Guan Shanjin away but was stopped.

"Will you run away from me again?" Guan Shanjin asked. He pulled half the rod out, listening to the sobs and wheezes next to his ear. The thin body in his arms jolted violently and finally shrank, shivering in his embrace. He was satisfied with this reaction.

Guan Shanjin was used to being high and mighty, and held himself superior to others. He didn't even care for the man sitting on the Dragon Throne. No one ever dared to embarrass General Guan, and yet this little adviser of such an impoverished place had the guts to cross him. It was unacceptable!

He should have come here earlier, but Rancui had the nerve to arrange for people to obstruct him. Guan Shanjin had to return to Horse-Face City to settle a problem with the Nanman invaders and ended up late in coming to Qingcheng County.

On his journey, he had ridden four good horses to death—and since Rancui was responsible for the journey, he owed him a debt. But really, the ultimate cause of this debt was Adviser Wu himself.

"No, no... I won't run away again..." Wu Xingzi had no idea what Guan Shanjin was talking about. He shook his head and sniffled, begging weakly, "Can you please let me come? It hurts..."

"It only hurts?" Guan Shanjin didn't believe it. Wu Xingzi's body seemed to be made for this. He suffered no injury, no matter how roughly he was treated. His recovery was astounding, not to mention his cooperation with any sex play.

"I need it!" Wu Xingzi wailed, as honest as usual. "Touch me, quickly! Touch me...please..."

As expected, Wu Xingzi was craving it. Guan Shanjin's lips curled up coldly. He hastily removed the jade rod from his urethra. Then he gripped Mr. D, pumping it fully in and out of Wu Xingzi's twitching, loosened hole. Every thrust brushed against the sensitive spot within, and he mercilessly ground the toy directly against that spot.

Guan Shanjin's other hand wickedly fondled Wu Xingzi's tight balls, and in a few strokes, Wu Xingzi came, fluids dripping from both his cock and hole. His mouth opened wide, and his eyes rolled to the back of his head as saliva drooled from the corner of his mouth.

"You're actually leaking down here, you dirty boy." Clicking his tongue in amazement, Guan Shanjin pulled Mr. D out. However, due to Wu Xingzi's orgasm, the spasming hole clenched down on the toy when it was almost fully out, sucking it all the way back in.

This made Wu Xingzi scream in shock, and he blacked out completely.

How slutty, Guan Shanjin mused.

He had to use some force to retrieve the toy from Wu Xingzi's body. Once he did, he carelessly tossed it aside.

Although Adviser Wu's looks were ordinary, his charming ability to lose himself in passion really tugged at one's heartstrings.

"Mr. Lu..." Guan Shanjin whispered.

Despite how different they truly were, Guan Shanjin could somehow still see the resemblance between the man in his thoughts and the man in front of him, whose face was red from crying. "Mr. Lu..."

Guan Shanjin hugged this man tightly. Lowering his head, he placed a gentle kiss on the plump and soft lips before him. His tongue brushed past neat rows of teeth and teased the familiar, soft tongue, entwining with it and sucking upon it.

The slightly cautious kiss gradually turned passionate as wet sucking sounds filled the room.

"Mm, oh..."

Kissed until he could barely breathe, Wu Xingzi regained his consciousness. He didn't understand what had happened to him, but he felt a pain in his tongue. He breathed haphazardly as an intoxicating sandalwood fragrance filled his nose, mingled with the scent of orange blossom. He could almost smell a vague trace of blood as the scent traveled all the way into his chest.

"You're awake?" Guan Shanjin asked, reluctantly ending the kiss. He pecked the tip of Adviser Wu's nose with a slight smile.

"Huh? Uhh... Mm..." Wu Xingzi regained his senses. He remembered he had fainted, and his body still ached. It was incredibly embarrassing.

"It's good that you're awake." Guan Shanjin lifted Wu Xingzi up into his arms, his smile blooming like a spring blossom. "Now it's time for us to play."

Wu Xingzi put his arms around Guan Shanjin's neck to steady himself. Though his face reddened, he didn't feel bashful. He was even confident enough to ask, "Can we forget Mr. D and the jade rod this time?"

Although he did enjoy the toys, there was no way his old body could withstand any further torture from those two objects.

Glancing at him, Guan Shanjin only smiled. Falling into bed together, he reached out and released the bed curtains.

Not long after, coquettish whimpers and moans drifted from the bed, interspersed with wet squelching and the loud smacking sounds of flesh against flesh. It was a beautiful night...

When Guan Shanjin willfully dropped everything and ran off to Goose City to take men to his bed, Vice General Man Yue became extremely busy. He accidentally put on weight, gaining even more resemblance to the full moon that was his namesake.

A few days ago, Nanman had suddenly created chaos at the border. Man Yue was unable to contend with their forces, so he had no choice but to hurriedly call the general back from miles away to settle the matter. When the general rushed back, Man Yue knew he was in trouble.

Who feared death so little that they dared anger the general of the Southern Garrison?

Man Yue couldn't deny his curiosity about the general's latest dalliance, especially after hearing from his associates that it was the general who'd suffered a loss this time. In his lifetime, Guan Shanjin had always been the one to come out on top—Man Yue had never heard of anyone who could make him come off worse in any kind of situation. Whoever this unknown man was, Man Yue really admired him!

Of course, Guan Shanjin's personal guards were tight-lipped, and Man Yue was unable to get anything more out of them. However, his heart itched to know. He wanted to ask the general himself, after he'd calmed down and vented his anger on Nanman, but in the blink of an eye, the general left again with his personal guards.

Was he going to catch that man, or was he going somewhere to let out his anger? Or catch that man *to* let out his anger...?

Despite his curiosity, Man Yue had no choice but to bitterly clean up after the general. His desire to see just how impressive this mystery civilian was grew day by day. Ever since Mr. Lu appeared, Guan Shanjin had never been interested in anyone else.

Over the past few years, Guan Shanjin had toyed with so many men who had a hint of resemblance to Mr. Lu. After they became infatuated with him, he would ruthlessly reject any relationship between them, maintaining a constant stream of Mr. Lu substitutes. Man Yue watched Guan Shanjin go through these men at will, leaving a trail of disaster behind him.

He tried many times to advise him, as he could no longer bear to watch, but Guan Shanjin wouldn't listen. There was nothing Man Yue could do about it. No one knew exactly how sharp that Chenyuan Sword was, but Man Yue really didn't want to test it with his own neck.

This was the first time someone had managed to make Guan Shanjin ignore Mr. Lu, even if it was simply to settle the debts between them.

Man Yue was quite optimistic about the matter. It would be for the best if this male civilian could capture Guan Shanjin's heart so he'd stop reaching for Mr. Lu.

"Vice General Man," came a voice. It was a voice so clear that it could refresh one's senses. However, Man Yue was not so easy to refresh. He looked up from his paperwork and gave a good-natured smile to the person standing by the door.

"Hua-gongzi, is there a reason you're looking for me?"

Beyond the door stood a young man dressed in blue. He seemed to have just come of age, and he looked very gentle and attractive. He stood tall and straight, his appearance fastidious, and carried with him a scholarly air. His smile was restrained but not distant, perfectly displaying his beauty and loneliness.

"I heard that the general returned from Goose City a few days ago?"

"He has left for Goose City again," Man Yue said, smiling brightly at the man in front of him.

The young man bit his lip. "Oh..."

"Is there anything else, Hua-gongzi?" Man Yue glanced at the paperwork on his desk, hinting that he had no time for pleasantries.

Hua Shu was an intelligent man, so he naturally understood Man Yue's intimation. He revealed a wry smile. "I'm afraid I've disturbed you, Vice General Man. However...you must know that I've been accompanying Mr. Lu for some time now. Seeing that Mr. Lu misses the general, I cannot help but look out for my master's best interests."

"Mr. Lu misses the general?" Man Yue was surprised, and his reply tumbled out thoughtlessly. "I thought Mr. Lu was coming along very nicely with the third daughter of the Yue family. Didn't he just return from Fragrance City...? So it turns out he still thinks about the general."

"Uhh..." A trace of embarrassment flashed across Hua Shu's face, but he quickly regained his calm and returned to a reserved, mild expression. "Mr. Lu has always held the general in a different light."

"That I believe." Man Yue nodded. "Hua-gongzi, is there anything more you'd like to discuss?" he asked with a grin. This was an explicit attempt to chase him away.

"I've been rude. Vice General Man, please forgive me." Hua Shu cupped his hands, his brows slightly creased. He hesitated for a moment before leaving the room.

When he was sure Hua Shu was far away, Man Yue sighed deeply. A female beauty was nothing. It was the male beauties that were exhausting!

Something major had happened recently in Qingcheng County— Adviser Wu of the magistrate's office seemed to have found a life partner.

Having some free time, Auntie Li grabbed a chair and sat outside her door, chattering away with her neighbors. "Aiyah, there's something all of you don't know about," she said. "Don't be fooled by Adviser Wu's honest face; his methods are out of the ordinary."

"What do you mean?" A-Niu's wife was still a girl of fifteen or sixteen. She could not help but be curious about the statement as she helped her mother-in-law strip the maize.

"Hah! Although Adviser Wu is a friendly person, you know what he's like." Auntie Li clicked her tongue a couple of times, a look of scorn on her face.

"But Adviser Wu's appearance is so clean and innocent," A-Niu's wife said. After she said this, her mother-in-law slapped her thigh. "Mother..." Full of grievances, she nearly started to cry.

"Shh! What do you know? Looking like he does, how can Adviser Wu compare to anyone else?" Her mother-in-law shot her a warning look and turned to echo Auntie Li. "Who knows how he managed to attract that god-like man. He must have used some shameful method."

"That's right!"

"You're completely right!"

The aunties all agreed with each other.

Seeing she had so much support, Auntie Li became even more pleased. She raised her chin. "The heavens really do have eyes! A few days ago, my boy woke up early to go to the mountain and happened to come across Adviser Wu with that god-like man! Aiyah, it was so embarrassing! The divine man wanted to leave, but Adviser Wu stopped him and refused to let him go, kneeling and begging. The man was too kind! Faced with Adviser Wu's pleading, he had no other choice but to stay."

"I had no idea Adviser Wu was so shameless!" Auntie Fang looked disgusted. "And to think he calls himself a scholar! He didn't live his life properly and look for a wife. Instead, he's chasing after a man all day. Has he been running to Goose City this whole time just to harass this man?"

"Who says he hasn't?" A-Niu's mother was deep in thought. "Didn't the Lius mention a few days ago that Adviser Wu was obsessed with making friends through the pigeon post? Hah! How do you make friends without seeing the other person? No way! He must have done something shameless to snag a man like that."

"But Adviser Wu is such a nice person..." The little daughter-in-law spoke up for the adviser, only to get smacked again by her mother-in-law. She didn't dare to speak again under the aunties' glares, lowering her head dejectedly to do her work.

"Auntie Li, what is the background of that god-like man? How was Adviser Wu able to deceive him into staying?"

"Hah! Let me tell you, this man is really extraordinary. Apparently, he moved here from the capital, and he hasn't been in Goose City for long. He's young and promising, with a good family and a great career! The emperor treats this man like no other. When this extraordinary man was going to leave the capital, the emperor personally saw him off for ten miles!" Auntie Li described these events in great detail, as though she had witnessed them herself. Her yearning and sighing made the other women all sigh along with her.

"It's too bad that he was deceived by Adviser Wu somehow. Such a noble stature, but he's living in that little house," Auntie Fang sighed with unconcealed jealousy in her eyes.

"Who knows? Adviser Wu is a scholar. He must have invoked some curse to blind the man. How vile!" Auntie Li's speculation roused everyone's agreement. She was extremely self-righteous.

"Bullshit!" A voice suddenly rang out, and a basket of kernels flew toward the aunties.

Auntie Li shrieked, falling from her chair. Groaning, she struggled to pick herself back up.

"Who's there?!" A-Niu's mother jumped a step away, snarling as she looked for the culprit.

"Who else but me!" Auntie Liu spat, rolling up her sleeves. She pushed away the few bystanders aggressively and rushed toward Auntie Li. Raising the broom she was holding, she started hitting her. "You cheap gossipmongers! Aren't you afraid the King of Hell will yank out your tongue?!"

"Aiyah! Why are you hitting us?!" Auntie Fang received a few swipes from the broom as well. She retreated in fear but was pushed back to the center by the bystanders.

"I'm going to beat all you gossipy old women! You're always troubling Xingzi with this and that. Auntie Fang, didn't your family look for Xingzi just a few days ago to get him to write a citation for you? The lot of you are worse than animals! At least animals know how to be grateful!" Auntie Liu angrily swung the broom in her hand, hitting Auntie Li and Auntie Fang until they cried and dodged her strikes.

"Why? Why?! If Wu Xingzi dares to do such things, he shouldn't be afraid of us talking about it! With his plain looks, how was he able to attract that god-like man? If he hasn't been using some nefarious method, how could he make him stay? Wu Xingzi is bad luck—his parents were cursed to death by him!" A-Niu's mother hid a distance away, but her mouth was merciless.

This made Auntie Liu extremely furious. She had watched Wu Xingzi grow up, and their families stayed rather close. Although she too liked to chatter about Wu Xingzi with the other women, she would never say anything harmful toward him. He was a good child. It was that mysterious man who seemed to have bad intentions!

In no time at all, the aunties all swarmed together, one digging at the other's eyes while another pulled at someone's hair. No one could stop them until their husbands heard the news and came running over, pulling them apart.

"I'll say it now! The moment I hear another ungrateful bitch speaking ill of Xingzi, I'll beat the living daylights out of her!" Naturally, Auntie Liu was the final victor. She emerged practically unscathed. Although her hair was messy and her face a little scratched, she still looked a lot tidier than the women who had fallen victim to her broom.

"As if we even want to speak of such filthy things!" A-Niu's mother, who hadn't been beaten as badly, could not let the matter go.

"What filthy things?" A new voice made the crowd fall silent.

"Hmm? What happened? What filthy things? We're all neighbors here. We should talk things out amicably."

This voice came from Wu Xingzi, dressed in a dark green robe. His forehead was covered with sweat—it seemed he had run over. Still panting, he had a warm and friendly smile on his face. The gossipy aunties all lowered their heads, not daring to respond.

Auntie Liu snorted out a laugh. "Who wants to admit what she has done now? Maybe she's also cast some curse to deceive others. This curse isn't very effective!" This time, no one dared to retort.

"Curse?" Wu Xingzi asked, perplexed. "Auntie Liu, you shouldn't believe those traveling Taoist priests so easily. If you have any trouble, I can help you."

"I know." Auntie Liu waved her hands, pushing the gossipy women to the back of her head. Warmly, she caught Wu Xingzi's hands. "I'm doing very well, don't worry. There's nothing going on here. You should head back now."

Nothing's going on? Wu Xingzi sneaked a peek at the mess on the ground and the disheveled aunties. Auntie Liu's basket lay on the ground, which looked like it had been broken under someone's foot.

"It's fine, really," Auntie Liu said. "If you don't believe me, you can ask them."

"Aunties, if you do have any trouble, please feel free to come to me," Wu Xingzi said sincerely.

"It's fine, it's fine," the beaten-up aunties all replied with a dry laugh. They had no choice but to swallow their pride. How could they mention the things they had been saying in front of Wu Xingzi?

"Look! Some people just have too much time on their hands. They get antsy if they don't get up to funny business," Auntie Liu said. "You won't be able to help with this. Who let them be so spiteful?" As one of the driving forces of conversation in Qingcheng County, her words could be more ruthless than a beating.

Wu Xingzi could only smile in response. He wasn't a fool—he could vaguely make a guess at what might have happened. Naturally, he didn't probe further. He was here because someone had gone to the magistrate's office, calling on him to settle this dispute, so he had to remain impartial.

After expressing some sympathy, Auntie Liu dragged Wu Xingzi away, as proud as a peacock. When they arrived at her place, Auntie Liu shoved a few steamed buns at him before letting him go.

He'd only walked a short distance away from the Liu family's home when someone embraced him from behind. Wu Xingzi hurriedly came to a stop, the tips of his ears tinting red.

"Y-you're here?" He snuck a glance to the side. Under the gentle afternoon sun, Guan Shanjin looked as though he was covered with a layer of golden gauze. Light glinted on his half-lidded eyes, scattering about with his breaths.

"Mm." Guan Shanjin curled his lips, hugging the man in his arms a little tighter.

"Look, Auntie Liu gave us some buns." Wu Xingzi waved the cloth bag in his hand. He felt a little restrained and uneasy, but he made no effort to struggle out of Guan Shanjin's embrace.

This feeling of unease lingered over Wu Xingzi as nearly a month passed.

One morning, Wu Xingzi woke up hungry, inhaling the aroma of food. He groggily opened his eyes, his body and mind feeling lazy. He was still drowsy, and if not for the fact that he was starving, he wouldn't have even been willing to open his eyes.

He and Guan Shanjin had indulged too much the night before, and Wu Xingzi felt that his hips no longer belonged to him. He was sore and numb. He tried to get off the bed but found himself unable to move. It scared him so much that he thought he was paralyzed, and he quickly pinched his thigh until a bruise formed and the pain nearly made him cry out loud. What a relief!

His door pushed open. "What are you doing?" Guan Shanjin had very sharp hearing and immediately noticed when Wu Xingzi awoke. He walked in with a bowl of porridge in his hands.

"Uh..." Wu Xingzi stared foolishly at this beautiful man holding a bowl of porridge, absentmindedly rubbing his eyes. "Wh-why are you still here?"

This was the second time already. Shouldn't Guan Shanjin leave after we...?

"Why do you always ask that?" Guan Shanjin's brows creased slightly, a somewhat resigned look on his face. "You must be hungry. Come have some porridge."

"Thank you, thank you..." Wu Xingzi cupped his hands, then tried his best to push himself up from the bed. However, his hand suddenly gave out, and he nearly rolled off. Guan Shanjin reacted quickly. In the blink of an eye, he was next to the bed, catching Adviser Wu in his arms.

"I've been too careless." Guan Shanjin's voice was gentle and mild next to his ear. Feeling the familiar warm breath, Wu Xingzi shuddered, his hips twitched, and his entire body flushed red in an instant.

"No, no..." The bowl of porridge was placed in his hands. Soon he was firmly supported between the mattress and a broad chest.

Wu Xingzi didn't know how to react, but he lowered his head and gulped the porridge down.

It was minced meat porridge. It tasted like rabbit seasoned with ginger and garlic, removing the gaminess of the meat but still leaving behind a rich and smooth flavor. The meat was minced very finely, but not to the point where it couldn't be chewed. Together with the porridge that was cooked to perfection, every mouthful tasted wonderful. Wu Xingzi whetted his appetite, finishing one bowlful after another. Only after four consecutive bowls did he feel satisfied.

"You clearly eat so well. Why can't you seem to put on any weight?" Guan Shanjin couldn't help asking as he watched him satisfy his hunger. Wu Xingzi's body was extremely sensitive, and it was one of the most enchanting ones the general had ever touched; however, he was very thin.

"Uh... I've always been like this..." Wu Xingzi said, dejected. Ever since he was a child, he could not put on weight. As a baby, his mother fed him without any sense of accomplishment. He drank twice the amount of milk compared to other children, but he remained smaller than other babies.

Even as an adult, Wu Xingzi ate well. Although his meals were simple, the quantity was not small. He did increase in height, but he stayed as thin as a piece of paper. It was hard to decide which was worse, his frail body or his lonely life.

"I'll have to feed you more in the future." Guan Shanjin shook his head as he left the room, his voice proper. However, those passionate eyes of his held a seductive charm. Wu Xingzi nearly blurted out, *Which mouth are you planning on feeding—the one on top or the one below?*

Fortunately, he managed to hold himself back. Otherwise, he really would have wanted the ground to swallow him whole.

Hmm? Hold on... What did he just hear?

"G-general Guan..."

"Haiwang." Despite the door between them, Guan Shanjin's voice was still crisp and clear.

"Hai, Hai, H-h-hai..." Wu Xingzi took a deep breath and tried to call out without any embarrassment. "Haiwang."

"Hmm?"

"Uhh... You said 'in the future'... What did you mean by that?" He sat half-reclined on the bed, cautiously trying his best to speak louder. *I definitely misheard him, right? The general of Horse-Face City must need to return to Horse-Face City in the future!*

Although...since he still hasn't left, maybe...

"What did I mean?" Guan Shanjin quickly finished washing the dishes. Coming back, he stroked Wu Xingzi's cheeks with his still-wet hands. "Why? Are you worried that I'll stay here in the future, or worried that I'll leave?"

Uh... Wu Xingzi chuckled wryly, not daring to respond.

He still had to go to Goose City today to collect *The Pengornisseur*! If Guan Shanjin remained, what was he to do about *The Pengornisseur*? That was fifty coins! And a hundred pages of prime pengornis!

"It seems you don't want me to stay?" He could clearly see what Adviser Wu was thinking. Guan Shanjin's face sank, and he pinched Wu Xingzi's cheeks hard. "You want to pull away after treating me like a whore?"

Whore? Th-this... Wu Xingzi's eyes rounded, and he could not help but rub at his ears. A beautiful man was beautiful no matter what he did—even the word "whore" sounded so elegant coming from his mouth.

"You're not admitting to it?" Guan the Beautiful smiled, and those white teeth sent a shiver down Adviser Wu's spine and left him breathless.

"I-I... I didn't pay you any money..." He didn't know why he mumbled this.

Guan Shanjin huffed an angry laugh. "How much do you plan on paying me?"

This old fellow dares to mention money? Together with what he has stashed away, he probably has less than ten silver taels to his name. How can he even think about using money to brush me off?

"Uh..." Adviser Wu couldn't say it was for free, as that was illegal...

"You could never afford my fees." Gnashing his teeth in anger, Guan Shanjin leaned into Wu Xingzi's face and bit his cheek. Leaving a mark there managed to quell his anger somewhat. "I'll be staying here until the debt is cleared."

What? Wu Xingzi was stunned. In a fluster, he waved both of his hands. "Uh...uh...uh...I'm bent over by your generosity!"

"Then I'll just continue bending you over. I know how flexible you are."

No! What does he want to bend? My waist? Last night's memories immediately flashed across Wu Xingzi's mind. His face reddened, and he had no idea where to put his limbs.

Last night, Guan Shanjin bent him in half and forced him to lick at his own little prick! His waist...

"B-but... I'm not good at cooking. I'm afraid that the general won't be pleased with my hospitality. It'll be t-too impolite..." Wu Xingzi was determined to reject this situation. He had originally planned on having only a casual fling with General Guan.

Instead, Guan Shanjin avoided the topic. "Wasn't the porridge you just had delicious?"

"It was..." Wu Xingzi licked his lips, wishing a little for more.

"I cooked it myself. I can take care of food." General Guan's beautiful eyes narrowed with a smile, licking his wet lips.

Wu Xingzi could not be any more astounded.

General... General... Such accomplishments on the battlefield, and such skills in the kitchen—is he even real?

"Then the matter is settled." Guan Shanjin smacked the table and leaned over to kiss Wu Xingzi.

Wu Xingzi didn't have the time or ability to reject General Guan. He officially moved in, suffocating Adviser Wu.

It was as the books said: a beauty's favor was the hardest to enjoy.

Wu Xingzi had many thoughts about this, and it felt as though his emotions permeated his bones! There was no way he would be able to return to the Peng Society. Guan Shanjin followed him around daily. They ate together, slept together—Guan Shanjin even tailed him to the magistrate's office. At first, the county magistrate planned on chasing the extraneous man away, but remarkably, they stopped upon seeing each other. Delighted, the magistrate quickly made his way toward them, bowing deeply at Guan Shanjin.

"Haiwang-xiong!" the magistrate exclaimed.

"Li Jian?" Guan Shanjin was surprised at first, and then he smiled. Wu Xingzi's stomach ached with curiosity as he watched, but he didn't even ask the magistrate about his past with General Guan, only knowing that his one remaining sanctuary—the magistrate's office—had fallen. This young and promising general was really taking the wind out of Wu Xingzi's sails.

Adviser Wu wearily walked into his office. With a sigh, he fell into introspection. What had he done wrong?

The books always said that people in high positions only had casual affairs with the common folk. They might take pity on them, or even like them, but they would never be reluctant to part from them.

He'd even finished reading the book that Manager Rancui had given to him and thought that he'd really met a general who only wanted a fleeting dalliance. Who would have thought that once the tryst was over, Guan Shanjin would refuse to leave? He would cuddle up with him on that narrow bed, cook for him every day, and even accompany him everywhere he went...

Thinking of Manager Rancui, Adviser Wu remembered *The Pengornisseur*, and his heart ached!

What exactly was Guan Shanjin thinking? Wu Xingzi sank into contemplation. He still had some self-awareness and was not under any illusion that Guan Shanjin liked him. He was old, ugly, old-fashioned, and timid. His lifestyle was boring, and he ate a lot. If he were Guan Shanjin, he wouldn't want to be with a person like himself.

"What are you thinking about?" Having finished reminiscing with the magistrate, Guan Shanjin entered the room to see Wu Xingzi in a daze, his eyes staring blankly at the files spread on his table.

The foolish look on his face did not resemble Mr. Lu at all. Guan Shanjin detested it, and so he reached out to pinch Wu Xingzi's cheeks.

"Ow!" In pain, Wu Xingzi jerked up. He rubbed his cheeks, a pitiful look on his face as he turned toward the man smirking at him.

Even though the smile was wicked, it was still as beautiful as a painting, and Wu Xingzi was entranced.

Guan Shanjin wanted to order this old fellow to never display such an expression—the reason the general stayed was for that little trace of Mr. Lu in Wu Xingzi. He had treated Wu Xingzi very well over these past few days because when he smiled, his shyness was very similar to Mr. Lu's. But more often than not, this old fellow had that silly, foolish look on his face instead.

Guan Shanjin felt unhappy with the situation, but on an impulse, he scratched at Adviser Wu's fleshy nose with a finger and smiled. "Why are you always in a daze?"

A beauty's scolding really was like poisoned wine! Wu Xingzi's face reddened, immediately forgetting all about how Guan Shanjin had been obstructing his life. He joyfully observed the beautiful man in front of him and shyly thought that it was also a good thing that the general's pengornis and his little hole could come together at night!

So, the two of them carried on for another month, each with their own thoughts on the relationship. The rumors spread even more wildly within Qingcheng County, erupting in a showdown between Auntie Liu and the other aunties.

Guan Shanjin knew about the rumors, but he wasn't bothered by them. After all, he was the god-like man everyone admired, and he didn't concern himself with obscene words spoken by vulgar villagers.

As for Wu Xingzi, he had long been subject to the villagers' rumors, so he naturally never paid attention to them. In the end, without his knowledge, half of the aunties were convinced that he could draw charms and cast spells, and that was why he'd been able to capture an otherworldly man like Guan Shanjin.

Ansheng had wanted to warn him, but for some reason, Ansheng felt like a quail with a noose around its neck whenever he was faced with Guan Shanjin. Pinned under those charming eyes, his voice stuck in his throat and his heart jolted. He was quite annoyed with himself for his cowardice.

However, he could see that Wu Xingzi was eating well and sleeping well, as well as getting along with Guan Shanjin, so maybe it was better that he did not say anything about it. Why should he speak of those rumors and upset Wu Xingzi? At most, he would observe the goings-on with Auntie Liu, and together they could think of another way to put the rumors to rest.

On the way home, Wu Xingzi asked the man in his arms, "I haven't seen you all day—are you busy with something?"

"Mm. I've received some news from Horse-Face City that needs to be dealt with." Guan Shanjin didn't hide it from him. He was a little gloomy, as the news mainly pertained to his military affairs and offered nothing much about Mr. Lu. Instead, Man Yue had told him about Hua Shu.

Guan Shanjin only had a vague recollection of who Hua Shu was. If not for the fact that he was someone close to Mr. Lu, Guan Shanjin wouldn't have even remembered his name.

But according to Man Yue's letter, Hua Shu had been asking after him quite frequently as of late. Apparently, Mr. Lu missed the general, and so, not wishing to see Mr. Lu turn melancholic, Hua Shu wanted to invite the general to visit Mr. Lu.

However, Man Yue also mentioned that Mr. Lu had recently been quite intimate with the third daughter of the Yue family. The two of them were constantly in contact with each other, and the Yue family seemed rather interested in becoming Mr. Lu's in-laws. Man Yue unceremoniously ended the letter by saying he was afraid that Mr. Lu didn't actually miss the general so much—at least not as much as Hua Shu did.

The letter vexed Guan Shanjin. He knew that Mr. Lu had always dreamed of marrying and settling down. He was already thirty-six this year, at the age where, even though he was a man, people would discuss his age behind his back. The Yue family was well-known in Horse-Face City, and they were always extremely deferential toward the troops based there. They always presented themselves humbly, and it was understandable that they would want a marriage alliance with Mr. Lu.

Each person had something they were looking to get out of the situation, and there was no way Guan Shanjin could interfere with the impending marriage. He was unwilling to make Mr. Lu angry with him, and he didn't want to leave Mr. Lu with the impression that he was the kind of man who coerced others with his power.

Already irritated, Guan Shanjin still had to deal with some middling military affairs. The entire day made him furious. He sent a reply, demanding Man Yue replace Hua Shu. Mr. Lu did not need such a scheming person at his side, and he didn't want this man to continue bothering Man Yue. After all, Man Yue had already sent a letter to him airing his grievances, and whether it was in public or private, he had to support his vice general.

However, seeing Wu Xingzi lessened Guan Shanjin's gloominess quite a bit. The expression this man had on his face right now did not bear a hint of resemblance to Mr. Lu. He looked like a silly little quail, so foolish that a person's heart would soften just by looking at him. One glance could make his heart melt.

"Is your military rank very high?"

This was the first time Wu Xingzi had asked about Guan Shanjin's personal matters, and for some reason, Guan Shanjin was delighted by this question. He hugged him even tighter before answering.

"It's not too bad. There's no one who has power over me."

"Even the great general of the Southern Garrison can't do anything about you?" Wu Xingzi was surprised. He held the Southern Garrison general in awe: that man was truly renowned. He heard that in the battle where Nanman was completely defeated, the ground flowed with three feet of blood, and the bloodstains could still be seen on the earth there.

Guan Shanjin smiled and kissed his face. "He can't."

Already used to such kisses, Wu Xingzi obligingly turned his head, allowing Guan Shanjin easier access to his lips.

The two of them went home holding each other close. Guan Shanjin headed into the kitchen to prepare a few dishes to accompany the buns, as well as to stew a pot of fish soup. The soup was a milky, creamy color, and it was extremely fresh and sweet, with a little spiciness from the ginger.

Wu Xingzi ate a great deal, so the few buns were not enough for two people. After cleaning his plate and finishing the soup, he felt there was still space in his stomach for more food.

"Do you want to go with me to Goose City?" Guan Shanjin asked as he reached out and rubbed at Wu Xingzi's soft belly, which felt a little hollow to him.

"Goose City?" Wu Xingzi blinked, tilting his head and considering it.

Tomorrow was an official holiday. Normally he would take the opportunity to help Auntie Liu out at her farm, then tidy up his own vegetable plot in his backyard. However, it was now winter, and all the crops had long been harvested. If he were alone, he could happily read some books at home and admire some pengornis illustrations, but how could he do that if Guan Shanjin stayed with him?!

Those drawings... No matter what, he could never let Guan Shanjin know about them.

"Sure. I'd like to visit Manager Rancui." He might even have the chance to ask him about the latest issue of *The Pengornisseur*.

"Let's go, then. It will only take three hours on horseback. We can even get something to eat while we're there." Guan Shanjin was a man of action. He swiftly retrieved some furs from the wardrobe and covered Wu Xingzi in them, before dragging him out the door.

Wu Xingzi was alarmed by Guan Shanjin's hasty decision. "Ah! Right now?" When he finally managed to ask the question, he had already been lifted into Guan Shanjin's arms as they ran through the trees.

"Of course. You're still hungry, right?" Guan Shanjin looked down and smiled at him. The last rays of the sun still shone, lighting Guan Shanjin's face with a warm glow. He really did look god-like; his beauty was incomparable.

Wu Xingzi was so entranced he forgot to ask further questions. He wasn't the kind of person who felt the need to get to the bottom of everything, anyway. Whatever Guan Shanjin felt like doing, Wu Xingzi would usually oblige him.

The horse was stabled on a hill a distance away, on an area of fertile grassland. However, this wasn't part of the territory of Qingcheng County. For some reason, all the soil in Qingcheng County always managed to be barren.

Wu Xingzi, of course, did not know how to ride a horse. Guan Shanjin carefully sheltered him in his arms and made sure to wrap him tightly in the furs. After making sure that he wouldn't suffer a chill from the wind, he kicked his horse off.

As a military man, Guan Shanjin's riding skills were impeccable, and his horse was one of the best in Great Xia. With the horse's considerable speed, they reached Goose City in two hours—just before the city gates closed.

"Where do you want to eat?" Wu Xingzi asked at last. He hadn't had the courage to turn his head to speak to Guan Shanjin before now—the horse had been running too fast. Even wearing Guan Shanjin's furs, he still felt a little of the cold wind cutting through. He could not fathom how the man behind him maintained his warm body temperature.

"Have you eaten at the House of Taotie before?" Galloping was forbidden in the city, so Guan Shanjin allowed the horse to amble through the streets at a leisurely trot. He only occasionally tugged on the reins to direct it.

"The House of Taotie?" Wu Xingzi gasped, and his eyes practically fell out of their sockets.

The House of Taotie was the most famous and expensive restaurant in Goose City! Even some of Goose City's top families didn't get the chance to eat there. This was not a matter of money, but due to the strange personality of the owner. If he didn't like a customer, he would refuse them service, even calling on his staff to chase them out. As for how he decided if he liked someone, the criterion was both easy and difficult: it was based on appearance.

Wu Xingzi turned to look at Guan Shanjin. All he could see from this position was his skin that was as fair as jade, his well-proportioned and marvelous neck, his chin that looked perfect from every angle, and a hint of his red lips that were like the petals of a flower.

Guan Shanjin was so beautiful that if he decided to demolish the restaurant, it was highly likely that the owner would joyfully stand back and watch him wreck the place.

However...

Wu Xingzi sighed, touching his own face.

"What? Afraid that the owner of the House of Taotie will chase you out the door?" Guan Shanjin saw through him immediately, and he let out a low laugh and bit Wu Xingzi's earlobe. "Don't worry. The owner is a childhood friend of mine. With you under my protection, he wouldn't dare touch you."

So, they're old friends... Wu Xingzi wasn't surprised to hear this. A few months ago, he would definitely have been shocked. Now that he knew Guan Shanjin was born to a top aristocratic family, it was expected that he would know these wealthy and powerful businessmen. It took Wu Xingzi no time to get used to it. It was remarkable how people could adapt!

The horse trotted onward, and they soon arrived at the House of Taotie. A staff member waited by the door. Seeing Guan Shanjin in the distance, he quickly ran over and greeted them warmly. "You must be General Guan. The owner welcomes you in."

"Mm." Guan Shanjin was calm. Hugging Wu Xingzi, he leapt off the horse and handed the reins over to the staff as he instructed, "Zhuxing has a fierce temper. There's no need to tie him up, he won't run away."

"Your humble servant understands. General, please make your way inside." The staff hurriedly gestured at someone inside. A middle-aged man who appeared to be the restaurant manager walked out slowly, his appearance clean and fair. He held an awe-inspiring air, attracting everyone's eyes.

"General Guan." The manager cupped his hands toward him. "The owner has assigned me as your humble servant. I welcome the general."

"Lead the way." Guan Shanjin glanced at the manager, not paying much attention to him. Instead, he looked down and helped Wu Xingzi straighten his lapels, drawing his finger across his nose. "What's wrong? You look like you're in another world."

But he was! The manager was gorgeous! Wu Xingzi looked at him, his face flushing slightly. Although he was principled, he did have an admiration for beauty. Why else did Guan Shanjin's appearance grip him so tightly? And Wu Xingzi had always preferred the sort of gentle, mild man that the manager seemed to be.

The manager noticed his gaze and reservedly looked at him with a slight frown. "If I may ask the general, who is this?"

"Adviser Wu from Qingcheng County," Guan Shanjin answered casually. Pulling Wu Xingzi into his arms, he headed into the restaurant.

"Forgive me, General, but the House of Taotie has its house rules. Adviser Wu has an outstanding temperament, but..." The manager's eyes looked cold, even a little disgusted, and he was unwilling to look directly at Wu Xingzi.

Wu Xingzi had always been aware of his appearance, and he didn't feel insulted by the manager's mindset. He only had a look of "I told you so" as he shrugged at Guan Shanjin.

Guan Shanjin burst out laughing at Wu Xingzi's attitude. "You were just salivating over the manager, and now he's looking down on you. Don't you know how to be angry?" Bending down, he kissed his brow, then turned toward the manager and spoke coldly. "You don't have the right to ask about who I want to bring here. Ask Su Yang to come out and speak with me."

"The owner is waiting inside for you. General, please..." The manager was about to continue, only to hear a soft sound of metal sliding against metal and feel a cold, sharp sensation on his neck. When he regained his wits, he realized there was a dark, gleaming sword pointing at his throat.

"Ask Su Yang to speak with me." Guan Shanjin's tone was soft, but he pressed on like an evil spirit. The manager broke out in a cold sweat and looked unsteady on his feet.

"I was wondering why you still hadn't gone in," a voice said. "You've even unsheathed your Chenyuan Sword?"

Following the voice was a man who seemed to have just come of age. At first glance, one couldn't help but think this exceptional man must have been crafted from jade. Adviser Wu, who loved looking at beautiful men, naturally could not drag his eyes away.

"Don't look." Guan Shanjin shielded Wu Xingzi's eyes, his voice full of scorn. "Not all that glitters is gold—looking at him will just hurt your eyes."

"Hah. If there were a contest to decide who is lower than filth... If General Guan declared himself to be in second place, no one in the world who would dare claim first," Su Yang, the owner of the House of Taotie, spat laughingly. However, when his eyes fell on Wu Xingzi, he made no effort to conceal his displeasure. "This is...?"

"Adviser Wu from Qingcheng County." Guan Shanjin cut Su Yang off. "He's mine, so you'd better think things through."

What he meant was "You'd better think about whether your throat can withstand my Chenyuan Sword."

Su Yang's brow creased as he reached up to touch his fair and flawless neck. He had no choice but to give in. "Please, come in. The food's waiting for you."

CHAPTER FIVE

EACH WITH THEIR OWN THOUGHTS

"You can't stay in Qingcheng County forever, right?"

As the general of the Southern Garrison, Guan Shanjin had been away long enough. It was truly time for him to return. However... "We've lived together for a month. Won't you even miss me a little?"

In the end, Wu Xingzi sighed. "But you still have to return to Horse-Face City," he said lightly. "Let's part amicably, shall we?"

In spite of himself, Guan Shanjin pressed his hand against his chest, and nearly vomited blood.

RETURNING CHENYUAN to its scabbard, Guan Shanjin wrapped an arm around Wu Xingzi—whose mind had drifted away—and stepped into the House of Taotie.

The interior was decorated tastefully. A few tables and chairs were scattered around in a seemingly random arrangement. The ceiling beams were quite high, and the resulting spaciousness was especially pleasing.

Besides a few antiques and several potted plants, the establishment was not extravagantly ornamented. It even looked a little simple—it was only after careful observation that one realized how exquisite everything was.

As they walked, Guan Shanjin quietly explained the history of some of the antiques to Wu Xingzi. His voice was gentle and pleasant, and his breath felt hot against Wu Xingzi's face as it grazed his sensitive ear—Wu Xingzi couldn't focus on anything Guan Shanjin actually said.

Su Yang led the way, occasionally turning back and narrowing his eyes at them. He seemed to disapprove of how considerate Guan Shanjin was to Wu Xingzi, and he was obviously very impatient.

"It's only a waiting hall. Do you plan on walking through it for the rest of your life?" Su Yang glared at Wu Xingzi, but the words clearly targeted Guan Shanjin.

Guan Shanjin didn't bother maintaining a veneer of politeness with his childhood friend. "Without anyone to appreciate them, all this stuff would just be junk."

Su Yang's eyes almost rolled to the back of his head. "I've never seen you be so considerate toward anyone. Not even toward that Mr. So-and-So," he grumbled sulkily.

This statement made Guan Shanjin's brow crease and his demeanor turn to ice. "It's Mr. Lu. He's my teacher—and he's different from Adviser Wu."

"I'd rather you bring Mr. Lu here instead. At least he's more pleasing to the eye." Su Yang smiled maliciously at the foolish-looking Wu Xingzi, hastening his pace through the hallway. "If you want to appreciate the antiques, I'll get my staff to bring them all into the room for you. If we don't eat the food now, it'll lose its flavor."

"There's no need for that. I only stopped to appreciate them on a whim. Adviser Wu doesn't like any distractions while he's eating, so don't come and cause trouble." Guan Shanjin waved off the suggestion, finally willing to follow Su Yang up the stairs.

The House of Taotie itself was not very big; it stood only two stories tall. However, it had an extremely spacious courtyard in the back. Instead of a pavilion, it featured a huge pond with lotus flowers, water caltrops, prickly waterlilies, and various other plants. In the summer, the staff harvested them to use in the restaurant's dishes.

Surrounding the pond was a clear dirt path without any stepping stones. Squares of vegetable plots flanked the left side of the pond, and seasonal weather did not disturb the vegetables. A row of bamboo plants stood along the peripheral area, giving off the leisurely air of a southern farmstead.

The House of Taotie only had private rooms—there was no shared dining hall. All six rooms had windows facing the courtyard. Looking out one of these windows was like viewing a vivid and elegant painting.

Entering the room, Su Yang pointed outside and curled his lips into a smirk. "You gentlemen came at the wrong time. It's cold and dark outside; the only barely presentable things are the lights reflecting across the pond."

"It hasn't been very long since we last saw each other. You've learned to be modest in that short time?" Guan Shanjin snorted. He brought Wu Xingzi to the windowsill and pointed out the various highlights of the courtyard to him.

At night, lamps shone around the pond. As the lotus-shaped lanterns floated across the water, the glowing lights evoked a unique feeling. Wu Xingzi was amazed by the view, and even a little befuddled.

Su Yang's sharp eye noticed the expression on his face. "What, do you have some advice on decorating the courtyard I've arranged so meticulously?" he asked.

"Umm..." Wu Xingzi scratched his cheek, looking somewhat uneasy. He glanced at Guan Shanjin, hoping for a way out. The beautiful man only smiled brightly at him, not lifting a finger.

"Just say it. Besides, this Guan fellow is now your ally—I won't be able to do anything to you." Su Yang's tone was very sour. He was unable to accept that such an ordinary, ugly old man had actually entered his House of Taotie. He waited to hear Wu Xingzi say something out of turn, hoping to use it as an excuse to vent his anger.

"Umm..." With his plea to the general falling on deaf ears, Wu Xingzi bowed his head and took a deep breath. "I was only curious why people in the city would enjoy this sort of scenery."

"What do you know? This is the flavor of the countryside! The view of peaceful scenery accompanied by the scent of fresh air and earth sets an idyllic scene for our guests to leisurely enjoy their food and drinks. This sort of relaxed, carefree atmosphere—I'm afraid Adviser Wu wouldn't understand a bit of it!" Su Yang laughed mockingly, wondering how Guan Shanjin became attracted to this sort of philistine.

Wu Xingzi truly did not understand the appeal. Ponds and farm plots like these could be found all over Qingcheng County. If a household had an empty plot, it was tilled to plant vegetables. They had no other choice; if they did not use the land wisely, it was very easy to starve to death in winter or in drought.

Goose City had only recently become prosperous. Despite the calm in Nanjiang, the well-maintained embankment dams, and the lack of drought in the past ten years, no one could rest easy when the memory of hardship and suffering lingered.

Wu Xingzi could not comprehend what Su Yang called the "flavor of the countryside." In his eyes, it was a matter of survival. City folks truly were a different breed. Adviser Wu marveled over it silently and did not say anything, cupping his hands at Su Yang and smiling warmly.

Su Yang's words seemed to have missed their mark. He'd placed quite a bit of venom behind his insult, but Adviser Wu wasn't swayed. Su Yang choked on his anger, his chest aching. With a huff, he sat near the table and asked the server to bring up the food.

"Even Su Yang can only eat his words in front of you." Guan Shanjin gave a low chuckle as he stroked Wu Xingzi's nose. However, his amusement did not reach his cold eyes.

How unfortunate that Wu Xingzi wasn't paying attention—he was busy watching Su Yang rub his chest in irritation. He wouldn't have missed the general's icy gaze.

"When did I make Su-gongzi eat his words?" Wu Xingzi blinked, his face blank. He had never liked arguing with others. Goose City was different from Qingcheng County, and it was hardly his place to object to other people's preferences.

Guan Shanjin smiled and shook his head. He brought him to sit at the table and poured tea for both of them.

The refined scent of tea wafted through the air, refreshing their souls. Guan Shanjin sipped it and praised the fancy brew. "It's Monkey Picked tea," he remarked.

"How is it?" Su Yang asked. "I spent a lot of effort obtaining it. Other than the pound-and-a-half that I've kept, I offered it all to the emperor." Su Yang looked proud as he too sipped the tea.

It definitely was an excellent tea. It was a little bitter at first, but a sweet aftertaste came later at the back of the throat. If the temperature of the water was not maintained perfectly, the tea would turn too bitter. It was clear and had a green hue, like Khotan jade. Sipping a mouthful of the aromatic tea, Wu Xingzi could tell how perfectly balanced it was.

"Do you like it?" Guan Shanjin asked Wu Xingzi.

"Mm..." Wu Xingzi nodded awkwardly, sipping at his cup a couple of times. It was delicious, even more flavorful than the tea he drank at the Peng Society. However, he felt it was a little difficult to swallow. "How much is this tea?"

"Don't talk about money—it's vulgar," Su Yang sneered. Having been born with a silver spoon in his mouth, he had never met a guest who dared to ask about the prices in front of him! How rude!

Wu Xingzi bit his lip and lowered his blushing face. He really had been somewhat too direct and impolite. Having interacted with Guan Shanjin for so long, he no longer experienced that initial shyness that had saved him from such blunders in the past. He had not felt this sort of awkwardness and embarrassment in a while, and he didn't know where to place his hands or his feet. How could he forget that Guan Shanjin himself was a high official's son, as well as the ungovernable general of Horse-Face City...?

While they'd been in Qingcheng County, Guan Shanjin was so amiable and approachable, even cooking for him every day. Now, Wu Xingzi was reminded how disparate their lives truly were. How had he unwittingly forgotten?

Looking at Wu Xingzi's reddened face and general unease, Su Yang finally felt vindicated. When the food came, he continued excluding Wu Xingzi from the conversation, making him feel too uncomfortable to eat. Wu Xingzi only took a few bites before he said he was full. He quietly sat in his seat and fell into a daze.

Throughout the entire meal, Guan Shanjin didn't say anything to help Wu Xingzi in any way. It was as if the man who had pulled out the Chenyuan Sword on Wu Xingzi's behalf earlier that night did not exist.

The meal took quite some time. Guan Shanjin and Su Yang rarely met, and they had many things to discuss. Although Su Yang was usually the one speaking, Guan Shanjin seemed happy to listen to him. Such intimacy made Wu Xingzi feel even smaller—he should never have shown his face in a place like this.

It was nine in the evening before Guan Shanjin bid Su Yang farewell.

Su Yang added his final words as he walked them to the door: "Next time, bring Mr. Lu." He had already guessed that Wu Xingzi was merely a substitute for Mr. Lu and was thus unwilling to let General Guan rest easy.

"Definitely." Guan Shanjin cupped his hands at him.

Wu Xingzi still did not speak, politely cupping his hands like Guan Shanjin and silently following closely behind him.

Su Yang looked at them again, then turned and headed back into the House of Taotie.

Guan Shanjin held Wu Xingzi's hand and guided the horse along as they walked through the quiet street. The Great Xia Dynasty did not have a curfew, but they would surely be hauled to the magistrate's office for a night if they disturbed anyone this late.

"Su Yang's words have always been harsh. Don't take it to heart." Guan Shanjin shifted his hand, wrapping his arm around Wu Xingzi. It seemed as though he had only just thought about comforting him.

"I didn't take it to heart..." Wu Xingzi sighed lightly, rubbing his belly. "I just didn't eat enough. The food was exquisite, but I had no idea what ingredients they used. I didn't really want to eat much of it."

"You don't blame me for reminiscing with Su Yang and neglecting you?" The question sounded tender, but there was a chill in Guan Shanjin's eyes that Wu Xingzi failed to notice.

Instinctively, he shook his head. "What blame is there? He's your friend, not mine. Naturally, there's nothing for us to talk about."

After all, Guan Shanjin hadn't spoken when they went to Ansheng's tofu stall.

"You're truly open-minded." Guan Shanjin was inexplicably gloomy. "It's my fault—I shouldn't have insisted on bringing you to the House of Taotie."

"It's not like that..." Wu Xingzi gazed at him. "You're a general. You even know our county magistrate. It's to be expected that you'd patronize places like this. You should bring Mr. Lu here next time."

Guan Shanjin stopped abruptly and looked at Wu Xingzi, his eyes somber. "Don't think too much about it. Mr. Lu is my teacher."

Huh? Wu Xingzi blinked, a vacant expression on his face. "I know that Mr. Lu is your teacher. I wasn't thinking too much." *Didn't Su Yang just specially invite Mr. Lu?*

"You weren't?" Guan Shanjin knew that Wu Xingzi was not a deceitful man. If he said as much, then he definitely wasn't thinking about it at all. Guan Shanjin suppressed the displeasure within him. He couldn't put his finger on why he was so annoyed.

"Since Mr. Lu is your teacher, he would definitely like the House of Taotie. As for me, it's just not my kind of place. I prefer simpler, filling food—porridge, noodles, buns. I'm not used to such exquisite meals."

The more Adviser Wu spoke, the hungrier he became. His dinner had been early, and he only consumed a small portion. The servings at the House of Taotie were far too small. They didn't serve any of the staple foods that could satiate him, and Wu Xingzi was now hungry beyond belief.

"Then why didn't you eat more in the House of Taotie?"

"I saw that the dishes and wine were really only enough for Su-gongzi and you. It's not that I didn't eat, it's just..." Wu Xingzi smiled placatingly, rubbing his stomach. "Why don't we look for a noodle or a porridge stall, and let me fill my stomach?"

"Are any food stalls still open?" There was hardly a soul on the streets at this hour. Guan Shanjin was unfamiliar with Goose City; he felt that it was troublesome to go hunting for food this late.

Wu Xingzi perked up. "There are. There's no curfew, so some stalls over at the square stay open late." This was something he had heard Ansheng mention to Constable Zhang. He didn't know if the stalls were any good, but that wouldn't deter him from tasting the food.

"Fine. There's no harm accompanying you to the square." Leading his horse along, Guan Shanjin walked toward the square, his arm still around Wu Xingzi.

The southern part of the city was split into two areas. The upper area housed an assortment of brothels, while the lower area was an entertainment district with abundant teahouses and restaurants. At this hour, all the shops in the lower area were closed, and the streets were cold and quiet. However, this was also the time when the upper area bustled with activity.

Since people gathered here in droves, numerous hawkers peddled their wares. Stores selling noodles and porridge were all open for customers. Whorehouses stood across the street, filling the air with pleasant music and fragrances. Handsome attendants and pretty ladies all smiled and laughed gaily at the doors, welcoming customers in. The night breeze itself seemed to be filled with the scent of perfume and the sound of ladies' laughter.

With an arm around Wu Xingzi's waist, Guan Shanjin strolled casually about the square. Even though he only wore a simple black robe, the quality and expense of the flowing fabric was evident to everyone around them. Despite his wealthy appearance, none of the attendants nor the ladies dared to call out to him—they all compliantly avoided him.

Wu Xingzi, however, did not notice such small matters. What caught his eye was the rows of stalls selling noodles, porridge, and snacks. Wiggling his nose slightly, he inhaled the aroma of food in the air.

"What would you like to eat?" Guan Shanjin asked as he brought Wu Xingzi to take a look at every stall.

The general's lack of interest was somewhat apparent. He had already eaten at the House of Taotie. Although the food there was light-tasting, every dish was perfect. The skill used to prepare the food was flawless, so naturally, the flavors were incomparable. It definitely lived up to Su Yang's reputation for indulgence.

Needless to say, the basic, boring food in front of him could not rouse his interest. However, watching how happy Wu Xingzi was, his slightly melancholy mood faded away.

"What should we eat?" Wu Xingzi asked after investigating every stall. Each one of them had something to tempt him. After all, these were the stalls across from the brothels, and their offerings were finer and more delicious than those of stalls found elsewhere. The stall selling dumplings was especially impressive— every shrimp dumpling looking fat and scrumptious, nearly as big as a baby's fist. The dumpling skin was almost translucent, and the fresh, juicy shrimp, chopped cabbage, and chives inside looked bright and lovely. Wu Xingzi's mouth nearly overflowed with drool.

"What about dumplings?" Guan Shanjin asked. He paid attention to Wu Xingzi's every move and noticed that he had taken a couple more glances at the dumpling stall than the others. It was clear what occupied his mind.

Delighted, Wu Xingzi nodded his head continuously. He took the lead and tugged Guan Shanjin over to the dumpling stall.

"Boss, I'd like a bowl of dumpling noodles," Wu Xingzi said. "What about you?"

"I'm full. Just order for yourself," Guan Shanjin replied as he patted the back of Wu Xingzi's hand. He found a table and led him there to sit.

The man selling the dumplings had a sturdy build and looked to be about fifty years old. He acknowledged the order loudly, then began to deftly prepare the noodles. In the blink of an eye, a steaming bowl of dumpling noodles was ready to eat. About seven or eight large dumplings bobbed in the seafood-based broth.

The bowl of noodles made Wu Xingzi's face brighten with joy. The way he looked enjoying the food made Guan Shanjin feel hungry out of nowhere, so he ordered a bowl of dumpling soup for himself. There were about half a dozen dumplings in the bowl, and Guan Shanjin couldn't finish them all. He transferred three of them into Wu Xingzi's bowl, and the old fellow's eyes lit up immediately. He thanked him profusely, as if General Guan had given him three pieces of gold and not three shrimp dumplings.

It had to be said that the dumplings were quite delicious, every bite bursting with flavor. The dumpling wrappers were thin and filled to the brim with top quality ingredients, each one skillfully crafted. The soup, made of seafood stock, was mouthwatering as well and tasted even better than the mushroom-stewed chicken from the House of Taotie.

The two men greatly enjoyed their supper. Rubbing his bulging stomach, Wu Xingzi looked satisfied, his cheeks dyed a pleasant pink.

To help digest their food, Adviser Wu and General Guan strolled about in each other's arms, exploring the nightlife of Goose City. Although Wu Xingzi didn't know where Guan Shanjin was taking him, he'd gotten used to being taken care of by the general over the past month, so he let him lead the way.

The way turned out to be pretty far. They walked all the way from the south of the city to the north. The northern part of the city was mostly made up of residential areas, and they were divided into eight squares. Qingyang Square was home to the upper class of Goose City, with each mansion taking up a large plot of land. The long, walled fences stretched so far, it felt as though they would never end.

Wu Xingzi had never been here before.

Unlike other squares, the doors to Qingyang Square closed an hour before midnight and opened at dawn. To enter or exit the square in the hours between, a waist tag issued by the magistrate's office was required. These tags couldn't be obtained by anyone but the owners of the mansions in Qingyang Square.

When they reached Qingyang Square, it was already past eleven. Wu Xingzi yawned, feeling a little tired. He didn't seem to think anything was amiss as he watched Guan Shanjin retrieve a waist tag and show it to the guards. *Just how luxurious are the inns in Qingyang Square?* he thought.

It was only when they walked up to the door of a mansion that Wu Xingzi realized the truth. Astonished, he asked, "You own property in Goose City?"

Guan Shanjin smiled but did not reply. He had bought this mansion just a couple of months ago, leaving it under the management of his four guards. He barely stayed in it himself.

Now that he thought about it, it made sense that he hadn't spent much time here. When he was seeing the accountant who lived in Sushui Village, he'd stayed in that village. This month, he was seeing Wu Xingzi—naturally, he'd stayed in Adviser Wu's little wooden house.

Without his having to knock, the side door opened, revealing a deathly solemn face. Wu Xingzi hunched into himself and shivered, hiding behind Guan Shanjin.

"General," the man greeted respectfully.

"Mm." Guan Shanjin waved him off indifferently. Catching hold of Wu Xingzi's hand, he walked through the side door.

The mansion was not monstrously large but had an overall spacious feeling. Its furnishings were simple, without any overly lavish decorations. Wu Xingzi soon calmed down and quietly observed the sizeable manor.

Guan Shanjin allowed Wu Xingzi to look around, following behind the adviser as he spoke quietly with his guard. After a short exchange, his brows knitted, and his attitude turned cold and stern. "Mr. Lu has already decided on betrothal gift arrangements with the head of the Yue family?" he murmured unhappily.

"Yes... General, isn't it about time we returned to Horse-Face City?" the guard asked. He was only asking casually; he shared the same opinion as Vice General Man, feeling that it was rare to see the general showering attention on anyone other than Mr. Lu. Whether his affection toward the adviser was sincere or simply a sham, the more time they spent together, the more difficult it would be to anticipate the future. It would be beneficial to take this opportunity to clarify the general's intentions regarding Mr. Lu.

This question was rather loud—Wu Xingzi overheard. His steps faltered, and he blinked at the dour-looking Guan Shanjin. The guard lowered his head, his expression unclear.

"You're...going back to Horse-Face City?" Wu Xingzi asked this question instinctively. He could not control the upward quirk of his mouth.

Could he finally collect the next issue of *The Pengornisseur*? This was great news!

"Why are you so happy that I'm leaving?" Guan Shanjin's lips frowned coldly.

"Uhh..." It had to be said that he was, of course, happy already. He had grown used to living with Guan Shanjin. He had the opportunity to look at a beautiful man every day, eat the food the beautiful man cooked, and play with the beautiful man's pengornis, but...

"Hmm?" Guan Shanjin's questioning sound was affectionate, but it caused shivers to go down Adviser Wu's spine and his hair to stand on end.

Having a tenuous grasp on how to handle Guan Shanjin's temper, Wu Xingzi shook his head forcefully. "How could I be happy? Once you leave, I won't have any pengornis to play with," he said placatingly.

Wu Xingzi knew at once that he had said the wrong thing. He obediently lowered his head, not even daring to exhale loudly. *Oh no. I'm dead.*

Guan Shanjin's expression was complicated. His brows creased tightly, and his mouth looked stiff. The cold look in his eyes was like a blizzard in winter. It seemed as though he wanted to say something but couldn't get the words out.

"You..." Guan Shanjin finally opened his mouth. "We've lived together for a month! And the only thing you'll miss is my *cock*?!"

His words were scathing; however, out of context, they were hilarious. At least, the guard next to them could not hold back his burst of laughter.

Aware of his blunder, the guard bowed his head. "General, I was wrong. I will go and punish myself," he said, admitting his wrongdoing. Still, the amusement in his tone could not be concealed.

"Go." What else could he say? If this had happened to someone else, Guan Shanjin would probably be laughing even harder.

He had stayed with Wu Xingzi for a month and lavished him with care and affection. Even his own parents had never enjoyed such meticulous and considerate treatment from him. This foolish old man usually looked so innocent—to think he was actually so hard-hearted!

If Wu Xingzi could hear the general's thoughts, he would've definitely cried out in defense of himself—at least, if he had the courage to do so.

Adviser Wu was deeply moved by Guan Shanjin's care for him. No one else had shown such affection in all the years of his life. Even when his parents were still alive, they had not been as meticulous as the general.

Still, it was clear to Wu Xingzi that it was impossible for him and Guan Shanjin to ever have a life together. Besides their age difference, the disparity of their family backgrounds was enough to cause a stir. In the Great Xia dynasty, no families whose members had official positions—no matter how small—would accept a male spouse. And with Guan Shanjin's strong family background, it was expected that his wife had to be someone who brought benefits to his family.

What did Wu Xingzi have? Two months ago, his life savings were worth ten silver ingots. Today, he had only nine and some coins to his name.

Wu Xingzi was very blunt and honest by nature, but he understood that he could never mention any of this out loud. It was fine if Guan Shanjin didn't care about Adviser Wu's lower status. However, if General Guan cared even a little, he might do anything to vindicate himself—all hell would break loose.

When the guard walked away, Guan Shanjin gentled his voice. "Why so quiet? Cat got your tongue?"

He was so clearly a general, and a northerner as well. So why was his voice always so soft and intoxicating? Wu Xingzi's ears flushed red as he stammered, "I, umm... I didn't mean anything by it, I j-just... don't want to be a burden to your work..."

"A burden?" Guan Shanjin drawled out. Wu Xingzi's limbs turned to jelly and his face burned as red as a tomato.

"Yes, yes... If you need to return to Horse-Face City, you definitely must have something urgent to handle. I understand. You can go back without any worries—you won't be missing anything."

At first, Wu Xingzi spoke only platitudes, but the latter part was what he actually meant. How could Guan Shanjin not have realized it sooner? His breath was stuck in his chest, almost unable to take in air.

A pair of beautiful, charming eyes glared harshly at Wu Xingzi, forcing him to avert his gaze, a look of innocent confusion on his face.

"You don't want me to stay?" Guan Shanjin asked through gritted teeth. He had always been the one to leave others out in the cold—this was the first time someone was so eager to abandon him.

Thinking about their one month of cohabitation, Guan Shanjin was so bitter that his chest hurt. He felt an indescribably intense reluctance to be parted from Wu Xingzi, as though ants were gnawing at his heart. How he wished he could swing his sword and dispel his unhappiness!

"You can't stay in Qingcheng County forever, right?" Wu Xingzi asked, startled. Unless there was a change in the garrison, soldiers couldn't just leave their stations whenever they pleased, could they?

Naturally, as the general of the Southern Garrison, Guan Shanjin had been away long enough. It was truly time for him to return. However...

"Have you never thought of coming with me to Horse-Face City?" Guan Shanjin asked.

"Why would I follow you to Horse-Face City?" Wu Xingzi was truly astounded. He'd always planned on living his entire life in Qingcheng County, Guan Shanjin already knew that!

"We lived together for an entire month. Won't you miss me—even just a little?" Guan Shanjin already knew the answer to his question. Wu Xingzi's feelings toward him never changed. He never begged him to stay. The only thing he seemed to be infatuated with was the physical aspect of their relationship. There was absolutely nothing else he was reluctant about leaving behind.

Faced with this question, Wu Xingzi experienced a rare moment of hesitation. It was inaccurate to say he would not miss him. He could never forget Guan Shanjin's cock. As for Guan Shanjin's care over the past month, he was not indifferent toward it—it was just... Everyone said that love was painful. He had not even started thinking about love, but he already had a headache.

In the end, Wu Xingzi sighed. "But you still must return to Horse-Face City," he said lightly. "Let's part amicably, shall we?"

Guan Shanjin could not help but press his hand against his chest. He almost vomited blood.

What the fuck!! Those were the words that the general always said to the shadows of Mr. Lu! How could this old man say the same thing to him?!

Finally noticing that Guan Shanjin looked a little unwell, Wu Xingzi grew anxious. "Y-you don't look so good. What's wrong?" Leaning over, he patted him on the chest in comfort. "Did you eat too much? You shouldn't have had that bowl of dumpling soup. Are you getting heartburn? Do you need a heart-calming pill?"

He might as well offer me a heart-resuscitating pill!

Guan Shanjin could no longer hide his anger. Swatting Wu Xingzi's hand away, he hoarsely said, "I'm not getting heartburn because of that bowl of dumpling soup, it's because of *you*, you foolish quail! Are you really so desperate to get rid of me?"

"That's not it..." Wu Xingzi waved his hands, looking entirely innocent. "You do have to return to Horse-Face City, right? We can still keep in contact through the pigeon post. When we go back into town, I'll give you a mail pigeon from the magistrate's office. We can even save some money that way! Letters cost a coin each through the Peng Society, and I have to travel to Goose City to collect the letter. What do you think about sending the letter straight to my office?"

"It's up to you..." Guan Shanjin really couldn't think of what else to say.

Throughout his life, he had been puffed up with his own pride. In his eyes, most things were unworthy of his attention. No one dared object to him: not his parents, not even the man on the Dragon Throne. This was the first time he had ever felt so helpless.

Of course, Wu Xingzi was physically weak—an old quail of a man. Guan Shanjin could probably pinch him to death with two fingers. However, Adviser Wu was too similar to Mr. Lu. No matter how frustrated Guan Shanjin became, he didn't dare to cause him any harm.

Guan Shanjin choked on his fury, completely and utterly vexed.

"You're...still upset?" Wu Xingzi wasn't blind. He could see that Guan Shanjin's alluring eyes were wild and his face flushed red as he gasped for air. His words were decidedly different from what he truly felt.

Wu Xingzi quietly leaned closer, tugging at Guan Shanjin's sleeves. "If...if it would make you happy... You can do whatever you want to me tonight."

Guan Shanjin immediately wanted to reject him. However, seeing Wu Xingzi's shy yet obliging expression made the flames of fury immediately morph into desire, lighting him up from within.

"You naughty old thing..." After scolding him harshly, Guan Shanjin pulled him into his arms and kissed him deeply.

His soft tongue deftly swept through Wu Xingzi's mouth, teasing at some of his sensitive spots, and then twined with his tongue as he sucked on it. He only pulled away when Wu Xingzi was breathless.

It was late at night, and the silver moon hid behind the clouds. There was only a vague, hazy light shining down on the two men. The lanterns in the courtyard were dim as they swayed gently in the air; Guan Shanjin's eyes shone brilliantly in comparison. Light danced brightly in those misted depths as he stared into Wu Xingzi's reddened eyes. Other than their panting breaths, neither of them made a sound.

Wu Xingzi didn't dare to ask Guan Shanjin what he was looking at. He remained in his embrace obediently and quietly, relishing the kiss they'd just shared. The tip of his tongue was tender and tingly, as though Guan Shanjin had almost swallowed it away.

A moment later, Guan Shanjin let out a low sigh. "What should I do about you?" he asked, his tone full of gentle affection. Wu Xingzi's ears burned red.

However, it was clear that Guan Shanjin did not require a response from him. He lifted him up and headed toward his room.

The courtyard didn't look big, but the walk from the entrance to Guan Shanjin's room took quite some time. When the general kicked the door open, Adviser Wu saw that the hearth within the room was already lit. The room seemed to be deliberately scented, and the air felt warm and toasty; it complemented Guan Shanjin's white sandalwood scent.

When Guan Shanjin placed Wu Xingzi on the bed, he didn't spend much time teasing him. Instead, he swiftly stripped them both of their clothes. He then retrieved a small, sealed container of lubricant from the cabinet next to the bed, his lips curving up in a slight smile.

"You'll really let me do whatever I want to you tonight?" Guan Shanjin asked.

The lid of the thin, shiny container was intricately decorated with a gold drawing of two dragons chasing a pearl. It seemed overly opulent for a jar of oil. Wu Xingzi glanced at it once and dared not look at it any further. He was afraid that he would start calculating how expensive it was and spoil the mood.

"Mm-hmm. Everything's up to you," Wu Xingzi said, submissively lowering his head. Even though he was so embarrassed that his entire face flushed, he made no attempt to conceal any part of his naked body.

"Good boy," Guan Shanjin said as he leaned forward to kiss him.

He twisted the container open. A sweet, cloying scent filled the air, permeating the entire room. The lubricant was red and slippery looking. Guan Shanjin scooped some up with fair, slender fingers, the red color standing in stark contrast to his pale skin. His fingers were positioned like a buddha in meditation, while he himself looked like a demon ready to take his soul. Wu Xingzi was unable to calm himself, his breathing becoming heavier.

Guan Shanjin flipped Wu Xingzi over on the bed with just one hand, positioning him with the top half of his body on the bed and his buttocks raised lewdly up in the air, his hips curving upward beautifully. General Guan's fingers slathered lubricant directly onto his hole.

After a month of intimate attention, Wu Xingzi's shy little hole had turned from its original pink and fair color to an alluring red, the tight creases slightly swelled up. With only a very light pressure, it swallowed up Guan Shanjin's finger immediately, the hole mouthing at it hungrily.

Guan Shanjin slowly and patiently applied the unguent to Wu Xingzi's hole. He paid special attention to the creases on the outside and the walls within, covering every inch with a layer of lubricant. As Wu Xingzi's body warmed and melted the oily substance, Guan Shanjin's fingers made wet, squelching sounds inside of him. Wu Xingzi could not help but cover his ears in embarrassment.

The unguent grew quite slippery as it melted, making Wu Xingzi's buttocks become shiny and oily. His skin was smooth and slick to the touch, and his hole gaped open slightly at a perfect finger's width. Glistening lubricant and lewd juices slowly dripped from his hole as it winked slowly at Guan Shanjin, as if welcoming him inside.

"What a hungry old fellow," Guan Shanjin scolded him with a laugh. His speech was somewhat coarse, but his tone was still soft and gentle; his words sounded like those spoken by a caring lover.

Wu Xingzi's hips shuddered, his hole suddenly itching. As he moaned and whimpered, his buttocks unconsciously started trembling. In between the fair, white flesh of his buttocks, his empty little hole clenched. It was immensely enticing, stirring a desire with General Guan to fuck him mercilessly.

Guan Shanjin had been hard for quite some time, to the point where it began to hurt. The head of his thick, savage cock was already oozing fluid, looking even weightier than usual. He dragged Wu Xingzi toward himself by the hips, and the tip of his cock rubbed against his cleft, grinding against the little hole. It clamped tightly upon the head, sucking on it as if eager to invite it in. Guan Shanjin allowed just the tip of his cock to enter, then pulled himself out without warning and brushed his dick against Wu Xingzi's balls.

"It itches..." Wu Xingzi whined pitifully, rocking his hips. His hole ached and tingled, desperately begging for something to soothe it. This itching desire was not only concentrated in his hole, but it also spread through his veins and into his limbs, even creeping into his head. He couldn't hold back his tearful pleas. "Haiwang, Haiwang! Please, help me soothe it, it aches..."

Guan Shanjin's wicked words became more passionate. "You're so obscene. What are we going to do about you?"

He barely pressed half the head of his cock into the hole, staining it with the melted oil. His forehead beaded with sweat and his breathing grew heavy from the effort of holding himself back.

His lean hips thrust against Wu Xingzi's, grinding his thick cock against his lover's pink and tender little member. Two cock heads of contrasting sizes dragged against each other as their shafts rubbed together in tandem. Wu Xingzi bit at the blanket in ecstasy, broken moans continuously tumbling from his throat.

Guan Shanjin was swept away by pleasure too, and he leaned over and wrapped Wu Xingzi in his arms. He incessantly rubbed his hard member against Wu Xingzi's dainty little cock. Perhaps because he'd rarely used it in the past—or maybe he was just born that way—Wu Xingzi's prick was silky smooth, and grinding against it was extremely pleasurable for Guan Shanjin. However, in the end, a cock was a cock; it was hard and slightly flexible, completely different from a soft and slippery hole. The feeling of friction as he thrust against Wu Xingzi's dick gave him overwhelming satisfaction, making Guan Shanjin groan aloud.

Wu Xingzi could barely endure it. Guan Shanjin's passionate moans mixed with his heated breath felt like a blazing fire, sending his body up in flames and turning his brain to mush. He released the blanket from his teeth, turning his head and kissing Guan Shanjin on the lips.

General Guan really was a seductive devil!

It was rare that the man below him initiated a kiss, and Guan Shanjin found no reason to refuse it. He allowed Wu Xingzi to nibble and gnaw at him, sucking on his tongue and refusing to let go. Saliva overflowed, sliding down from the corner of his mouth as they loudly kissed.

"Haiwang... Haiwang..." Adviser Wu kissed and kissed the man on top of him, his body tingling all over. He ground his buttocks against Guan Shanjin's cock as he begged, "I'm aching deep inside. Help me soothe it, please... Help me soothe it..."

"What do you want me to soothe it with?" Guan Shanjin growled, the passion within him about to boil over. The tip of his tongue drew lightly against Wu Xingzi's tongue, then his lips; he then kissed toward his sensitive ear. He sucked and bit on his soft earlobe. "Use your words."

Wu Xingzi was embarrassed, but the flames of desire overwhelmed him, and he was very straightforward in his request. "Your cock... I want your big cock to soothe it..." His buttocks ground enticingly against Guan Shanjin, and his little pink cock rubbed torturously against the thicker one. A large bead of fluid welled up and leaked out from the head of his prick, soaking the blanket.

Guan Shanjin clicked his tongue and slapped Wu Xingzi's ass. A lewd, pained sob came from below him as he grasped those writhing hips, inserting his thick shaft into Wu Xingzi's sopping wet hole.

"Ah—!" Wu Xingzi cried as Guan Shanjin slammed straight into his sensitive spot. He trembled as his orgasm was forced from him.

"You're really as obscene as I said you are!" Guan Shanjin exclaimed. Wu Xingzi's hole convulsed constantly around his cock in the aftershocks of his orgasm. For a moment, Guan Shanjin could not move. It felt as if thousands of little mouths were sucking at his cock at once. It felt so good that his forehead dripped with sweat, his alluring eyes narrowing as he gasped.

"S-slow down," Wu Xingzi pled. He didn't realize how overstimulated he had become. His pleasure didn't decrease even a little after he came; instead, the movement of General Guan's thick, sturdy cock made him so sensitive that he burst into tears.

Guan Shanjin ignored his pleas, grabbing his hips. "Patience," he said softly, "I'm not all the way inside you yet."

Guan Shanjin spread Wu Xingzi's convulsing buttocks apart and thrust his entire cock inside. It felt like he was thrusting right into his stomach. He didn't always enter so fully when he'd fucked Wu Xingzi in the past, but today, he wasn't going to let him off so easily. Pressing down the writhing and crying Adviser Wu, he caressed his soft belly as he pushed himself further inside.

"Ah, ah!" Wu Xingzi cried out sharply, collapsing onto the bed like a dead man. General Guan's cock made part of his stomach bulge out. His little prick ejaculated again, the thin white fluids staining both the blanket and his own belly. A warm hand wiped the fluids away, sweeping past that frightening bulge.

"Don't do this, Haiwang... Have mercy on me!" Wu Xingzi shouted with such force that his entire body shuddered. Together with the aftershock of his orgasms, he was on the verge of fainting.

"Stop spouting nonsense," Guan Shanjin snarled. His chest lay against Adviser Wu's back as he held him around the waist, supporting him. A powerful thigh spread Wu Xingzi's legs apart so that he was practically sitting on Guan Shanjin's cock.

Wu Xingzi propped himself up against the headboard, his slender, fair legs feebly hooking around Guan Shanjin's thighs as the general once again rubbed at his bulging stomach. Before he could make a sound, Guan Shanjin thrust in again, his heavy balls slapping loudly against Wu Xingzi's slippery, smooth buttocks as his cock reached a depth that no one had ever explored. Wu Xingzi howled, his voice quavering. His slender legs went limp, and his toes curled.

Guan Shanjin fucked Wu Xingzi with rhythmic thrusts. The older man could barely make a sound, his hole loosening with the brutal movements. His little hole tried its best to tighten around the savage shaft, but it was being stretched relentlessly. Wu Xingzi could only weakly let the general have his way with him, his abdomen bulging out with every thrust.

However, Guan Shanjin was still not satisfied. His heated palm pressed against Wu Xingzi's swelling belly. It felt like masturbating through a thin layer of skin, and the sensation gave him so much pleasure that his eyes darkened. Guan Shanjin bit harshly into Wu Xingzi's thin neck, trailing bruises and bite marks along his nape. Wu Xingzi groaned at every stinging press of his teeth.

It wasn't long before Wu Xingzi came again. This time, his cum was thin as water. His head tilted all the way back and his cry was soundless. His eyes rolled all the way to the back of his head, looking like he might lose consciousness.

Guan Shanjin did not relent, shoving himself inside again. His palm pressed down harder on Wu Xingzi's stomach. Still in the throes of climax, Wu Xingzi could not withstand such sweet torture. After a few violent convulsions, he lost control of his bladder, piss dripping onto the bed. Stimulated by the pungent odor and the intense clenching of Wu Xingzi's hole around him, Guan Shanjin fell over the edge, delightedly spilling inside of Wu Xingzi.

General Guan ejaculated a substantial amount, the warm cum making Adviser Wu twitch. It took a long time before he finally exhaled and fainted on the bed.

Guan Shanjin did not immediately pull out. He had no idea what was going through his own head. Wu Xingzi was filled with so much cum he looked as though he was three months pregnant. Guan Shanjin caressed the man's belly, turning around and hugging him as he lay on the bed. At the moment, he had no plans on cleaning up the mess they'd made.

Within the bed's canopy, the pungent smell of sex filled the air. The sweet scent of the lubricant still lingered, as well as Guan Shanjin's white sandalwood scent. A faint herbal aroma emanated from Wu Xingzi.

This scent was not exactly pleasant, but to Guan Shanjin, it was intoxicating—he couldn't tear himself away from it. Some part of his heart softened, and he felt a trace of satisfaction along with quite a bit of indignation.

"You really want to leave me?" He hugged Wu Xingzi, his half-hard member wetly sliding out a little. The man sleeping beneath him moaned aloud a couple of times. Snuggling into Guan Shanjin's arms, he fell into a deeper slumber.

Ah, forget it. We'll talk tomorrow, Guan Shanjin thought, kissing the man in his arms. Although he was reluctant to pull out, he got up from the bed to clean up.

After staying in Goose City for a few days, Guan Shanjin apparently had some military duties to handle. After assigning a guard to follow Wu Xingzi, he disappeared.

Wu Xingzi wouldn't let such a rare opportunity go to waste. Waking up early, he headed for the Peng Society with General Guan's guard following behind him.

When the familiar-looking salesman saw that it was Adviser Wu, he approached them with a warm demeanor. "Adviser Wu! Our manager has been thinking about you these past few days."

"I'm grateful that Manager Rancui thinks of me. May I ask if he's available to meet?" Wu Xingzi cupped his hands at him. He had been dreaming about the next issue of *The Pengornisseur* for so long.

"Of course. The manager always reminds us that if we see Adviser Wu, we must invite him in for a chat." The salesman's friendliness made Wu Xingzi bashful, yet happy. It was good to be missed—even more so, he supposed, when fifty coins were involved.

It was evident that General Guan's guard knew what the Peng Society and *The Pengornisseur* were about. He silently followed five steps behind Wu Xingzi. If not for the salesman's glance toward him, Adviser Wu would have forgotten the guard was there.

The salesman recognized this guard. Last month, when Manager Rancui tried to stop the general from traveling to Qingcheng County, they'd exchanged quite a few blows. "And this is?"

"This is..." Wu Xingzi was unable to answer. He looked at the guard apologetically and said, "I've been negligent. Sir, how should I address you?" Wu Xingzi only knew that he was Guan Shanjin's guard.

"I'm Hei-er," the guard replied respectfully, cupping his hands toward the salesman. "The general commanded me to protect Adviser Wu. I fully trust Manager Rancui, but since I can't defy orders, please bear with me."

"Uhh..." The guard was very polite, and the salesman was unable to criticize him on any point. He also recalled all too well the alarming skirmish that had broken out last time they'd met. A few pavilions in the courtyard still needed repairs. "I can bring you along, but when the manager speaks with Adviser Wu, you must stand further away!"

"I understand. Thank you very much."

Since the guard was hell-bent on following him, Wu Xingzi allowed it. He put all his focus on *The Pengornisseur* and Rancui.

The salesman led the two men toward a familiar pavilion. Manager Rancui was already seated within it, sipping his tea. When he looked up and saw Adviser Wu, he revealed an exquisite smile.

"Adviser Wu." Putting down the teacup, Rancui stood up and cupped his hands at Wu Xingzi in welcome. Looking behind Wu Xingzi, his smile turned colder. "Commander Hei. We meet again."

"It's Hei-er. I caused you a disturbance a while ago." Hei-er bowed his head, and his expression couldn't be made out. He stood at a distance, but his voice was loud enough to hear. Rancui snorted, an icy look on his face; he then turned to Wu Xingzi and gave him a friendly smile.

"Please take a seat, Adviser Wu," Rancui said. "I haven't seen you in a month."

"Thank you for thinking of me." Wu Xingzi hurriedly cupped his hands in thanks, cautiously taking a seat. "Manager, I'd like to ask about *The Pengornisseur*..." He turned his head and glanced at Hei-er. He lowered his voice before carefully continuing. "I was unable to come and collect last month's *Pengornisseur*. Here are the fifty coins for next month's edition." He furtively procured a small coin pouch and pushed it toward Rancui. His face flushed red, and he felt uneasy and excited at the same time—as if he'd been caught doing something naughty.

"What do you mean, exactly?" Rancui did not accept the little coin pouch. He gestured at the salesman outside the pavilion.

The salesman instantly understood and walked over to Hei-er, to distract him with conversation.

"I'd like to continue receiving *The Pengornisseur.*" Adviser Wu's face reddened further, but he was very determined. Rancui eyed him for a moment before the smile on his face turned even more radiant.

"Didn't you plan to become life partners with General Guan?" Rancui had been furious from the moment he brought it up. A month and a half ago, after confirming with Adviser Wu that it was only a tryst, he had immediately handled the matter with General Guan. It ended up causing some trouble in Nanjiang. Although the small commotion would not affect the lives of the civilians, Guan Shanjin had still spent some effort settling the matter.

That little incident with General Guan was supposed to be a secret, but Rancui knew about it. A man whose heart was already occupied with other matters was unsuited for making friends through the Peng Society. However, this was the exact reason Rancui's boss wanted Guan Shanjin to participate—he wanted to stir the pot. He had said that if someone like Guan Shanjin could meet his life partner through the Peng Society, then the society's future success would be even more assured.

Rancui didn't know if the general would be able to find a life partner, but it was undeniable that Guan Shanjin had brought trouble to the Peng Society's members. He'd left the accountant in Sushui Village brokenhearted, and that poor accountant had ended up marrying a woman. Two days ago, Rancui had received the dowry cakes, and in a fit of anger, he'd eaten them all. His stomach still ached slightly.

Seeing as General Guan never had true feelings for anyone, Rancui thought that after settling the commotion in Nanjiang, he would simply forget about Adviser Wu. Not only did he not forget he even returned to Goose City and demolished half Rancui's courtyard. Pointing his Chenyuan Sword at Rancui's throat, he threatened him with a cold smile that Rancui shouldn't reach his arm out too far, or he would chop it off.

Truthfully, Rancui had completely lost all hope. Especially after Wu Xingzi hadn't come the previous month to collect *The Pengornisseur*, he had thought that perhaps Adviser Wu would send dowry cakes—hopefully a little blander, so Rancui would not suffer a stomachache after eating them. Who would have guessed...?

"No, no," Wu Xingzi said, waving his hands as he blushed. "General Guan and I are not on the same path in life. How could I ever go above my station like that?"

"Adviser Wu doesn't have to be so modest. In my eyes, General Guan is the one going above *his* station." After demolishing the courtyard, the general had tossed enough money at them to build a whole new manor. However, that did not quell Rancui's anger. He had done scrupulous work for the Peng Society these past ten years; he had never imagined that in two short months, two members would have their hearts broken at the hand of one man! What a slap to Rancui's face!

"Manager, can I collect last month's edition?" Wu Xingzi did not have any interest in arguing over who was going above his station. All he was concerned about was *The Pengornisseur*.

"Of course, that's not a problem. However, you're still living with General Guan, correct?" Rancui glanced over at Hei-er. The guard still had his head lowered. The salesman chewed his ear off, but he still stood there motionlessly, towering over the salesman. Rancui did not know if he could hear their conversation.

"Yes, yes..." Wu Xingzi sighed as he rubbed at his nose. He was a little unhappy, but soon he perked up again. "He's about to return to Horse-Face City. Why don't I come back and collect *The Pengornisseur* once he leaves?"

"We can do that," Rancui replied with a smile. However, he was very curious, and could not help asking: "General Guan's departure doesn't bother you?"

In fact, it seemed that Wu Xingzi looked forward to it. Although Rancui disliked Guan Shanjin, he could not deny that the man was very attractive. He was very successful in matters of romance—who knew how many hearts he had trampled?

But surprisingly, Adviser Wu didn't look as though he had fallen for the general.

"Even if it did bother me, he still has to leave, and I don't want to move away from Qingcheng County. You'll laugh hearing this, but I've already selected my gravesite. Qingcheng County is a great location for my ultimate resting place."

Adviser Wu's wistful expression made it seem like he was describing a scenic spot, rather than his grave.

"I never thought that Adviser Wu was so free-spirited," Rancui said. Wu Xingzi had struck him as a lonely man of great affection. He thought he was the type to fall in love easily, who would struggle to shake those feelings without difficulty.

Looking at him now, not only did Wu Xingzi not seem to have any great affection for Guan Shanjin, it was as though he did not even have a place for him in his heart.

"You think I'm free-spirited?" Wu Xingzi blinked, picking up his teacup and drinking from it. He gave a wry smile. "Not really. I'm not free-spirited. It's just that it's impossible for some people to be together forever—so why go through all the trouble?" This sounded logical, but there was a poignancy to it.

Rancui did not respond to Wu Xingzi's statement. Instead, he asked Wu Xingzi to enjoy the snacks.

The two of them chatted for a little while longer. When another Peng Society member arrived, Rancui pushed the coin pouch back into Wu Xingzi's hand, speaking gently, "Adviser Wu, take these fifty coins back. It was the Peng Society's inadequacy that allowed General Guan to find you. Fortunately, you weren't harmed, but the Peng Society has to compensate you. Until you find your life partner, *The Pengornisseur* will be provided to you for free. Please accept it."

"How can I accept that?" Wu Xingzi anxiously pushed the coin pouch back to Rancui, but Rancui had already stood up, signaling that he would not take the money.

"Adviser Wu, you're an important customer of the Peng Society. Don't worry about it—and please accept our apologies. The cost of this little book is nothing worth mentioning. I hope to hear good news from you soon." Rancui motioned the salesman over, instructing him to lead Wu Xingzi out.

Seeing that he was unable to object, Wu Xingzi cupped his hands and thanked him. He didn't leave until Rancui had disappeared from sight.

When he exited the Peng Society, it was already a quarter to two in the afternoon. Wu Xingzi rubbed his belly. Although he'd had some snacks and tea, his stomach still felt empty. He said apologetically to Hei-er, "Commander Hei, I've been inconsiderate. You must be hungry. Why don't we look for a food stall and fill our stomachs?"

"The general instructed that once you're done at the Peng Society, I must bring you to the Restaurant of Songs to meet him. Also, you may simply address me as Hei-er."

"Uh…" Adviser Wu scratched at his nose. He was only a commoner, an adviser of a little county. How could he just call the commander by his name?

"You're involved with the general, so you're my master. There's no need to be bothered by it." Hei-er bowed his head, his tone respectful, and it made Wu Xingzi feel even more baffled. Seeming to notice his unease, Hei-er dropped the subject and led Wu Xingzi toward the Restaurant of Songs.

The Restaurant of Songs was one of Goose City's most famous restaurants. It was also the oldest one, and its prices were reasonable. A meal with three dishes, one soup, and half a pot of rice could be purchased for around ten coins. The cooking style was simple and grounded, and the restaurant never cut corners or did things carelessly. Wu Xingzi had eaten there twice before. Guan Shanjin's choice of restaurant made him feel relieved, and he grew even hungrier.

Although it was past mealtime, the Restaurant of Songs still bustled with customers. Seeing Hei-er and Wu Xingzi, a server came up immediately and welcomed them cordially. "Hello, gentlemen. You're here for a meal?"

The Restaurant of Songs had something that set them apart from other restaurants: they had a license to brew alcohol, so they could supply their own liquor without purchasing from other merchants. Their exclusive Kongsang liquor was brewed from mulberries. Its color was similar to wine, but a little lighter, like carnelian. It tasted slightly sour and sweet, and held a lingering spiciness. It was warm and mild upon drinking, but the throat tingled as the liquid slid down, feeling a little piquant. It heated the stomach like a glowing fire, bringing a kind of comfort to the drinker. Many customers came just to sample the liquor and didn't order any food.

"We're looking for Guan-gongzi," Hei-er told the server.

"Guan-gongzi?" The server thought about it for a moment, and his smile turned warmer. "Guan-gongzi is waiting for the two of you in the Room of Rain. Please follow me."

They climbed the stairs all the way to the top. The building that housed the Restaurant of Songs was the tallest in Goose City, with a bird's-eye view of the surroundings below.

There were only four rooms on the top floor, and they were all very spacious. The Room of Rain was the first room on the left. It had the best view, so it was no wonder the server smiled until his eyes crinkled.

Opening the door, the first thing Wu Xingzi saw was Guan Shanjin's tall and slender figure. The general sat by the window, dressed in black. Hearing the door open, he turned his head toward them. His beguiling eyes looked hazy, with just a faint glimmer in them. Seeing Wu Xingzi, they curved slightly. Although he did not smile, his face looked even more enchanting than if he had. His expression held a lingering affection. Wu Xingzi couldn't drag his eyes away. His face flushed deeply, and he practically floated toward Guan Shanjin.

Only once he smelled the general's cool scent did Wu Xingzi stop and stammer, "H-have you been waiting for long?"

"Not too long. I've only had one flask of liquor." Guan Shanjin reached out to pull him into his arms, stealing a kiss.

Wu Xingzi could taste the sweet and sour flavor of the liquor on Guan Shanjin's lips. He had yet to drink anything, but he already felt slightly intoxicated. Perhaps it was because he knew Guan Shanjin was about to leave, but Wu Xingzi started to treasure their time spent together.

He took the initiative to lick across Guan Shanjin's lips. His tongue was promptly caught and sucked upon. He only started struggling once he was short of breath.

Guan Shanjin released him. "Why are you so obedient today?" he asked, raising his brow. Adviser Wu lowered his head shyly and did not speak.

Guan Shanjin had no intention of forcing an answer out of him. He was in a good mood from having drunk a flask of wine. He asked the waiter to serve the dishes and called Wu Xingzi to eat while he sat by the window, drinking. Next to him sat a Go board, which he contentedly played with.

Soon, the entire table of dishes was wiped clean. Wu Xingzi patted his belly in satisfaction and sipped his tea. He seemed rather interested in Guan Shanjin's game, dragging a chair over to watch.

"Do you know how to play Go?" Guan Shanjin was playing both sides, the black and white pieces strewn all over the board. However, the white pieces seemed to have the advantage, hiding their power and biding their time. Without any warning, the white pieces engulfed the black pieces.

"Isn't it boring to play by yourself?" Wu Xingzi asked. The white pieces would know what the black pieces were going to do and vice versa. Wouldn't victory be decided before the battle even began?

Guan Shanjin smiled. "Playing Go by oneself uses the same logic as arranging the formation of one's army," he explained. "During war, you cannot focus only on your own formation; you must understand the enemy's formation as well. Mapping out a strategy now means success in the future. A battle does not determine who has the superior martial arts, but who is more astute, more vicious, who can react faster, and who is more blessed."

"Who is more blessed?" Wu Xingzi tilted his head in confusion. He could understand what Guan Shanjin said at the beginning but relying on luck seemed foolish. Fortune was out of the control of mortals—they could only pray to the heavens.

"I didn't think that Guan Shanjin believed in such mystical things." He didn't realize that he'd said that out loud. Guan Shanjin laughed cheerfully. "Why wouldn't I believe in them? Going into battle is a risky endeavor. Once we're there, we never think about coming back. In this world, there's no such thing as a perfect strategy or formation. Men are fallible; there's always bound to be an exploitable weakness. If I'm speculating on their next move, won't they be doing the same to me? After seeing so much of life and death, I've learned that many victories and losses don't depend on how detailed a strategy is, but who is more blessed. It's difficult to put into words, but most of us do give credence to the mystical."

"Oh, I see." Wu Xingzi nodded, although he didn't fully comprehend Guan Shanjin's explanation. He watched as the white pieces finally demolished the black pieces, while Guan Shanjin looked gentler and more relaxed than ever. There was faint amusement and unlimited charm in his eyes.

"This game is modeled after the battle where I conquered Nanman. I captured the king of Nanman and delivered him to their capital. Our cavalry stampeded into the king's throne room, and the eldest son of the king had no choice but to surrender. I also conveniently helped deal with a few of his disobedient brothers." Only a small pile of black pieces remained at the southernmost part of the board. They looked pitiful and lonesome as they lay scattered.

"Do you miss those days? Killing your enemies on the battlefield?" Wu Xingzi felt that these weren't quite the right words, but he'd noticed a hint of pride in Guan Shanjin's eyes.

Nanjiang had been calm for five years, and under the defense of the Southern Garrison, it was unlikely that Nanman would be able to cause any major trouble for the next twenty or thirty years.

Other than the occasional suppression of bandits, the soldiers who had grown accustomed to war had to feel a little aimless.

"Why would I? Battles are treacherous, and one careless mistake can mean your death in an unfamiliar place. The price civilians have to pay is even greater. Who enjoys war?" Guan Shanjin sighed as he separated the black and white pieces. "Want to play a game with me?"

"I'm not good at Go." Wu Xingzi blushed slightly. He had played Go for a few years with his father. However, he was very young at the time, and he only played for fun. After the flood, he was alone. It wasn't exactly busy in the magistrate's office, but he had no desire to play Go; it no longer held any enjoyment for him.

"It doesn't matter, we can just play it for fun." He pushed the white pieces toward Wu Xingzi. "I'll even give you a twenty-five-piece advantage."

"Thank you, thank you." Adviser Wu rubbed at the tip of his nose and decided not to stand on ceremony. He'd seen what was going on in the previous game, and he knew he couldn't compete with Guan Shanjin's skills, but this was just playing a game with the general.

After they'd arranged the pieces properly, the game started. In less than fifteen minutes, Guan Shanjin had all but annihilated Wu Xingzi. It looked like he had no chance to recover at all, holding out until his very last breath. It happened to be Wu Xingzi's turn, and he randomly put a piece down, not looking at the board at all.

This was not the first time he had done this. After placing his twenty-five pieces, Wu Xingzi played with a sort of relaxed and carefree attitude. Not only did he not speculate about Guan Shanjin's strategy, he didn't even look to see where Guan Shanjin placed his pieces. Adviser Wu wasn't just relaxed, he was completely detached from the game, and not the least bit concerned about the results.

"Why did you make that move?" Guan Shanjin asked, weighing the piece in his hand. His pale fingers stood out against the shining black pieces made of eye-catching agate. Guan Shanjin's beautiful brow knitted in concern. His expression wasn't unhappy, but he seemed to be deep in thought.

"There's not really a reason. I'm bad at Go. I just put it down where there was a space." Wu Xingzi looked down and rubbed his nose, face flushed.

His father told him once that his nature was unsuitable for Go. It had nothing to do with talent; his personality was too indifferent, and he had no hunger for victory. For a person like him, winning or losing did not matter, only pleasing one's opponent.

"Is that so?" Guan Shanjin tossed the piece back into the box. "It's impossible for you to win now. I'll beat you in seven moves. We should just stop here."

Sighing a breath of relief, Wu Xingzi happily packed up the Go set. He was more interested in the material used to make the set than in playing the game itself. Reluctant to put the pieces down, he touched them a few more times before packing them all up.

"Would you like a drink?"

When Adviser Wu emptied his hands of the Go pieces, Guan Shanjin pulled him into his arms, and both men admired the scenery outside the window.

CHAPTER SIX

IN VINO
VERITAS

"*If you don't want me to leave, then I won't.*"

"*No, you can't... You can't...*" Wu Xingzi's tears continued to flow. "*You have to rush to the capital for the imperial examination,*" he mumbled. "*I can't cause you any delays...*"

Rush to the capital for the imperial examination? Guan Shanjin's brows creased, and his mood turned bitter.

The person Wu Xingzi was crying over, the person he dearly missed—wasn't him?

D ESPITE THE BLEAK WINTER, the distant mountains were still a dark, lush green.

"I only drink a little bit every now and then." Wu Xingzi licked his lips, sounding a little regretful.

"If you want to drink, just drink. I'm here. Hauling a drunkard back home is no problem for me." Laughing gently, Guan Shanjin pressed a cup into Wu Xingzi's hand and filled it up with Kongsang liquor. "This is finely aged liquor. You wouldn't be able to drink it even if you had the money. The owner of the Restaurant of Songs is a great friend of Su Yang—he spared me a quart and a half. There's no more, even if you wanted it."

The fragrance of the drink filled their noses, with its distinct, sour-sweet note of mulberry. Wu Xingzi recalled the taste that he had licked from Guan Shanjin's lips a moment ago and hungered for more. He quickly drank a large mouthful, tasting it carefully with the tip of his tongue.

As expected, the flavor was rich yet mellow. Compared to the common Kongsang liquor available in the restaurant, there was an additional silkiness to this aged version. The refreshing spiciness as it entered the throat felt as smooth as a river pebble, yet there was no loss of intensity.

"It's very tasty." In less than three mouthfuls, Wu Xingzi drank the cup dry. He smacked his lips, his face reddening. His gentle eyes had brightened, like they had been washed clean. His stomach felt comfortably warm, and the heat soon traveled through his veins and diffused throughout his body. The warm glow wrapped around him like a thick blanket, so cozy that it made him giggle.

"Another cup?" Guan Shanjin filled Wu Xingzi's glass to the brim again. The adviser smiled foolishly, not rejecting the general's offer. He emptied his cup with another sip.

Adviser Wu ended up downing three cups. Drunk and dazed, he nuzzled his red face in Guan Shanjin's chest, mumbling about how warm he felt.

Taking the cup back, Guan Shanjin poured himself some of the liquor to drink. As he patted the disgruntled man in his arms, he looked out at the mountains.

The Kongsang liquor was dry, tart, and sweet, and its aftereffects were very strong. If not for Guan Shanjin's formidable strength— and the fact that he did not get drunk easily—there'd be no way he could remain clearheaded after finishing a flask and a half by himself.

Wu Xingzi fussed about for a while, finally burying his face into Guan Shanjin's neck. In a drunken stupor, he sniffed at the general, murmuring, "You smell good... I like your scent..."

"If you like it, I'll have someone prepare a box for you." Wu Xingzi's attentions were making his sensitive neck itch, but Guan Shanjin allowed him to continue.

His gentle promise made Wu Xingzi tremble. "No need. I... I'm all right..." The adviser's giddy smile faded away, and he hunched over dejectedly.

"What's wrong?" Unease welled in Guan Shanjin's chest. Looking down, he brushed the fleshy tip of Wu Xingzi's nose. Out of nowhere, he found Wu Xingzi's ordinary face—now red with drunkenness—adorable. But Guan Shanjin wasn't especially bothered when this thought flashed through his mind. As long as Wu Xingzi carried a hint of Mr. Lu, it was only natural to find him pleasing to the eye.

"You don't have to give me anything..." Wu Xingzi scrunched his nose, his face earnest and a little dazed. He seemed worried, repeating, "Don't give me anything. You mustn't give me anything."

Guan Shanjin tightened his arms around him. "Why? Don't you like the incense I use?" He was too curious not to probe further. "Tell me the reason, and I'll decide whether I'll give it to you."

Perplexed, Wu Xingzi blinked. "Tell you the reason?" He reached out and wrapped his arms around Guan Shanjin's neck, pulling that beautiful face closer and staring at him in concentration. He smiled bashfully as he admired Guan Shanjin.

"What's wrong?" Guan Shanjin asked.

"You're really handsome," Wu Xingzi sighed, emotional. Pouting, he placed a kiss on Guan Shanjin's petal-pink lips. He could not stop smiling foolishly.

"Do you like me?" Guan Shanjin asked, setting his cup down. Feeling cheerful, he snaked one arm around Wu Xingzi's slender waist and pinched his chin with his other hand.

Wu Xingzi giggled. Looking at him for a moment, his eyes low-ered feebly, but he didn't answer the general's question.

This was starkly different from his usual demeanor. Normally, Wu Xingzi was shy and timid. He had an inferiority complex, he was artlessly blunt, and he always acted like nothing troubled him. Even when the villagers talked about him behind his back, it didn't bother him. He never let anything affect him. Not even Guan Shanjin could spur him to selfish behavior. All he really thought about was *The Pengornisseur*.

But now he looked dispirited, avoiding Guan Shanjin's gaze. He seemed to have sobered slightly, his eyes carrying a trace of desolate sadness. His entire body stiffened, staying silent as he bowed his head.

The general's intuition told him that this sorrow had something to do with Wu Xingzi's nonchalant attitude. He could not resist lifting Wu Xingzi's face up with his fingers, coaxing him gently, "Why are you sad all of a sudden? Tell me what's wrong."

"Tell you?" Wu Xingzi blinked slowly, staring straight at Guan Shanjin. A moment later, he opened his mouth. "Aren't you already leaving?"

"You really want me to leave?" Guan Shanjin's expression dark-ened as he recalled the conversation he'd had with Adviser Wu a few days ago. This old fellow wanted him to hurry off so he could go collect *The Pengornisseur*, and he still thought that Guan Shanjin was none the wiser. He had purposely assigned Hei-er to follow him—as a warning to Rancui, as well. General Guan had yet to tire of Adviser Wu, so nobody should even think about touching what was his.

"No...I don't want you to leave." A tear suddenly rolled down Wu Xingzi's face. Guan Shanjin's anger dissipated, his heart aching; he held Wu Xingzi to console him, patting his back.

Other than in bed, Wu Xingzi had never cried in front of Guan Shanjin before. He didn't seem prone to tears. Guan Shanjin had asked Li Jian, Qingcheng County's magistrate, many things about Adviser Wu—he had a rather thorough understanding of this man. Adviser Wu was friendly yet detached. He was very caring toward everyone, but he also never let anything affect him emotionally. He'd been living in solitude for twenty-odd years, and he led a calm, ordinary life. He'd even happily picked out a gravesite a few years ago.

"If you don't want me to leave, then I won't." Guan Shanjin hadn't expected Wu Xingzi's tears to make his heart hurt so much. Wu Xingzi outwardly seemed so unaffected by his departure, yet he felt such a loss internally. It made the general feel terribly tender toward him. Kissing him softly, he said, "I'm not in a hurry to return to Horse-Face City. Man Yue can handle things. It's no trouble for me to accompany you for a few more months—don't cry."

"No, you can't... You can't..." Wu Xingzi submitted to his embrace, his tears continuing to flow. Soon, Guan Shanjin's chest was wet. The warm tears felt like a blistering flame, painfully burning his skin.

"I can. I decide everything in Horse-Face City. You don't have to worry." A gentle kiss landed on top of Wu Xingzi's head. Guan Shanjin felt a little panicked. He tried his best to make a promise to Wu Xingzi, but he still could not stop the adviser's tears.

Adviser Wu sobbed softly. "You have to rush to the capital for the imperial examination," he mumbled. "I can't cause you any delays... I'll wait for you. I'll wait for your return. Whether it's one year or two—or even ten—I'll be waiting. You will definitely return with honors!"

Rush to the capital for the imperial examination? Guan Shanjin's brow creased, and his mood turned bitter.

The person Wu Xingzi was crying over, the person he dearly missed—wasn't him?

Who exactly *was* this person? He knew very well that ever since Wu Xingzi's parents had passed away when he was sixteen, there had been no one else by his side. He'd had a fleeting crush on the tofu seller, Ansheng, but once he knew that Ansheng and Constable Zhang were life partners, he'd put those feelings to bed. It was almost as if he had immediately and completely forgotten about Ansheng.

But it turned out that Wu Xingzi was not so uncaring—he already had someone in his heart!

Who the hell is he talking about?! General Guan was furious. Pressing his hand against his chest, he nearly tasted blood.

Adviser Wu, drunk and disoriented as he was, only choked pitifully as he betrayed his true feelings. "I-I know that your greatest wish is to bring honor to your family name, Zaizong-xiong. You're so talented and smart—this little Goose City can't trap a mighty bird like you. You're a legendary fish in such a tiny pond. You should go to the capital and become the top scholar!"

Zaizong-xiong? This name sounds awfully familiar...

Guan Shanjin did not interrupt Wu Xingzi's chattering. He mentally searched for the identity of this man as he pieced together the story tumbling from Wu Xingzi's lips.

"You don't have to worry about travel expenses. I have some silver ingots saved up, and I'm the only one left in my family. You can take the money." Wu Xingzi lifted his head, his face full of sincerity.

Guan Shanjin looked at the earnest face in front of him. Although Wu Xingzi's gentle, shining eyes gazed at him, his thoughts were captured by another man entirely. Guan Shanjin could not hold himself back from pinching Xingzi's cheek.

"Ow!" Wu Xingzi cried out in pain. Guan Shanjin did not control his strength, nearly leaving a bruise on Adviser Wu's face. He hurriedly let go, feeling utterly irate.

Since Wu Xingzi mentioned going to the capital to participate in an imperial examination, this was clearly not something that had happened in recent years. General Guan was well aware of how little money Adviser Wu made. Who knew how long it had taken him to accumulate a measly ten taels?

It sounded like this Zaizong-xiong had not returned from his trip to the capital. Perhaps he'd died on his journey. Maybe he'd failed the exam and was too ashamed to return. It was possible he'd got lost in the luxury of the capital. Perhaps he'd achieved great results in the exams and found an ideal marriage, burying Wu Xingzi in the back of his mind.

However, the name sounded familiar to Guan Shanjin. If he recalled correctly, a man named Zaizong-xiong had entered the emperor's court. His position was quite high, at least a fourth-level official or higher.

What right did this disloyal man have to let Wu Xingzi pine over him for so many years? What right did he have to make him cry?

He looked down to see Wu Xingzi coltishly nuzzling into his arms. His face was tearstained and his eyes were tinted red, but at least he had stopped crying.

Guan Shanjin pondered over it for a moment and decided to further investigate the matter. He could vaguely guess that something had happened to Wu Xingzi back then, and that was why he'd become so unwilling to be close with anyone. That Go match had bothered him. It was true that some people did have an aloof personality and were not interested in competition, letting the chips fall where they may. However, Wu Xingzi was not simply going with the flow of things. He did not plan on asking for anything, ever; being so passive was the only way he could be at ease. Whether it was a Go game, a marriage, his livelihood, or even his own reputation, the first thing he looked for was an escape route. He would never take a step forward of his own volition.

Even though he liked Ansheng, going so far as to buy a jade hairpin in preparation for his confession, in the end, he could only bury his feelings with the hairpin under his bed. If he needed money, he would dig it up and sell it; he was not reluctant to part with it. Wu Xingzi had not hidden this matter from Guan Shanjin. In fact, he spoke about it openly in front of him as he brought the pin out. He had looked at the jade hairpin, sighing, "The color of this jade is really quite nice. How many coins do you think I could sell it for?"

"You're not keeping it?" Guan Shanjin took the dirty box, casually sizing up the dull object. This pin looked to him like something an older maid in his house would use. However, for Wu Xingzi, it was a treasure.

"I wanted to keep it, but..." Wu Xingzi bit his lip, darting a swift glance at his wardrobe next to him. *There's no point in holding on to this thing now that I have the pengornis drawings. Keeping it buried is such a waste.*

Guan Shanjin noticed this but did not take it to heart. He had no idea what Adviser Wu was currently thinking.

"Don't sell it yet. Bring it to Horse-Face City! Horse-Face City doesn't have a lot of luxuries like Goose City does. Even though it's common jade, you'll be able to sell it for a higher price." Guan Shanjin replaced the lid on the box, brushing the dirt away before returning it to Wu Xingzi.

"Horse-Face City?" Wu Xingzi blinked, and then burst out into laughter.

At the time, Guan Shanjin had yet to mention leaving Qingcheng County, and Wu Xingzi hadn't brought up the subject.

Thinking about it now, something didn't seem quite right. Guan Shanjin did not understand how he could he have been so blind to everything. No matter what, Adviser Wu was most similar to Mr. Lu out of all the men he had found, and he wanted to keep him by his side for a little while longer.

In any case, he had not paid close enough attention. General Guan had mixed feelings about it all. He signaled to Hei-er, who had been standing guard outside, to come in. He instructed him to bring a basin of warm water as well as a clean washcloth.

Not realizing that his mood was different from usual, Guan Shanjin replaced the liquor with tea, feeding Wu Xingzi little mouthfuls. He had already formulated a plan.

"Xingzi." He called Adviser Wu's name gently. The man in his arms shivered, bashfully lifting his head up in acknowledgment.

"You said that you wanted to cover my traveling expenses. How much?"

For scholars who lived farther away from the capital, the local authorities provided a certain amount in travel subsidies, as well as the use of a horse. For the scholars of Goose City, it was a three-month journey to the capital. Ordinary scholars tended not to know how to ride a horse, so most would choose to ride in an ox cart or even walk there. Fifteen silver taels were usually provided to finance their expedition.

Still, expenses in the capital were high. Although the journey itself might not cost fifteen silver taels, staying in the capital in preparation for the exam, as well as while one waited for the release of the test results, required a large sum of money. It was not uncommon for people to have spent so much on their excursion to the capital that they were unable to make their way back home.

Hearing Guan Shanjin's question, Wu Xingzi squinted. He seemed to be studying the man in front of him with great concentration. Thinking that Wu Xingzi had sobered up, Guan Shanjin was a little disappointed that he might not be able to get to the bottom of this.

But he was surprised to see a smile bloom on Wu Xingzi's face. "I have eight silver taels. Just take them all, Zaizong-xiong," he replied earnestly. "It's not much, so don't worry about it. You have great talent—you can't just stay among us commoners."

"Eight taels?" Guan Shanjin's voice deepened a little. This amount was not a small sum for Wu Xingzi. He currently had less than ten silver taels in his stash!

"Zaizong-xiong, if it's not enough, I'll go borrow some more for you." Wu Xingzi's tone was eager, not wanting his Zaizong-xiong to be unhappy. "The county has some money set aside for scholars. Nobody touches it. We're waiting for the day a candidate from the county can successfully participate in the imperial examinations. The taels are to aid him in bringing some honor to our county. Although you're from Goose City, I'll try and mention it to the magistrate. He might lend me some."

Wu Xingzi froze after saying that, looking dazed. Then he mumbled, "I-I b-borrowed fifteen taels for you, Zaizong-xiong. I know you will achieve great results in the imperial examination, but I... Zaizong-xiong, did you get married? Are you never coming back?"

Married? Guan Shanjin felt a pain in his heart as Wu Xingzi remained submerged in the ocean of his memories. Guan Shanjin opened his mouth, wanting to pull him to the surface. However, he was too slow, and Adviser Wu continued.

"I still remember the first time I saw you, Zaizong-xiong. It was spring, and the peach blossoms outside Goose City were in bloom. I was delivering a letter on behalf of the magistrate and saw you dressed in a Confucian robe. You stood there like a pine tree amongst the peach blossoms, looking far off into the distance. Can you tell me what you were looking at? I've always wanted to ask, but I never dared. I didn't want to startle you."

Wu Xingzi's face glowed softly. Guan Shanjin could easily picture how this Zaizong-xiong had enchanted a young Wu Xingzi. Using the gentlest words, he described the man like he was the world's most beautiful, colorful gem.

General Guan could not help but recall the day he saw Mr. Lu for the first time. The only thing that stood out against the dull gray surroundings was a figure dressed in white, smiling at him. He looked just like the Banished Immortal, Li Bai. The sight alone was more than enough to leave Guan Shanjin dumbstruck.

"After that, I often found excuses to go to Goose City. I only saw you amongst the peach trees twice out of ten trips. I thought perhaps you were the god of the peach blossoms, and it was only due to the good fortune I'd accumulated in my previous life that I could see you. But the peach blossoms were about to wilt, and I was so very anxious! So I gathered up my courage and spoke to you, Zaizong-xiong..." Wu Xingzi chuckled faintly, looking very embarrassed. "Ah, that was the bravest thing I had ever done. Fortunately, Zaizong-xiong, you were very kind with me, and you didn't mind that I had offended you."

"Why would I mind? Anyone can discern your thoughts when you act so foolishly," Guan Shanjin snorted, feeling resentful. Wu Xingzi's contented appearance irritated him, so he leaned in and bit his nose.

"Ow! Zaizong-xiong, why do you keep biting me today?" Wu Xingzi whined, covering his nose. Although he was a little shy, there was no dishonesty in his behavior; it was clear that he was used to interacting like this with Zaizong-xiong.

"Continue what you were saying," Guan Shanjin ordered, extremely gloomy. Adviser Wu had never whined like this to the general before.

"Continue?" Blinking, Wu Xingzi obediently continued, "After that, we became good friends. Zaizong-xiong, you're gentle and knowledgeable, and your presence is captivating. You shouldn't be trapped in a tiny place like this. My heart aches for your hardships—neither of us has any family left. In this crowd of people, who can understand that loneliness? Don't be afraid. I'll care for you. I always will."

"As you cared and cared, you fell in love?" Guan Shanjin's voice was glum. Hei-er just happened to return with the basin and washcloth right then. Guan Shanjin glared at him fiercely, making the guard break out in a cold sweat. He swiftly put the items down and scurried away.

"Why are you angry?" Wu Xingzi hunched his shoulders, shivering. He seemed to be sobering up as he stared at Guan Shanjin's face. "Hey, you're really good looking. You smell nice, too." He buried his nose in Guan Shanjin's neck, sniffing in satisfaction.

"I'm not your Zaizong-xiong." Guan Shanjin pushed him away, soaking the washcloth before wringing it dry and wiping Wu Xingzi's face and neck. Adviser Wu moaned in pleasure, and he could not stop shifting about in the general's arms.

"Look at you. How useless. You deserve to be abandoned."

Wu Xingzi giggled. He found a comfortable position and lay there, not moving a muscle. There was no point in trying to reason with a drunkard. Guan Shanjin could only sit there and stew in his own anger. He thought hard, trying to recall every minister of the court. He decided that once he found out who this Zaizong person was, he would not let him off easily.

"Originally, I didn't realize I had feelings for you." Wu Xingzi tightened his arm around Guan Shanjin's trim waist. "Wouldn't it be great if I had stayed that way?" he said morosely.

"But in the end, you knew. That was why you were willing to give him so many taels, right? You foolish old man!" Guan Shanjin scratched gently at Wu Xingzi's nose.

"I didn't expect you to like me. Although it's allowed in Great Xia, and many people have committed to being life partners...you're going to be an official. I don't want to make things difficult for you. But...when I gave you the taels, you gave me a perfume sachet. I'd seen that perfume sachet before. It was always tied on your waist, embroidered with pine trees. A stern yet elegant pine tree that remains upright in winter—it was just like the figure I once saw amongst the peach blossoms."

Near the end, Wu Xingzi's voice deepened, sounding vaguely weepy. His eyes reddened, but tears did not fall. Instead, he said, "I remember you told me that your mother had sewn it for you, and it was the only thing you had left to remember her by. Your parents were old when they had you, and they always pampered you. They hired the best teachers for you, giving you the best possible life. Although your mother's eyesight wasn't good, she still sewed such a lovely perfume sachet for you. You gave it to me as a memento, asking me to wait for your return, saying that you would come back and take care of me...that you would definitely take care of me..."

Wu Xingzi exhaled heavily, remaining in a daze for quite some time.

"Don't think about it anymore. It's all in the past. You're drunk, you should sleep it off. If not, you'll get a headache later." Guan Shanjin was about to tap a pressure point to put him to sleep. He could roughly guess what came next in Wu Xingzi's story without hearing it. That Zaizong-xiong, who'd promised to come back and take care of him, had not come back in the end; instead, he'd married a woman and had a child. He'd risen rapidly in the court, and he had no plans to ever return those twenty-odd taels to Wu Xingzi.

"No, no... I believe you! I really believe you!" Wu Xingzi became agitated, clutching Guan Shanjin's hand tightly. His grip was so strong that even the battle-hardened general winced in pain.

Wu Xingzi's eyes were unfocused, but they were bright, and his breathing was fast and hurried. "I carried that perfume sachet with me every day. I was afraid that people would ask about it when they saw it, so I even sewed a bag to store it in, and I kept it right next to my skin," he rambled. "Every day I looked at that perfume sachet, remembering your face, wondering exactly what you were gazing at in the peach blossom trees. Why did I happen across you? I missed you every day, praying to the heavens to let you pass your exam in one try. I never wished to be life partners with you. I understand that the court can be treacherous to navigate, and you have to be flexible. It was enough for me to simply be next to you." He sounded as if he was sobbing, but no tears fell.

"I waited for a year, but I didn't hear any news from you. That was fine—the capital is far away. After your success in the examinations, you were probably occupied with many things. You had no family in Goose City, and it was normal to not have any news delivered back home. I waited for another year, and another year... Three winters passed, and I was scared, worried that something terrible might have happened to you. However, I told myself to remain calm, since you were a person blessed with good fortune; you might just have been very busy." Adviser Wu paused again. He had a faraway look in his eyes as he shook his head slightly. His hold on Guan Shanjin's hand tightened even further. His nails left crescent marks on the general's fair skin, nearly tearing into flesh.

Guan Shanjin did not interrupt. He could see that Wu Xingzi was possessed by his emotions. If he did not allow him to let them out, they might overwhelm him entirely.

It took some time before Wu Xingzi spoke again. He sounded soft and hoarse, as if he dreaded what came next. "During the spring of the fourth year, the peach trees bloomed. Since I missed you, I took a walk through the blossoms. On my way back, I wanted to buy a little something for Auntie Liu—you know how she's always been so good to me. When I entered Goose City, I heard that a merchant had just come from the capital to sell some interesting little trinkets.

"Why did I have to be curious?" Wu Xingzi mumbled to himself, but there was no answer to this question. "The merchant brought along news about the Assistant Minister of Official Personnel Affairs, saying that the position had been given to someone from Goose City. He said that the man was good looking and well educated, and the emperor liked him very much. Three years ago, he was named a top scholar. He gained the emperor's trust very quickly. He was promoted every year, and he married the daughter of the Minister of Revenue last year. This year, he even had a child. As for me, I knew a long time ago...that if you were still alive, it meant that you didn't want to come back. I already knew... But you still left me a memento, didn't you?"

A faint smile appeared on Wu Xingzi's ordinary face, but he looked terrible—even worse than when he was crying. He chuckled, then, and the more he laughed, the giddier he seemed. He looked as if he was about to descend into madness.

Guan Shanjin reached out to apply pressure to his sleep point. He could not let him continue to drown himself in this pain, this wound buried so deeply within. No matter how apathetic Wu Xingzi had seemed in the past, he could no longer hold himself back.

However, before Guan Shanjin's finger could tap the point, Wu Xingzi began to mumble. "I saw the perfume sachets the merchant was selling. They were exactly the same as the one you gave me... There were dozens of them...dozens..."

Guan Shanjin deftly pressed his sleep point, and then wrapped his arms tightly around the adviser's cold, sleeping body.

He finally knew the identity of this Zaizong-xiong. He was the son-in-law of the ex-Minister of Revenue, the previous Assistant Minister of Official Personnel Affairs. The ex-Minister of Revenue had retired, and his son-in-law had become the new Minister of Revenue—Yan Wenxin. Zaizong was his courtesy name. He had been born in Goose City, and he was a current favorite of the emperor. A staunch follower of the crown prince, he had once tried to cozy up to the protector general. When Guan Shanjin lived in the capital, he had received a drawing of Yan Wenxin's eldest daughter for his consideration.

Hmph! Damn you, Yan Wenxin! A demonic smile appeared on Guan Shanjin's beautiful face. It was enchanting and terrifying all at once. "As soon as I get the chance, I'll come for you!"

Guan Shanjin held Wu Xingzi as the old man took a short nap. Hei-er knocked on the door. Without waiting for Guan Shanjin to respond, he pushed the doors open and entered, his aloof, solemn face looking a little dark. Seeing the sleeping Wu Xingzi in the general's arms and that the adviser's nose was still red, and the corners of his eyes were still slightly damp, Hei-er hesitated. He kept his mouth shut.

"What's the matter?" With the exception of Man Yue, Hei-er and the other three guards were Guan Shanjin's closest subordinates. He normally wasn't very strict with their discipline, even in the barracks, so he wasn't that bothered by Hei-er's interruption. Most likely, Man Yue had sent another letter urging for his return.

"Vice General Man has sent a letter." As expected, that was the first thing Hei-er said. However, it seemed like he had more to say, so Guan Shanjin lazily opened his eyes to look at him.

Hei-er took a deep breath, glancing again at Wu Xingzi, who was sleeping fitfully. He lowered his voice before continuing. "In Vice General Man's letter, he said that Mr. Lu fell from his horse two days ago and broke his leg. He also has some minor internal injuries..."

Alarmed, Guan Shanjin stood up, and the man sprawled in his arms nearly tumbled to the ground. General Guan paid no attention. Instead, it was Hei-er who rushed to support Wu Xingzi, preventing him from crashing onto the floor.

"Mr. Lu is injured?" Guan Shanjin's glinting eyes narrowed. The anxiety in them was obvious. "Why are you only telling me now?" His sharp, icy tone made Wu Xingzi shudder and let out a muffled groan. A tear slid down his pale face, but Guan Shanjin didn't seem to care. "We'll return to Horse-Face City immediately. Tell Man Yue to call on Doctor Tu."

"Vice General Man has already brought Physician Tu over. In his letter, he said that Mr. Lu's injuries are not very serious. He'll be able to get out of bed after about two months of rest." Hei-er paused for a moment. He took Wu Xingzi, who had clearly been forgotten by the general, into his arms, steadying him so that he would not fall and injure himself.

Guan Shanjin snorted. "He needs two months of bedrest, but it's not serious? Man Yue resents Mr. Lu. I'm sure he'll take this opportunity to pester him further. I must go back at once. The four of you will finish dealing with matters in Goose City first. Don't slow me down." Guan Shanjin's smile was grim. None of his close subordinates liked Mr. Lu. It was likely that Mr. Lu would feel profoundly uneasy during this recovery period.

The more he thought about it, the more concerned he became. Guan Shanjin didn't even bother leaving the Restaurant of Songs through its front doors. Instead, he used his qinggong skills to leap out of the window. He didn't want to delay his departure for even a second.

"General!" With Adviser Wu in his arms, Hei-er was unable to chase after the general. He could only watch as the black-robed figure disappeared into the distance.

Hei-er looked down at the pale-faced, despondent man in his arms and sighed internally. *We're in for it now.*

He had overheard Adviser Wu's story as he stood guard by the door, and naturally noticed Guan Shanjin's tenderness for him. Adviser Wu obviously had a special place in Guan Shanjin's heart— anyone with eyes could see it. However, no matter how much Guan Shanjin liked Adviser Wu, he could never compare with Mr. Lu, the man the general had pined after for so many years.

Man Yue had given special instructions in his letter. They must return to Horse-Face City right away, and they must immediately inform the general about Mr. Lu's injury. But Hei-er didn't understand why.

Mr. Lu was about to seek a marriage alliance with the Yue family—and now this happened. The timing was too coincidental. If it wasn't for Man Yue insisting over and over again that they ought to return, Hei-er would have dragged it out for a few more days before telling Guan Shanjin. Now, what? Was he supposed to send Adviser Wu back to Qingcheng County, or should he bring him along to Horse-Face City?

Hei-er wasn't inclined to give it any further thought. Guan Shanjin's attitude was unsurprising, and Man Yue definitely had his own agenda in giving him those orders. Great—now Hei-er had to be responsible for Adviser Wu.

Hei-er carefully wrapped a cloak tightly around Wu Xingzi, then pulled the doors open and summoned the server, giving him a few instructions. He then jumped out through the window just as General Guan had, carrying Wu Xingzi. He returned to the manor in Goose City and happened to see the back of Guan Shanjin riding away on his horse, Zhuxing.

"Hei-er." Fang He, a man with a big beard, came up to him. "What's going on? The general instructed us to bring Adviser Wu to Horse-Face City and then left. Yesterday, didn't he say he was going to stay here for a few more days?"

"Vice General Man sent a letter saying that Mr. Lu injured himself falling from his horse. How could the general stay here?" At least the general had spared a thought for Wu Xingzi. Hei-er was a little gratified.

"Falling from his horse at this time?" Fang He said, shocked. His eyes were full of unbridled contempt. "Isn't he about to marry into the Yue family? I heard that he's planning on confirming the marriage alliance before the new year. This new year is going to be tough."

"Exactly..." Hei-er sighed, shifting the man in his arms. "If we're going to bring Adviser Wu with us, should we go to Qingcheng County first? Or do we just take him with us while he's still asleep?"

He suspected that if they waited for Adviser Wu to wake up, it wouldn't be easy to take him with them. Secretly, Hei-er wanted to let him go—once they returned to Horse-Face City, it was unlikely that Adviser Wu's life there would be easy.

"Would Adviser Wu be willing to go to Horse-Face City when he awakes?" Fang He asked the question, but he also shook his head with certainty.

The four of them all knew that Adviser Wu was not at all reluctant to part from the general. Even Manager Rancui probably held a higher position in Wu Xingzi's heart than the general—or rather, the general's cock. How would he ever be willing to leave Qingcheng County?

"We can only beg the adviser's forgiveness later," Hei-er sighed. His entire life had been spent in the military, so obeying orders had become almost an innate part of him. Moreover, this order came from Guan Shanjin. Hei-er had to follow his orders, no matter how he felt about them. Not everyone could stand up to the general like Man Yue could, with excellent tactics, a soft, plump figure, and a silver tongue.

"Adviser Wu is pretty feeble, so he won't be able to handle a difficult journey," Fang He said. "You should go ahead with him in a carriage. As soon as we've settled everything here, we'll follow behind you. If we arrive too long after the general reaches Horse-Face City, I don't know if he'll even remember this guy." Fang He shook his head compassionately, turning around to prepare the carriage.

It would be better if he didn't remember! Then the adviser could return to Qingcheng County in delight, spending his days peacefully with *The Pengornisseur*.

An hour after Guan Shanjin's departure, the carriage was ready. Although the four guards were rough, hardened men, they were very meticulous. Inside the carriage lay comfortable cushions and bedding. Although it was a little cramped, it was warm and cozy. There were books, scripts, and paintings to stave off boredom, and plenty of snacks and tea. They'd even prepared a few sets of clothes, neatly and tidily packed within the carriage drawers.

Wu Xingzi's creased brow relaxed when he felt the soft bedding. His lips curved faintly into a smile as he snuggled into a cushion and fell into a deeper sleep.

The carriage itself was well constructed, and Hei-er was a skilled driver. They barely felt any jolts on their journey, and the mild swaying of the carriage only made the journey more pleasant. Wu Xingzi slept all the way through the night.

When he woke up the next day, he stared blankly at the space around him. It was even tinier than his own small bedroom. He was enveloped by bedding that was as soft as a cloud, and for a moment, he thought he was still dreaming. He reached out and pinched himself on the thigh to make sure. He winced in pain and almost cried out loud before letting go.

Where... Where am I?

Before he could recover his wits, a ray of sun shone upon his face. A figure towered over him, blocking some of the light. "Adviser Wu, you're awake already. Would you like something to eat or drink?"

Wu Xingzi squinted. The sunlight wasn't especially bright, but the eyes of a man who'd slept for an entire day and night were naturally sensitive. It was glaring enough for him to start tearing up.

"Warrior, you're..." Wu Xingzi hurriedly sat up within the bedding. He could finally see that he was in a carriage. How had he ended up in a carriage? Had he been kidnapped by thieves? "I'm the magistrate's adviser, Wu Xingzi from Qingcheng County. Warrior, are you seeking my money or my life?"

Hei-er paused for a few breaths before laughing cheerily. "It's Hei-er," he said, "and I want you alive."

"Uh... C-Commander Hei?" Wu Xingzi rubbed his eyes, and he could finally make out the person in front of him. Letting out a huge sigh of relief, he bowed his head, feeling embarrassed. "I'm sorry, Commander Hei. My mind wasn't awake yet. I mistook you for a thief. Please forgive me."

"It's fine. And you can just call me Hei-er." Hei-er tied up the curtains of the carriage, allowing the rare glimpse of warm winter sun to shine through, hoping to give the adviser's pale face a bit of a flush.

"You haven't eaten for nearly two days. Would you like some food?"

As soon as food was mentioned, Wu Xingzi's stomach gurgled in hunger. Blushing, he pressed his hands against his belly and bashfully replied, "I am a little hungry. Do you have rations to share, Commander Hei?"

"Why don't you call me Hei-er, and I'll call you Adviser? Our current form of address feels very distant." Hei-er felt helpless. In his letter, Man Yue had asked him to build a good rapport with Wu Xingzi, and that it would be best if the adviser acclimated to having a personal guard before they reached Horse-Face City. Even if Wu Xingzi couldn't bring himself to treat him like a subordinate, they had to at least interact as peers. He was not to let Wu Xingzi demean himself.

Hei-er sighed. He hadn't expected this mission to be so difficult.

"Uh..." Wu Xingzi faltered. He was only a commoner, and he had a deep-seated fear of military personnel. Moreover, the commander had to be at least a fourth-ranked official! Compared to ordinary folks like Adviser Wu, they might as well be separated by heaven and earth! How could he ever have the guts to just casually call him by his nickname?

"Let's agree on it. I wish to interact with you as your equal—please grant me that." Hei-er decided to be direct. Adviser Wu was blunt, honest, and sincere. It would be useful to quietly get him used to this change during their journey now instead of allowing him to ponder over it endlessly.

"Uh..." Wu Xingzi scratched his cheek. He really didn't have the courage to cause Hei-er any loss of his dignity, so could he only nod his head wildly. He stammered, "H-Hei-er..."

"Hey." Hei-er smiled at him. He handed over a wax-paper bag, and Wu Xingzi hurriedly accepted it. The bag was warm in his hands, and he could smell a tempting aroma wafting from it. Gulping down his saliva, he didn't bother with proper etiquette any longer as he tore into the bag. Inside were four big meat buns. The fragrant bread and the rich aroma of the meat filling rushed out, and Wu Xingzi's stomach, which had been empty for so long, gurgled loudly.

Blushing heavily, Wu Xingzi sneaked a peek at Hei-er. Seeing that he had already turned back to face to the front and drive the carriage, he patted himself on the chest in relief.

The buns were still steaming. As Wu Xingzi bit into one, the juices of the meat dripped down his chin. It was so hot that his tongue went numb. The bun was fluffy and stuffed completely full with finely chopped meat, and the flavor was well rounded and pleasant. It had a hint of ginger spiciness, but it wasn't overpowering. The bun was so delicious, like blossoms soaked in the juices of the meat—he practically wanted to swallow his tongue down along with it.

These buns were somewhat different from the ones you could get in Goose City. They were chewy yet fluffy, and the meat inside was extremely juicy, but not overly tender. Wu Xingzi couldn't stop eating the fresh, salty buns. He finished three in one go, and then stared at the fourth, not daring to touch it.

"H-Hei-er, I'm sorry. I was so hungry, I ended up eating some of your share."

With four buns, he figured there were two for each of them. Hei-er had a fit and muscular body, so he probably ate more than Wu Xingzi did in order to maintain his physique. Wu Xingzi desperately wished for somewhere to bury his face in embarrassment.

"Adviser, what are you saying? Those are all yours. I already ate." Hei-er turned and consoled him, handing him a flask of cool water. "There should be tea leaves in the drawers. If you'd like some hot tea, I can boil water for you later."

Wu Xingzi quickly waved his hands. "No need to go to all that trouble..." He wasn't used to being taken care of like this, and in such strange surroundings, too... He looked around outside as he bit into the last bun. The carriage was quite speedy, and the unfamiliar scenery rushed past continuously. The two horses pulling the carriage were extremely spirited, with shiny, sleek coats and sturdy, muscular bodies. The clatter of their hooves beneath sounded smooth and powerful.

Although he wanted to ask Hei-er where they were going, Wu Xingzi wasn't a fool. Thinking about it, he could guess what was happening—this was definitely the path to Horse-Face City!

Oh no, his *Pengornisseur*! Would Manager Rancui know that he had been taken away from Qingcheng County? And his rattan case of erotic drawings! His toy, Mr. D!

At his wits' end, Wu Xingzi sat up on the bedding. Licking the leftover meat juices from his fingers, his heart ached so much that his mind reeled.

Because of how drunk he'd been yesterday, Adviser Wu had long forgotten what had happened in the Restaurant of Songs. He didn't want to think about how he had somehow gotten into this carriage heading for Horse-Face City, or why he saw no sign of Guan Shanjin, who had been following him around relentlessly as of late.

The only thought in his head was that the weather had been quite cold recently and there weren't many bugs around, so the insect-repelling scent pouch in his rattan case should be able to last for a few more days. But if he couldn't return to Qingcheng County before New Year, his pengornis drawings might be in danger! Each and every one of them was worth a coin! Every piece represented a beautiful night, and the more he thought about it, the more his heart ached. Tears threatened to roll down his cheeks. The flush that usually came after having food and drink was nowhere to be seen; instead, his face had an ashen look to it that spoke of utter anguish.

Hei-er noticed Wu Xingzi's expression, but he mistakenly thought that the adviser was upset at discovering Guan Shanjin's absence. He tried to comfort him. "Adviser, you don't have to worry about the general. He had something to attend to, so he went ahead first. You'll be able to see him once we arrive in Horse-Face City."

"What?" Wu Xingzi blinked, looking blankly at Hei-er. In his mind, he was still flipping through each phallic illustration from his memories. He looked completely lost, not seeming to pay any attention to what Hei-er was saying. He simply nodded his head along.

"Also..." Hei-er saw how sad Wu Xingzi looked, and he could not bear it, deciding to remind him of the general's feelings for him. "Don't worry about Mr. Lu too much. Although the general is unable to get away for now, you're still in his heart."

"What?" Wu Xingzi heard Hei-er, but he didn't understand what he was saying. His dazed expression made Wu Xingzi seem even more pitiful. He looked like a drenched quail, a little pile of feathers huddled on the bed.

Sighing, Hei-er solemnly made a promise. "I'll help you," he said, hoping that this man would not be hurt too badly.

A carriage wasn't the fastest way to travel. In consideration of the state of Wu Xingzi's fragile body, Hei-er paid extra attention to him. By the third evening, the other three guards had caught up to them on their horses.

It was immediately obvious that all four of these tall, sturdy men had been thoroughly tempered on the battlefield. Their expressions were cold and stern. Although they were good looking, their icy milieu could not be concealed, their eyes glinting with traces of bloodlust. One guard had a long scar which split his mysterious-looking face into skewed halves.

Wu Xingzi remained huddled up in the carriage. He had always been timid. He would even unconsciously detour around the head constable and his team, to say nothing of these military men who had spent so much time enacting deadly violence in battle. Adviser Wu wasn't exactly afraid of them, but it was more like holding them in awe and respect, and he had no idea how to interact with them.

Fortunately, all four guards knew about his disposition. They silently spurred their horses forward as they kept a watchful eye on him. Other than Hei-er, no one else tried chatting with him. Of course, these were all specific instructions expressly given by Man Yue. The guards didn't understand the reasoning behind the orders, but still they obeyed.

After a few days, Wu Xingzi got used to the guards, and acted less reserved. He could even carry a short, casual conversation with Hei-er, inquiring about the scenery of Horse-Face City.

When they were about half a day away from Horse-Face City, Fang He sent off a pigeon with a report for Man Yue. The journey lasted a little longer than usual; they'd been on the road for seventeen days. They were ten full days behind Guan Shanjin, and the four guards were all a little puzzled. Man Yue didn't want them to hurry, but to slow down—and he didn't want them to stop the general, either.

No one knew exactly what Man Yue was scheming. If not for the fact that everyone knew Man Yue had never liked Mr. Lu, they might have thought he was trying to solidify Mr. Lu's position by deliberately rejecting Adviser Wu.

Half a day later, the group arrived at the gates of Horse-Face City. From afar, they could see a tall, handsome red horse, its coat speckled with silver. On its back sat a round, plump officer in silver armor. Under the sun, he was exceptionally striking.

"Vice General Man." The group quickly made their way over. Thousands of thoughts ran through their heads. They felt like complaining a little.

"I'm glad you're back. Follow me," Man Yue said, glancing at the carriage. At the same time, Wu Xingzi happened to lift up the curtain to look outside. Their eyes met, and Man Yue gave him a simple and honest smile. The adviser felt relief wash over him, no longer as nervous. This man who looked like a smiling buddha turned out to be the Vice General Man Yue that everyone was talking about. He looked like a good person, completely lacking the air of brutality that most military men seemed to hold.

"Vice General Man," Wu Xingzi said. He moved to cup his hands at the vice general, forgetting that he was still in a carriage, and ended up staggering and nearly falling out. Luckily, Hei-er was fast enough to catch him, deftly nudging him back into the carriage.

"Please be careful, Adviser," Hei-er said.

"Ah... Thank you, thank you. Sorry to trouble you again." Wu Xingzi blushed and rubbed his nose in embarrassment. He didn't dare to move again. Only his eyes darted about curiously, taking in this border city that shared no resemblance to Qingcheng County or Goose City.

Horse-Face City was originally called Nan'an City.[9] However, Nanman had staged a long, aggressive campaign against the city, so that it barely experienced any days of calm or tranquility, unlike its original name that spoke of peace.

Any able-bodied young men in the city who hadn't been permanently disabled from battle were part of the troops stationed there. Most of the citizens were either very old or very young, and those who were able to leave had done so long ago. Now, it was mostly women left in charge. Therefore, in Horse-Face City and its four surrounding counties, female authority was highly respected. In fact, the status of female citizens was no less than that of male citizens. Sometimes they were even of a higher status.

As there were so many deaths, Horse-Face City did not bury their dead, but cremated them instead. They would store the ashes in little earthen jars and bury them under their beds at home. This way, they could prevent the enemy from digging up the graves and tarnishing their ancestors, and it was much safer for them to pay their respects. However, in the eyes of outsiders, it seemed profoundly creepy to have remains buried under people's beds—even if the ashes belonged to family members.

Over time, this strange practice came to be known as Horse-Face, shortened from "Ox-Head and Horse-Face," after the two animal-headed guardians of the underworld. After using this name

---

9   Nan'an (南安) means "southern peace."

for a long time out of habit, the city became known as Horse-Face City.

The folk customs of Horse-Face City never wavered. Although peace had returned five years ago and the city now flourished, there were still strong, fortified buildings as far as the eye could see. Practicality outweighed everything else, and there were barely any decorations. Everything had a grayish, muddy tone, with no sign of the elegance that characterized the south.

By the road, women could be seen with exposed arms. They were dressed in trousers, with their shirts tucked into their waistbands. Huffing and puffing, they hauled goods up to the ox carts. It seemed like no one found it strange to see them mixed in with the men.

It really was an eye-opener. Wu Xingzi looked left and right, his body leaning further and further out, and he nearly tipped out of the carriage again. Hei-er sighed lightly, deciding to just help Wu Xingzi out of the carriage and sit beside him. In a low voice, he introduced Wu Xingzi to the sights of Horse-Face City.

After traveling for about the time it took an incense stick to burn, the group finally arrived at the estate of the Southern Garrison general. Wu Xingzi stared at the bold and uninhibited writing on the plaque, his mouth falling open so wide that two eggs could have been stuffed inside it. He forgot how to blink.

A moment later, he heard himself ask, "Hai—H-H-Haiwang is the Southern Garrison general?"

"Yes." Man Yue smiled at him, his eyes curving. "Did the general never mention it to you?"

"No..." Wu Xingzi shook his head stiffly. Something Guan Shanjin had said before suddenly flashed through his head: that no one in Horse-Face City had power over him... That was true—no one could do anything to the general of the Southern Garrison! How had he not realized that?!

Wu Xingzi patted himself on the chest as he heaved a sigh of relief; he had been lucky to escape deeper feelings for the general. An inexplicable wistfulness welled up within him at this thought.

He did not dare to think about why he had always avoided speculating about the possibility of Guan Shanjin being the famed general of the Southern Garrison. The general's reputation had spread far and wide, and discussions about him even reached Qingcheng County. Other than being famed for his prowess in battle, many often mentioned how young and promising the general was.

Shouldn't he have guessed it long ago? He was the right age, and he had an impressive family background. Although his appearance wasn't savage and frightening like the rumors described, and he didn't even have any scars on his face—in fact, he had god-like beauty—all signs pointed to Guan Shanjin being the Southern Garrison General. It was Wu Xingzi who'd been unwilling to draw the conclusion... His slender shoulders slumped slightly, and he urgently wanted *The Pengornisseur* to soothe himself.

Although he was unwilling to admit it, Guan Shanjin's care and concern over the past month had made Wu Xingzi lower the barriers around his heart quite a bit.

"The general has arranged for Mr. Wu to stay in Shuanghe Manor in the west. Please follow me." Man Yue seemed to completely ignore Wu Xingzi's apprehensive expression. He simply led the adviser into the estate. "Right, the four of you, go see the general. Quickly."

"Yes, sir."

Unintentionally, Wu Xingzi looked at Hei-er. Since they'd returned to the general's estate, Hei-er was no longer as warm as he had been during their journey. He acted even colder and sterner than when Wu Xingzi first met him, turning and leaving at once. Wu Xingzi felt even more uneasy. He was in an unfamiliar place with unfamiliar people. Although Man Yue seemed easy enough to get along with, he was still a stranger. Wu Xingzi twisted his sleeves, almost ripping them apart.

"Don't be nervous," said Man Yue, comforting him at the right moment. "We're all good people here at the general's estate." No matter how Wu Xingzi looked at it, Man Yue's smiling, cheery face was warm and friendly. He gradually calmed down, shyly nodding at Man Yue to express his gratitude.

Shuanghe Manor was a rather small compound, and the rooms were very simple. A patch of mallow plants grew in the yard. There were even some vegetable patches. Despite the overflowing weeds, the sight was familiar enough to allow Wu Xingzi to breathe a sigh of relief.

"The general is especially afraid of you getting bored. Horse-Face City doesn't have much by way of entertainment compared to Goose City, but by tending to the vegetables, you should be able to while away the hours. The soil here is quite fertile. Just let me know what sort of vegetables you'd like to plant, Mr. Wu." Man Yue led Wu Xingzi around the compound, then pushed open the doors and brought him inside.

The scent of wood rushed into his nose. It was obvious that the furniture within was brand new, and it all seemed cozy and comfortable.

After pushing the windows open, the house seemed even brighter. The plum blossom tree outside the window had just started budding. When it was in full bloom, the rooms would definitely be filled with its scent.

Horse-Face City was further south than Qingcheng County. As long as the rain wasn't falling and the wind wasn't blowing, it didn't feel like wintertime at all.

Wu Xingzi liked this little house very much. Each decoration and furnishing was to his liking, and there was even a small kitchen to the side. He didn't know if it had always been there, or if they had built the kitchen after the rest of it.

"Mr. Wu, please rest. Later on, I'll get Hei-er to bring two maids to come take care of you." Man Yue was about to leave. He was, after all, the busiest person in the general's estate. If he hadn't wanted to scope out the sort of person Wu Xingzi was, he would never have shown up to handle these kinds of matters.

"There's no need for any maids!" Wu Xingzi hurriedly refused him. What status did he have to need any maids?

"That's not possible. In the general's estate, we cannot slight any important guests. Don't worry, Mr. Wu. The maids I've selected are smart and capable girls. They won't disturb you." Man Yue smiled, but his tone brooked no argument. Wu Xingzi stood in stunned silence, his mouth agape; he could only nod his head and accept the situation.

Man Yue's round and fair figure vanished quickly into the distance. The courtyard immediately quieted. The wind occasionally brushed against the mallow plants, the faint scratching sounds making Wu Xingzi shrink into himself in unease.

After contemplating it for a moment, he decided to ignore all the anxiety he felt. Since he was already here at the general's estate, he should just go along with it. All he had to do was wait until he saw Guan Shanjin, and then he would ask him to send him back to Qingcheng County. He would be able to return home before the new year... Right?

After exploring the entirety of Shuanghe Manor, Wu Xingzi finally stopped in front of the vegetable patches. Picking up the corners of his robe and tucking them into his belt, he started to earnestly pluck out the weeds. The soil of the vegetable patches was dark and fertile. The smell of fresh dirt felt so much like home that Wu Xingzi almost forgot that he was in the general's estate.

When all the weeds were cleared, Wu Xingzi piled them up by the side of the vegetable plots. He entered the kitchen to look for a flint, wanting to burn the weeds to make fertilizer.

Having finally managed to find some flint, when he returned to the yard, he saw an unfamiliar man. He was pretty and had a refined appearance. He seemed as gentle as flowing water, like a weeping willow tree.

Adviser Wu, who always appreciated a beautiful face, couldn't help but stare at the man. When the man frowned slightly at him in displeasure, though, Wu Xingzi quickly lowered his head. With a red face, he cupped his hands in apology. "I'm so sorry for the offense."

"Mm," the man murmured in acknowledgment. The sound was extremely pleasant; even the owner of the House of Taotie, Su Yang, didn't have a voice as melodious as him. This man's voice was like a bubbling brook, or the sweet song of a nightingale. The tips of Adviser Wu's ears reddened slightly.

"You're the man from Qingcheng County?"

"Yes, yes, yes. I'm Adviser Wu Xingzi from Qingcheng County. It's a pleasure to meet you." *Ah, his voice is really lovely. Almost as good as Guan Shanjin's.*

"Wu Xingzi," the man recited his name softly, ending with a mocking lilt. "This name is something special."

"No, no. My father named me on impulse. There's no profound meaning behind it, it just sounds smooth when you say it."

Wu Xingzi blushed a little. His name had no special relation to any works of literature; the name simply came from his parents' sincere love for their child.

"I'm Hua Shu," the man said.

"Hello, Hua-gongzi."

"I'm Mr. Lu's caretaker," Hua Shu said. "The general will be staying at Mr. Lu's abode for the next few days, so he may end up neglecting you, his honored guest. Mr. Lu specially sent me here to seek your forgiveness. He hopes you do not get the wrong impression about the situation. He sends his best wishes and hopes to prevent you from any distress." Hua Shu raised his fair and sharp chin slightly in a haughty display. A pair of clear eyes peered slowly over at Wu Xingzi, and his lips curled in a faint smile.

"What?" Adviser Wu blinked at him. He could tell that Hua Shu looked down on him, but that didn't bother him. After all, Hua Shu was someone from the general's estate! It was natural for him to be arrogant. He didn't really understand what exactly Hua Shu was getting at.

On his way here, Hei-er had told him that Guan Shanjin had rushed back to Horse-Face City because Mr. Lu fell and broke his leg. Since Mr. Lu was currently recovering from his injury, it was human nature for Guan Shanjin to spend more time with him. Were they not mentor and student? A mentor was like an adoptive father. The younger generation should take good care of the older generation.

Wu Xingzi quickly cupped his hands together and answered Hua Shu. "I hope Mr. Lu will recover well," he said. "As they say, a disciple should serve his teacher. Haiwang is the student. It's expected of him to stay by Mr. Lu's side."

Adviser Wu did not expect Hua Shu's face to suddenly change.

A dark glimmer flashed across his crystalline eyes, and he snorted coldly. "Mr. Wu has a very sharp tongue."

What? Wu Xingzi was confused. Did he say something out of turn?

"You think that the general has really fallen for you?" Hua Shu continued. "Hmph! In the general's heart, you can't even compare to a single hair on Mr. Lu's head. You should hurry up and learn your place—and stop daydreaming!" Hua Shu shook his sleeves out fiercely before turning around and storming off.

Left behind once again, Wu Xingzi was at a loss. He didn't have a chance to defend himself and could only foolishly stand there and watch Hua Shu leave.

He sighed heavily. "Let's just plant cucumbers."

The people of this city had terrible tempers!

With a garden to tend, Wu Xingzi's days in Horse-Face City went quite well.

Not long after Hua Shu left that day, Hei-er led two maids into the house. They were a pair of twins. The elder twin was called Mint, and the younger twin was called Osmanthus. They were local girls born and raised in Horse-Face City, around thirteen years old, and they were quick with their work and very familiar with handling a garden. Every day they would collect water for the plants, pull out the weeds, and remove any bugs. They were even better at the job than Wu Xingzi.

Guan Shanjin seemed to have left some instructions for them. The two maids were supposed to go to the main kitchen every two days to collect some vegetables, meat, eggs, rice, and noodles. The three of them would then cook in the kitchen of Shuanghe Manor; they never ate anything directly from the main kitchen.

Wu Xingzi was satisfied with this arrangement. The first day, he ate noodles that Mint cooked. They looked like slippery little white fish. After they were cooked and drained, the noodles were mixed with chili, vinegar, soy sauce, coriander, bean sprouts, and other seasonings. It was delicious, but so spicy that it made Wu Xingzi's lips swell. He slept fitfully, even waking up in the middle of the night with diarrhea. He woke up the next morning feeling as though he had wilted. This was how he learned that the food of Horse-Face City was heavily seasoned.

This was especially evident with the chili peppers that had recently been imported from overseas. They were red and pointy; in fact, they looked rather adorable. However, they were spicy enough to raise a man from the dead. The tongue-piercing pain added a finishing touch to the seasoning; the unique spiciness was incredibly addictive, and the people of Horse-Face City couldn't get enough.

Qingcheng County was located rather far away, and it tended to be a somewhat closed-off community. The people living there were not that interested in spicy food. At most, they would use a little bit of cherry dogwood for flavoring. They barely had any dishes that used chili peppers, and Wu Xingzi had never really taken to spicy food.

It was no wonder, then, that Guan Shanjin specially prepared this small kitchen for Wu Xingzi to cook for himself. Otherwise, if the spiciness didn't kill him, the diarrhea would.

After that incident, the two maids prepared food that was a lot lighter in flavor. They always meticulously prepared any broth they made, which enhanced the intrinsic flavor of the ingredients. At first, Wu Xingzi felt bad that the two girls had to accommodate his palate, but after he saw them pull out a little jar of pickled chilis to add to their own food, he felt more at ease.

A month passed for Wu Xingzi, mainly spent farming, eating, and occasionally strolling about Horse-Face City with Hei-er. Soon, New Year was just ten days away.

In the past, Wu Xingzi had always spent the holiday alone. His New Year's dinner was always very simple; he celebrated it with just a fried fish.

As for decorations and gifts, he never paid special attention to them. After pasting some paper-cuttings on the windows, writing a spring couplet for his door, and buying some dried fruits, his preparations would be complete. The dishes that he prepared as offerings to his ancestors were also very basic, mainly because if he could not finish the food himself it would be wasted.

During the entire New Year period, other than visiting some friends and saying his prayers on the first day, he spent his time at home reading. The books were all old ones that he had already read. Before he joined the Peng Society, Adviser Wu hadn't bought any new books in ten years. Each new year, he would reread the books that he had fortunately rescued from the flood—the books that once belonged to his father.

The water damage and the age of the books had caused the words inside to smudge, no matter how carefully Wu Xingzi took care of them. This was especially the case for the comments that his father wrote in the margins, as the ink he had used was not of a very good quality. About eleven or twelve years ago, the words had blurred into an indistinct smear. However, Wu Xingzi still treasured them and looked through them annually. After the holiday was over, he would carefully wrap them in a few layers of waxed paper and store them with insect-repelling herbs.

Looks like it's too late to go back and get the books this year. Adviser Wu sighed, feeling a little lost and disappointed. *And what should I do about the offerings? I'm the sole remaining descendant of my family. How can I let my parents and my ancestors go hungry this year?!*

Wu Xingzi started feeling anxious.

Fortunately, Hei-er happened to bring him some New Year goods, and he hurriedly caught hold of him. "Hei-er, is the general busy at the moment?"

"Uhh..." Hei-er couldn't really say that the general was busy, but neither could he say he wasn't. It was just that Guan Shanjin had been spending all his free time with Mr. Lu. After a moment of silence, Hei-er resolutely shook his head. "He's not very busy. The New Year is approaching, so there are significantly fewer official duties for him to handle. If you'd like to see the general, I'll ask him for you."

"Thank you, thank you. Please check with him as quickly as possible." Wu Xingzi heaved a breath of relief. However, he soon quickly wrung his hands uneasily. "What should I do if the general doesn't have the time? In that case, can Vice General Man see me?"

"I'm afraid Vice General Man is truly too busy." After all, the busiest person in Horse-Face City was Man Yue! Thinking about that man—who had accidentally put on a few pounds again—Hei-er's face twitched, trying to hold back his laughter.

"Oh..." Adviser Wu could not let this rest. Even a fast horse would need eight to nine days to travel from Horse-Face City to Qingcheng County. He didn't know how to ride a horse, so Wu Xingzi's journey was bound to be delayed even further. According to his estimations, if he wanted to go home for the new year to pray to his ancestors, as well as change the sachet of insect repellent for his pengornis drawings, he needed to leave within the next couple of days.

"Please help me contact the general. I just want to tell him something."

"Definitely. You have my word." In his heart, Hei-er believed that Adviser Wu missed the general. He'd stayed in Horse-Face City for many days but had not seen the general even once. No matter how composed the adviser was, he must feel a little resentful!

Hei-er really didn't know what the general was thinking. Why did he ignore Adviser Wu after making arrangements to bring him here? If the general no longer held affection for the adviser, why would he ask after him every few days? Of his own admission, Hei-er was not the most intelligent of men. After puzzling over the matter a few times, he decided to simply let it go.

"Thank you, thank you." Wu Xingzi kept bowing in gratitude, forcing Hei-er to run away from Shuanghe Manor before he stopped thanking him.

The twin girls were eavesdropping nearby. Seeing that Hei-er had left, Mint asked, "Sir, are you thinking about the general?"

Over the past month, the two sisters hadn't seen or heard their gentle, friendly master mention the general even once. Instead, he had mentioned the grave that he had selected for himself three times already, talking about the trees there, about the shade available, the luxuriant grass and plants, and how it was truly a great place to be laid to rest. The girls didn't understand what he was describing, as the dead in Horse-Face City were cremated and buried under their family's beds.

When Vice General Man had selected them to serve Mr. Wu, they had thought he was the general's lover. Although he was somewhat older, the girls adored his gentle, friendly aura. Compared to Hua Shu and Mr. Lu, he was much nicer to be around.

But as the days passed, they soon realized that they had no idea what was going on between the adviser and the general. Mr. Wu had apparently come to Horse-Face City from Qingcheng County because of the general, but the general spent every day with Mr. Lu. When the two sisters went to the main kitchen to collect food for Shuanghe Manor, they'd observed the general's close interactions with Mr. Lu a few times. The general was exactly the same as in the past—his captivating, romantic eyes were still full of undeniable love for Mr. Lu.

So why had the general decided to bring Mr. Wu with him?

What made the sisters even more uncertain was Mr. Wu's obvious lack of interest in the general. No matter how they looked at it, these two people seemed like total strangers! How did they end up together?

"I'm not exactly thinking about the general." Wu Xingzi scratched at his cheeks, smiling awkwardly. He could not tell these two young girls that he was preoccupied with thoughts of his parents, his predecessors, and his penis pictures!

"Sir, the next time you see the general, you must grab hold of his heart!" Osmanthus implored him, a solemn look on her face. Her hand, occupied with removing bugs from the garden, clenched with a *crack*.

"That's right, sir. After the New Year, Mr. Lu is to be married. Just endure him for a few years. Spend some quality time with the general, and then twist him around your little finger," Mint chimed in, buzzing with excitement.

The girls had listened to a number of romance stories. They weren't quite sure what love really meant, but they still yearned for it. They especially loved the stories where the little maid was not only the master's meticulous caretaker, but also his clever confidant, suggesting ideas for their master to gain favor with his beloved. They had long been itching to play this part.

Adviser Wu smiled wryly. He didn't want to disappoint the girls, but he really did not need any sort of advice! In the end, there was no love or affectionate indulgence when he was with Guan Shanjin. Their time together was only an extension of their tryst.

Wu Xingzi had no choice but to change the topic. "Little girls should work hard and talk less. Don't end up killing off my cucumbers!" he said, pretending to reproach the two girls.

Having long come to understand his temperament, Mint and Osmanthus giggled, completely unafraid of him. Still, they dropped the subject.

That evening, Wu Xingzi, Mint, and Osmanthus prepared pies for dinner. They were kneading dough when Hei-er arrived.

"Adviser," Hei-er said, looking somewhat haggard.

"Hei-er?" It had only been a few hours since he last saw the man; how did he end up looking like this? Wu Xingzi was shocked. He casually tossed the dough in his hands aside, leaning closer to look at him. "What happened? Are you feeling unwell?"

Silently, Hei-er took half a step back, hanging his head. "Thank you for your concern, Adviser. I'm very well. The general has asked me to pass on a message to you. At noon tomorrow, you'll have lunch together, and anything that needs to be said can be spoken face-to-face."

"At noon tomorrow?" Wu Xingzi nodded and made a mental note of it, finally breathing a sigh of relief. He knew that it was very likely that Guan Shanjin had already forgotten about him. If Adviser Wu left without saying anything, it wouldn't cause any trouble. However, he felt that after living in the man's estate for a month, he ought to at least express his gratitude. Furthermore, he needed to borrow a horse.

"Thank you very much, Hei-er. Would you like to have dinner with us tonight? The girls are clamoring for pies, and it's no trouble to make a few more."

"I appreciate your consideration, Adviser." Cupping his hands, Hei-er took three large steps back, looking a little panicked. "I still have duties to attend to, so I must bid you farewell."

"Oh, I see." Watching Hei-er take those huge steps backward, Wu Xingzi was befuddled. He had gotten quite close to Hei-er during their journey to Horse-Face City—why was there this distance between them again?

He wanted to ask, but he couldn't bring himself to be so direct. As such, he could only cup his hands back at Hei-er, bidding him farewell. A little sullen, he went back to the girls, kneading the dough with considerable vigor.

Detecting that Wu Xingzi was not in a good mood, the girls didn't disturb him. They purposely left the dough to him and went to the side to prepare the meat filling.

Adviser Wu was not the sort to hold himself down with negative memories. As he kneaded the dough, his mood improved, and while waiting for the dough to proof, he even taught the girls to recite poems:

"They cook the pig; the fragrance flows throughout the land.

Hungry crows are in the trees; the elders wait by temple gates.

Though their offerings are small, the ancient customs still stand.

Drunk, they leave the meat on the young ones' plates."[10]

The girls didn't know how to read, and they listened to Wu Xingzi explain the poem after he recited it. Mint covered her mouth and laughed, "It's already winter, and the year is coming to an end. The meat is already gone."

"There is some pork left, so hopefully cooking it will bring some luck." Wu Xingzi had started reciting the poem on impulse. Now, he happily chatted with Mint and Osmanthus, forgetting about that unhappy matter with Hei-er.

---

10   *Poem by Southern Song Dynasty poet Lu You.*

Little did he know that outside the compound, a pair of eyes stared at his reddened, smiling face. Those eyes belonged to quite a gloomy man.

"You're not going in?" Man Yue asked, holding a court bulletin that he had only halfway read. He glanced over at Guan Shanjin.

"We're meeting tomorrow at noon anyway." Guan Shanjin was dressed in black as usual. With his half-lidded eyes, he looked a little listless, but it was to conceal the sadness in his eyes.

"Then you could've just waited! Why did you have to drag me here to peep at him?" Man Yue was so busy, he desperately wished he could grow another pair of hands and four more pairs of eyes. He didn't have the time to stroll about with the general!

"I wanted to come and see why he suddenly wanted to meet with me."

Man Yue could not help but look at the general disdainfully. "You're so simpleminded!" he replied, annoyed. "What if Adviser Wu asks why you're ignoring him in front of Mr. Lu tomorrow? What do you plan to do then?"

"Would he ask that?" Guan Shanjin gritted his teeth. He had deliberately ignored Wu Xingzi for a month. He did not expect the old man to be living so happily. There was no trace of weariness in him at all, and he'd even formed a friendship with Hei-er! Guan Shanjin snorted. He had seen Hei-er's dick before, and it was nothing compared to his own.

"What sort of dirty things are you thinking about now?" Man Yue really knew Guan Shanjin too well. With a glance, he frowned, scorning him.

"Cocks," Guan Shanjin snorted coldly in reply.

Man Yue's hand shook, and he nearly dropped the bulletin in his hand, coughing unnaturally a few times. "The night is still young.

If you're really that eager, just ask Mr. Lu to pull his out for your amusement."

"The hell are you saying?!" General Guan spat, his brows creasing. His eyes were again drawn to the thin figure in the yard.

Wu Xingzi really had a strange body. Despite access to better food and eating it more often, he seemed to have lost even more weight. Guan Shanjin stared at him for quite some time. Only when Wu Xingzi carried a large tray of pies into the kitchen did Guan Shanjin look away.

Finally done with the bulletin, Man Yue looked up. "Did you find anything valuable? You've certainly been searching for quite some time," he said, the mockery evident in his words.

"I found an old quail," Guan Shanjin said, somewhat astonished. He didn't understand why he dragged Man Yue over to peer into the yard, either. Wu Xingzi was only a shallow replacement for Mr. Lu, but lately they seemed more and more different.

Now that the general was back at Mr. Lu's side—and the traces of Mr. Lu vanished from Wu Xingzi more and more—he should have long since sent the adviser back to Qingcheng County. Why was he so reluctant to do so? Unless it was because of Mr. Lu's impending marriage... Was he looking for someone to fill his place?

That was probably the case. Barely managing to convince himself of this, Guan Shanjin left, dragging Man Yue away with him.

Mr. Lu had yet to fully recover from his injuries. Whenever he swallowed his food, his chest hurt. Guan Shanjin worried about leaving Mr. Lu in Hua Shu's care, so he'd go back and feed Mr. Lu himself. Delays weren't good for his body.

Man Yue allowed Guan Shanjin to drag him along, but he still had to get a last jab in. "Hah. I bet Mr. Lu anxiously awaits your return."

"Stop talking nonsense." Pinching Man Yue's fleshy chin, Guan Shanjin secretly wished that Mr. Lu *would* feel anxious. However, he was acutely aware of Mr. Lu's indifferent demeanor. Mr. Lu had always been very tactful in his handling of matters and people. Guan Shanjin hated it. How could he ever feel anxious about the general arriving a few minutes late?

Man Yue snorted and flung Guan Shanjin's hand away, urging him on in irritation. "Go, go. Go feed that darling of yours with the broken leg. I'm hungry as well, so I won't accompany you any longer!"

With shocking nimbleness, Man Yue vanished into the night.

CHAPTER SEVEN

ᲡUNREQUITED LOVE AND THE ONE ᲥHAT GOT ᲐWAY

"Why are you always thinking about leaving me?" Guan Shanjin asked bitterly. In his heart, Wu Xingzi was merely a shadow of Mr. Lu. He had been more conscientious toward Wu Xingzi than any of his previous lovers—even Mr. Lu had not inspired such meticulous care from him before. However, Wu Xingzi still behaved as though he wasn't a part of this relationship. He acted like his heart had never been moved by Guan Shanjin...

WU XINGZI WOKE UP LATE. It was already past nine when he was awakened by someone, either Mint or Osmanthus, knocking on his door. "Sir! Sir! Are you up yet?"

Opening his eyes blearily, Wu Xingzi stayed in a sleepy stupor for quite some time. Hearing the girls outside the door anxiously discuss whether or not they should break his door down, he answered in a fluster: "I'm up! I'm up!"

"Sir is up!" This voice sounded like it belonged to Osmanthus. She exhaled in delighted relief. "Sir, the general has sent someone to invite you over."

"The general?" Wu Xingzi's mind had yet to become fully alert. Pulling an outer robe on, he stumbled over to the door and opened it. His bones ached a little; perhaps he had slept in for too long.

"Yes, the general is inviting you over." Mint saw that Wu Xingzi was still in a daze. He stared blankly at the twins. Mint could not stop a burble of laughter from escaping as she shook her head. "Sir, you should quickly go and wash up. Today, you must grab the general and hold him tight!"

"Hold him tight?" He couldn't do that! He had to go back home and pay respects to his ancestors.

At last, he was fully awake. Wu Xingzi smiled awkwardly at the two girls in silence. He took the water basin from Mint and headed back into his room.

The girls were already used to Wu Xingzi handling everything by himself. They opened the wardrobe and took out a silky, dark green robe, along with a rose-red belt woven through with glinting threads. They paired it with a light blue inner robe, its collar embroidered with a bird pattern. His clothes looked simple, yet exquisite.

Osmanthus found a few accessories. The girls tried them out on Wu Xingzi's belt with doubtful looks on their faces.

Done with washing up, Wu Xingzi started to comb and tie his hair up in a bun. However, Mint quickly came over and took his comb away from him. Pushing him toward the vanity and sitting him down, she skillfully combed some osmanthus-scented oil through his hair.

Uhh... Wu Xingzi was stunned. The smell of the osmanthus oil was a little thick, making him sneeze a few times. A somewhat sardonic expression appeared on his face when he made a vague guess about the reason behind the girls' actions.

"Umm, I'm not..." *I'm not seeking any affection from the general. I just want to go home for New Year, that's all...* But Wu Xingzi was unable to say it out loud. Besides, the odds were good that the two girls wouldn't listen if he did. Wu Xingzi sighed, resigned to let them do whatever they wanted. He only hoped that Guan Shanjin would not misunderstand the situation.

"You were supposed to have lunch together, but now the general is inviting you over early. There must be something going on."

Osmanthus added a fragrance to the clothes she had laid out. The scent was pleasant and refreshing, making Wu Xingzi feel at ease.

"Maybe he has some military matters to deal with," Adviser Wu said. The two girls snorted heavily at his suggestion.

"More like he's worried about delaying Mr. Lu's mealtime," Mint said, cleverly twisting his hair into a bun. She inserted a hairpin the color of warm jade. The style was neat and simple, with not a hair out of place.

"That must be the case." Osmanthus pouted, upset. "Mr. Lu broke his leg, not his hands! Why does he need the general to feed him every meal?!"

"I heard Physician Tu say that Mr. Lu has internal injuries. That's probably why the general is so worried." Mint glared at her younger twin in warning. As servants, it wasn't their business to speculate on such matters.

Osmanthus stuck her tongue out. She obediently brought over the clothes that she had just perfumed and began to dress an entirely stiff Wu Xingzi.

"Sir, you look like an outstanding talent with delicate beauty," Mint said, looking at Wu Xingzi in satisfaction. After some dressing up, the gentle, ordinary-looking middle-aged man now glowed with a fairly ethereal aura. He had lost a touch of his friendliness and warmth, but there were now additional traces of elegance.

Wu Xingzi could only give a droll smile. This was more than he'd signed up for. No matter how sincere and straightforward he was, he figured he was in for some trouble.

The person Guan Shanjin had sent over waited patiently in the parlor outside, not hurrying them at all. By the time the two girls dragged Wu Xingzi out, nearly one hour had passed.

"Ah, it's Fang He. Hello, Commander Fang..." Wu Xingzi recognized him immediately. He was one of the four guards who had escorted him to Horse-Face City, and his huge beard was still quite striking.

"Adviser Wu." Fang He cupped his hands at him. "The general has requested your company. Please follow me."

"I've troubled you," Wu Xingzi said, quickly walking forward. "I've made you wait too long, Commander Fang."

"Don't worry, it's nothing." Fang He waved him off politely before turning and leading Wu Xingzi away.

Wu Xingzi stumbled quite a few times along the way. Fang He's footsteps were quick, and the path to the general's manor was filled with twists and turns. If he looked away for a second, he could easily lose track of Fang He. Wu Xingzi truly had to expend all his effort to maintain a distance of four steps behind Fang He. He nearly tripped and fell several times. When they finally reached the garden where Guan Shanjin waited for him, Wu Xingzi was gasping with exertion, looking haggard.

"General, Adviser Wu is here."

"G-general...this civilian humbly greets you," Wu Xingzi said, panting. He felt a stitch in his side and his legs wobbled. Despite it being the middle of winter, he was sweating heavily.

"It's Haiwang," Guan Shanjin said coldly. He stood several steps away, looking up at the budding peach tree. "Leave us now. No one is allowed to enter without my command," he told Fang He.

"Understood." Fang He obeyed and left. As he walked past Wu Xingzi, his eyes darted toward him, his face expressionless.

Wu Xingzi happened to be wiping his sweat with his sleeve, still trying to calm his breathing. He completely failed to notice Fang He's meaningful look.

In an instant, there was no sound from anyone else in the garden. There was only the rustling noise of the wind blowing through the plants and trees, and the gradually steadying breaths of Adviser Wu.

Guan Shanjin could not wait any longer. "Do you have something you want to say?"

"Hmm? Ah! Yes, yes, yes. I have something that I would like to tell you." Without any outsiders listening in, Wu Xingzi's tone relaxed. Despite not having seen Guan Shanjin for a month, his warmth for the general had not faded away so easily.

"Go on." Guan Shanjin glanced over at him. When he noticed his clothes, his expression changed to one of subdued delight.

"Yes, yes. Uhhh..." Somehow, Wu Xingzi found it difficult to say what he wanted, carefully rubbing his nose.

"Just speak your mind. No need to keep hemming and hawing," Guan Shanjin said. His attention had long been drawn away from the peach tree. His hands, hidden inside his sleeves, clenched slightly, and for some reason, they were a little sweaty.

He waited for Wu Xingzi's response. Maybe he would say that he missed him; maybe it would be a complaint, or perhaps he would whine gently... Guan Shanjin had spent all of last night trying to guess what the man in front of him would say today. He had been unable to sleep, and while having breakfast this morning with Mr. Lu, he had been somewhat distracted. He wouldn't have been able to endure waiting until noon to see Wu Xingzi, so he'd anxiously pushed their meeting time forward.

"It'll be New Year in a few days. I was thinking, maybe..." Before Wu Xingzi could finish, Guan Shanjin suddenly raised his hand, gesturing for him to stop talking. Guan Shanjin's brows creased slightly, and he looked a little unhappy.

I didn't even say anything yet! Wu Xingzi thought.

"Someone's here," Guan Shanjin said.

Just as the general finished speaking, Fang He sped over, looking nervous. With his head bowed, he cupped his hands toward Guan Shanjin. "General, Mr. Lu wants to see you."

"Why is he here? Quick, let him in," Guan Shanjin said, shooting past Wu Xingzi and vanishing in the blink of an eye.

Wu Xingzi remained where he was, looking foolish as he and Fang He stared at each other.

Fang He sighed. "Adviser Wu, please don't be bothered. The general is only worried about Mr. Lu's leg."

"It's all right. I understand." Wu Xingzi wasn't bothered at all by Mr. Lu. Instead, he was bothered by the way Fang He looked at him. Was that pity in his eyes? Could it be that Fang He also thought that there was some unspeakable, secretive affection between him and Guan Shanjin?

Before he could explain, he heard a torrent of footsteps coming from behind him. Reflexively, Wu Xingzi turned toward the sounds.

The sight was incredible. Adviser Wu, who had grown up in the poor and barren Qingcheng County, was fully entranced by the sight before him.

An entourage of about seven or eight people headed toward him, attending to Guan Shanjin as well as a man dressed in white. Guan Shanjin held the man in his arms. This must be the famous Mr. Lu!

Wu Xingzi could not be blamed for staring at the captivating spectacle. Apart from Guan Shanjin, Mr. Lu was the most gorgeous person he had ever seen. Even the owner of the House of Taotie, Su Yang, paled in comparison next to him.

If he had to describe Guan Shanjin's beauty, it was the sort of charming, seductive appearance that felt almost demonic. A single flirtatious glance from him was enough to make someone melt down to their bones. As for Mr. Lu, he was like a river in the moonlight. He had the benevolent and ethereal appearance of an immortal being, firm and unyielding.

Mr. Lu finally noticed Wu Xingzi. He struggled slightly in Guan Shanjin's arms, only to be held even tighter. It was as if Guan Shanjin was worried that the treasure in his arms would fall and shatter into nothingness.

Mr. Lu closed his eyes. "Put me down," he said, his elegant voice sounding more pleasant than an orchestra.

"I'll put you down when they've arranged the chairs, Teacher," Guan Shanjin said, gesturing with his chin to the servants behind him. They immediately set up a chaise longue in the shade of the peach tree, along with a tea table and some other items for Mr. Lu's comfort.

Only then did Guan Shanjin gently place the man down on the longue, arranging the cushions for him. The general then sat down on one corner of the cushioned bench, shifting Mr. Lu's injured leg onto his lap and warming it up with a hot water bottle.

"This is...?" Mr. Lu asked. Only now did the group finally shift their attention to Wu Xingzi, who had nearly been crowded out of the garden. He stared at Mr. Lu with a slight flush on his face, enchanted by the man's beauty.

"This is the man I mentioned to you a few days ago—Adviser Wu from Qingcheng County," Hua Shu responded with some amusement as he stood behind the chaise lounge on the right. He was currently placing some snacks and tea on the table for Mr. Lu.

"Adviser Wu." Mr. Lu smiled gently at Wu Xingzi. "I keep hearing Haiwang mention you."

"Oh, really?" Adviser Wu blinked, incredulous. "Why would he mention me?"

This was not good! He had thought that Guan Shanjin had already forgotten all about him. He'd already decided to head home today after thanking him and borrowing a horse!

"He definitely must think of you often," Mr. Lu said, his tone very gentle. He seemed to have thought of something interesting, tapping on Guan Shanjin's shoulder and laughing lightly. "Last night, he told me that he would be seeing you today. His eyes shone brightly, just like a child. He was completely distracted as we ate breakfast this morning. This is truly the first time I've seen him regard someone with such importance."

"But he's very meticulous toward you, Mr. Lu! Previously, in Goose City, he thought of you—he wanted to bring you to the House of Taotie! When he heard that you were injured, he rushed back immediately... Ah, right, is your injury better now?"

Hearing Wu Xingzi speak, the expressions of the crowd grew strange. Mr. Lu was the only one whose face remained unchanged, still smiling softly.

"Haiwang is simply acting like a doting son. He sees his teacher as an adoptive father of sorts—he takes care of me. Adviser Wu, don't think too much about it. It's not the same."

"I meant it that way too," Wu Xingzi said. "It's always good to respect one's teachers."

"Don't talk so much," Guan Shanjin reproached Wu Xingzi sourly, unable to hold himself back. "If you have something to say to me, say it. Mr. Lu has yet to fully recover, and he cannot stay out in the wind for long."

Guan Shanjin knew that every word Wu Xingzi spoke was sincere. The adviser was always earnest, and did not intend to speak with hidden insults... So why did Guan Shanjin's chest feel so tight?

"Sorry, I've been inconsiderate!" Wu Xingzi hurriedly cupped his hands and apologized. "I only wanted to thank the general for housing me here, and to borrow a horse to go back home."

"Go home?" Guan Shanjin's voice cooled. He glared at Wu Xingzi, asking in a dangerous tone, "You want to go back home?"

"Yes, yes, yes. I've already lazed about in the general's estate for a month. The year is about to end, and I'm the only one left in my family. I have to go home and pay respect to my ancestors!"

"Wu Xingzi!" General Guan yelled. He no longer cared that Mr. Lu was sitting right next to him. He gritted his teeth, ready to spew flames. "Damn you, Wu Xingzi! You've lived here for a month, and the first thing you say is that you want to leave? Great! Just fantastic!"

Guan Shanjin's vision darkened. Blood surged through his body, his chest aching; his mind buzzed, and he tasted copper at the back of his throat. Someone next to him shouted in alarm, throwing the group of men into chaos.

"Haiwang!" Mr. Lu exclaimed.

Mr. Lu's worried call sobered him up a little. Dizzily, Guan Shanjin opened his eyes and discovered something trickling out from the corner of his lips. Standing a distance away, Wu Xingzi looked scared stiff, staring at him in panic.

Guan Shanjin wiped away the blood from his mouth and began to calm down. Pulling a handkerchief out from his robes, he cleaned his fingers. He spoke in a low voice to Mr. Lu: "Teacher, I have something to say to Adviser Wu. I can't accompany you right now. I'll have the servants take you back."

"Are you all right?" Mr. Lu reached out and caught his hand.

Taking the stained handkerchief, he gently wiped away traces of blood from the corner of his lips.

"I'm fine. You don't have to worry about me, Teacher." Guan Shanjin moved Mr. Lu's injured leg from his lap, then gave instructions to his men. "You must be careful. Don't cause Mr. Lu any pain."

"Understood."

Guan Shanjin then walked over to Wu Xingzi, gnashing his teeth. "You. Follow me."

"Oh..." Wu Xingzi didn't dare to refuse, obediently following Guan Shanjin.

Once the two men had walked a distance away, Hua Shu leaned over and whispered into Mr. Lu's ear. "Mr. Lu, what sort of background do you think this Adviser Wu has? He really just made the general..."

Mr. Lu calmly glanced at Hua Shu. "Even a pet can be frustrating when it isn't obedient," he said.

"Ah, yes..." Hua Shu's face paled. He looked down, his voice a little glum. "Mr. Lu, let's head back!"

"Mm." Mr. Lu placed a hand on Hua Shu's shoulder and slowly stood up. A servant pushed a wheeled chair over and helped him take a seat. "Thirty minutes from now, go and tell Haiwang that my chest is uncomfortable and I can't drink my medicine. Let him know that you came secretly, and that I didn't allow you to tell him."

"Understood," Hua Shu said.

Without uttering a word, Guan Shanjin strode ahead. Wu Xingzi was worried but dared not speak. He kept sneaking furtive glances at the man in front of him, his back as straight as a board. Adviser Wu's mind still dwelled on the trace of red at the corner of Guan Shanjin's lips.

Why did he spit up blood? Wu Xingzi's footsteps slowed down as he kept imagining all sorts of scenarios. Was there too much heat raging in Guan Shanjin's body? Perhaps he was feeling weak or suffering from exhaustion. Could it be a relapse of an old injury?

Despite how furious Guan Shanjin was, he couldn't help but pay attention to the old man behind him. Hearing his shaky footsteps drifting further and further away, Guan Shanjin quashed the conflict within himself and stopped to glare at Wu Xingzi.

"Do you not know how to walk?" the general spat.

"Uhh..." Wu Xingzi hurried over, smiling placatingly. "I got distracted for a moment. Sorry about that."

For the first time, Wu Xingzi's placid and clear eyes seemed to reflect Guan Shanjin within them. Inexplicably, the general's moroseness dissipated considerably, and the corners of his lips curved up slightly.

"You don't like Horse-Face City?" Guan Shanjin asked. Now that his mood had somewhat improved, he no longer walked gloomily by himself. Holding onto Wu Xingzi's hand, he casually sat down on a bench, tilting his head and looking at him.

"I can't say if I like it or not..." Wu Xingzi scratched his cheek, carefully glancing at Guan Shanjin's aloof expression. He felt a little helpless. "Ah, remember how I said we could remain in contact through the pigeon post? I personally trained all the pigeons at the magistrate's office. They're intelligent and obedient. They won't lose any letters."

"Why are you always thinking about leaving me?" Guan Shanjin asked bitterly. He really did not understand why he was so upset. In his heart, Wu Xingzi was merely a shadow of Mr. Lu. It was especially apparent in his choice of clothing today; his scholarly, elegant appearance was almost godly, and strikingly similar to Mr. Lu. When he saw him for the first time today, his palms became sweaty, and he felt jubilant—as if he finally held Mr. Lu in his arms.

He had been more conscientious toward Wu Xingzi than any of his previous lovers. During that month in Qingcheng County, there had been practically no limit to how he pampered the old fellow. Even Mr. Lu had not inspired such meticulous care from him before. However, Wu Xingzi still behaved as though he wasn't a part of this relationship. He acted like his heart had never been moved by Guan Shanjin... Could it be due to his past with Yan Wenxin?

Thinking about Yan Wenxin, his improved demeanor immediately darkened again, and his expression turned ugly.

"What's wrong? Does your chest hurt again?" Wu Xingzi said, worried. After some hesitation, he asked, "Shall I rub your chest for you?"

"Why must you rub it for me? What position do I hold in your heart, Wu Xingzi?" It sounded less like a question and more like a troubled plea. Guan Shanjin had never been so lost and bewildered in his life. This man in front of him made him feel as though he was only punching at cotton, his efforts futile. Everything he did was like pebbles thrown into a lake: they caused a reaction on the surface, but in the blink of an eye, the ripples would all disappear.

If Wu Xingzi had absolutely no interest in him, it wasn't a bad thing; that meant there was a weakness for him to exploit. The same logic could be applied in battle. What soldiers feared was not the strength of the enemy, but that the enemy would only dodge their attacks, circling about. This meant the soldiers were now mired in a bog, unable to free themselves and unable to display their prowess in battle. Instead, they would be dragged to their deaths.

Wu Xingzi froze, not knowing how to answer. He'd never expected Guan Shanjin to ask such a question.

"Do you care for me? Are you tired of me, or..." Guan Shanjin started again, but ceased his question abruptly. Closing his eyes, his long eyelashes cast a shadow on his cheeks that fluttered as he breathed.

Do you not even see me at all?

Ever since he was a child, Guan Shanjin had always gotten his way. He was gifted and talented, always finding a way to overcome obstacles. The brilliant and commendable Guan Shanjin, who held everyone's favor, had come to the startling realization that he was not even an afterthought for Wu Xingzi. He couldn't decide if he was upset or simply disappointed. This was the first time he'd closely examined his own feelings toward Adviser Wu.

In the end, what exactly did he hope to get from Wu Xingzi?

Was he chasing that shadow of Mr. Lu, dismayed that he could not grasp it? Or was it simply Wu Xingzi himself?

Adviser Wu's mouth was half open. It seemed like the general's question confused him. As he stared at Guan Shanjin, even his breathing seemed wary.

Glancing at him, Guan Shanjin forced himself to wave away all the turbulent thoughts in his head. He did not plan on forcing Wu Xingzi to answer the question; instead, he changed the topic. "You want to return to Qingcheng County?"

"Ah, yes, yes." Wu Xingzi, still looking absent-minded, shook his head casually.

"To pay respects to your ancestors for the New Year?"

"That's right, that's right. That's what I'm doing." Wu Xingzi blinked, snapping out of his daze. Once again he put a placating smile on his face, but worry could be clearly seen in his eyes.

Snorting, Guan Shanjin pinched his nose. He watched in satisfaction as Wu Xingzi's ears turned red. "You're the only one left in the Wu family, then?"

Guan Shanjin's hand itched, and he was unable to resist pulling Wu Xingzi into his arms to caress him. This courtyard was remote; he and Man Yue were the only ones who had access to it. Up ahead was his study, and within it were various papers and reports containing confidential military intelligence. If anyone were to trespass here, they would be flogged to death.

Knowing this, Guan Shanjin's actions became bolder. In a flash, he stripped Wu Xingzi of his robe, leaving him in only his inner clothes.

"Oh! We're out here in broad daylight..." Wu Xingzi was very shy. He twisted about in an unsuccessful attempt to wriggle free. Then he buried his face into the crook of Guan Shanjin's neck, as if nothing would happen if he couldn't see it; this allowed Guan Shanjin to do as he wished.

Wu Xingzi had to admit that after a month apart, he did miss Guan Shanjin a little, especially when he smelled that aroma of white sandalwood and orange blossom. His mind went vacant at the scent. With weak limbs, he clung onto the strong, muscular man in front of him, and the lower part of his body started to simmer.

"Broad daylight is good. I can look at you properly." Guan Shanjin laughed as he kissed his hair. His nimble, slender fingers slid down Wu Xingzi's back through the thin material.

The fabric had been chosen carefully. It was thin and comfortable, and it felt like flowing silk. The tailor was someone Guan Shanjin specifically brought back from the capital to make clothes exclusively for himself, Man Yue, and Mr. Lu, and his skills were unmatched. After Wu Xingzi arrived, all his clothes had been carefully tailored for him too. Although he was still thin and weak—his waist was so slender that there was barely anything to grab onto—he no longer looked so hollow and feeble. Now, he resembled a literary scholar.

Despite ignoring him for a month, Guan Shanjin had secretly gone to Shuanghe Manor many times to watch Wu Xingzi. It satisfied the general to see Wu Xingzi looking respectable and proper, but it rankled him that the adviser was able to go about his merry life without a care.

"What's there to look at?" Wu Xingzi trembled slightly as Guan Shanjin caressed and stroked him. The large hand on his back burned like a flame and every touch lit him ablaze. He didn't feel the cold of winter; he was so warm, in fact, that he nearly broke out in a sweat. This heat seeped deeply into his skin, spiking his temperature even higher. It was as if insects bit at his bones, and he panted in desire.

"I just like to look," Guan Shanjin said with a quiet chuckle. He slid his hand into Wu Xingzi's clothes, now in direct contact with his reddened, sensitive skin. He could almost feel Wu Xingzi's heart pounding away.

The pale inner robe fell to the ground. Wu Xingzi's bare body glowed a light pink, and tiny goosebumps emerged where the wind brushed his skin. However, Wu Xingzi only felt hot. He wanted to push Guan Shanjin away to catch his breath; however, the general's pleasant scent had seduced him, and he was unwilling to draw away. He didn't even realize he was heaving deep breaths and kissing Guan Shanjin's neck, moaning and whimpering.

"Your body is always so open to me." Guan Shanjin tilted his head, nibbling and licking at Wu Xingzi. His teeth nipped sensitive skin, and the man before him groaned uncontrollably. With how painfully the bite tingled, it was bound to have left a mark. The place he bit into would be easy for others to see, but Guan Shanjin didn't care at all.

The two of them twined together, and Guan Shanjin deftly removed his clothes, laying the robes on the ground to cushion them both. He let Wu Xingzi lie on top of him, saving him from the chill of the icy ground, and he wrapped his cloak around Wu Xingzi to shelter him from the wind.

The two men kissed out in the open, unable to part from each other, their tongues tangling together. Guan Shanjin slowed down, as if he intended to retreat from this pent-up passion, but Wu Xingzi immediately deepened their kiss, unwilling to stop. In a rare moment of boldness, he forcefully licked his way into Guan Shanjin's mouth. Holding onto the general's beautiful face, he deepened the kiss, practically swallowing him down.

Wu Xingzi himself didn't know why he was doing it. Perhaps he really did desperately miss Guan Shanjin's cock.

His trousers had already been stripped away. Guan Shanjin guided those bare, slender legs to straddle his strong waist. Wu Xingzi's buttocks ground against Guan Shanjin's crotch, and soon he felt something hot and hard pressing against his ass through the general's clothes.

"You..." Wu Xingzi managed to remove his tongue from Guan Shanjin's mouth, a thin, delicate thread of saliva dangling between their lips. In a daze, he stared at the beauty under him; Guan Shanjin smiled seductively and licked away the embarrassing trace of moisture with a red tongue.

"You started the fire—now you have to put it out."

A smack fell on his buttocks, and Wu Xingzi averted his eyes, his body twisting away uneasily. He thought Guan Shanjin would catch him and pull him back. After all, according to past experience, this man was savage in bed. How could he ever allow Wu Xingzi to pull away? However, this time, Guan Shanjin had no plans on moving. He only grinned at Adviser Wu, his eyes clouded with desire.

It seemed like Wu Xingzi couldn't back down this time. With a red face, he shifted about awkwardly, sliding away from Guan Shanjin's waist a little.

He should do something now, right? Unexpectedly, Guan Shanjin stayed put, continuing to look at him with a steady gaze. If not for the few drops of sweat beading on Guan Shanjin's forehead, Wu Xingzi would have thought that the man had been replaced by someone else. But since there was no one else, it definitely meant he was just as wicked as before.

"I..." Swallowing, Wu Xingzi's throat felt especially dry. Although shy and easily embarrassed, he was remarkably lascivious and daring in bed, and desire slowly welled up within him. "I don't really know how to ride a horse..."

Oh, fuck. Guan Shanjin nearly exploded. He was so enchanted by this darling, filthy man in front of him that he wanted to swallow him whole and absorb him into his bloodstream so as to prevent him from trying to run away all the time.

"Don't worry. This horse is very obedient." He caught Wu Xingzi's hand, moving it to rub at his lower torso. "Look at what a handsome horse it is."

"Yes, it's handsome. Very handsome..." Wu Xingzi stroked and stroked, unable to pull his hand away.

Guan Shanjin was well built. Since he was young, he had either been training in the army or fighting in the battlefield, waging wars for many years. He never skipped a single day of training, and each and every one of his muscles was strong and firm. They weren't overly bulging or exaggerated, but smooth and quite suited to his frame—which concealed how truly strong he was.

His breathing turning flustered, Wu Xingzi slowly shifted his buttocks back to their original position. Grinding and writhing, the frightening phallus beneath him leaked copiously. A large, wet stain formed on the general's trousers; the material looked ready to burst open.

"You're not going to saddle this horse?" Guan Shanjin's husky voice was bewitching. Wu Xingzi looked a little lost, and his hands shook as he undid Guan Shanjin's trousers. *Slap!* A thick length smacked across his round buttocks. The tingling pain made Wu Xingzi shudder. His mouth fell open as he gasped for air, his saliva dripping down from the corner of his mouth. His appearance was absolutely obscene.

As Wu Xingzi sprawled across Guan Shanjin's chest, the heated cock beneath him slid between his ample buttocks. Wu Xingzi twisted his hips, grinding himself against it. He moved a little too wildly, and the hard, wet tip jabbed at his taint, forcefully sweeping along it. Wu Xingzi released a long, lewd moan, and he sped up the movement of his hips.

Soon, his ass was wet with fluid from Guan Shanjin's cock. There were a few times the head glanced across his hole, putting some pressure on the tight little entrance and almost pushing inside. Unfortunately, there was no lubricant to ease the way, and Wu Xingzi was unable to get the general's cock where he wanted it, always missing the mark. That part of his body slowly throbbed with desire.

It happened so many times that Wu Xingzi felt his lust was going to destroy him. Lying on Guan Shanjin's chest, he moaned, "I can't saddle my horse... He's too naughty..."

"Blame the saddle, not the horse," Guan Shanjin said. The filthy fellow in his arms was going to tease him to death. There were a few moments where he almost lost control, nearly reaching out to hold the old quail down and thrust himself inside.

"Help me..." Wu Xingzi raised his hips, shifting about. The tip of Guan Shanjin's cock brushed past his hole again and again; it ached so much that he was close to tears. Restless, he urged, "Help me! I can't saddle the horse. How am I going to ride it?!"

"You dirty boy!" Guan Shanjin could no longer hold himself back, groaning as he grasped Wu Xingzi's buttocks and kneaded them a few times. He used his fingers, plunging them into the hole that was now slick with his pre-cum. Although his hole was a little tight after a month without being fucked, when Guan Shanjin's finger nudged at that little sensitive spot within, Wu Xingzi immediately collapsed on him with a shuddering wail. His juices gushed out, dripping onto Guan Shanjin's hand and his cock; everything became extremely slippery.

Gritting his teeth, Guan Shanjin pulled his fingers out. Gripping the trembling buttocks, he spread them apart, his hole gaping open. He then shoved his cock inside so forcefully that it hurt.

"Ahh!" Wu Xingzi shrieked, twisting about. He wanted to escape. After all, it had been some time since he had such an intimate exchange with a pengornis, and the sudden impalement made his tight hole burn in pain. He did not dare ride this handsome horse.

However, now that the horse had been saddled, he definitely was not going to get the opportunity to run away! Guan Shanjin tightened his hands around his narrow waist, giving him no opportunity to break free. "Be good," he consoled Wu Xingzi sweetly.

"It hurts... Gentler, gentler..." Wu Xingzi choked back tears as he bit at Guan Shanjin's shoulder. Guan Shanjin gently pinched his waist, and somehow, it no longer hurt as much. Instead, a burning ache came over him, and he started writhing his hips in an effort to take the general's cock in even deeper.

As Guan Shanjin expected, this man was truly salacious. He laughed lightly, cooperatively pushing himself in deeper. Soon, he reached Wu Xingzi's core. If he were to press on further, he would be pressing into his stomach. Part of his cock was still outside, but Wu Xingzi whimpered and groaned, refusing to take in any more. Thrashing around, he started riding his handsome horse.

Wu Xingzi lifted his ass, leaving only the tip inside, then he sat back down as he exhaled, swallowing the cock up until it reached his core. He sometimes supported himself on Guan Shanjin's chest, twisting his buttocks to get Guan Shanjin's cock to grind against his sensitive spot.

Rocking back and forth, Wu Xingzi was really enjoying himself. Although he wasn't experiencing multiple orgasms like when Guan Shanjin would catch hold of him and fuck him, this was better in the sense that he could control the speed. The pleasure made him moan and tilt his head back. His insides clenched, sucking on the thick, heated member as his juices gushed out. His face was alluring enough to enchant a man's soul.

Of course, Wu Xingzi's gentle approach and retreat was not enough to satisfy Guan Shanjin—but the astonishing coquettishness on display left him bewitched. He felt as though something sweet and cloying had ruptured within him, flowing through his bloodstream. His mind went blank as a completely different kind of satisfaction filled him utterly.

Wu Xingzi didn't have great stamina. He hadn't been riding Guan Shanjin for long before he was gasping and trembling. He thrust himself back a few more times, gritting his teeth and a white, sticky fluid shot out from his pink cock. Weakly, he fell into Guan Shanjin's arms.

The intense clenching of his orgasming muscles pushed Guan Shanjin over the edge, causing him to shoot his load into Wu Xingzi. The fluids were so hot that Wu Xingzi cried out, and an extraordinary amount of cum once again leaked out from his little dick. He lay there, convulsing.

Panting, Guan Shanjin hugged Wu Xingzi for quite some time before he finally pulled himself out. A mixture of juices and semen flowed out, smearing across both their lower bodies.

When Wu Xingzi regained his wits, he was so embarrassed by his obscene actions that he didn't want to be seen. He simply collapsed on Guan Shanjin's chest, pretending to be dead.

Laughing to himself, Guan Shanjin did not expose him. Remarkably satisfied, he was in a spectacular mood; he forgot all about how Wu Xingzi had enraged him earlier. Gently, he patted the man in his arms.

"I'll go with you to Qingcheng County tomorrow! It's too lonely to spend New Year alone."

Wu Xingzi felt an unexplainable joy—followed by despair.

Oh no... How was he going to change the sachet for his pengornis drawings?

However, this was not the time to worry about his penis pictures. The adviser certainly had his fill of horseback riding, but the general had not! As the famed general of the Southern Garrison, Guan Shanjin had spent half his life on horseback; his riding skills were incomparable.

When the man in his arms had rested sufficiently, Guan Shanjin spread his slender, fair legs apart. It was his turn to ride. Wu Xingzi clung onto him so gently; every moment of the ride was exquisite.

He rode his old horse until he spurted both at the front and in the back, filling him up with cum. With General Guan's endless thrusting, Wu Xingzi couldn't stop climaxing. He cried until his voice turned hoarse. Only then did Guan Shanjin carry him into the bedroom next to his study, still pounding into him. Their bout of fucking only ended when Wu Xingzi pissed himself.

After a month of abstaining, Guan Shanjin finally had a chance to feast. The general devoured Wu Xingzi to his utmost satisfaction, licking his lips and savoring the aftertaste. The adviser had been ridden hard and put away wet—he was practically half dead. Collapsing pitifully on the bed, he fell into a deep sleep.

As always, Guan Shanjin meticulously cleaned Wu Xingzi. Wrapping him up in his own outer robe, he pulled the blanket over him, preventing him from catching a chill. Only after taking delicate care of the adviser did he finally go wash himself up.

When he walked out of the room with wet hair, he saw Man Yue's plump figure in the study, reading through reports. He looked up at Guan Shanjin upon hearing his footsteps. "You're worse than a beast," he remarked.

"Thanks for the compliment," Guan Shanjin said with a smirk, raising a brow. He walked over and snatched the report from Man Yue's hand. "Why are you here? Is there someone outside looking for me?"

"Uh-huh." *If there wasn't, do you really think I'd have the patience for you to finish your...business?*

"Who?" Guan Shanjin pretended not to notice Man Yue's accusing eyes. In truth, Man Yue was also taking advantage of this opportunity to take a break. There were too many people outside looking for him. With how he'd been running about the entire day, he'd barely even stopped to drink water.

"Hua Shu." Man Yue looked at Guan Shanjin expressionlessly as he placidly passed along the message. "He said, 'Mr. Lu's chest feels heavy, and he is unable to drink his medicine. Because he's worried that the general would be concerned, he refused to let me inform the general. However, with Mr. Lu's current condition, how can he not take his medicine? I had no choice but to secretly come and tell the general. Please let the general persuade Mr. Lu.' I didn't change a single word, nor add a single one. He's been kneeling outside for four hours already."

Guan Shanjin's expression changed. He stood and began to head outside, not bothering to tie up his hair.

"Hold on, hold on," Man Yue said. "Do you really think I'd let your Mr. Lu wait for four hours to take his medicine? I already asked Physician Tu to go and take a look. The problem isn't serious. The blood flow in his chest is just sluggish. He only needed a few acupuncture needles—his blood is flowing normally now. He took his medicine and is now asleep." Man Yu reached out and grabbed onto the general, giving him a mischievous wink. "As your vice general, how could I let such a small matter alarm you? I heard that you'll be traveling with Mr. Wu tomorrow to honor his ancestors. That's a very important matter. Have you prepared your luggage yet?"

"You were eavesdropping again?" Guan Shanjin spat out. A thought quickly flashed through his mind. Instantly, his face darkened. "Did you...see his naked body?" Just as he finished speaking, Chenyuan whistled out, the cold, sharp point of the sword directed right at Man Yue's short neck.

"Fuck! Could you give me a warning before you wave that sword of yours around? Give me a chance to explain!" Man Yue yelled in alarm as he dodged the sword, bounding up to the ceiling beams in an attempt to escape. Despite how quickly he moved, he wasn't faster than Guan Shanjin. Chenyuan continued pestering the rotund man, steadily pointing firmly at his throat, the distance never wavering. If the sword moved just an inch closer, blood would have been spilled.

Man Yue seemed to deflate, breaking out in a cold sweat. He stared at the black, cold blade, not daring to look away. His shoulders shrank.

"Explain." Guan Shanjin's lips curved into a striking smile. His sword inched forward, and Man Yue could feel the sharp sting of Chenyuan. The cold blade brushed past his throat, leaving a trail of pain behind.

"Just wait a minute. I'll explain right now," Man Yue said cautiously. He didn't dare to speak loudly, almost mumbling. "After you left with Mr. Wu, Hua Shu came looking for you less than half an hour later. Because you had entered your study, there was nothing he could do about it, so he came to me instead. I only came here to look for you, as I didn't want anything to happen to your precious sweetheart. It was a coincidence that I heard Adviser Wu talking about riding a horse! Please have mercy!"

After a flash of dark metal, Man Yue fell backward, bumping into a pillar. Narrowly avoiding Chenyuan's blade, he waved his hand pathetically, bellowing, "I didn't hear or see you and Mr. Wu having sex! I turned and immediately left to go look for Physician Tu! How else do you think your precious Mr. Lu could have taken his medicine? How else would he be sleeping right now?"

By now, Man Yue had tumbled out of the study. His face dripped with sweat as he glared resentfully at the beautiful General Guan, who stood at the door of his study wielding his sword. Man Yue did not even blink, afraid that Chenyuan would pierce a hole in his body.

"What great timing. You even knew to return only when Adviser Wu had finished riding the horse, hmm?" Guan Shanjin himself did not understand why he was this angry. He didn't want anyone to hear the old quail's moans or witness his wanton eroticism.

"You think I wanted to eavesdrop? Hua Shu is kneeling out there waiting. I *had* to come in and deliver his message! It's not my fault that I overheard! Why didn't you go indoors?"

The indistinct moaning from the courtyard had stopped before Man Yue dared to sneak over to deliver the message. How could he have possibly expected that he would end up eavesdropping on their sweet nothings? It wasn't his fault!

"Once I heard you tell the adviser that you wanted to ride the horse as well, I fled immediately. I didn't hear a single sound of what happened next."

Man Yue's throat still bore the mark Chenyuan had left last time. He took several large steps backward. His face—that normally looked like the Smiling Buddha—twisted up in distress. This was entirely unfair. Mr. Lu had not caused a mishap this time, but a catastrophe.

"If Mr. Lu has already fallen asleep, why is Hua Shu still kneeling outside?" Guan Shanjin asked. He was still angry, but he didn't actually want to injure Man Yue. Since he had already achieved his objective of cowing him into submission, with a twist of his hand, he returned Chenyuan back to its scabbard. He hooked his finger toward Man Yue, motioning him to come over.

Man Yue patted his chest a few times to calm his breathing before returning to the study, the frightening memory of the sword's attack still lingering in his mind. Cold wind blew past his sweaty body, making him shiver. He quickly headed to the hearth and stood next to it to warm himself. It wasn't until he'd poured himself a cup of hot tea and drunk it that he calmed down.

"Hua Shu says he'd like to see you, and if he can't, he'll continue kneeling there. I don't know what his intention is, but it's probably because of Mr. Lu." Man Yue smacked his lips. Guan Shanjin's tea was brewed with quality tea leaves brought in from the capital. Since Man Yue had the rare opportunity to drink some, he would help himself to as much of it as possible.

"Because of Mr. Lu?" Guan Shanjin frowned. He did not remember much about Hua Shu, or how he had started following Mr. Lu. Having seen him many times, he did remember what he looked like, and he also knew that Mr. Lu trusted him implicitly and relied on him heavily.

"Do you remember when you wanted me to get rid of Hua Shu?" Man Yue asked casually. He had no expectation that Guan Shanjin would still remember a small matter like this. As expected, General Guan shrugged at Man Yue, pouring himself a cup of tea and sipping it.

"Anyway, a while ago, you asked me to get rid of Hua Shu. He was gone for less than two days before Mr. Lu got him back again, saying that he was used to him and did not want a different servant. He wanted me to tell you that he would apologize on Hua Shu's behalf."

"He would apologize on Hua Shu's behalf?" Snorting, Guan Shanjin's agitation was evident. "Fine. Since Mr. Lu is used to him, we don't have to bother about this small matter. If he still doesn't know how to remain obedient, then we'll sell him to Nanman."

"So...would you like to see to this small matter?"

"If he wants to kneel, let him kneel. It'll prevent him from going back and disturbing Mr. Lu's rest." Guan Shanjin never liked anyone who got too close to Mr. Lu. Everyone he had assigned to Mr. Lu understood this, and they didn't interact with him often. Hua Shu was the only exception.

"Are you really going back to Qingcheng County with Mr. Wu tomorrow?" Man Yue asked.

"Yes. Why?" New Year was fast approaching, and the affairs at the border were a lot more relaxed. Even Man Yue managed to get a reprieve in his duties, and Guan Shanjin was even more at ease.

"What plans do you have for Mr. Lu? He hasn't fully recovered from his injuries. The third-youngest daughter of the Yue family has been visiting every day out of concern. If not for you, she might have just brought him to her home to take care of him there. You're fine with seeing this happen?"

This was not how Guan Shanjin normally handled things. In the past, anyone who dared to get close to Mr. Lu or tried to make overtures toward him would be struck with some sort of misfortune. By now everyone knew about General Guan's soft spot for Mr. Lu, so no one dared to touch him.

This third daughter of the Yue family was childish, pampered, and willful, and she took no heed of Guan Shanjin. She was the only one who dared pursue Mr. Lu so daringly and publicly—and she actually succeeded.

It was possible thanks to Guan Shanjin's inaction, seemingly permitting the progress of the matter. Up until now, he had no intention of making a move against the Yue family. The head of the Yue family knew how to take advantage of this opportunity. He encouraged his daughter's constant coddling of Mr. Lu, planning on using this relationship to tie himself to Guan Shanjin. This way, he might even be able to gain connections to other nobles in the capital.

"Mr. Lu has always wanted to marry and settle down, to find a wife and have a child..." Guan Shanjin laughed bitterly, his hand tightening around his cup. Under his enormous strength, the jade-colored porcelain cup turned into dust. Patting his hands to get rid of the powder, he looked up and smiled at Man Yue. "You wouldn't tell me this sort of thing just for the sake of gossip. Your attitude is making me suspicious. You normally don't care about Mr. Lu, but you've helped him out quite a bit lately. Man Yue, what are you planning?"

Guan Shanjin said it so plainly, but Man Yue still shrugged, smiling shamelessly. "I'm not planning anything. I'm just afraid that you'll explode in anger over our dear Mr. Lu. There's no need for me to remind you who's behind the Yue family, right? Yue Dade can't read the situation. What an idiot. Because of his good son, he's about to be eradicated, and yet he's still foolishly giggling away."

"It's too late." Guan Shanjin revealed a supremely gorgeous smile. Leaning over, he pinched Man Yue's full and fleshy chin.

"Too late?" Man Yue grew alarmed. He pushed at Guan Shanjin's hand. "Why would you say that? Why is it too late?" he asked, his tone serious.

"I've already decided to take care of the man behind the Yue family," Guan Shanjin said calmly. "Some people piss me off just by looking at them. Dealing with them will improve my mood."

"What did he do to you? Is it because of Mr. Lu?" Agitated, Man Yue leapt up from his chair, pacing the room. "Haiwang, it's been five years since you left the capital. You know very well how complicated and treacherous the situation there has become. When you stopped Nanman, the protector general didn't say a word—even the emperor never urged you to return. You should know the reason even better than me! If you make a move, you'll definitely be stirring the hornet's nest. Why put yourself in so much trouble over Mr. Lu? If you really dislike the Yue family, I'll just come up with a plan to get that third daughter married off."

"Don't touch her. Since Mr. Lu is willing to marry her, then he should marry her. I don't want him to resent me." Thinking about this marriage filled Guan Shanjin's heart with despair. However, if he didn't endure it, he might not be able to see Mr. Lu in the future. He would definitely find a way to keep Mr. Lu by his side by the time the third daughter of the Yue family gave birth to a child.

"Then why do you still want to move against the Yue family?" Man Yue asked, puzzled. Taking out the head of the Yue family was hardly a difficult feat. With the combined might of Guan Shanjin and the protector general, he could be dealt with easily.

Still, the power structure amongst the officials in the capital was an intricate web. Pulling a single thread might cause a ripple throughout the entire echelon. For generations, the protector general's position had been a shining bastion amid the corrupt muck, and everyone was desperate to find a crack in his fortress. Even if they couldn't take the seat of power for themselves, they'd still try their best to destroy the man sitting in it.

If he were to make a move against the Yue family, the flaws of the protector general were bound to be exposed; it might even stir up some trouble. Although Guan Shanjin was arrogant and impertinent, he wasn't the type to just do as he pleased and ignore the bigger picture. Why else would he have obediently stayed in the south as the local tyrant?

"I must deal with him, as well as the people behind him." Guan Shanjin bared his teeth in a grimace, a bloodthirsty gleam appearing in his eyes. He looked like a demon considering his next meal, and chills ran down Man Yue's spine at the sight.

"Why?"

"Because I want to." Guan Shanjin glanced into the bedroom. Thinking about the man sleeping inside, he smiled softly. "Anyway, I'll be accompanying the old fellow back to Qingcheng County tomorrow. If that young lady wants to take Mr. Lu to her home, just let her do it. Mr. Lu would be happy with that arrangement."

"Guan Shanjin, are you possessed?" Man Yue asked.

"Stop talking nonsense." Guan Shanjin rolled his eyes and waved him off rudely. "Now, scram! Since you know who I'll be targeting, why are you still standing there? Do you still need me to tell you how many schemes we'll have in play during the New Year's banquet?"

"Guan Shanjin, you're a fucking scumbag!" Man Yue left in a huff. It didn't matter how uneasy he felt, General Guan had already made his decision: as the vice general, Man Yue had to follow his lead.

He didn't understand what the power behind the Yue family could have done to antagonize the god of death that was General Guan. He could only remember one man who'd aggravated him like this—the Minister of Revenue, Yan Wenxin, who had once proposed a marriage union between his daughter and Guan Shanjin in an attempt to gain a connection with the protector general. Before anyone could even finish discussing the matter, though, Guan Shanjin had released a statement saying that he would only marry a man. Thinking about it, wouldn't Yan Wenxin be the one to hold a grudge against Guan Shanjin for *his* despicable behavior?

Miss Yan did marry quite well later on, to the Assistant Minister of War. In private, this man had gathered the battalions in charge of the capital's defense; he essentially had a noose tied halfway around the capital.

As for Yan Wenxin, he was highly favored by the emperor. It was no exaggeration to say that the entire capital was in the hands of the Yan family.

Why would Guan Shanjin invite disaster like this? Mr. Lu was truly the root of all misery!

Once they'd agreed to leave together, Guan Shanjin packed both his and Wu Xingzi's luggage. He didn't plan on staying in Qingcheng County for too long, as he had to immediately return to Horse-Face City after the New Year to help Mr. Lu prepare for his wedding. He only packed a few sets of clothes and a handful of taels.

He also sent a letter to Su Yang in Goose City to ask him to prepare New Year goods.

Wu Xingzi awoke to the smell of food. He lazily opened his eyes, rubbing his belly. Nose twitching, he followed the enticing aroma to its source at the table. He didn't even notice that he was dressed only in thin inner clothes, and by the time he realized, he didn't have time to pull on a robe.

While Adviser Wu was deeply asleep, Guan Shanjin had brought him back to his own wing of the estate. The furnishings and structure were similar to Shuanghe Manor, and Wu Xingzi was still too bleary-eyed to have noticed anything amiss.

He only vaguely registered that he seemed to be taking a longer time than usual to reach the side hall. Only when he arrived did he snap out of it, realizing that there were two people sitting by the round table of delicacies. One was Guan Shanjin, and the other was Mr. Lu, who he had just seen not too long ago.

One was dressed in black and the other white, so harmonious that it looked as natural as breathing. Wu Xingzi was dazzled by the sight of them. If not for the hunger growling in his stomach, he would have been more than willing to simply continue gazing at the two of them.

"Mr. Lu." If Guan Shanjin had been the only one around, Wu Xingzi would have simply taken his seat. They were comfortable with each other, so they weren't very fussy about appearances. However, with Mr. Lu here, Wu Xingzi felt a little more awkward. In front of these two people, he was the outsider. He had no idea how he should behave.

Mr. Lu gave him a faint smile and called out to him gently. "Mr. Wu. Quick, take a seat. Haiwang guessed that you'd get hungry and wake up around this time. He specially asked the kitchen staff to prepare your favorite dishes. Come, eat! Don't let the food get cold."

Guan Shanjin had certainly made an accurate guess. Wu Xingzi glanced at Guan Shanjin, feeling pleased. Most of the dishes on the table were truly his favorites. They were simple, plain, and not too elaborate, but they still looked absolutely delicious.

Wu Xingzi instinctively sat down at the chair designated for the lowest-ranking person in the group. He didn't notice the crease of Guan Shanjin's brows; although it wasn't obvious, Guan Shanjin's eyes were cold. He stared straight at Adviser Wu—who presently was only concerned with the food—and watched the man unconsciously stick out the tip of his greedy tongue to lick his lips.

"Why is Mr. Wu still so distant?" Mr. Lu noticed Guan Shanjin's icy expression. With an elegant smile, he spoke to Wu Xingzi. "I'm very aware of the relationship between you and Haiwang. There's no need to deliberately sit apart."

Hmm? Wu Xingzi didn't pay close attention to what Mr. Lu was saying. He was very hungry, and all he could think about was—*those braised pork trotters look very delicious! So fatty and tender. The oil will definitely seep out when I bite into one... Should I take one and daringly chomp on it? Or just daintily pick some meat off the bone to nibble?*

Guan Shanjin had some idea of what was going through his head, and it was making him gloomy. But he couldn't throw a tantrum in front of Mr. Lu. Was Wu Xingzi purposefully avoiding anything that might arouse suspicion? When it was just the two of them, they always ate next to each other. With Mr. Lu present, the old fellow became quite shy...

Now that he'd worked out why Wu Xingzi was so avoidant, Guan Shanjin's mood improved. He noticed Wu Xingzi staring at the braised pork trotters with shining eyes; he picked up one piece and placed it in his bowl. "Have some. You must be hungry."

"Yes, yes." At first, Wu Xingzi was troubled about how he would start eating, but the sight of food in his bowl completely eradicated his hesitancy. Delighted, he picked up the trotter with his chopsticks and took a bite.

As expected, the meat had been braised until it was soft and tender, but it didn't lose its shape. The flavorful juices of the meat burst as he bit into it, and some of it spilled out from the corners of his lips. The meat melted in his mouth, but there was no loss of the texture of the pork. The taste was well rounded, a combination of wonderful flavors.

It paired very well with rice, but simply eating it by itself was its own kind of pleasure. Wu Xingzi's blissful expression made Guan Shanjin's stomach rumble in hunger. He picked up his rice bowl, selecting some stir-fried lily bulbs, vegetables, and other lighter-tasting fare for Mr. Lu before eating some of it himself.

Mr. Lu glanced at Wu Xingzi. The grease staining the adviser's mouth and hand made him look unattractive and boorish. However, when he glanced at Guan Shanjin, he discovered that his student, who had always been graceful, and a stringent follower of etiquette, didn't seem to be bothered by Wu Xingzi. Not only did he quietly eat, he continuously placed food in Wu Xingzi's bowl.

Inexplicably flustered, Mr. Lu picked up his chopsticks and took a bite of the vegetables. When he swallowed, he felt pressure in his chest. He dropped his chopsticks and frowned, rubbing at his chest.

"Teacher, are you still feeling pain in your chest?" Guan Shanjin noticed his discomfort. Concerned, he no longer paid attention to the happily eating Wu Xingzi, instead turning to help Mr. Lu rub his chest.

Guan Shanjin's elegant hands were broad and warm. Held against Mr. Lu's chest, they felt like a small flame, helping assuage the pent-up pain. Mr. Lu looked relieved, and he gave his thanks in a low voice. He then pushed Guan Shanjin's hand away, instead of letting the general soothe him for a while longer like he usually did.

Guan Shanjin's expression stiffened slightly as he registered Mr. Lu's rejection. A little helpless, he quietly tried to persuade Mr. Lu, "Teacher, your chest still hurts. Please let me help you with your blood circulation. Wu Xingzi isn't the type to gossip, and he wouldn't think much of it. Please don't worry."

"Nonsense." Mr. Lu still rejected him, picking up his bowl and chopsticks while deflecting Guan Shanjin's hand. "After all, your relationship with Mr. Wu is different. Anyone would mind, even if you don't. Although you're doing the right thing, people still have their biases."

These enigmatic words made Guan Shanjin hesitate. His love for Mr. Lu was his life; he never wanted him to suffer, not even a little. He was willing to suppress his reluctance and sadness about Mr. Lu's impending marriage in the spring. He just wanted Mr. Lu to live a happy and free life.

Although Wu Xingzi was only a shadow of Mr. Lu, it was impossible for Guan Shanjin to ignore the old fellow. Furthermore, the adviser had yet to cultivate deeper feelings for him, even now. It was a good thing Wu Xingzi had yet to realize Guan Shanjin's intentions—if not, he would have run from him much sooner.

Mr. Lu was right that people's hearts were biased: this old man's heart was biased toward *The Pengornisseur*!

Guan Shanjin couldn't help it, he kept glancing at Wu Xingzi over and over again where he was munching away. He looked so much that he made Wu Xingzi thoroughly uncomfortable. He foolishly stared back, biting his chopsticks.

"What's wrong?" he asked. During mealtime, Wu Xingzi focused entirely on eating, probably because he was so used to living alone.

He hadn't heard the quiet conversation between the other men at all, completely unaware of the intimate actions between the two. If not for Guan Shanjin's scorching gaze, he might not have ever noticed anything was amiss.

"It's nothing," Guan Shanjin said with a superficial smile. He himself wasn't exactly sure what he wanted. He definitely wouldn't like it if Wu Xingzi were to inquire about Mr. Lu. However, Wu Xingzi's complete disinterest upset him too, leaving him restless and fretful. "Mr. Lu has yet to recover from his injury. With the pain in his chest, he has trouble eating and sleeping. I'm only helping him improve his blood circulation—don't think too much about it."

"You're his student, after all!" Wu Xingzi replied. "Mr. Lu told me that you respect him like an adoptive father. It's your duty to aid him." Wu Xingzi didn't understand what Guan Shanjin was rambling about, but considering that it was human nature to help one's mentor, it wasn't difficult to respond to him.

In contrast to Wu Xingzi's cheerful indifference, Mr. Lu's pale face flushed red. "There's no need," he objected. "Haiwang is just too cautious. It's only a small injury. I simply have to take medication—I'll gradually recover."

"But I heard the girls say that you fell off a horse and suffered internal injuries," Wu Xingzi said.

"It's nothing major. I can only blame myself for my poor riding skills. Thank you, Mr. Wu, for your concern." Mr. Lu lowered his eyes, concealing his shame and resentment. He firmly believed that Wu Xingzi was implying something with his words. This old man looked honest, but he had a sharp tongue.

Mr. Lu didn't want to make himself look as though he was fighting for favor. He knew perfectly well who held the highest place in Guan Shanjin's heart. After the time they'd spent together over the years, Mr. Lu was more aware than anyone of Guan Shanjin's feelings for him. He knew what Guan Shanjin wanted from him, but he was very miserly in giving him what he wanted—he relied on Guan Shanjin's esteem, after all.

Any man would understand the logic: a wife would always lose to a concubine, a concubine would lose to an affair, and an affair would lose to someone you could never have. Guan Shanjin had never been a sentimental person, not even toward his own parents. He was very respectful, but he was never that concerned about them. What more could those around him expect? Mr. Lu had seen this clearly for a long time now.

"Oh..." Having been rebuffed by Mr. Lu, Wu Xingzi was brought out from his food-focused daze. Embarrassed and befuddled, he glanced at Guan Shanjin.

"Just eat. Why are you talking so much?" Guan Shanjin shoved a quail egg into Wu Xingzi's mouth, preventing the old fellow from saying something else upsetting.

Wu Xingzi munched on the quail egg, feeling falsely accused. *Wasn't I already eating quietly?!* he thought. *Ah, the yolk of this quail egg is so smooth and tender—it's not dry at all. Delicious!*

He took another two eggs and placed them in his bowl. If Mr. Lu and Guan Shanjin didn't like him speaking, he was more than happy to bury his head in his food. He sampled every dish and didn't leave a single one out.

As for the other two men, their moods were not as good as his.

Mr. Lu suffered pain in his chest, and thus was unable to eat. He felt as though his chest was congested and stale air was stuck in his throat. He was neither able to swallow it down nor release it; it was like being suffocated. His entire body felt uncomfortable, and his internal injuries seemed to have worsened. None of his comments seemed to have made any impact on the men eating with him. He hadn't created any ripples in the water—not even a tiny splash.

Guan Shanjin was well used to Wu Xingzi's carefree attitude, but he didn't feel any better. He had lost his appetite; he simply let the servant clear his bowl and chopsticks. Why had he deliberately gathered Mr. Lu and Wu Xingzi to have a meal together? In the end, only the old fellow benefited. He happily ate the entire table of delicacies by himself.

"Teacher, you should still have a bit more. Taking medication on an empty stomach is bad for your body," Guan Shanjin persuaded Mr. Lu gently. His heart ached seeing Mr. Lu without an appetite, sitting there ashen faced.

"Mm." Mr. Lu gloomily had a few more bites of vegetables before putting his chopsticks down and refusing to eat any more.

Guan Shanjin had no choice. He summoned a servant over, asking him to instruct the kitchen to prepare some porridge and to send the medication a little later. He then helped Mr. Lu up, wanting to hasten him back to bed.

"Ah, are both of you done eating?" Wu Xingzi hurriedly swallowed the food in his mouth and stood up in a panic.

"There's no need to be concerned, Mr. Wu. My body is weak, so I must be rude and leave first." Mr. Lu pushed at Guan Shanjin, a faint smile on his pale face. "You should stop concerning yourself with me, too. Don't you have to accompany Mr. Wu tomorrow to his village and make offerings to his ancestors? You should treasure him more. I have Hua Shu to serve me."

"Accompanying you back to your room won't cost me any delays, Teacher," Guan Shanjin said. He thought about how once he left for Qingcheng County with Wu Xingzi, the third daughter of the Yue family would come and take Mr. Lu away with her. After that, it would be a long time before he'd be able to be this intimate with Mr. Lu. He couldn't help but feel sour.

"I've been a fool in front of Mr. Wu." Mr. Lu stopped declining Guan Shanjin's help. He had yet to recover from his leg injury, which affected his ability to walk. Now, he leaned heavily in Guan Shanjin's arms, allowing him to support his weight. "Mr. Wu, please continue with your meal. There's no need to see me off."

Guan Shanjin turned his head, speaking to Wu Xingzi with a cold expression. "Wait here and don't go running off. You didn't even wear a robe—you'll catch a cold! Are you planning on making me worship your ancestors on your behalf?"

Wu Xingzi blushed. He obediently sat back down, continuing his mission to conquer all the dishes on the table.

When they stepped out of the hall, Guan Shanjin lifted Mr. Lu up in his arms, so as to prevent him from aggravating his injuries. In this position, Mr. Lu's head pillowed right into the crook of Guan Shanjin's neck. Above the collar on his fair and beautiful neck, there were many red marks. The marks extended into his clothes, as though Guan Shanjin had been bitten by insects. There were some marks all by themselves, as well as some clustered together, and there was even a faint impression of teeth.

Mr. Lu became distressed. How could he not realize what sort of marks these were? Guan Shanjin had never allowed anyone to leave these kinds of marks in such a visible area, either, which troubled Mr. Lu even further. He reached out to touch them, making Guan Shanjin stop for a moment. His emotional, enthralling eyes lowered, meeting his gaze.

"Teacher?"

"Mr. Wu has taken a bite right here." With a serene expression, he scratched at the patch of skin with his finger. "Since you like him, you must be good to him. I've always wished for your happiness."

"You know who's in my heart, Teacher." Guan Shanjin shifted his neck away from Mr. Lu's finger and averted his eyes. "I've instructed the kitchen to prepare some porridge for you. Take your medication after you've eaten some. I'll be back after New Year. When you're at the Yue Manor, Teacher, please recuperate well."

Guan Shanjin gently placed Mr. Lu down on the wheeled chair that a servant pushed up outside. He covered him tightly with a feathered cloak, protecting him from the chill of the wind.

"Don't concern yourself with me. I'm pushing you aside to get married to the third daughter of the Yue family... I'm the one who has done you wrong. Don't be so good to me anymore. Mr. Wu is an honest man—don't let him down." Mr. Lu held Guan Shanjin's hand, patting it softly. Even though he'd finished speaking, he didn't let go.

Surprisingly, Guan Shanjin was the first to pull his hand away. "Teacher, you should head back quickly now," he said. "Spending too long out in the wind is no good for your body."

"Mm." Mr. Lu looked at his empty hand, and a wry smile appeared on his face. "I'm the one who has treated you poorly. You're a good child; stop thinking about me." He gestured for the servant to push him away, without waiting for Guan Shanjin's response. Only when the slender figure in the wheelchair vanished from sight did Guan Shanjin return back indoors.

In the side hall, Wu Xingzi had eaten to his heart's content. He joyfully rubbed at his bulging stomach, the plates on the table in front of him nearly empty. Guan Shanjin was satisfied at the sight, but also vaguely irritated. He walked up and stroked Wu Xingzi's stuffed belly, causing him to cry out in surprise and nearly fall off his chair. Guan Shanjin then pulled Wu Xingzi into his arms.

"All you ever do is eat, so why aren't you putting on any weight?" Wu Xingzi's frame was not big, and his muscles were soft and tender. It felt sublime to caress and touch him, but sometimes Wu Xingzi's bones would dig into him uncomfortably.

"Why didn't you accompany Mr. Lu?" Wu Xingzi figured that Guan Shanjin would need at least two hours, and he could take the opportunity to digest his food. That was why he was clumsily sprawled across his chair, rubbing his belly—he didn't expect to be caught doing it! He didn't know how to hide his embarrassment.

"Mr. Lu wants me to treasure you more." Guan Shanjin lowered his head to bite at Wu Xingzi's fleshy nose. His teeth itched for more. Feeling unsatisfied, he went down further and bit at his lips, which tasted of braised pork trotters. Oily and plump, his lips were even more delicious than the food.

"Ah..." Wu Xingzi felt stifled. Even Mr. Lu had misunderstood the nature of their relationship...

Guan Shanjin decided to stop mentioning Mr. Lu, and instead earnestly informed Wu Xingzi of their travel plans: "We'll head out early tomorrow morning. Since you're not good at riding, you'll share a horse with me."

"You're really going to return with me to pay respect to my ancestors?" Wu Xingzi kept feeling that it was a little improper; something about it didn't feel quite right. He didn't plan on seriously objecting to the general's proposal, though. The confused feeling in his gut wasn't very strong, but he was unable to explain it.

"Haven't we already agreed on it?" Guan Shanjin said. He pulled Wu Xingzi's lip between his teeth. The intensity of the flame in his heart grew—he just wanted to push him down and have his way with him.

Wu Xingzi was a little bashful about Guan Shanjin's reply. He evaded his question and picked up one of the pork trotters.

"Are you going to eat? Let me tell you, the braised pork trotters are really delicious. I've left two for you, so don't waste them," he said. "I'll help you tear the meat off so that it's easier to eat. You're such a big man, you shouldn't go hungry."

"You're going to feed me?" Guan Shanjin rested his chin on Wu Xingzi's narrow shoulder, wrapping his arms around his slender waist. His eyes were full of amusement as he watched Adviser Wu carefully tear the meat from the bone. The pile of streaky, shiny meat in his bowl looked absolutely appetizing.

When he turned his head to look at Guan Shanjin, Wu Xingzi felt somewhat vulnerable. He didn't know what was going on with him, but he had a feeling that the general's attitude toward him had shifted.

Fine, I'll just feed him! "Here, open your mouth," Wu Xingzi instructed him. Guan Shanjin had washed his private parts for him before—feeding him was nothing!

When a man was fed and warmed, his sexual desires often came to the forefront. Once he was fully fed, Guan Shanjin's cock started to tent his pants. After all, the man in his arms was only dressed in his inner garments, and he was so soft and sweet.

Consequently, when a servant from Mr. Lu's courtyard came rushing over with a message that Mr. Lu had started retching up bile after taking his medication, Wu Xingzi was heartlessly left to stand outside in the wind. He was not lucky enough to view the coming of spring that took place inside.

THE BULL AND THE COWHERD

HERE WAS A COWHERD in Qingcheng County who wasn't exactly young anymore, but he was all alone. He had no elders in his family, no wife, and no children. His years were spent in poverty, his appearance was ordinary, and his personality was tinged with timidity. None of the girls liked him—so, at over the age of thirty, the cowherd had no one else around him but an old bull, not even a friendly neighbor.

This wasn't anyone else's fault, really. Although the cowherd was a gentle person, he was very shy and easily embarrassed, so he wasn't good at interacting with other people. When he was asked a question, it would take him quite some time to respond. Who would have the patience to chat with him? The cowherd would actually speak to the old bull now and again, perhaps because he spent so much time with it.

In the past, plenty of people hired the cowherd to herd their cattle. However, for the past couple of years, the cowherd had not herded any cows other than his own bull. The people did not know how the cowherd survived, and they couldn't be bothered to ask, either. After all, the village was situated within forested mountains, and food could be found everywhere.

The cowherd and his bull lived just beyond a small patch of trees, a distance away from the village. Barely anyone passed by, so naturally no one realized there was something going on with the cowherd.

At night, when everywhere else was quiet and still, a man could be heard panting away in the cowherd's home. Mingled with heavy breaths were the alluring sounds of soft gasps and moans that faded into trembling keens. The noises were enough to make anyone's heart pound, and even a fool would know what was happening inside that house. If the house hadn't been situated a distance away from the village, they would have long been discovered by the villagers.

In the dim lighting indoors, a tall and muscular man pressed a fair, thin man down onto the bed. Moonlight streamed in through the window, the rays reaching just a few inches beyond the bed, casting a hazy glow across the lust-stricken faces, as though enshrouding them in gauze.

Lust hung thick in the air, and the scent of desire lingered everywhere. A man's heavy panting mixed with the yearning moans. The harsh breathing came from the man pressing the cowherd onto the bed. Muscles corded thickly along his body; his back was broad, and his waist was slim. As he moved, the firm muscles of his back shifted and flexed, and beads of sweat rolled down the sharp lines of his body. Several faint red scratches from the cowherd's fingernails could be seen across his back, but he seemed not to feel them at all. Rocking his powerful hips, he thrust vigorously into the cowherd beneath him.

The man's strength was crude and rough, his muscled arms holding firmly onto the cowherd's plump buttocks. Every time he entered, he would thrust himself in deeper, wanting nothing more than to shove everything inside that swollen, gaping hole.

The cowherd had been fucked for most of the night, and his hole looked like a fruit dripping with juices. Each time the man pushed inside him, fluids seeped out, mingled with semen left inside of him, soaking the bedclothes underneath him. Wrapping an arm around his belly, it wasn't clear if he was begging for mercy or for the man to go harder; his screams stayed stuck in his throat.

The bed threatened to break from all the movement. The tall, muscular man would practically pull himself all the way out every time, leaving only the head of his cock inside before pounding right back in. His cock was extraordinarily large, with veins running across the head; the shaft was so long it reached all the way to the cowherd's abdomen with every thrust, creating a huge, visible bulge through the skin.

This bout of fucking left the cowherd gasping for air. He had climaxed a few times already, and his little cock could no longer ejaculate—it shriveled into a pitiful little ball within his pubic hair. However, the man on top of him did not let him off so easily. Instead, he trapped the hands trying to push him off and fucked into him even harder. The bulge in the cowherd's belly pushed up far enough to brush against the man's muscled abdomen, leaving the cowherd hoarsely begging for mercy.

"I-It's too much... Have mercy... Have mercy on me..."

The man gave a low chuckle before pressing their lips together, shoving his tongue into the cowherd's mouth and licking across every sensitive inch within. His tongue was strangely long, reaching all the way into the cowherd's throat—his kisses made the cowherd gag. The cowherd's eyes rolled to the back of his head and tears rolled down his face as he convulsed, climaxing once more.

The man bellowed in pleasure as the cowherd's hole clenched tightly onto his cock during his orgasm. He again thrust into the cowherd using the strength of his trim and muscular torso, deep and fierce, and it felt like he even managed to force his balls partway into the cowherd's hole.

If not for how accustomed the cowherd had become to getting fucked like this the past few years, he would probably be bleeding.

But even though he wasn't injured, this was exceeding what the cowherd could endure. Summoning the last of his energy, he made a final struggle to escape the man's hold—and this time, he actually freed himself. Not only did he manage to escape the suffocating kiss, he even pulled away from the colossal cock inside him.

The cool, tranquil moonlight streamed across the bed, casting a soft, hazy glow onto the cowherd's pale body and the mysterious man's muscular form. At the same time, it highlighted how extraordinary the man's lower half was.

That cock was really, truly long—it was no wonder it could reach all the way inside the cowherd's stomach, practically piercing through him. It was rock hard and slick with the cowherd's juices, looking even more savage and terrifying. However, its shape was different from that of most men.

First, the head of the cock was a lot thinner than the rest of the shaft, sharp and pointed like the head of a venomous snake. The shaft gradually grew wider closer to the root. At its thickest, it was wider than a child's arm, and overall, it was very weighty and solid. Accompanied by two huge balls, the entire organ looked like a terrifying weapon.

The cowherd had long been exhausted from all the fucking. Trembling, he shifted up the bed, his limbs like limp noodles. However, his hole still twitched and pulsed, cum slowly seeping out from his movements. The sight of the red, swollen hole smeared with thick, white fluid caused the other man's eyes to darken. Grabbing hold of the cowherd—who had only managed to move a few inches away—he began anew, fucking right into him.

"Ahhh—!" A heart-pounding, lustful scream came from the cowherd. He wanted to reach out and push at the man's chest, but his arms were so shaky that he couldn't exert any strength at all. His eyes rolled to the back of his head, and he lay limply on top of the messy bedspread, shivering and jolting. With his tongue hanging loose between his lips, he looked half dead.

"Be good. Let me finish fucking you, all right?" the man said as he hovered over him, forcing his immense cock all the way inside. He reached somewhere even tighter and warmer, exhaling in satisfaction.

"Bull... Bull..." His words muddled, the cowherd called out to his bull.

The man fucking vigorously into him kissed his lips, intimately responding to his call.

Seeing the cowherd left in a daze from all the fucking, the man was filled with tenderness.

This man was actually a magical beast. When he was about to ascend to the throne and become the king of all magical beasts, his enemies plotted against him, causing him to return to his original form. He had no choice but to hide amongst the humans to heal his wounds. Just like that, he came across the cowherd, who had only been ten years old at the time.

At first, he had planned on absorbing the child's vitality to heal himself, but he did not anticipate that the foolish child would give up so much for him. He even chose to surrender all rights to any land when his family members divvied up their inheritance, just to keep the bull with him.

Despite being full of scorn for this young fellow, the bull bathed in the warmth of his grand gesture. Unknowingly, he started to see the youthful human as his responsibility, and he used all means at his disposal to help him lead a comfortable life.

As a powerful magical beast on the cusp of reaching kinghood, his strength was abundant. Although he had not been able to turn into his human form at the time, he was still able to divine heaven's secrets. He knew that the daughters of the heavenly emperor planned to secretly descend into the mortal realm to play, and thus he decided to teach the cowherd how to keep one to be his wife.

The bull had thought that he would need to explain himself at length to convince the cowherd that he wasn't going to harm him, and that he should trust him. However, the moment he opened his mouth, the cowherd blushed happily, hugging him tight and refusing to let go. Then, no matter what the bull said, the cowherd refused to marry any of the heavenly fairies, only wanting to spend the rest of his life with the bull.

Tsk. He actually came across a strange man who liked bulls. Perhaps this was fate!

*A*N INTERVIEW

Behind The Scenes of Blackegg's Work,
and How the Story Came About

QUESTION #1: **How many years have you been writing? What does writing mean to you?**

A: Saying how long I've been writing is rather embarrassing. I'm no longer young, so for now, I'd like to maintain an aura of mystery for a little while longer.

I was in my third year of elementary school when I became interested in writing novels. At the time, I had started to read Jin Yong's wuxia novels, and so I only thought about writing wuxia. However, at this point in my life, I much prefer "sword fighting" between two men. *laughs*

Writing is completely ingrained in me. After all, I've been walking this path for twenty years. If I were to step away from writing, it would leave a huge, empty space in my life. I once thought about giving it up, but in the end, I couldn't harden my heart enough to commit to it. I'll continue writing for the rest of my life.

QUESTION #2: Why did you choose Blackegg as your pen name?

A: This name came about after many ups and downs. When I first started posting on PTT's BB-Love forum, I did not use Blackegg as my pen name. However, I won't be telling anyone what my pen name was back then. That's something that's completely sealed and locked up in history!

In any case, when I was using my original pen name, I didn't get good reviews. As I was still young then, I felt that the bad reviews were due to my pen name, and so I decided to try changing it. At that time, I happened to be studying in Japan, and I suddenly had an intense craving for century egg tofu. Hence, without any further consideration, I chose the name Blackegg.

That's right, there was no further consideration. Blackegg was entirely a stroke of inspiration. Only two or three years later did I realize that I should explain to everyone that the reason I chose the pen name was because I'm actually a century egg!

QUESTION #3: How do you find your inspiration? How did you come up with the idea for *You've Got Mail: The Perils of Pigeon Post*?

A: The birth of *You've Got Mail: The Perils of Pigeon Post*—or rather, the inspiration—came out of nowhere. Before I started writing YGM, I was stuck in a very long slump. I pretty much had no new works, and only worked on extras for my old works. I always wanted to write a new novel, and I'm very grateful to my readers and friends who continued encouraging me during my slump and never left me.

Unfortunately, the gods never grant one's wishes! Despite having many ideas, none of them came to fruition. It was only one day, while chatting with a friend—I've already completely forgotten what our main topic of conversation was—we happened to talk about dating apps. Somehow, one of us started talking about how these days, many guys like to send girls photos of their dicks without any warning, even being very proud of their "very impressive dicks."

My friend said, "Ah, it would be so much more interesting if guys were to send guys their dick pics."

And so we kicked off a writing session imagining a scenario about dating apps, where men send each other dick pics and end up having sex.

My friend then said, "Hey, since there's such a perfect story idea here already, you should write it! Just write it, even if it's only a thousand words long!"

I thought that my friend was right, and I should write it. As such, I prepared an outline, but as I worked on it, I quickly grew bored. It wasn't fun at all to write about exchanging dick pics through dating apps in modern society, since that's so ordinary and commonplace. For a novel, it would either be very realistic, or it would turn into an uninhibited story that was just about sex. Neither option lit up my desire to write.

I originally planned on giving up...but at that moment, the god of inspiration seemed to have taken some sort of drug (and I hope the god keeps taking this drug). Anyway, I suddenly decided to set this story in ancient times—in a time without dating apps. So, how were people supposed to find hookups, and how were men going to find other men who wanted to have sex? I felt that this would definitely be interesting! So after spending two days coming up with the setting, I started writing YGM.

Why did I need to spend two days preparing the setting? This is a habit of mine. Before starting to work on a novel, I must first prepare the world where it takes place. Friends who were following YGM when it was ongoing might have seen me mentioning something about the setting in an extra I linked on Facebook a long time ago.

Simply put, there was a limit to using the pigeon post.

First, the pigeons had to be trained, and pigeons that had been trained would not fly wherever you wanted them to. They were only trained to fly from Point A to Point B and back—they could only fly between two places. Flying to Point C or D would be impossible, as they would neither be able to fly there, nor fly back.

Furthermore, at the end of the day, pigeons are only birds. They can't fly too far, and it's unrealistic for them to fly across the entire country, especially in novels set in ancient times. The places we imagined were usually quite big, and pigeons are unable to fly these distances. As such, if the letters were to be sent even further away, it wouldn't be using the pigeon post, but posthouses instead.

With these two limitations, how was making friends through pigeon post going to be realistic? This was something I needed to spend time considering.

In the end, *The Pengornisseur* wasn't a book that had the same version throughout the entire country. Instead, every district had their own version. Members could choose to receive versions from only their own district or from other districts depending on their financial ability. People who were rich enough could say, "Ha ha ha, I want the nationwide edition." As such, what Xingzi got was a copy of the nationwide edition that he could use for the rest of his life. The sending of letters wasn't restricted to just the pigeon post, but included other methods that required a little more time and money. Normally, the size of a district was decided by how far a pigeon could fly within a week, which meant that one would need at most two weeks to receive a response. Beyond this distance, one would need to use postal services.

Because of this, when you're reading, you'll be able to see the mention of many districts' versions of *The Pengornisseur*. However, I didn't elaborate too much about this in the novel. This can be considered a detail that exists mostly in my head, and I'd probably need to write another book in the same universe before I can put this detail into play.

Please stay tuned for more!

THE STORY CONTINUES IN
You've Got Mail: The Perils of Pigeon Post
VOLUME 2

Character & Name Guide

Characters

WU XINGZI 吴幸子: A lonely, gay thirty-nine-year-old in a dead-end clerical job who's decided to die at forty.

GUAN SHANJIN 关山尽: The renowned and formidable young general of the Southern Garrison; a playboy who only has space in his heart for Mr. Lu.

PEOPLE IN QINGCHENG COUNTY

ANSHENG 安生: Wu Xingzi's crush, who introduced him to the Peng Society.

OLD LIU 柳老头: Wu Xingzi's neighbor, who provides transport to Goose City.

AUNTIE LIU 柳大娘: Old Liu's wife, a gossip who is fiercely protective of Wu Xingzi.

CONSTABLE ZHANG 张捕头: Wu Xingzi's colleague in the magistrate's office, and Ansheng's life partner.

AUNTIE LI 李大婶: A gossipy woman who doesn't think much of Wu Xingzi.

PEOPLE IN GOOSE CITY

RANCUI 染翠: The manager of the Peng Society.

SU YANG 苏扬: The owner of the restaurant House of Taotie; a childhood friend of Guan Shanjin.

PEOPLE IN HORSE-FACE CITY

MAN YUE 满月: Guan Shanjin's vice general and childhood friend.

HEI-ER 黑儿: One of Guan Shanjin's bodyguards.

FANG HE 方何: Another of Guan Shanjin's bodyguards.

MINT 薄荷 **AND OSMANTHUS** 桂花: Sisters who work as maids for Wu Xingzi at Guan Shanjin's compound.

MR. LU 鲁先生: Guan Shanjin's teacher and his unrequited first love.

Name Guide

Diminutives, Nicknames, and Name Tags:

A-: Friendly diminutive. Always a prefix. Usually for monosyllabic names, or one syllable out of a two-syllable name.

DOUBLING: Doubling a syllable of a person's name can be a nickname, e.g., "Mangmang"; it has childish or cutesy connotations.

DA-: A prefix meaning big/older

XIAO-: A diminutive meaning "little." Always a prefix.

-ER: An affectionate diminutive added to names, literally "son" or "child." Always a suffix. Can sometimes be a fixed part of a person's name, rather than just an affectionate suffix.

Family:

DI/DIDI: Younger brother or a younger male friend.

GE/GEGE/DAGE: Older brother or an older male friend.

JIE/JIEJIE: Older sister or an older female friend.

Other:

GONGZI: Young man from an affluent/scholarly household.